AUTUMN CTHULHU

Edited by

Mike Davis

It was the best time of the year but it was also the saddest. Because winter was coming.

~ Lawrence Block, *In the Midst of Death*

And in the autumn of the year, when the winds from the north curse and whine, and the red-leaved trees of the swamp mutter things to one another in the small hours of the morning under the horned waning moon, I sit by the casement and watch...

~ H.P. Lovecraft, *Polaris*

Beware the autumn people.

~ Ray Bradbury, *Something Wicked This Way Comes*

For Danielle and Logan.
You are the sun and the moon.

Table of Contents

The Night is a Sea *by Scott Thomas* 1

In the Spaces Where You Once Lived

by Damien Angelica Walters 24

Memories of the Fall *by Pete Rawlik* 41

Andy Kaufman Creeping through the Trees

by Laird Barron 47

There Is a Bear in the Woods *by Nadia Bulkin* 77

The Smoke Lodge *by Michael Griffin* 92

Cul-De-Sac Virus *by Evan Dicken* 116

DST (Fall Back) *by Robert Levy* 137

The Black Azalea *by Wendy N. Wagner* 151

After the Fall *by Jeffrey Thomas* 166

Anchor *by John Langan* 181

End of the Season *by Trent Kollodge* 258

Water Main *by S.P. Miskowski.* 271

The Stiles of Palemarsh *by Richard Gavin.* 290

Grave Goods *by Gemma Files* 309

The Well and the Wheel *by Orrin Grey* 335

Trick... or the Other Thing *by Joseph S. Pulver, Sr.* 347

A Shadow Passing *by Daniel Mills.* 371

Lavinia in Autumn *by Ann K. Schwader* 383

Introduction
by Mike Davis

Halloween, 1977. Two months previously, my family had moved from Texas to Iowa. I was six years old, used to hot Octobers, and Halloweens that still felt like summer.

This was different.

It was dusk. I exited our house and was completely unprepared by the scene that greeted me. Everywhere, costumed creatures roamed the neighborhood. A chill was in the air. Red and orange leaves whispered to me from the sidewalk, from the street. I could smell a wood fire. A cold, light rain was falling.

It was beautiful and sad and mysterious and lonely...and I couldn't take my eyes off of it. A longing suddenly filled my heart, a feeling that I didn't understand, but that somehow felt right. I knew that this was *me*. I think this was the moment that I became what Ray Bradbury called "an autumn person, thinking only autumn thoughts." I fell in love with the fall, with Halloween, and almost forty years later, that hasn't changed.

Though I read voraciously throughout my childhood, I didn't discover Lovecraft until my early twenties. Since then, it has slowly dawned on me that autumn and cosmic horror are a natural fit. Halloween, after all, is a time when the veils between worlds are the thinnest, when the *aos sí* could more easily enter our world. And what is the *aos sí*? Many scholars believe that they are versions of ancient gods.

Sounds pretty Lovecraftian to me.

In this book, you'll visit a house that is haunted...but not by ghosts. You'll take a scary walk in the autumn woods. You'll discover the horrors of living on a cul-de-sac, witness the beginning of the end of the world, and meet an actual monster. You may even spy Andy Kaufman. He's creeping through the trees.

Is it fall as you read this? Maybe, maybe not. But no matter the time of year, in my heart, it's always autumn, and it's always raining. I'm guessing you feel the same way.

Autumn is the best time of the year, as Lawrence Block wrote, but it's also the saddest.

Because winter is coming.

The Night is a Sea

by Scott Thomas

ONE:
Merritt House

I was standing in front of the brooding Victorian where Evelyn Merritt had died. Seasonally speaking, with Halloween creeping closer, it was one of those moments that just seemed perfect. The house was both stately and foreboding, a high shale-colored thing bordered by maples and looming against the watercolor purple of October dusk. I felt like a trick-or-treater rather than an intrepid reporter as I approached the lit porch, making my way through noisy leaves that a recent frost had hastened to flight. Rather than a pillowcase or plastic jack-o-lantern, I carried my trusty camera and paused to take a photo for my news column, *Emerson Bridge's Journeys on the Border*. The picture of the house came out rather dark because of the failing light, but that made it look all the more menacing.

To say that Evelyn Merritt had actually died may have been oversimplifying things. According to the news reports from the autumn of 1984, Merritt, who was 60 at the time, had locked herself in a strange little attic room of her Eastborough, Massachusetts home, going so far as to nail boards across the door. While there were no gas lines in that part of the house, there was an explosion that blew a jagged hole through the roof of the building. All that could be found of the woman was a hand clutching the shriveled black page of a book. Some in esoteric circles liked to believe that Evelyn, an eccentric who spent a great deal of time indulging in mysterious arts, had vanished rather than expired.

I mounted the porch stairs, passed between two glowering pumpkin sentries, and rang the buzzer. The door was impressive, set with an oval stained-glass window commissioned by Evelyn the summer before her death (or disappearance). Done largely in somber shades of purple and blue, the collective sections suggested an opening from which several milky faces were peering. Something moved behind the glass, and I felt a shiver.

The door sang a shrill little note when it opened, and a short, round sixty-something man welcomed me with a smile. It was Gavin Maynard, the owner, looking sufficiently professor-like in horn rims and a cardigan.

"Hello, Emerson! Come on in," Maynard greeted me heartily.

There is always a paradoxical sense of dread and thrill when I enter a place where some alleged horror has occurred, and I had heard enough about this house to know that it was considered very haunted. Luckily for me, the place was owned by someone who didn't mind having it featured in an article about the most frightening places in Worcester County.

The house was gloomy enough on the inside, but cozy as well, and there was a pleasing aroma of Cavendish in the air. Maynard had created a suitable ambiance using candles to light the rooms, and a ceramic skull sat watching me from atop an antique card table in one of the parlors.

The professor took obvious delight in telling me all about the place, how it went back generations in the Merritt family, about the architect who built it, about the carriage house that had been crushed in the tornado of 1953, and of course about Evelyn and her proclivities.

I was given a tour of the first and second floors before we made our way to the attic. A dim, claustrophobic stairway led up to a landing where a small window gazed east. The glass was watery with age, and I could see a blurry hand of maple leaves reaching for the panes or perhaps beckoning to me. The dusk had made a strange color of the foliage. More steps curved up from the landing, and we thumped up these to the door of the third floor. Maynard unlocked it (*he kept it locked!*) and we went in. He fumbled for a string, and a dangling bulb glared to life and swung slightly, making dizzy things of our shadows.

"The attic isn't all that sinister to look at," the professor said nonchalantly, gesturing. We were standing in an area that made me think of a double parlor, open on the left and on the right, neither space filled with enough clutter to suggest that my host was a hoarder. "This floor was rented out as an apartment for a time in the forties and fifties. You can tell from the paint colors. But, the room where it happened was specially built after Evelyn started to get deeper into her mysteries. You do want to go in, of course, right? Some people won't go in. They flat out refuse."

"Oh, yes." I smiled bravely. "I want to go in."

Maynard chuckled. "Of course you do!"

The door was unremarkable, not the original that had been damaged when police kicked it in while responding to the blast that shook the neighborhood. While not an ancient door, it creaked when it opened, just as a door in a haunted house should creak. I think I'd have been disappointed if it hadn't.

I peered in. Evelyn's odd little room was unlit and could hardly have measured more than 6 feet by 6 feet. The walls were blank but for the back one which bore a simple design, and the ceiling, in contrast to the splintered maw my mind had envisioned, was smooth and plastered.

Maynard remarked, "Not a lot to see, just the holes in the frame where she nailed the boards across the door."

"I've heard that there was no blood. Is that true?"

"That's what I've always heard, though I've never gotten my hands on any of the police reports."

"That doesn't seem to make sense. A person blown apart and no blood?"

Maynard wagged his head. "Nope, and if the explosion was so intense that it incinerated all of her but for a hand, you'd think there would have been serious fire damage, but all they found was some ashy black on the shattered boards and that burnt page in her hand. Apparently she'd removed her clothing, because it was lying in a heap on the floor, and there were no traces of scorching on it."

"That's odd," I said. "Could it have been a lightning strike?"

"Nope. There were no storms that night. It was clear and cold."

We both stood gazing for a moment, and then the professor urged, "Go on in and see if you can sense anything."

I gave a little laugh. "Sure. Okay."

Two steps and I was in. I imagined that it was cooler there than in the attic proper, and I shuddered when I thought about the possibilities of what had taken place that autumn night in 1984. Had someone died horribly on the very spot where I was standing, or had something stranger than death occurred?

Evelyn Merritt had painted a plain symbol on the back wall of the room. It was done in black, an oval with lines emanating out from it. A sun? I had seen a picture of it once in a blog piece about Evelyn, but I had not been able to find a similar image in any of my occult references.

"Feel anything?" Maynard, who stood in the doorway, asked.

"I'm not sure. Do you sense anything peculiar when you're in here, Professor?"

Maynard squinted. "Difficult to articulate it, really; though interestingly, while I have great cellphone reception everywhere else in the attic, when I'm in there all I get are weird sounds that make me think of the recordings folks have made of whales communicating. Give it a try and see if you get it on yours."

I took out my cellphone. The screen fluttered uncharacteristically, the blue light almost harsh in the small, dark room. It caused my eyes to blur for a second, and in that second I thought I saw a pale figure – like a whisper made of light – peer briefly from behind Professor Maynard's shoulder.

"No signal," I observed.

"No whale sounds." Maynard noted.

"Let's see if it works outside of the room," I said, actually glad for an excuse to get out of that chamber. As soon as I was through the doorway my phone regained reception.

Maynard took me back downstairs, and we had fireside coffee in one of the parlors while he told me about his ghostly experiences there at the old Merritt house. I was riveted! The hours got away from us, however, and it eventually came time for me to leave. Maynard walked me out onto the porch where our conversation returned to Evelyn Merritt.

It had begun to rain, a soft rain scented in a way that only October rain can be scented, an inhaled epitaph of apples and dying leaves, of wood smoke and weary fields. It ran delicate fingers across the roof of the Victorian's porch and made a dull orange haze of the trees nearest the streetlights.

I studied my host and asked, "Tell me, Professor; what do you think happened that night?"

Maynard puffed pensively on his pipe. "I've heard and read a variety of things, conflicting things, speculation largely. I don't know...maybe she messed up somehow, or got more than she bargained for in doing whatever magical experimentation she was into. It's possible that she achieved exactly what she wanted to achieve. She was fascinated by the theory that certain rituals could open doorways into neighboring dimensions. But, she had mental and emotional issues and hated just about everyone and spoke of wanting to kill the planet. "

"May I ask your personal opinion about the explosion explanation?"

A church bell on a near street began to count ten. The sound was muffled in the damp air.

Maynard blew a Cavendish plume out of the corner of his

mouth and said, "The physical evidence doesn't support a conventional explosion, Emerson. There were no gas pipes near that room, no traces of combustible substances found, and there was nothing to suggest that she would have had a bomb, or a meth lab for that matter. No, the explosion conclusion doesn't hold water. If there was an explosion in that room, then the boards and debris would have blown upward and out, but the damage showed that the boards were broken *inward*."

"Oh, my word!" I had not heard this before.

Maynard squinted into the rain and said, "It's like something from the sky punched a hole through the roof and snatched her."

TWO:
October Rituals

"We know now that in the early years of the 20th century this world was being watched closely by intelligences greater than man —" the unmistakable voice of Orson Welles spoke from my refurbished 1930s cathedral radio. I was partaking of an October ritual, sitting in the jack-o-lantern-scented darkness of my little study listening to the Mercury Theater on the Air's 1938 radio offering *The War of the Worlds*.

A fellow named Ben Meyer hosted a weekly radio program, *Nostalgia at Midnight,* on a community station a skip down from NPR on the dial. He broadcasted old time radio plays, and each October, to my delight, drew from his fecund archives of spooky shows. The Welles classic was an annual treat.

Two days had passed since I had visited the Merritt house, and I had spent another fruitful day working on the article about the scariest places in Worcester County. My ghost pieces for the self-consciously edgy alternative paper *Free Worcester* had become a yearly tradition, and this one was shaping up to be the best yet.

I had driven down to woodsy Sutton, to an orchard on the grounds of the Federal period farmhouse where Zaccheus Winch had killed his wife and three daughters in the October of 1791. Winch had been one of the town's most prominent citizens, but something went wrong that autumn. The man stopped going to church and took to carving strange symbols into the trees of his woodlot, and in his diary he wrote that something terrible was coming and that the sky was going to bend down and eat his family if he did not save them. He "saved" them with an ax and then killed himself with a dueling pistol.

I interviewed the current owner of the Winch house and then climbed the hill that hosted a knobby coven of yellowing trees. The branches looked pained beneath the weight of their ruddy late-season fruit. Local folklore maintained that the apples tasted like blood and that they contained human teeth instead of seeds. It was also alleged that a person walking among the trees might see dangling apples that had been carved with crude skull-like features as if small red jack-o-lanterns. A picture of one taken by a local ghost hunting group stirred interest for a time, but most wrote it off as a hoax.

I had to sample one of the fruit, of course! It was actually very nice. No taste of gore and no teeth biting back. Even so, there was something in the air there that I find difficult to express, and crazy as it seems, I felt as if the stark blue sky above the hill was somehow watching me. This strange sense lingered with me as I drove home. The old New England houses, patient among their colored trees, looked alternately cozy and haunted, and the sunset that draped about them was the color of candlelit cider.

"The Roma Wine company of Fresno, California, welcomes you

again to this weekly half-hour of Suspense!"

The pumpkin-toned dial of my radio stared from the darkness as the *Suspense* episode *Fugue in C Minor*, staring Vincent Price and Ida Lupino, came to me from the speaker as if through a time machine. I had completed and sent in my article earlier in the evening, so I thought that I owed myself a bit of seasonal indulgence. It was comfy there in my study, and I was warmed by the Cyclops glow of the radio and the twitching light from the jack-o-lantern squatting on one of the bookcases.

A brief news update followed *Nostalgia at Midnight*. I was only half-listening until the newscaster read the last story, "Authorities in North Brookfield are searching for a 64-year-old dementia patient who walked away from a long-term care facility on Friday and who has not been heard from since.

"Celeste Merritt was last seen wearing a green jacket, gray blouse, and dark pants. She disappeared from Ivy Hill Assisted Living on James Road sometime between eight and nine p.m. Merritt does not have access to a vehicle and is believed to have left on foot. She has shoulder-length grey hair, green eyes, stands five-foot four and weighs about one hundred and thirty pounds.

"Anyone who spots Merritt should call the West Boylston police at – "

"Celeste Merritt," I said aloud.

Celeste Merritt was the niece of Evelyn, who had either died in or vanished from the strange little room in the attic of her Eastborough Victorian in the autumn of 1984.

THREE:
Wachusett

October mornings transport me back to childhood, when I would walk to school along sidewalks strewn with dry foliage, or mornings after a rain when the drowned leaves in puddles made crimson Rorschach shapes. *The world towered around me then...the high brick school where I attended first grade, the two enormous grey trees that seemed half plant and half dinosaur*, the sky more vast and mysterious than any ocean. That morning when I set out to join the volunteers preparing to search for Celeste Merritt, the heavens were a pale pristine blue, but winter, or perhaps something more inexplicable, was lurking behind the facade of autumnal serenity.

A few months earlier, I had heard that Celeste, a respected professor at Wellesley College, had suffered a severe mental breakdown. She had participated in some sort of psychic experiment held by members of The Brinklow Society, a group interested in the theories of Simon Brinklow, a British fellow who during the 19th century investigated mysteries of the supernatural and who, prior to vanishing under strange circumstances, purported that otherworldly dimensions abutted our reality. While I had yet to learn the details about what happened that night, it was known that several of those attending were struck with dementia, and poor Professor Merritt ended up in a nursing home.

I drove to West Boyltson and parked across the street from farmland where rows of pale cornstalks shuddered in the wind like an army of unraveling mummies. Quite a few people had shown up to join the search for the missing professor, and we gathered for a briefing and instruction from the local authorities. We were told that someone driving in the area shortly before midnight the evening before had reported seeing a person who resembled Celeste walking in the vicinity of the Wachusett Reservoir, thus the search was going to be focused on the forestland surrounding that expansive body of water.

We broke off into pairs and headed out onto a series of

snaking trails. My partner was a local volunteer fireman named Frank. The woods were dark with shade, fraying as the tired year dictated. Leaves rasped underfoot, though the deciduous trees that had deposited them were a minority amidst the dense population of evergreens. Even so, there were spotty exclamations of color, proof that the October paint box had not exhausted its supply of oranges and yellows.

"I'm worried about hypothermia," Frank said. "It got down into the thirties last night, and she only has a light jacket with her, they say."

"And, it's supposed to be cold again tonight," I said, my concern all the more acute when I pictured the pleasant, intelligent face and mannered grey hair of the woman pictured on the MISSING flyers.

While initially I had been heartened by the number of folks who turned up for the search party, I began to wonder if there were far too few of us. The woods were so sprawling, so thick with branches and shadow that a group of a thousand or more might not be enough to find Celeste Merritt, and what if her intent was *not* to be found?

Off in the distance I heard another searcher, a woman's watery voice calling out, *"Celeste! Celeste, where are you?"*

Not to boast, but I tend to regard myself as something of a walking encyclopedia when it comes to Worcester County weirdness, so when I found myself at the Wachusett Reservoir, my thoughts naturally turned to the Rev. Benjamin Coddington house, a gable-fronted colonial structure with a rather curious history. Abandoned for decades, the place had become a magnet for ghost hunters and was famous for being the site where the Ice Sisters were discovered back in August of 1949.

Built as a parsonage, the house resembled other two-story houses of the day until the reverend built a high, peaked tower, a private sanctuary where he, according to his dairy, "sought the voices of the heavens that the common man shuns."

As for the Ice Sisters… A boy searching for his missing dog found three dead women dressed in colonial mourning gowns lying in the middle of a field on the Coddington property. They were spaced evenly apart with their heads nearly touching, though their hair and faces could not readily be seen. Each had a dark wooden box enclosing her from the neck up, and underneath, shaped to the dimensions of the boxes and further encasing the women's heads, were blocks of ice. Somehow the ice had not melted, though the day was very hot. The young women were all lovely with dark hair and eyes, though their petrified expressions suggested that they died in mid-scream. None of the three were ever identified.

I mention this because we came to a spot where the woods thinned, and an open area could be seen, a pumpkin patch, and beyond that the grey relic of the Coddington house sulked between haggard maples. Peaked and windowless, the adjacent tower built by the reverend reared like a missile of rotting wood.

My search partner and I were looking out across the tangles of withered vines, and the orange globes their leaves tried to hide, when a call came in on the walkie-talkie. Frank responded, spoke for a few minutes, and then turned to me.

"Well, it sounds like we're wasting our time looking in the woods. A guy who runs a tattoo place over on route twelve just noticed one of the posters in town and said that a woman who looks a lot like Celeste came in and got a tattoo yesterday afternoon before walking off down the road like she was headed for Shrewsbury."

I was curious of course. "What kind of tattoo?"

"Sounds odd. She got it right in the middle of her forehead. Something sort of like a spider. A circle with lines. He claims she hardly spoke a word, but when she was leaving she smiled at him and said something about the sky killing the world."

We turned away from the pumpkin patch, and the Coddington house beyond, and started back on the trail. The cooler air imparted the scents of the forest in a way that only October could convey them. The earth, the vegetation, the breezes all bore the melancholy essence of a resigning year.

Frank looked to me at one point and said, "Oh, the tattoo guy also said that the woman was missing one of her hands. Is Celeste Merritt missing one of her hands?"

FOUR:
The Holloway Phone

Much as I am fascinated by the things that humans have yet to logically explain or understand, the concept of fate troubles me. I mean, to think that the episodes of my life that I like to believe are (relatively) shaped by choice, will power, and intention might actually be connected dots governed by some great unknown is terribly unnerving. For example, I loathe the expression *everything happens for a reason*. But, bewilderingly, there are times when something fate-like, or at least in sync with Jung's theory of synchronicity, pops up to rattle my comfortable perception of reality. So, imagine the thoughts that went through my mind when the woman I had spent the day searching for in the West Boylston woods *contacted me*, to say nothing of the way she did it!

My income being what it is, I have only been able to afford a meager assemblage of strange/mystical collectibles. I own, for example, a 19th century candle bearing the imprint of a ghostly child's hand. Other items include a glass eye that once resided in the head of the Vermont medium Davis Bartlett as well as a desiccated mouse - one of thousands - that rained down on a farm in Grafton, Massachusetts, in November 1959, and a copy of the rare pear-shaped grimoire *The Quartz Bride*. But, most prized among these objects is the black 1930s Bakelight telephone used by Col. William Holloway to communicate with the dead during the composition of his book *Voices from Never*. I purchased it at the annual auction held by the Society of Esoteric Antiquities, and it has stood in a place of honor atop a bookshelf in my study ever since.

The phone, to my understanding, was inoperable and had never made a sound during the time that I possessed it, so I was utterly astonished when it suddenly began to ring. I picked up the hand piece and stuttered out a *hello*. A combination of fizzing and words hissed into my ear. It was a woman speaking.

"*I am Celeste Merritt...saw your article...my aunt has returned...pumpkin too heavy...need your help...to stop her.*" The voice began to warp, to dissolve into a blizzard of static. I could only distinguish two more words: "*Coddington house.*"

The last sounds from the Bakelight reminded me of the noises that whales make, and then the line went dead.

FIVE:
The Impossible Baby

It was Halloween dusk, and all the New England houses were haunted. They watched as I drove along the dimming streets, beckoned to me with the warm light of porches, tempted me with the promise of chocolate. But I could not stop. En route to the Coddington house, I was like a leaf on a breeze, carried by chill currents without question or choice.

There were ghosts in the chimney smoke that scented the air, and as sunset reduced to a line of cool copper behind shadow trees, I thought of another Halloween. On October 31ˢᵗ, 1993, shortly after the publication of his book, *Voices from Never*, Col. William Holloway was visited by something more unsettling than masked children. He arrived home from work to find a large pumpkin sitting on his front porch. Seemingly intact, the gourd was shaking as if something was trapped inside. Holloway carried the orb into his house and carefully cut into it, revealing the contents. In his journal, in a trembling script, he wrote: *How can this be possible — a living baby lacking facial features, ears or developed limbs! It is like a great pale maggot writhing in a soggy womb of pumpkin guts and seeds.*

Holloway placed the creature on some towels atop his kitchen table, and before he could even collect himself enough to call the police, witnessed three dime-sized wounds spontaneously opening on the visitor's white belly. Inexplicably, he was reminded of the eyes of a triops, a crustacean often compared to the trilobites of old. The holes were dark and bloodless, and words which seemed to be German were whispering out from them. He was able to make out: *die nacht ist ein meer*, which translates to *the night is a sea.*

The final journal entries that Holloway penned are chilling: *I've lost power — found flashlight, but baby is gone from table — sounds in woods around the house — like whales — phone won't work.*

Holloway's scrawls became more frantic, some of the words hard to decipher. He told how he found the baby: *Long leafy tendrils of rockweed sprouted from the wounds — stretched up and attached to the ceiling, lifting it above my head where it dangles, convulsing.* But there were other more pressing matters to tend to.

Someone was hurling pumpkins through his windows, and scrawny, half-glimpsed figures were darting about in the woods that enclosed his secluded little Cape.

Holloway wrote: *Scarecrows — bony twig figures — surrounding —*

windows breaking – whale sounds – I hear them inside now – going to get pistol and shoot baby.

We don't know if Holloway managed to find his gun or get off any shots, for neither he nor the baby nor his pistol were ever seen again. There were, however, ragged effigies, bony tangles of dark bombazine cloth and birch snared in the bushes outside. One was halfway through a smashed window, and another was sprawled on the kitchen floor amidst a scattering of slick seaweed strands and broken pumpkins.

Part of my brain, upon remembering Holloway's final Halloween, urged me to turn the car around and race back to the safety of home. But I was compelled by something other than reason, and I continued along the darkening roads, staring ahead as lonely breezes sang and orange bats danced across my windshield.

SIX:
The Night

The sky at Halloween seemed larger than it did on other nights. Perhaps it was just that so many leaves had left their hosts, or maybe the darkness was a vast witch's cloak or an upside down ocean of melted bats and unlucky cats. It hung above the puny towns and peered with icy eyes as the inhabitants below dabbed coy toes into a blackness they only dared to glimpse on an annual basis.

Below that immeasurable drapery, the houses fell away as I approached the Wachusett Reservoir. The trees looked cold for their lack of leafy garments, though I came to an area where densely clad evergreens stood shoulder to shoulder on either side.

The effect made the street seem thinner, and with a little imagination I could visualize myself driving along between two immense, furred creatures. The forsaken stretch led me to the Coddington house.

The spired colonial appeared suddenly in the intrusive glare of my headlights. Ancient and abandoned, it was the perfect place for ghosts, or sad capsized poets with moonlight for blood. It loomed amidst gaunt maples, and despite its gray disrepair demanded a certain respect, a measure of fear and awe. It embodied the autumnal sadness and thrilling mystique that since childhood had spoken to me from the black and orange heart of Halloween.

I climbed out of my car and stood there in front of the structure not knowing what to do. It was quiet but for some leafy sighs of wind until I heard a voice rasping, calling my name.

"Emerson Bridge!"

I shivered.

"Emerson Bridge. Help me!"

I turned toward the pumpkin patch, uneven, sprawling, and vague against the darker backdrop of reservoir trees. The sound came from there.

"Hurry! She is here! Evelyn is here!" It was the voice of Celeste Merritt.

I found myself running, inexplicably wishing I'd brought the pistol that I kept in a drawer at home. There were no streetlights, no moonlight, just the beam of my flashlight to guide me. Pumpkins like orange turtles hugged the earth, crouched half-hidden under crippled leaves and brittle vines. My steps crunched and my heart thrummed.

At first glance the woman seemed a scarecrow there in the middle of the field, her shoulder-length hair like wild straw, her loose windbreaker flapping in the breeze. She turned as I approached, her face stark and desperate in the harsh illumination. There was no doubt that this was Celeste Merritt, the woman from the MISSING posters. She did not have a tattoo on her forehead, nor was she missing a hand. She was pointing at a pumpkin that lay like a great ribbed egg.

"This is the one," she breathed.

The pumpkin was shaking as if something was trapped inside.

"What do I do?" I asked, bewildered.

"We have to take it to the tower," Celeste said.

"Why?"

"To save the planet."

Most others would have dismissed the woman as mad, considering she had been placed in a nursing home after what appeared to be a mental collapse, but I found myself handing her my flashlight and then kneeling and lifting the gourd, freeing it from the shriveled umbilical cord that had nourished it. How much of the trembling came from my hands and how much from the pumpkin, I could not say. I held it to my chest and followed Celeste as she started for the house.

A soft, bluish light fell upon the empty old parsonage, emanating from somewhere up in the endless October sky. It was strange considering there was no moon that night. But I was too busy to give it much thought, too busy trying to keep my nerve, busy holding that restless globe against my torso, and trying not to trip. Celeste had gotten ahead of me, because she had the flashlight and could better see where she was going.

One of my feet thudded hollowly against something, and I stopped, nearly fell forward, nearly dropped the pumpkin. I looked down. I had kicked the side of a dark wooden box, a rectangular box that encased the head of a woman in a black colonial mourning gown who was lying on her back in the grass with her arms stiff at her sides. I gasped and took a step back.

The figure rose up onto her feet with hardly a bend or any seeming effort, like a marionette tugged to attention. Off to my right, I glimpsed more movement, heard vines rustle as another woman lifted from the patch. She, too, had thin arms and full skirts of antique black, and her head was hidden like that of the other. The third sister wakened from her own bed of hissing leaves and stood ghastly just yards away on my left. There were no eye holes in the boxes that obscured the women's heads, but they all stared nonetheless and proved intent on following when my feet had the sense to move.

I had never run so quickly in my life. My feet and heart pounded, and moments later I found myself just behind Celeste as she creaked up the wooden steps of the Coddington house. Blue light was more noticeable now, an eerie cast on the clapboards, on the mysterious windowless tower that aimed at the heavens. I glanced above the tall old place and saw what I took to be the moon, a gentle round radiance. But how could it have been the moon when there were two similar orbs on either side of it?

My mind was rushing. Three blue moons. Three dead women moving behind me, following us, nearing the edge of the pumpkin patch that abutted the overgrown Coddington yard. My plump orange charge was shuddering against me – what was inside? I could hear something tapping insistently.

Celeste got the door open and looked back, gesturing for me to hurry. As we entered the blackness of the parsonage, we heard what I first took to be the kind of spooky organ music that some folks like to play for trick-or-treaters. But, as we ventured deeper into the vacant old rooms, it more resembled the dirge-like noises that whales make. The place almost vibrated from the strange, deep tones.

"This way to the tower," Celeste said.

We were in a parlor with raised paneling on the fireplace wall, and she had opened a door and was shining the flashlight up a staircase of extremely steep stairs. I noticed then that she had a knife in her other hand. That was when fingers like an icy spider closed on the back of my neck and pulled me backwards off my feet.

My chest broke the pumpkin's fall, but my back hit the floor hard, and my head bounced against the wide pine planking. One of the Ice Sisters folded over me, snatching at my face with barbed white hands as the others came like breezes out of the shadows and swooped in, set on taking the pumpkin. I yelled and launched up, and ducked swiping fingers and the dark arms that moved wildly as if branches in wind. Still clutching the pumpkin, I dashed into the stairway behind Celeste.

Those long, mournful notes that I had mistaken for organ music rumbled through the claustrophobic dimness of the tower. They grew louder the higher we went as our feet thumped frantically on the steps. We climbed up one set, reached a little landing where the stairs turned, then rushed up some more before turning again. This seemed to go on and on as if the tower had no end, and I was straining, carrying the heavy pumpkin, trying not to let the dizzying blood in my head get the better of me. And, the Ice Sisters were wordlessly making their way up behind me, their long, wide skirts brushing against the walls and over the thin stairs with ghostly little hisses.

Celeste looked back down at me, her grey hair falling crazily about her face.

"It's begun," she cried.

The whale sound became a terrible, almost deafening drone, and the old boards that comprised the upper part of Benjamin Coddington's tower began to warp impossibly outward, groaning, creaking, and ultimately snapping as one after another was sucked away into the night leaving openings in the walls. The whole tower trembled violently, and I tried to hang on to the pumpkin and keep from falling back down the stairs, tried to keep pace with Celeste as she headed for the structure's top compartment.

Cold fingers clawed at the back of my leg. I swiveled and kicked hard. My heel struck one of the box-faces dead on, and I saw a figure tumble back, heard a commotion on the stairs, domino bodies tumbling.

Celeste aimed the beam of my flashlight up into the tower room. I bent to look around her, and saw what I first thought was a skeleton. It was Celeste's aunt, Evelyn Merritt, who had vanished in the autumn of 1984. She was naked and haggard, though she looked no older than she had been at the time of her disappearance, a woman of 60. She was lacking her left hand, and there was a tattoo on her forehead, an oval emanating lines. Evelyn was standing there swaying with her eyes closed, and she was chanting something to herself, though I could not make out the words or even the language, for the whale song had become a roar, and the building was being peeled away, noisily, all around us.

The roof and large portions of the sides that had comprised the tower room tore free, went spinning off into the darkness, and there above were the objects that had first seemed to be three moons. Looking up through the opening that lead to the disintegrating chamber, I saw them for what they truly were, and I shuddered in awe as Celeste shone the light at them. The roundish, blue-glowing objects had merely been the tips of three side by side gargantuan icicles that hung from some undetermined source miles above, somewhere in the black heavens. An ocean's amount of water shaped into terrible spears.

These three monstrous formations flared from their narrow tips, widened enough to encase what appeared to be a multitude of unevenly-spaced black colonial mourning gowns, bodiless and gracefully petrified bombazine garments looking like they had suddenly frozen while floating. The glimmering ice fangs were steadily lowering toward the Earth as Evelyn chanted with increasing passion, swaying and raising her hand and stump to the sky.

I startled when Celeste spun around and brought her knife down toward my chest. It sank into the pumpkin, and a rich seasonal scent came up into my nose as she cut a circular opening. She plucked off the lid and aimed the light into the globe. I expected to see some horrible little baby, but there seemed to be nothing extraordinary inside, only what one would expect to find in a pumpkin…stringy pulp and white seeds. But the seeds were not seeds, after all. They were the size and color of pumpkin seeds, but they were tiny fossilized trilobites.

"Dance!" Celeste, called into the opening. "Awake and dance!"

The woman pulled back, and the pumpkin jerked in my arms as the trilobites flew up and out of their Halloween womb. Like an upside-down hail storm, the seeds slashed directly to where Evelyn stood on the floor of the tower chamber. They sliced through her bloodlessly as if through mist and continued on into the sky. Evelyn opened her eyes in horror.

"Noooo!" The older Merritt howled.

The naked woman began to convulse, her body pulsing with luminosity as if lightning were coughing through her veins. Her corporeality began to falter and blur, and within seconds she came apart, her soft fragments blowing away like dandelion spores.

The mammoth icicles began to pull back into the vast blackness above them, and as they did so they began to melt into mist. Great spectral clouds boiled out and writhed, and floating in these in a lovely, dance-like way, were the mourning gowns disinterred from their icy prisons. They swam in the clouds like witches' cloaks until the clouds dispersed and the fangs faded away and stars peered down like the eyes of a million distant jack-o-lanterns.

SEVEN:
Silence and Song

Celeste Merritt, to my understanding, has not spoken again since that night in October. She resides once again at Ivy Hill Assisted Living in North Brookfield. Every week I go to visit her. We sit in the sunny community room and have tea. I read to her, and sometimes she draws pictures. It's hard to tell what level of intelligence remains or if she remembers much about that night at the old Coddington house, but her drawings, which are fairly well-rendered, consistently depict 18th century mourning gowns. The garments hover on the paper as if gracefully dancing to a song that only Celeste can hear.

As for the three dead women found at the bottom of the stairs of the broken Coddington tower on November first, none have been identified. Like those discovered on the property in the August of 1949, each had a dark wooden box enclosing her head, and underneath, shaped to the dimensions of the boxes, were blocks of ice. The young women were all lovely with dark hair and eyes, though their petrified expressions suggested that they were screaming when they died.

I have considered writing a book, or at least a series of articles, about the events I have described here. But, I am hesitant, partly because I want to spare Celeste the intrusive glare of publicity. The woman deserves some peace and privacy considering the fact that she saved the world from something that I can't even begin to comprehend. I don't know what the future holds for Celeste, but I feel a certain protectiveness toward her, our lives forever united by the strange events of that Halloween night.

As you might imagine, the inexplicable happenings at the Coddington house found their way into my dreams. This must also be the case with Celeste Merritt, for while she has not spoken since we climbed down from the ruins of the tower that night, I hear from the nursing staff at Ivy Hill that she makes strange noises in her sleep. Low, mournful sounds echo out from her room and haunt the hallways, sounds that remind those who hear them of the songs of whales.

In the Spaces Where You Once Lived

by Damien Angelica Walters

A doe picks her way from between two trees at the edge of their back yard, keeping to the narrow path, her legs moving with a dancer's grace. Helena holds her breath, even though she and the deer are separated by a wide expanse of lawn, a deck, and locked French doors. Somehow, it seems the right thing to do. Her hand instinctively reaches for Jack's, touches empty air instead. They say it takes twenty-one days to break a habit; the heart knows nothing of such things.

The doe lifts her head, tips it in Helena's direction. Its eyes seem wrong, pale where they should be dark—blind, perhaps? Or ill?—and several patches appear to be missing from its fur. Helena squints and leans closer to the glass, but before she can take a good look, the animal's ears twitch and it turns tail and disappears back into the woods, moving too surefooted to be blind. A few orange leaves spiral down from the trees, as if marking the doe's passage, but as yet, the branches hold more than they've shed. The temperature is still mild, and Helena longs to follow the doe into the deeper woods. Maybe if she were younger; maybe if circumstances were different.

Their house sits on the southern edge of the woods surrounding Loch Raven Reservoir, the largest body of water entirely within Baltimore County. The woods contain nearly seventy miles of hiking trails; over the course of their forty-eight years in the house, most of the trails have worn their footprints, their daughter's, and more recently, those of their grandsons.

Autumn was always Jack's favorite time of the year for hiking. "For a little while, Lena," he'd say, "everything is different, like the world is opening up to show us its secret side."

"Then winter comes to hide it away again," Helena whispers. Tears prick her eyes, and she blinks them away. Too many of those these days, far too many.

From behind her Jack says, "I can't find my keys."

He's wearing a wool scarf, a windbreaker, pajamas, and slippers. His hair resembles the quills of a porcupine; it's too long but when she tried to trim it three weeks back, he pushed her hand away as soon as he saw the scissors. She hasn't had the heart to try again, and, frankly, the length of his hair is the least of her worries.

"You moved my keys again," he says, his voice heavy with accusation. "I need to pick up my wife, and I can't find my damn keys. Where did you put them?"

She recoils from the force of his words; *her* Jack rarely cursed. "I got a ride home from Naomi today because your car is in the shop. Remember?"

A necessary lie—his car was sold months ago—but guilt clings bitter to her tongue nonetheless.

"Oh," he says, his face softening. "Oh. I guess I forgot again."

She twists the wedding band on her finger. It doesn't move nearly as easily as it did a year ago. Jack has lost both the weight she's gained and his wedding band; the former is easily explained, the latter still a mystery as to how and where.

"Did you finish reading the newspaper?" she asks, her voice holding a tone similar to the one she used when Cathy was small.

"It came already?"

She nods. "It did."

"Today's paper?"

"Yes."

"Oh."

His gaze flicks from her face to the window. The sun is only beginning to set, but the room holds the suggestion of shadows. Helena bites back a curse—at her own forgetfulness, not his—twists the kitchen window blinds closed, and pulls the French door's drapes tight.

"Did the newspaper come today?" he asks.

"Yes, it did. It should be on the coffee table."

His brow creases. "Okay."

She moves toward him. "Do you need any help—"

He yanks his arm away before she makes contact. "Help? To read the newspaper?"

"No, how silly of me. Of course you don't need help, but would you like to help me shut the rest of the curtains?"

He glances at the window again, shakes his head.

"Okay, well why don't you go ahead and read the paper while I take care of the curtains, and then we can have some dessert." She thinks of mentioning his scarf and jacket, but decides not to. It takes so little to upset him these days; he'll take them off if and when he wants.

"Before dinner?"

She catches her lower lip briefly between her teeth. "Well, we had dinner already, but if you're still hungry, there's some chicken left."

His brow creases again, deeper this time, but instead of responding, he retreats back to the living room and once she hears the crinkle of the newspaper, she takes a deep breath. Then she starts the nightly routine of shutting the rest of the curtains and turning on all the lights, hating the way it makes the house feel closed-in, hating the way it will affect him if she doesn't.

When Jack gets up in the middle of the night, Helena snaps awake. The wandering is a recent development and odd, too, given his newfound fear of the dark, but after the first time, when he stubbed his toe hard enough to tear half the nail away from the bed, she's started to leave a handful of lights on. He uses the toilet (luckily, he's only had a few minor accidents thus far), and then his feet take to the stairs. She debates whether or not to stop him, to try and guide him back to bed, but her forearm still wears the ghosts of finger-shaped bruises from her last attempt, so she follows him instead.

He skirts the living room furniture with ease, pausing in front of their wedding portrait hanging on the wall. They were both so achingly young, so vibrantly smiling, and she can't bear the thought of the hole in his memory where that day should live. In the kitchen, he opens the curtains to the French doors and stands with his hands behind his back; his posture reminds her so much of the days before the disease, before he started forgetting, a lump takes hold in her throat.

"This is the wrong door," he says, and she startles. "This isn't my house."

"Jack, honey, it's late. Come back to bed. It's still dark outside, that's why it looks different, but it's the same house we've lived in for a long time."

He shakes his head. "No. This is the wrong door. The right one is out there." He reaches for the doorknob; before she can move toward him, he takes his hand away. "Okay," he says softly. "Not yet."

She steps close. "Let's go back to bed, okay? Everything will look right in the morning."

His eyes narrow and his lips tighten, then he moves past her and heads back upstairs. She stares out the window, elbows cupped in her palms. The sky is just beginning to lighten at the edges, a lessening of dark as opposed to real light, and wind rustles through the trees, turning the leaves to a rippling fan of orange, red, and yellow. Autumn, like Alzheimer's, turns everything strange and unfamiliar, and when you look for the shape of the real hidden within, you find only a promise of the winter to come.

There's another stir of movement in the woods, back

where the path curves into the trees, and Helena catches a quick glimpse of ears, legs, and tail. She waits, but whatever was there, if not a trick of the shadows, has moved on.

When she returns to their bed, Jack is already asleep; she clasps her hands beneath her breasts and stares at the ceiling, knowing she won't fall back to sleep.

"How is everything, Mom?" Cathy asks.

Helena looks up from the dinner plate she's scraping into the sink. In the back yard, her grandsons are playing catch while Tim, her son-in-law, watches from the deck. Jack stands nearby, and Helena wants to think he's watching the boys, too, but his gaze is trained on the woods.

"Much the same. He has good days and bad, and luckily, today is a good one."

Cathy takes the plate from Helena's hand and slides it into the dishwasher. "Not with Dad. I mean how is everything with you?"

"Everything's fine, sweetheart." Helena smiles, and even though it feels too small and too tight, she does her best to make it convincing.

"Is that the real answer or just the one you want me to hear?"

Helena waves one hand, grabs another plate.

Cathy makes a sound low in her throat. "I see dark circles under your eyes and you only get that way when you're tired, really tired. Are you sure you don't want me to arrange for someone to come in and sit with Dad so you can get some rest?"

"Really, I'm fine. Your father woke up in the middle of the night a couple times, that's all, but he slept through last night.

It'll take me a little while to catch up on my beauty sleep." Another small lie, another false smile, both more palatable than the truth.

"Seriously, you don't have to do it all."

"I know, but I'm afraid a stranger coming here will only make things worse for him, especially on the not-so-good days."

"I can talk to my boss, take some time—"

"Hush. You have your hands full with your job and Tim and the boys as it is. I'm perfectly capable of taking care of your father right now, and if things get too bad, I'll call someone in."

"Do you promise?"

Cathy's youngest son barrels into the kitchen. "Mom? Nana? We're gonna go for a walk, okay? Pop-Pop wants to go, and Dad said to ask you guys."

"Are you okay with that?" Cathy asks.

A nervous twinge stirs in Helena's belly. Jack is still steady enough on his feet and she trusts Tim, but Jack's good day can change in an instant without provocation.

"How about if I go, too?" Cathy says, catching Helena's eye.

"Please, Nana?"

Helena nods, although the twinge bites again.

Cathy smiles. "Good. Leave the rest of this until we get back, okay? Go sit down and read the paper or watch TV or even take a nap."

Helena watches them take the path, Cathy gently holding her father's arm. When they disappear into the woods, she leaves the dishes on the counter and sinks into her corner of the sofa. She'll rest her eyes for a moment, then she'll finish cleaning up. It's been ages since she had the opportunity to take a catnap.

The door bangs open, and Helena, still on the sofa, blinks awake.

"Nana, Nana! We're back."

Once jackets have been shrugged off and set aside,

Helena touches Cathy's shoulder. "Was everything okay?"

"Yes, pretty much. Dad got a little upset at one point because he said he couldn't find the right place, but then we started to come back and he seemed better. He did say that you don't let him walk in the woods anymore." She says this last with a small smile, but there's a kiss of sadness on her face, too.

After breakfast, Jack starts pacing from room to room, now and again pausing to cock his head. Helena lets him make three full circuits on the first floor, including the half-bath, but when he shows no signs of stopping, she says, "Jack, what's wrong?"

He brushes past her, keeps silent. In the foyer, he pauses again, his mouth moving in silent conversation.

"Jack?"

According to his doctor, he isn't truly hearing voices or seeing things; his brain is misinterpreting reflections in windows, house noises, or sounds from outside. Still, it's unnerving. He comes to a stop in the living room and whirls around to face her.

"This isn't my house," he says, his voice razor-sharp. "I know it isn't."

"Would you like to watch a movie?" She keeps her voice bright, cheerful.

"Stop talking to me. I know what you're doing, but it won't work. This isn't the right house."

She takes a deep breath. Redirection doesn't always work, but it's the best technique to use to keep his irritation from becoming true anger.

He cocks his head again. "But I'm tired of waiting."

"What?"

"I'm not talking to you. I'm talking to *them*. Leave me alone."

Another deep breath. "What if we take a walk into the woods, like you did with Cathy and the boys?"

He smiles then, and all she sees is *her* Jack, and she fights against the sting of tears. He allows her to help him with his boots and his coat, waits while she dons hers, but when she tries to take his arm, he shrugs her off. She lets it go but keeps close to his side as they cross the yard to the path, not speaking. Focusing on the pleasant chill in the air, the smell of pine and earth, the vibrant oranges and reds and yellows of the leaves around them, some of her tension falls away. No holding hands, true, but it could be a normal day, a normal walk with her husband. Even Jack's posture changes: his strides grow longer and easier, his arms swing, his eyes gleam with purpose instead of confusion or ire. Fallen leaves crunch and whisper beneath their soles.

His fingers brush hers, and then again; the third time, he entwines them with hers and she bites the inside of her cheek to hold in a sob. The path becomes a wider trail littered with small twigs that crack with each step. Sun glimmers through the trees, speckling the ground with bits of bright like crushed glass. Day stars, she thinks. He always called them day stars. The words linger on her tongue, but she's afraid to say them aloud and break the fragile spell, for this, his hand around hers, his easy walk, is a kind of magic. The best possible kind.

A thick branch lies across the trail, and Helena pauses, wondering if they should go back, but Jack tugs her hand, helps her over. Their gazes lock, and once more her throat tightens. Warmth radiates in his eyes; more than that, recognition, familiarity. This is the Jack that stood beside her and said "I do," the man who cried with her when she had her first miscarriage and her second and her third, the man who cried even more when she gave birth to Cathy, healthy and whole. This is the husband whose weight she felt atop hers more times than she could count, whose hand she held at funerals, at weddings, at birthday parties. In this moment, she is companion, not caregiver. *Please. Let him stay Jack for a little while longer. Just for today, let him remember, let him stay.*

Around them, the shadows grow, but they continue to walk. Her boot begins to rub against the smallest toe on her right foot, and although she knows there will be a blister to pay, she says nothing, tries only to shift her foot as she places it down.

Jack pauses. His fingers tighten around hers; his head turns this way and that. His mouth moves, forming silent words, then his hand relaxes and he starts walking again. She bites her tongue. A small misstep, not worth the mention, not worth the worry. For all she knows, he did hear something she missed.

They come to a slow incline; halfway up, he freezes in place, and she does the same. At the top, half hidden in the brush, stands a doe. No, not *a* doe, but the doe with white eyes and missing fur. The animal is so thin its ribs resemble a xylophone, its remaining fur is dull, and threads of frothy spittle dangle from its jaws. Her mouth turns to desert; her fingers to ice. Her body jolts, and beneath her heel, a twig breaks, the sound loud and sharp. The doe doesn't run as expected, but slowly turns and disappears down the other side of the incline. Helena shudders.

Jack pulls his hand free, shakes it as if removing the memory of her touch. "We have to go back. It isn't time yet," he says.

"Time for what?"

The Jack mask falls; in its place, an angry old man with narrowed, suspicious eyes. "We have to go back. Now."

"Okay, Jack, okay. We'll go back." She shoves her hand in her pocket, the warmth of fabric a pale substitute for the warmth of skin.

Several times on their way home, she feels the weight of unseen eyes, but when she casts a glance over her shoulder, she sees nothing unexpected, nothing save trees and falling leaves.

She wakes to find the bed empty and panic fills her mouth. Upstairs, Jack is nowhere to be found. As she takes the stairs as quickly as possible, the blister on her toe bursts wet and warm against the adhesive bandage. Her breath comes fast and harsh, easing when she finds Jack in the kitchen, once more standing at the French doors with the curtains partially open.

He mumbles something and frowns. He speaks again, his words tangled and indistinct. The tone of his voice is strange, thick and yet somehow liquid, as though he's speaking around a mouthful of half-set gelatin. A cold chill dances the length of Helena's spine.

He frowns yet again, followed by another slur of words, and turns toward her.

"Soon," he says, his voice perfectly measured, perfectly *normal*, and leaves her alone in the kitchen.

She waits until the upstairs floorboards creak before she moves to shut the curtains. There, at the end of the yard, the white-eyed doe. More patches of fur have fallen out; the bare skin beneath holds a strange grey cast. Her arms go all over goosebumps, and the icy waltz makes a second spin on her back.

She doesn't know if diseases can pass from deer to human, doesn't understand why it keeps showing up or how it can even find its way, but most of all, doesn't want to believe that Jack was holding an imaginary conversation with the animal.

"Go away," she whispers.

As if on command, the doe turns and slips back into the woods. Her goosebumps remain.

Jack refuses to get dressed in the morning, and after tempting him with several shirts that were once favorites, she gives up. What's the real harm in letting him keep to his pajamas and slippers? He sits at the kitchen table without argument, though. A small victory.

While the coffee is brewing, she asks, "Jack, last night, when you woke up and came down here, you said, 'soon.' Do you remember? What does that mean? Is something going to happen?"

He smiles. "I'm waiting for the door, the real one, to my real house, and it's almost time. They can fix everything, they can fix *me*. They said so."

"Who said so?"

He looks down at his hands. "I can't tell you."

"Can't or won't?"

"Are we having eggs today? I think I want eggs."

She puts away the box of pancake mix. "Yes, of course we can have eggs."

Midday, while Jack is napping, Helena dials Cathy's number but hangs up the phone before it can ring. What's she going to say? Your father is talking crazy, and there's a doe that keeps coming to the house, a doe with white eyes and missing fur? Oh, and I think your father is talking to it, too?

She shakes her head. It's the disease; she knows it is. The disease and the toll it's taking on her, his paranoia bleeding into her, and the deer is obviously ill; sick animals usually remain close to familiar areas until they find a place to die. And Jack isn't talking *to* the deer, but *at* it, as if it were a newspaper or a television show. Soon enough, he'll be fixated on something else.

The truth is, she can't handle this; she can't handle Jack on her own anymore. She needs to put aside her own pride and bring someone in to help because it isn't going to get any easier and she knows what's coming: more anger, more confusion. The disease will continue to strip every bit of Jack away, and when it's done, it will destroy his body. Like an autumn tree, he's shedding his leaves, leaving bare branches behind, but for him, the new growth of spring will never come.

She wishes for a stroke or a heart attack, something quick to end his suffering—and hers—but as soon as the thought takes shape in her mind, guilt drapes itself across her shoulders, and she scrubs her face in her hands. This is the way the world breaks you. It takes everything you know and love and turns it inside out. It leaches the color from your hair, yellows your teeth, and curves your spine, and even though you wish you were the same person you've always been on the inside, you go grey and stained and frail there, too.

Stop. Get hold of yourself. You need a good night's sleep, that's all.

Tears burn in her eyes and she lets them fall, unsure if she's weeping for Jack or for herself or maybe for them both.

He's pacing again. Living room to dining room to kitchen and back again, pausing at each window to peer outside, muttering incoherencies all the while. She does her best to ignore it, but when he shows no signs of stopping, she asks if he wants to go for a walk.

"No," he says.

"Would you like to watch a movie with me?"

He tips his head to the side, then nods. "Okay."

Once settled on the sofa, he pats the back of her hand. "Lena, I'm sorry I'm so forgetful sometimes."

Her name. He used her name. A knot tightens in her

chest. "It's okay, Jack. I love you."

"I love you, too."

She cups the side of his face in her palm, and although he doesn't lean into her touch the way he used to, he doesn't pull away.

Arms around an empty laundry basket, Helena walks past the bathroom and grimaces. Jack's toothbrush, still holding a bright blue swoop of toothpaste, is on the edge of the sink, but there's no sign of Jack. Leaving the basket in the hall, she checks their room, but it's empty, too. She was only in the guest bedroom long enough to put the freshly washed sheets back on the bed. How did he get past her without her hearing a thing?

Once again, she finds him downstairs by the French doors.

"Jack, what are you doing? It's time to get ready for bed."

"No," he says, reaching for the lock. "It's time for me to go. They said so."

"Let's go back upstairs now. You need to brush your teeth."

He whirls around, his face a snarl. "You can't stop me. This has nothing to do with you. It's only for me."

She takes his arm. His mouth twists again; he puts his hands on her shoulders and growls. "No," he shouts, shoving her away.

Her arms flail, but she grabs only air as she falls, landing hard on her tailbone with a sharp cry. The door thumps shut, and she struggles to her feet, breathing through her mouth, ignoring the starburst of pain in her lower spine. Her fault, this is her fault. She should've replaced the locks with keyed dead bolts. What if he falls, what if he gets lost and hurts himself? Or worse?

The night air is chill, full dark with no hint of sunrise, and clouds veil an almost-full moon. Too dark to see much of anything but shadows and the pale blur of his pajamas.

"Jack, please stop. Come back. It's too dark outside."

But he doesn't stop, doesn't look back, simply keeps moving across the lawn faster than she's seen him move in years, moving as steady and sure as if it were a sunny day. He reaches the path and, with a flash of striping, disappears into the trees.

She scrambles across the kitchen to the junk drawer, pawing frantically through the contents. At the very back she finds what she's looking for: a small flashlight. "Small, but bright," Jack said when he bought it at the hardware store, long before his diagnosis. She pauses by the phone; she should call Cathy or even 911, but no one will arrive in time and if he wanders off the path... She checks to make certain the flashlight works and shakes her head. No, Jack won't go far. He *won't*. Not in the dark.

Beneath her feet, the ground is cold and her nightgown isn't nearly warm enough, but she's wasted enough time already. She sweeps the light across the lawn; the last thing she needs is to trip and fall. Pressing her lips together tight, she takes to the path. A few steps in and the shadows hang even heavier. She scans the trees with the light. No Jack.

Impossible. He has no light. He can't have gotten that far. She trains her light on the path and keeps moving, her back awash in a cold sweat, her mouth a sharp slick of panic. She calls out his name, gets no response. The path turns to trail, and still she sees nothing but darkness and shadows. No sign of her husband. The woods are silent, strangely so. Shouldn't there be small animals scurrying about or something? This quiet is absolute and terrifying.

She nearly stumbles over his discarded slippers, but they alleviate some of her panic, for even in the dark he's managing to stick to the path. On the other side of the branch Jack previously helped her with, she sees both foot and handprints. The shake of her hands makes the light bounce, but there's no blood on the ground, so if he fell, maybe he didn't fall hard.

"Jack?"

When she reaches the bottom of the incline, she calls his name again, hot tears coursing down her cheeks. She needs to go back and call for help. She was a fool to try and find him on her own. *Stupid woman. Stupid, prideful woman.*

Then she hears Jack's voice, low and unintelligible, but distinctly his. A wave of relief crashes over her.

"I'm coming, Jack. Stay there. Please stay there."

"I'm here," he says.

On the incline, her thighs start to burn, and her feet slip on twigs and scree. Halfway up, she hears Jack say, "Will it take me to the right house? Is it the right door?"

"It is all doorways," another voice says, a guttural, inhuman voice, one she doesn't hear with her ears but with her bones, each syllable pressing its shape into her marrow. Every instinct says run, but she can't. She *can't.*

"You will carry it until it's time," the inhuman voice says. "The animal wasn't strong enough."

A pale, sickly light spills over the top of the incline.

"Oh," Jack says.

Ignoring the ache in her legs, Helena scrambles the rest of the way up. Jack stands at the bottom, his arms slack at his sides, and in front of him, the doe. The light is seeping from the corners of its white eyes, the way sun finds the edge of a window blind. There's no sign of the speaker, no sign of anyone or anything else.

The doe's body ripples, its eyes expand, and more light spills out, a greenish-yellow light that hangs heavy in the air. The sound of tearing fabric—no, worse than that, tearing flesh— breaks the quiet, and the doe's body topples, landing with a soft thump. In its place hovers a fist-sized ovoid of the blackest black haloed within the strange light. It begins to slowly rotate, absorbing the light and expanding to the size of a basketball. When the light is gone, the sphere resembles an oil slick dotted with flickering lights. Starlight, she thinks, but it isn't that exactly. It's something more, something bigger than she can put a name to. A truth, a nightmare, a *doorway*.

Yet for what?

Jack holds out his arms.

"No," she cries, but the word shivers into the air and is silenced.

The sphere collapses, draping over his skin like a blanket of space. It seeps into his flesh one galaxy at a time, leaving strange whirls and spheres in between, patterned as if they, too, are galaxies, but those her eyes are not able—or not allowed—to discern. A scream tears its way from her lips, but if it holds a sound, it lives only in her mind. Pressure thuds behind her temples, sharp jabs blade through her head, and she falls to her knees, dropping the flashlight to cover her eyes with her hands. She hears: a slow thrum, a symphony of voices speaking in a language she wasn't meant to hear and can't understand, the sound of strange and ponderous bodies moving through water.

Her ears pop and silence falls once more. She scrabbles in the dirt for the flashlight and rises on rubbery legs, her breath a rasp of sandpaper laced with sobs. The air is thick with the stench of a rotting carcass; underneath that, the impossible salt tang of an ocean.

"Jack?"

He turns toward her voice, his shoulders slumped. As far as she can see, no trace of the black remains.

"They couldn't fix me," he says. "I'm too broken."

A lump in her throat steals her voice away.

You will carry it until it's time.

Looking down into his eyes, all she sees is Jack, lost and

afraid, but she feels the presence of something else, something *other*.

What is he carrying inside him, and what will happen when it's time? How is she supposed to pretend everything is fine? This isn't fair. It isn't right. He's too old for this, whatever this is; they both are. Haven't they suffered enough?

She swallows hard, her thumb tracing a circle around the flashlight's on-off switch. She could turn around right now and leave him here. No one would know. She could call the police in the morning and tell them he wandered out sometime in the night without her hearing. He wouldn't be the first, or the last, to do such a thing.

But how can she do that to him? Even if he isn't wholly Jack, he hasn't been Jack for a long time. Still, she remains where she is, staring into the shadows.

"I'm cold," Jack says, his voice trembling. "And I don't feel well. I want to go home now. Please, Lena, can we go home?"

Memories of the Fall

by Pete Rawlik

As the door shuts, the light bulb switches on. I only have a few moments to remember the day, to reinforce it, to make it the dominant image in my mind, – just a few moments to try and stay sane.

They let me spend a few minutes in the courtyard while the children scurried to class. The air was crisp and there was an aroma of smoke and burning leaves. It's a damp kind of smell, the kind that should linger for hours. I took a deep breath through my nose and let the scent fill my lungs and my memory. I wanted to savor this, let it roll around on the back of my brain and imprint itself there.

Throngs of children, all ages, all colors, all heights, all shapes, all sizes, and all in the same uniform, marched past me, babbling to each other in their sing song voices. The flood of youth brought a new cavalcade of odors: laundry detergent, wet grass, and more wet leaves, but also the scents of dogs, cats, and rabbits. There are wafts of sausage and oatmeal, warm milk and cocoa. I miss the foods of childhood. A boy wandered by chewing on an egg and cheese sandwich on toast, and I had to fight the desire to snatch it from him.

A clutch of girls strolled around me carrying dried flowers. There were corn stalks, gourds, spiky gum balls from sweetgum trees, cattail heads, and other things I recognized but couldn't name. The girls were laughing the sweet laughter of children having fun without a care in the world. Their coats were covered with a variety of hitchhikers, as if they had walked to school through the tall dry grass, the last ants and crickets of the season scurrying out of their way.

The principal and teachers did their best to keep these children contained and controlled, but it's like trying to herd cats, organized chaos; a losing battle against a juvenile throng.

The bell rang, it was electronic, too loud, and it hurt my

ears. Kids took off at a run, scattering, and the courtyard emptied; they left nothing in their wake except echoes of footsteps pounding down halls beyond closing doors. Seconds pass and the electronic tone is replaced by a female voice distorted by a bad microphone and aged speakers. I couldn't understand what she was saying, but I recognized the rhythm of what was said. I placed my hand over my heart and I mumbled out the Pledge of Allegiance, or at least what I remembered of it.

The pledge was followed by announcements muffled and garbled. I think they were in English, but given what I could hear above the popping and clicking of the static they could easily have been in Swahili. Suddenly, Mrs. Kennedy appeared by my side. It's been a year since I've seen her or talked to her. She reminds me of the waning moon: thin, pale, and sharp. I followed her into the cafeteria which doubles as an auditorium.

There were eight tables, maybe six kids per table, which made about fifty or so children. There were other teachers besides Mrs. Kennedy, but they didn't bother to introduce themselves. Mrs. Kennedy raised her voice and demanded order in a strict, raspy tone that sent shivers up my spine. The class, or maybe it is three classes, quieted down quickly. Did they respond out of respect, or was it out of fear? Does it matter?

The walls of the room were decorated with construction paper cutouts. Orange and black were dominant colors. There were pilgrim dolls, skeleton cutouts, and pre-printed cornucopias on the walls. Toilet paper ghosts hung from the ceiling. I tried to think about what day it was to no avail. I think I'm before Thanksgiving, but am I before Halloween, or between the two? I let the frustration show on my face.

I was introduced – it's cursory, and even though I've done this for more than a decade, they still have no idea how to properly work with me. It's alright. I took control at the first opening. I got the kids interested by asking them question. What are you reading? What are your favorite scary stories? The answers came quickly, and most of them I didn't recognize. Thankfully, some of them have read the classics: Poe, Stoker, and Wells. I spent a few minutes on Wells, focusing on his use of science fiction to express his concerns about class struggle and the dehumanization of the poor. I didn't mention that he was a socialist. I talked about Poe and his emotional state expressed through poetry. I avoided the fact that he was an alcoholic.

I moved the conversation toward writing, mentioned metaphor, foreshadowing, irony, and a few other cheap tricks writers employ. After ten minutes of this, I needed a mental break. I pulled some pages from my coat pocket and read from them. Three stories, not my best work, but not my worst either. They were safe stories with just a twist of darkness, and a hint of violence, suitable for the young – not at all like what I've been writing for the last ten years. Afterwards, there was some applause punctuated with nervous, macabre laughter. One boisterous young man suggested that my work should be made into a film. He appreciated the subject matter but preferred it in another medium. Doesn't anyone just read anymore?

The class really opened up after that. An excitable girl with dark features named Madeline wanted to be in one of my stories; another named Victoria, with glasses that nearly cover her entire face, told me she really wanted to be a writer and for me to be her editor. I didn't have the heart to tell her the sacrifices we have to make; the conditions I have to work under; the things I must do for my art.

I did a trick with punctuation using the phrase LETS EAT GRANDMA, and showed them the importance of comma placement. They laughed at the variations so I did another about cowboys and panda bears. In an instant I was a rock star, at least amongst twelve year olds.

I winced when the bell rang; I'd lost track of time. The teachers had the children thank me before they filed out in another example of organized chaos. One of the teachers, a young man with a head like a mop, stopped in front of me. He took me by the hand and for a moment looked me deep in the eyes. "I'm sorry," he blurted before racing out the door. I wanted to respond but a flood of children suddenly surrounded me and I lost any chance at conversation.

They let me eat in the teacher's lounge. Lunch was cafeteria food; mystery meat smothered in gravy, reconstituted mashed potatoes, milk, and a slice of pumpkin pie. The pie was heavy and the filling thin. It ran across my plate, spreading like a glob of orange slime that had seeped into the world from some nearby hell dimension. I took my plastic spoon and ate it greedily.

I wandered the school for a while; I don't know how long, I don't have a watch. At first I thought they had forgotten me, but as I drifted toward the main entrance the maintenance man appeared. He had a mop with its head buried inside one of those buckets on wheels. He stood between me and the door. The mop came out and swished around on the floor. It was all I could do not to panic and run. Instead I turned and marched back down the corridor. Ten years and I still don't know my way around this building. I think they change it a little each time just to confuse me.

By chance I found the library. The room was quiet, and at first I thought it was because there were no children, but then a slight movement caught my eye. Something the size of a large dog, something with pale skin and a dingy brown sweater, moved down one of the rows. I tried to follow but balked as I look where I thought it went. The row between the shelves of books faded into a distant, dimly-lit part of the room. Something moaned and gibbered as it retreated from where I was standing, and I stumbled backwards into the light.

The librarian caught me and with a gentle and aged hand on my side and pulled me away from the murmuring dim. I was shaking. She found me a seat by a window. She made me a cup of tea—not Earl Grey, but it did what was needed. I stared at the world beyond the glass. An occasional car crept past the gates, a trail of exhaust smoking behind it in the chilled air. My breath steamed the window. With my finger, I drew a smiley face and the words HELP ME. I let them sit there for a second and then in a panic I quickly used my sleeve to wipe it all away.

The evidence of my transgression eliminated, I leaned back in the chair and fell asleep. I didn't dream.

I am wakened by the sound of someone saying my name. They weren't yelling, just repeating it over and over and over again in a calm, systematic way, as if I were waiting for an appointment at the DMV. When I finally struggled back to consciousness, I apologized profusely. Mrs. Kennedy put her hand on my shoulder and told me it was time. I felt like a mouse caught in the claw of some predatory bird. I asked if I could spend another hour, perhaps talk to another class, but she just shook her head no. School was almost over; there were no more classes for the day. Resigned to my fate, I followed her down the halls because I really had no choice. The sea of children headed for busses parted before us. In mere moments, I was far from the cafeteria, far from the classrooms, in a wing of the building where children aren't allowed.

My moon-pale escort opened a door marked STORAGE. Inside, a single bare light bulb, a wooden chair, and a metal cot with a thin mattress and a thinner pillow welcomed me home. In the corner a shelf held a stack of paper and a jar of pencils nearly worn down to the nubs. The far wall was bare, unpainted concrete.

I went inside and sat down and watched as Mrs. Kennedy took the stack of what I had written this past year. She is not a fan of my work, but under these conditions what else can I be expected to write except cosmic horror. As she closed the door, the hall light reflected her smile, a malevolent grin that I hate. I hated it ten years ago, and age has not improved my feeling. Then the door closed, the key turned in the lock, and the light sputtered to life.

The memory of my day comes to an end, and tears fill my eyes. The far wall shudders and then dissolves. It melts away like wax and leaves behind an open window to the eternal howling void at the heart of our galaxy. Black stars burn cold in the night. Dying stars dump clouds of cosmic ash that seep down between the barren rocks that once were planets. Something shadowy passes between me and the stars. I scream. I scream until my lungs nearly burst and my throat is raw. I scream until I am no longer sane and the madness takes control. In this place, sanity is a detriment, and madness is a survival skill.

Then I grab what is left of my pencil and I try very hard to write coherently. Perhaps if I produce something more marketable, they will let me spend more time away from this place. I write. I write desperately, madly, and try to think of what I shall do for Mrs. Kennedy and her students when she lets me out next year. The memory of autumn still lingers in my nose, on my tongue, and in my brain. They can't take my hope. They can't take my memories away. I watch as a world of sentient butterflies with gossamer wings collapses in on itself spewing radioactive proto-matter in my direction that burn my retinas.

I cling to the memory of crisp autumn air and try to pretend that the stench of death and destruction that surrounds me is the scent of damp leaves smoldering in the distance.

Andy Kaufman Creeping
through the Trees
by Laird Barron

Autumn, 1998

Senior year of high school isn't the best of times. It is totally the other way. And how shall I count the ways? Cancer is eating my father alive. He's got six months, a year, it's anybody's guess. How many of those days will be worth a damn? He's sort of a tough-as-shoe-leather guy and I bet he'll make it hard on himself, on us all. Both our dogs, Little Egypt and Odysseus, bit the dust from old age during summer vacation. Not enough drama? The last week of August I almost kill myself on the new trampoline. Okay, technically, I fly off the trampoline and do a half-gainer into the side of our house. Instant KO.

Why does this even happen (and why me)? Solution: The Universe is a real bitch. Sometimes she smirks and gives you what you want. My heart's desire is a full-sized trampoline to practice cheer moves on. Well done, cosmos, you perverse whoremaster. A neighbor lost his job way up north in the Prudhoe Bay oil fields and put basically everything he owned out on the lawn at fire-sale prices. The neighbor kids cried when we loaded the trampoline into the bed of our truck. Flash forward twenty-four hours and it's me singing the blues.

I get cocky and bounce hard near the edge and *Kaboing!* Thank Satan the rhododendron bush cushions the impact. Also, thank you, dearly departed Anton LaVey, our Lord and Savior, I am alone for this debacle. None of the other girls bear witness to my humiliation. Dad has passed out drunk earlier than usual and doesn't hear the thud or the shattering china. Also kinda bad, though. I lie stunned for a few seconds, then angry yellow jackets swarm from their nest in the bushes and sting the ever-loving hell out of me.

Neck brace, knee brace, swollen face. The knee is the worst, although sharing Renee Zellweger's squinty pout for a week is not to be envied. The upshot being one of my rivals (probably trailer park queen Reline Showalter) will lead the cheer squad when our boys pillage their way to state again. Grr! Is it too petty of me to hope the team suffers a rash of injuries and misses the playoffs?

Damn our soon-to-be ex-neighbor and his stupid discount trampoline he bought for his stupid brats. Damn the universe and all its devices, such as gravity, colorectal cancer, and children.

The mound of get-well cards is impressive. So many flowers and gift baskets, it becomes tedious to sort them for the contraband. Chocolate! Stuffed toys! Poppers (bless you Benny Three-Trees)! Porno disguised as *Cosmopolitan, Girls' Life,* and *Seventeen!* Rob Zombie and Weezer CDs!

I'm blonde, taut, and hot. Everybody loves me and everybody else hates me. I know who's who—pals write, *Hey Julie V, get well, babe;* the fools call me Julie Five, or Stuck-Up Bitch, and say, *too bad you only sprained your neck.* It's vital to know the sides. High school is a cold war no more or less a game than East versus West. Most of the girls, pro or con Julie Vellum, are super smooth and you can't go by kind words or a friendly smile. If you don't keep the factions and the alliances straight, you'll get a knife between the shoulder blades. Been there (middle school), no thanks.

Human nature; what are you going to do? After my tragic accident and the initial flood of sympathy, even my tightest friends avoid me like I'm Typhoid Mary. A knee brace or an arm cast can be sexy if you work it right. *Neck* braces, visible swelling, and contusions are totally uncool. Emotionally, I'm not well-equipped to cope, even if my upbringing suggests otherwise.

Being an only child kinda sucks when it doesn't totally rock. My shrink (Mom's idea), an ex-pill dispenser to the stars, says ugly sibling rivalries are transferred to my peers and blown up on the stage and that I should watch it. She's right despite her ignominious status as a Beverly Hills refugee – I sharpen these claws on classmates and it's earned me a bit of a reputation for being a super-bitch. Meanwhile, Grandpa says acting snotty is a cover for weakness and it's too bad I don't have a brother to keep me in check. He seldom wears shirt or pants and handily out-drinks Dad, believe it or don't.

I take this wise counsel in stride.

Haters can talk smack all they like, I am *not* an entitled high school slut cheerleader. I am a regal and voraciously *sexual* high school cheerleader. Besides, I didn't actually do the deed until Rocky Eklund, then the backup quarterback, popped my cherry after the team took state last fall. Junior freaking year. Yeesh. Ask Robin Sloan or Indra Norse when they first gave it up. Ask those skanks, Jessica Mace and her cousin Liz Lochinvar. *I* was practically a cloistered virgin before the dam broke. Unless we're counting hand jobs and BJs. In that case, it would be fifth grade and weird, so let's not.

A week of school convinces me that I'm in a political exile. Woman without a Country. The second tier girls and hangers-on occupy my table in the cafeteria; talk about a come-down. Greetings range from nervous to frosty. Nobody looks me in the eye. Smiling the hard smile Jackie taught, I seriously worry my face will get stress fractures. I read the history of the Borgias during lunch and fantasize about a mass poisoning.

Rocky has football practice (I'm giving my beau his space; got to provide him political cover until I shed the scaggy collar) and then beers and pool at Mike Zant's house after Thursday class. Doc won't let me drive until I can turn my head again.

I catch a lift with Steely J. We have business anyhow. His ride is a Toyota wagon with Visqueen taped over the rear side windows; hundred and thirty thousand miles on the odometer. He keeps the wagon spiffy as a military bunk, oddly enough, and daisy-sweet with a cluster of air fresheners rubber-banded to the rearview. Nonetheless, I spread a handful of cafeteria napkins on the passenger seat. My hunch says a blacklight would paint a very different picture of the environment.

Steely J resides in the friend camp. He's in the friend camp for *most* of us, not to be confused with a buddy or a pal or a member of the crew. Dude is like Australia or Switzerland; up for hijinks and not the teeniest bit judgey. He's a fixer and you don't have to like a fixer to love one. Tall, really quiet, although not broody, he-man quiet; closer to a great white shark cruising through the shallows. And white is right—he's whitey McWhite cream cheese complexioned. He walks soft, sorta hunched in his lumpy sweaters, buzz cut, black frame glasses, and sneakers for sneaking.

A man of unexpected facets, he's obsessed with ancient aliens (Greys built the Pyramids!) and a hundred and one doomsday scenarios. The universe is a hologram and the only real gods are likely horrifically evolved humanoids or giant blobs of sentient protoplasm. His father worked for a pharmaceutical company and had taken his whole weirdo family on months-long business vacations to Borneo and the Amazon Basin when the kids were little.

We've shared bizarre conversations. Craziest exchange happened after I paid him to get the test key to Math finals. Apropos of absolutely nothing (although I had the sniffles), he said, *Wonder why I never get sick?*

Not really. Fair question though. Granted, the pasty bastard isn't an exemplar of health, yet I don't recall him ever missing school from the seasonal crud.

I bleed myself.

Like Dark Ages bleeding? Smoke enemas? Barf me out, dude.

Dark Ages is recent history. Bleeding goes back to the Hellenic. In the 1920s, missionaries brought it here from South American death cults. Got to propitiate them old black gods with rivers of blood, y'know.

I'm quite sure I don't.

Bad blood out, fresh blood in. Ever want to give it a whirl, I've got the kit. Make a superwoman out of you for real.

Fresh blood in? What did that even mean? I decided I didn't give a shit. I'd let it return to haunt me at some future 3AM.

He doesn't do sports despite his "perfect" health and even though he'd wallop most of the boys with his bizarro, predatory grace. Elmer D. said there was an incident at wrestling tryouts and Coach Grinky eighty-sixed Steely J hardcore.

Side note: I fooled around with Elmer the summer of our junior year, but have since nixed our romance. His dad wrecked their truck this past winter. Mr. D. burned and Elmer survived with some wicked scars. Pitiable or not, I pretend he doesn't exist because now I'm rolling with Mr. Future-All-State-full-ride-to-some-powerhouse-football-town. JV be trading up.

Steely J is solid with the rich kids (especially Fat Boy Tooms). Rumor is, he gophers for them since he can pass for legal, has a boss fake ID, knows no fear, and, most importantly, is scruple-free. You want weed, booze, or heavier stuff, you call Hostettler or Benny Three Trees. You need somebody to hold for you, alibi for you, or step-'n-fetch-it, Steely J is your prole. He makes book on sports events and makes unwanted pets vanish. He's the source for cheap designer clothes, "borrowed" power tools, scalped tickets, and VIP invites to password-at-the-door-parties. It's this last detail that interests me at the moment.

I hit him with the lowdown. "Okay, dude, look. My dad. He has cancer." This confession has the opposite effect from what I expected. My stomach tightens. The bile in my throat must be remorse.

"Sorry to hear it." Steely J speaks in a monotone drawl that pitches slightly to indicate his mood. In this case, it descends toward baritone. He gives a perfunctory shit. "What kind?"

"The way he guzzles Maker's Mark, you'd think cirrhosis, but nope. Rectal cancer."

"Huh."

"This is eyes-only need to know, so keep your lips zipped."

"Not planning to do a press release. Damn."

"Good, or it's your balls."

"Sure your purse has got room for 'em?"

"It's a coin purse. Plenty of room for your junk. I need a favor."

"Heck of a way of asking."

"My dad's birthday is October ninth. He loved Andy Kaufman, see. Absolutely adored him, is more to the point. Dee Dee Andersen says her brother knows a guy at the Gold Digger who saw the booking sheet for Halloween. That lounge singer character Kaufman did in the '70s is on the schedule—"

"Tony Clifton."

"Yes, Tony Clifton. Live and in person. What I need—"

"*The* Tony Clifton...Here, in Anchorage?" Steely J's monotone pitches higher.

"Uh, yeah, sure."

"Fucking A! Who's playing him? Zmuda, I bet. Has to be Zmuda."

"*One* of Kaufman's buddies, obviously. That's not the important—"

"You'd assume one of his compatriots. On the other hand, it's possible Clifton exists. True story, Kaufman and

Zmuda planned to work on a film biography of Clifton and how Kaufman originally discovered him at a hotel in Vegas and they got to be friends, and so on. Fell through because *Heartbeeps* didn't sell enough tickets. Bummer." He drives like turtles screw so we've apparently got all the time in the world.

"You should write a book."

He doesn't react to my sarcasm. "Comedians tap into the infinite. Black Kryptonite."

"Fascinating, not really, but—"

"Kaufman faked his own death. Something hinky about these random gigs Clifton does. Think about that—fourteen years and he's still dropping in to do his old routine and for what? Nobody except fogies like your dad even remember him. The whole setup is hinky. Kaufman might've been sick of the limelight. Fame gets some people down. *Heartbeeps* was pretty bad. Okay, it reeked. That's why he faked his death and retired to a South Pacific island and he comes around to yank our chains every once in a while. It's possible, right?"

"For the love of…No, J. Neither of those are possible. I can't even." My lips hurt, we're way off in the weeds, and I'm about to blow a fuse. The pressure of being Julie Vellum can be crushing.

He licks his cheek. "Yeah, yeah. I know. It would be cool."

"Please pay attention. Dee Dee says the show is a hush-hush exclusive. One night only. There's a secret list. I want Daddy on that list."

He smiles. His incisor is silver. The smile doesn't change his expression much more than a lone cloud moving across the sky. "Clifton rules. Best character Kaufman ever did, easy. I'll make some calls, see if it's legit."

"Super. What's it gonna set me back?"

He flicks a glance my way. His tongue protrudes again, tasting the possibilities. "I dunno. BJ?"

I tap the brace that ratchets my neck and chin so severely it might as well be one of those Elizabethan collars the vet puts on a dog. My eyes and nose are still swollen and my lips are fat enough I'm still taking vital nutrients through a straw. "You probably play the lottery, too. C'mon, dude. I'm in no condition. *You're* in no condition. Blowing you is against the Geneva Convention."

"Well, you look like a walking glory hole. Fifty bucks. Plus whatever the tickets go for, if this is legit." Fifty bucks is his asking price for everything from shoplifting eyeliner, to scoring tickets, to committing grand larceny or felonious assault.

"Deal!" I almost shake his pallid, sweaty paw before I come to my senses. His parents own a place on the hillside. Didn't mom and dad J relocate to the Midwest in '95 and basically abandon the property? Rings a bell. He's got a litter of younger siblings. Pale, snot-nosed ankle-biters who look like they should be floating in jars of formaldehyde. Did his family abandon him? You can attend public school until the age of twenty-one. I think he's close. Does he sleep in his car? In the trunk (a coffin)? Is he communicable? He wears the same sweater several days in a row. Dirt under his nails is a given. Drops of blood crust the toes of his sneakers. His favorite all-weather ensemble is a Seahawks track suit, plus a goose down parka when the mercury dips. He smells ripe and his cheap aftershave is insufficient to the challenge. He habitually sips I don't have a clue what from a mason jar jammed inside a grody Starbucks cup holder. His breath is raw as fuck. He appears pudgy unless you've been around ball players and weightlifters and recognize there's earth-moving brawn under the panda-bear-softness. Why do his eyes make me think of fish? I consider these mysteries for half a second and we're home sweet home.

Steely J says as I open the car door, "Ever have an imaginary friend? When you were a kid?"

"Jesus," I say.

Mom insists I call her Jackie. It's a Unitarian thing, maybe? She and Dad lived in California right out of high school. Jackie got knocked up, then she got religion. She was too busy giving birth to me to finish college. By the time I entered Kindergarten, she'd ditched the whole stay-at-home-mom routine (bailed on the church, too), took a few night classes in business, and embarked on a career as a hotshot saleswoman of water purification systems.

Dad couldn't hack UCLA no matter how he tried. He slunk home to Girdwood, Alaska, in defeat. Grandpa gave him a superintendent job at the chemical plant in Anchorage. Dad's name is Jeff. He doesn't let me call him Jeff; he's not a Unitarian and the Valley didn't rub off on him. Mom, I mean, Jackie, got the full dose and passed it along to me.

Jackie travels the globe. She stays on the road two weeks out of every month. She's an absentee parent, which makes her pretty damned rad. Sure, it blew chunks (and to whom it may concern, I don't suffer from bulimia; my athletic figure is purely genetic) during pre-adolescence not having a mom to teach me how to navigate middle school and getting my period and so forth. Past is the past (Grandpa says it's prologue). I've come to appreciate the combined arms power of benign neglect and guilt. Besides, when she is around, she displays the demeanor of an indulgent queen dishing boons willy-nilly. Boys? *Just be careful, dear. Here's a variety pack of condoms.* Money? *Let's tack another twenty onto your allowance.* Out late? *Be home by dawn.* Can I have a car for my sweet sixteen? *Tell your father to take you to the dealership. Nothing too fast, okay?* Best part is, once I grew tits I magically became eligible for her Machiavellian advice, which she dispenses freely.

Fun and games notwithstanding, there is a single ironclad rule. On my first morning as a freshman at Onager High, Jackie drove me to the front entrance and we sat in the car bopping to "Black Hole Sun" and verifying our makeup. A dark-haired girl in a leather jacket, jeans, and combat boots got out of a stone age Ford truck.

Jackie grabbed my arm real hard and said in a witchy, hateful voice that surely belonged to someone else's mom, *See that little twat dressed like a Jet? That's Jessica Mace. Her bitch mother is Lucius. Redneck losers. Stay away from them or you'll be sorry.*

I didn't have the slightest clue as to her damage (and the fact a lot of people consider *us* to be barely one step out of the trailer park made me wonder if dear old ma was projecting). My arm hurt with those talons squeezing tight. Why the drama? Yeah, I could tell the Mace chick was trouble from the way she stood, all badass nonchalant with her mouth crimped like Lee Van Cleef, or somebody who carried a switchblade. Still, I could handle it. *Jeez, Jackie. Get real. I'm not scared of redneck trash.*

Fear me, then.

What? I'm not scared of you either.

Pow! Jackie backhanded me and smashed my lip. Prior to that shocking moment, she'd never lifted a finger to check my antics. Dad did the discipline in our house. I sat there in shock while she dabbed the blood with a hanky and straightened my hair.

We're copacetic? She smiled, gangster-hard. Nobody ever really knew her, or this is why Dad drinks.

I swallowed my tears and bailed. Had to slink past Mace loitering on the sidewalk. The girl appraised me with narrowed eyes and a smirk.

You've got something on your face.

Jackie needn't have worried. I hated Mace already.

Three years on and we haven't revisited the topic. Everything seems rosy between mother-dearest and me. Jackie may be less creepy than Steely J, however that doesn't make it easier to read her. She is, after all, the one who assigned *The Prince* as bedside reading. *Smile, then stick it to them, honey. Instead of wrist-wrist, elbow-elbow, it's smile-smile, stab-stab. It is totally better to be feared than loved.*

She recently returned from a trip to the Midwest, hell-bent as ever on expanding her empire conference by grueling conference. I haven't told her of my plan to surprise Dad with Tony Clifton tickets. Maybe I will, when I get some more courage. Since Dad got diagnosed with the big C, she acts as if she almost loves him again. Freaks me the hell out.

Dad's on a permanent vacation from the plant. He drinks more than ever. Surrounds himself with cartons of Natty Light and Maker's Mark and slouches in the den in the dark watching horror flicks with the sound low on his pride and joy RCA box— he doesn't need the volume; he knows the script by heart and mutters his lines with the embittered diligence of a failed actor. He surfaces for dinner that Jackie or I cook (defrost). Sits at the head of the table (at least two beer cans or a whiskey next to his plate) with a drowning man's grin and asks how our day went. Doesn't slur, although he speaks slowly and his eyes are bloodshot.

Today, he's absorbed in the *Montel Williams Show* and oblivious to me limping past on the way to my bedroom. Bunko, the grizzled tomcat, follows at my heel, same as he always does. Jackie feeds Bunko, Dad kicks him, and *I* pet him and give him love. He's as close to a brother as it's going to get around here.

By the way, the reason I'm an only child is Jackie had two miscarriages and an abortion before she gave birth to breech-baby me. According to her, she'd argued with Dad about whether to keep me at all. I'm not sure which of them was pro or con Julie. My foes say she conceived me in the backseat of Dad's jalopy and that she kept me to keep him leashed. For the record, she doesn't deny it.

Reflecting on grade school, I realize how lonely our home was due to Mom's relentless travel schedule. Dad let me stay up late and watch *Taxi* reruns with him when she was away. Sloppy Joes, Tang, and an ice cream sandwich for dinner on a TV tray on the couch in my Cabbage Patch Kids PJs. Movie of the week or a western or some stand-up comedy from his stack of VHS tapes. I'm not exaggerating—he loved Kaufman, and Robin Williams, and Bill Hicks (grooved on horror by Lewton, Carpenter, and Romero, but decided I was too young to go that heavy). The rough stuff did it for him – brutal satire and white man madness fumed from those comedians. Except for the profanity, most of it went over my head. No worries; those were the rare occasions that I got to be Daddy's little girl instead of a piece of furniture.

He cried his eyes out the day after Kaufman passed away. Drank himself into a stupor in honor of Hicks a decade later. Dad didn't shed tears over Hicks, though. I'm not sure he had any left after 1984.

Whatever our problems, he's my dad and he's dying and I have to believe it's a signal from the universe that Dee Dee Andersen told me about Clifton's forthcoming surprise appearance. I'm infamous for deviousness not imagination. Until this opportunity, I haven't thought of a single meaningful gesture to show Dad I care the way a daughter is supposed to care (even though my heart feels kind of numb). I'm selfish and big enough to admit the failing.

I lie in bed and crank the Matthew Good Band. I do a couple poppers and hope they can help sort out some of this bullshit. My prayer is, *Save the day, Steely J, you weird, weird dude.* Bunko nuzzles under my jaw, where the brace seam is snuggest, and purrs. He loves the shit out of my cone of shame.

Rocky calls on my rhinestone-studded telephone in the wee hours after Dad has fallen asleep in front of the TV and Jackie disappears into her bedroom lair downstairs to consult spreadsheets and headshots. Rocky's favorite topics are football and his Iroc-Z in no particular order. Tonight is more of the same. Eventually he remembers to ask how I'm doing. Am I already an afterthought? Did he call so late because he took one of my many, many rivals on a cruise of the Eklutna Flats in his damned midnight-blue Iroc-Z? Time for another popper. Bingo-bongo, better.

Rocky says, "I ran into your pal, Steely J, at the store. Freaky you should ask him to score Clifton tickets. You and him are Kaufman nuts?"

"Hey, now. I wouldn't exactly say I'm a nut—"

"Fucker gives me the willies."

"Steely J isn't for everyone. Still, where would you get your discount 'roids without him?"

"I meant Kaufman."

"Kaufman's definitely not for everyone either," I say. "You're in luck, considering the fact he's dead as a doornail, Jim. Supposedly, haha."

"He was evil."

"How evil was he?"

"Caveman in a cave raping all the cavewomen evil. Freeze frame his face next time you watch one a his old shows. Pure, violent malevolence." Rocky breathes heavily, the way he does after a hard practice or a screw-session in his Iroc-Z. "The others have other ones. These .celebrity haunts. Jim Morrison. Jim Belushi. Freddy Mercury. Bette Davis. Charlie Chapman. Gilda Radner. Marilyn Monroe. Elvis."

"Uh, baby? Is this a joke?" I'm losing my pleasant buzz with a quickness. Rocky isn't the sharpest knife in the drawer. I would not have guessed "malevolence" is within a million miles of his vocabulary. His jokes concern bodily functions and referring to his rivals as faggots. If this isn't a joke, I'm not sure I want to know what it is.

"Stifle yourself and listen. There's an entry with a roster in the black almanac, but I haven't read it, and maybe it's a lie. I knew one unlucky kid who claimed visitations from Peter Lorre. Makes my blood run cold and mine is bad enough. Sometimes I see Andy Kaufman creeping through the trees outside our house. He shows himself when something awful is on the way."

"Uh, you see Andy Kaufman. Lurking. Am I hearing you right?"

"You're hearing me right. Months go by and nothing, then poof! He's every-damned-where. Follows me home from school and stands under my window and grins. Winks at me through the stacks at the library. I know he's real because I've seen his tracks and because it's happened to members of my family going back generations. How far? How deep? Deep as a snake, black-slipping into its hole? Is it just entertainers? Maybe it's all sorts of dead famous people. Did the pale visage of George Washington vex my child grandfather as he huddled with his Boy Scout troop around the fire? Did Ben Franklin meet the Bard on some lonely deer path in Virginia? The way Franklin doped and drank and forswore a Christian deity, I bet it is so."

Visage? Vex? This is pod person talk. Has my boyfriend had a brain transplant? I let the silence stretch. "Rocky, have you been hitting the nitrous again? You sound totally fucked up."

"I'm high on plasma. Speaking of fucking. To be honest, babe, I *had* to get my rocks off. Today was a real stressor. I drove Reline to the flats and banged her like a drum. Didn't mean anything. She's a skank. I double-wrapped my junk." He waits for me to respond; I don't because my heart is a lump of ice in my throat. He eventually goes on, "Don't be pissed. You are, aren't you? I get it. I was disgusted with what I'd done and I thought about capping her on the spot, just crack her open and dump the whole mess into the bay. I've done it before. Usually I stick to dogs because nobody misses them. Nobody makes a federal case over a dead animal. You still there?" Rocky laughs and it's not his laugh, it changes. Steely J says, "Sorry, JV. Just messing with you. I've got a natural talent for mimicry."

"Holy shit, you asshole. Be sure to put that in as your yearbook quote. *A natural talent for being a douche.*" I can't tell if I'm having a heart attack. Bunko wakes from whatever cats dream of and his fur puffs. He yowls, swipes a claw at my phone-hand, and leaps from the bed.

Steely J laughs again and says in a not-quite perfect imitation of Rocky, "For the record, your boyfriend is a schmuck. Two to one he *is* taking a cruise with Reline as we speak. Probably imagines he's spiking a puppy instead of a football whenever he scores a TD. It's in those beady eyes. What I said about Kaufman is also true. He really started coming around my place one dark autumn. For my dad it was James Dean. I'll tell you the whole story later."

He hangs up before I can answer with a stream of profanity. Amazement overcomes my immediate anger. Got to hand it to the freak—it's an epic prank. I laugh it off like I'm supposed to. Not so deep down, I wish there was someone like a friend to call and unburden myself.

I ditch the neck brace and my lips finally deflate to regulation air pressure. Better than a poke in the eye with a sharp stick (one of granddad's top five apothems), although the way my luck is running, the pointy end of a stick might have my name on it.

After a week with no contact, I track Steely J to the

school stadium. It's lunch period. He's hanging with Jessica Mace on the football stadium bleachers. Surprising, given their history of mutual animosity. During seventh grade, he snapped her bra strap on a dare from Nolan Culpepper. Mace clobbered Steely J with a bicycle pump. Thirty stitches and no truce. Yet here they are, thick as thieves. Like I said: high school is global politics in microcosm. Factions are ever-shifting ice sheets, calving, drifting, merging.

Mace rises with languid insolence and blocks the path. She wears a faded shirt that reads ANCHORAGE WOLVERINES ROLLER DERBY SQUAD 1978. Her mom's blood is still spackled in the fiber. Lucius Lochinvar (her maiden name) had skated under the handle Scara Fawcett. A goon. Jackie knew her, even back then—whatever happened with them led to a twenty-year feud. Violence is my bet. Thuggishness seems to be a Lochinvar-Mace trait.

Down on the field, my girls of Raven Squad are drilling— *Raven Power! Let's go, Ravens, Let's Go! Raaa-ven Power! Juke To The Left, Juke To The Right! Beat Em Up, Beat Em Off, Fight-Fight-Fight! Raven Power! Raven Power! Rat Shit, Bat Shit, Yay Team!* Something along those lines.

"Hey Julie Five. How's tricks?" Mace smiles, and like Steely J, it means less or more or worse than you'd think it does. She may as well have a storm cloud boiling overhead. Her eyes are fierce. Eyes of a drunk or a woman who just had angry sex. Her fighting rings glint—three on the left, two on the right. The death's head could crack a bone.

My inclination is to smack her with my crutch. I rein in the impulse.

She puts her hands on her hips. "Julie, you're a cooz and I'm calling you out."

"What's up your ass?"

"Elmer's a dear personal friend of mine. You kicked him to the curb. Broke his heart. I'm going to do unto you by breaking your face."

"Think so?"

"Know so."

"Isn't this is a teensy bit out of the blue?"

"Been on my honey-do-list for a while."

I flash a sneer to cover the fact my knees are knocking. "Real brave picking a fight with a girl halfway in traction."

"Don't worry, sweetie. I like cold dishes. This'll wait until that chicken leg is out of the brace. Just be sure to keep your veterinarian on speed-dial. You're gonna require his services."

"Fuck you in the ear," is my witty rejoinder as I squeeze by.

Mace chuckles and sticks a cigarette into the corner of her mouth. "Save the date, bitch."

Steely J sits on a bench, filming the cheer squad with a handheld movie camera. He doesn't glance at me as I collapse beside him. "Jessica M. is in a bad mood. Might want to avoid her." His lips barely move. He did a ventriloquist routine at the school talent show once. His dummy had lacked a lower jaw and its sundress costume was rotten with mold. He'd called her Veronica. Have I mentioned Steely J is an odd duck?

"Nice, thanks. What are you doing, perv?"

"Picking out victims."

"Hello?"

"Annual sacrifice to the death gods is nigh. If I'm gonna be the American Fulci, got to get my hands bloody."

"Sick. Start with Showalter. You could be right and the twat is gunning for my spot at the head of the squad."

"Only a virgin sacrifice will do."

"The death gods are going to starve around here, I guess."

"Sometimes terror is enough. Put on the mask of the dark of the moon and wander the earth."

"Damn, Steely, you say some loco bullshit. Ought to hang

with the Goth kids. They'd love your shtick."

"I'm too edgy. The Goths don't feel me."

"Go figure. Anything on those tickets? You're supposed to be hooking me up. You gonna come through, or is your rep bullshit?"

He sets the camera in his lap. "Meant to tell you, I checked with my sources. Clifton isn't on the schedule."

"Dee Dee swears he is."

"Dee Dee got suckered by secondhand info. It's smoke. Somebody probably thought it'd be a great joke to start the rumor. Classic Kaufman."

I close my eyes and imagine the last time I kissed Rocky. Two days before the trampoline debacle. We've fucked thirty or forty times and it's okay, although I never come. Is it me, or is my stud merely adequate? A busload of other girls would love to double-check my findings and that's why I don't complain. I imagine tripping Mace down the concrete staircase on the other side of the cafeteria. I've only seen her cry once after her brother was in a car accident. The memory of her ugly tears keeps me warm on long arctic nights.

Steely J says, "There's another possibility. We could get creative. Do some community theater. My audition was convincing, right?"

"This a "creative" way to separate me from fifty bucks?"

"*One hundred* bucks."

"Where the hell am I going to get a hundred dollars?"

He mimes sucking a cock. "Seriously, though. I'll need a week or two to rehearse. Perfect the delivery."

"Rehearse? Rehearse what?"

"A command performance."

"How come you're so great at imitating voices?"

"Told you—it's natural talent. I meditate at night. Sit in the middle of my room and open my mind to the cosmos. All kinds of shit is floating around in the dark. Seeps into us every minute of the day. I just figured a way to make it happen faster."

"Anybody can meditate."

His expression slackens by one or two turns of a screw. His pupils expand. Funny how a millimeter or two can change someone's face so dramatically. "See, I'm really into it now. Used to take all night in full lotus. I can slip sideways at will." He wriggles his tongue and says in a Don Pardo voice: "Would you care to hear my idea?"

"I'm all ears." A glib pronouncement that belies serious misgivings regarding my deepening association with Steely J, Man of a Thousand Voices. I should have obeyed my instinct to tell him to piss up a rope.

Diehard leaves in the birch trees turn yellow and drop after a real cold snap toward the end of September. A few minutes past six and dark. I'm pacing in front of the window, nervous as a freshman awaiting her prom date. Hilariously, Jackie and Dad figure from the way I'm behaving Rocky is going to pop the question. Dad has spent a significant portion of the afternoon sharpening a Bowie Knife from the display case in the basement. He's only half drunk. There's an ominous portent for you. Jackie warms him a TV dinner. The gusto with which he attacks his Salisbury steak confirms he'll adjust to his inevitable group home environment with aplomb.

Steely J's car parks with one tire on the curb. Even though he'd warned me, I'm jarred by his radical transformation from oafish, pervy teenager to the hulking schlub in the Vegas lounge singer suit who strolls up the walkway. Middle-aged, pale, bad toupee, worse skin, tinted glasses, ruffled shirt and bowtie, gut overhanging his belt, disco pants, and scuffed loafers. He carries a case sheathed in red velvet in his left hand. The change wouldn't be more complete if he'd transformed into a werewolf.

I open the front door and do a double-take. It's really Tony Clifton, or at least someone who resembles Clifton. No way, no freaking way – Steely J has to be under there somewhere, right? Unless he's paid one of his pals to act as an accomplice and *really* sell the gag. He knows everybody and one of them could be a frustrated actor.

"J, is it you?" I whisper as he grips my fingers near the tips and gives them a shake the way you do with a toddler.

"Tony C, baby. Tony C plays live." His accent is nasally and he smells like he took a bath in Aqua Velva. I still can't decide. "Course, you've invited me in, I can return anytime I wanna." He says it deadpan.

Jackie comes around the corner. Her stare wavers between bewilderment and horrified recognition. Mommy dearest is a control freak. She dislikes the unexpected. "Who is this, dear?" That stilted tone reminds me of the time she slapped my mouth. She's wearing a red blouse and a black skirt and the shoes she won't be caught dead in away from the house. I also know she knows Tony Clifton from her conversations with Dad over the years. I hate it when she plays coy. She truly does take Machiavelli to heart.

Steely J winks. "Hi, toots. Be a doll and fix me a drink, will ya."

Before she can yell at him, I tell her it's Dad's big surprise. Step aside and let the magic happen, Mom! She frowns and departs for the kitchen to mix a tray-load of cocktails. Monday is Caribou Lou night at the Vellum casa. Steely J, or whoever the fuck, ambles after me into the den and there's Dad slumped on his La-Z-Boy throne, a yellow Husqvarna ball cap tilted back. Blue light from the oversized TV screen glints in his eye as he regards the spectacle of Steely J unpacking a karaoke box and microphone.

After a few minutes of strained silence, Dad gestures at me with his knife. His expression is similar to Mom's. Expectant with dread and willfully ignorant. "Honey, what the Sam Hill is going on?"

I take his free hand and say in a well-honed baby-girl voice, "Daddy, a friend of mine heard you're a major fan of Tony Clifton. Tony's in town for a couple of nights and—"

"Don't bore your old man to death, sweetheart," Steely J says and the accent slips. However, his patronizing contempt is one hundred percent authentic Clifton. "You're giving me an earache. Where's my highball?" He snags a glass from Jackie's tray as she edges by and swats her ass hard enough to make her bunny hop.

I'm astonished. A) the jerk has the nerve, and B) my mom blushes and keeps stepping as if she's a cocktail waitress pulling a shift in a 1960s club. What the fuck, over?

My heart flutters – Dad will blow sky-high; aggression and territorial pissing are hardwired into him. Instead, he smirks and a trapdoor opens in the collage of my memories of childhood. Sure, I'm used to their civil antipathy. Nonetheless, there's a rawness to Dad's smile; his hatred is laid bare. Things with them are more complicated and bitter than I'd dared to imagine.

Steely J leans over and his pants ride his crack. He switches on the sound. After a burst of feedback piano keys tinkle, building. "All right, all right, everybody park your caboose so's I can get this show on the road. I can't stay here all evening, I got a gig in Anchorage. My manager lined up this charity crap or else I'd be at the Gold Digger squeezing pole dancer titties and drinking real booze. You know it, cousin."

Dad guffaws. "Gimme some Pat Boone."

"Shuddup, wiseacre. I'll sing what I wanna sing." Steely J clears his throat. "As it happens, I wanna do a number by Pat B." He proceeds to sing, or kind of sing, "Speedy Gonzalez," including the cartoonish bridges by Speedy and his put-upon wife. Visualize, if you will, a flat affect teen mimicking a dead comedian imitating a middle-aged crooner who enunciates through his nose imitating a faux Spanish accent and fucking the lyrics over just enough to sprain your brain, and you get the picture.

"Sweet baby Jesus, what am I hearing?" Jackie mutters through her clenched teeth. She grips my elbow while smiling to shame a constipated beauty queen. "Who is this idiot?"

I return the grin with interest. "Tony Clifton, Ma. None other. Look how happy Daddy is."

"Speedy Gonzalez" wraps. The lull segues into an instrumental. Steely J huffs and puffs. Sweat makes tracks in his makeup. He sips the highball and nods at Dad. "Alaska, huh? Land of the Midnight Sun. Where men are men and so are the women. That wife of yours, buddy. Whadda ya do? Kidnap a mountain goat and slap a dress on it? Lady, another round and keep 'em coming." He hands Jackie (who looks like she's chewing tenpenny nails) his empty as the intro for "Green, Green Grass of Home" kicks in.

At this point, I'm naïve enough to hope it's going to be a success. Alas, during the instrumental, Steely J says to my dad, "Last time I did a charity set, it was at a children's ward. Cue-ball central. Really pathetic, I tell ya. Now, you look pretty good for a guy with the big C. Really good, really vibrant. Can't tell what's under your hat. Looks like a full head a hair. You got some meat on your bones. Got a nice gut goin', hey? Dunno, maybe beer has cancer-retarding qualities and that's why your hair hasn't all fallen out yet. Cancer of the ass, right?"

"Jeff isn't on chemotherapy," Jackie says coldly. She directs a withering glance at me. "Julie, I don't know who this…lout is, or if he's a friend, of yours, but I've had quite enough—"

Steely J snickers and waves dismissively. "'Quite enough?'

Way you stomp around the house in your fuck-me pumps, you ain't had *any* in a while. Amirite, Jeff? Cancer of the asshole does take a man's zest for life out of the equation. How you supposed to concentrate on shtupping the missus when you're distracted by a burning ring of fire?"

"Oh my." I cover a horrified smile with my hand. I can smell the brimstone. The roof is sure to collapse and bury us alive any second. Such is my desperate plea to a non-existent god, at any rate. Dad and Jackie appear dumbfounded.

"Christ almighty, I'm thirsty." Steely J tosses the mike and does his penguin-strut out of the den.

"He has to leave. Immediately!" This from Jackie. She grips a shelf for support. Weakened and shocked, she'll assume her ultimate form in a minute, I have no doubt.

"Mom—"

"Fine! I'm calling the police!" Strength returning. Rage will do the job.

"Overkill, Mom. Overkill."

"No, that's it. I'm calling 911."

"Mom, Jackie, what do you want the cops to do?"

"What do I want? What do I want! I *want* him to take his crappy karaoke box and get the hell away from us!"

"I'm gonna stab him," Dad says thoughtfully. He hasn't moved, and his expression is sort of dopey rather than furious, but he's white-knuckling the Bowie knife. "Jackie, I don't like how he's talking. I'm gonna slice his neck."

I tell them to cool their jets and stay put for the love of god. I go after Steely J. He's not in the upper living room or the kitchen. I'd run through the back door if I were in his shoes. Not the dude's style. His car remains parked on the street. He's the sort to hang his head and absorb whatever verbal or physical punishment is dished at him. At the moment, it's the physical punishment that Dad will inflict that has me worried.

The door to the half bath is wide and there's Steely J on

all-fours, head dipped into the toilet. His foot twitches as he gurgles and laps with the rabid gusto of a hound attacking his favorite bowl.

I kind of scream and he shudders and gazes over his shoulder, water dripping from his askew fake mustache.

"Yeah?" He says in a voice I haven't heard before this moment. It isn't Tony Clifton's and it isn't quite his own.

"My parents are straight tripping. Holy shit. Get your ass out before Dad stabs you or my mom calls in SWAT." I'm convinced he's got to go for several reason. Imminent injury will suffice. "Are you...Are drinking that?"

He paws his smeary lips and cracks his neck. "I'm due a commission." Almost in character, although his pancake makeup is ruined.

"Please, dude. I'll catch you with the dough later."

"Fine. Pay Steely J." He rises unsteadily. His bulk crowds the whole bathroom. The front of his suit is soaked.

"Just beat it before I hurl." Well, too late on that count.

I expect a mushroom cloud and nuclear fallout. Instead, Jackie tiptoes through the house with a sheepish expression. We mumble weather-related factoids. Dad continues to marinate. I hobble around campus and grit my perfect teeth (thank you, retainer manufacturing company!) when I hand Steely J his hundred bucks. He's cool; just counts his money and walks away like nothing.

I tell the adventure to Rocky Friday night after a hot and heavy session on the Eklutna Flats. The neck brace is history and I'm looking fly, so we're on again. It's cold and he lets the engine idle. Stars are embedded in the steamy glass. Every passing set of headlights on the highway illuminates the interior of the Iroc with a spangled glow.

"Toilet water?" Rocky says. "Sounds like a laugh riot. Bet your parents lost their shit. Eric Michaels told me Steely J's Dad and Zane Tooms's parents are asshole buddies with a whole slew of Chinese investors. They fund illegal hunting expeditions in Africa and Siberia to snuff endangered animals and drive up the prices of sex drugs and diet pills. The Asians think powdered rhino horn will get their shit hard. Anyway, these guys are betting that once a bunch of animals go extinct, their market share is gonna pay big bucks. Pretty cold, huh?"

I agree it's pretty cold.

"I hope you didn't pay for the Steely J con."

"What else was I going to do?"

"Tell him to blow it out his ass. You owe him dick."

"Nobody crosses Steely J on a debt."

"Yeah, but the punk didn't come through as promised. No deal."

"I don't know, Rock. He came to the house and did his routine. Technically, we're the ones who pulled the plug—"

"Screw that noise." His hair is mussed and sweaty. His shirt is unbuttoned. He reeks of me. He sets his jaw with gung-ho stubbornness. "What's going to happen is, you're receiving a refund. Right now. We'll roll up to his pad and get him with the program."

I don't bother to argue. Rocky has the brains of the aforementioned blood-crazed rhino and there's no point. "It'll keep until tomorrow. How about we go another round, champ?"

"Another round." He glances at his crotch with a flicker of doubt.

"Ding-ding."

And that's how I start along a path that teaches me there are worse things than calamitous domestic scenes or getting accidentally knocked up.

Rocky cruises by my place the following afternoon. Mike Zant idles behind him on Mike's dad's Kawasaki motorcycle. Mike is varsity fullback, totally hot, and a lunkhead among lunkheads—exactly the type of goon you bring along when you're planning something stupid. Rocky dares not approach the front step (he is familiar with Dad and Dad's knife). He honks until I get it together and walk over to see what he wants. He tells me to hop in. After some back and forth, I do.

And we're off to see Steely J with intentions of malice. I spend the next twenty minutes half-heartedly trying to convince Rocky this is a bad idea. I stole the hundred dollars from Jackie's sock drawer, she doesn't miss it, and so on. Nothing doing. He clenches his jaw and presses harder on the gas. Eventually I hunker in my seat and get quiet. Lots of hairpin turns on the road up the mountain to the house of J. Lunkhead Mike won't wear a helmet over his majestic afro. The way he's laying the bike over on curves trying to match Rocky's pace, I'm worried he'll miss one and crash among the spruce.

Much as I protest against this trip, the cruel bitch inside of me hopes Rocky and Mike have to slap Steely J around. He embarrassed me in front of my parents and I'd love to have the money I stole from Jackie back in my hot little hand; there's a shoe sale on at the Dimond Center Mall in Anchorage.

The house lurks at the end of a steep drive (rutted and broken pavement), eighty or ninety feet off the main road. Funky shake roof and siding peel from the house. It might have been tits a decade ago, but the place is going to hell fast. Mother Nature rules Alaska. Lower floor is a daylight basement wedged into the hillside. Cruddy, brown-yellow curtains are drawn. Trees everywhere. Last mailbox I noticed is a mile back, at least. Steely J's Toyota is angled next to a state trooper cruiser on blocks. The cruiser may have been in a fire. Smashed in windows and busted light bar. Nearby, a rotting doghouse, but no dog. Reminds me how much I miss mine. Spruce branches, shorn by the last few windstorms, lie tangled in the dead grass. A raven perches on a splintered, disconnected telephone pole and gives me a knowing eye.

I pretend the hood of the Iroc is a piano and lounge atop it (awkwardly) while Rocky and Mike move up the driveway, climb a flight of rickety stairs, and knock on the front door. The door opens and they step inside. The door closes. It's much cooler here. Sunlight slants through the canopy, feeble as a candle in a huge, wrecked mossy cathedral vault. Too chilly. I huddle in the car for a while. Problem is, Rocky took the keys and now my feet are totally freezing. Worse, no tunes.

This drags along for an unbearable while until Dee Dee's number beeps on my cell phone. Bored and vengeful I answer. Just the twat I want to ream. She asks if my Dad enjoyed the show at the Gold Digger and I tell her to cram it where the sun don't shine. She's genuinely taken aback—*Say what? Why you trippin'?* and like that. I thank her for the false info, and ruining my Dad's birthday, fuck you very much.

"Whoa-whoa—I didn't feed you any bullshit."

"You said your pal was in the know about Clifton. Only the guy was never scheduled to appear. Nice, real nice."

"Julie, Julie, calm down. I told you, it was a private show. Clifton played—10PM sharp. My parents went. Dude's an asshole. Everybody loved it. Dad got an autographed photo. You're really spun, girl."

I tell her to blow a goat and end the call. Oh, dear dog, my wrath toward Steely cocksucker J has reached a crescendo. Murder is a possibility. The conniving bastard failed to secure tickets and concocted the whole performance to cover himself and charge me double. Fuming and plotting, I glance toward the house and notice the door has swung open again.

Somebody yells my name. The muffled cry doesn't repeat and leaves me guessing. My imagination runs wild—Steely J's fat face getting knocked in by Mike's fist; Steely J's nads getting kicked around like a hacky sack. This is a pleasing fantasy, except... What if the boys go too far? What if they beat him to a pulp and forget to collect the loot? This situation practically begs for a woman's touch.

My knee is better every day. Rage makes a beautiful painkiller. I ascend the grade and climb the steps with less difficulty than I'd feared. Gets my heartrate going is all. Gawd, the house, though. Steely J carved something, maybe a crescent moon, into the wooden door panel. Inside, Lemon Pledge partially masks an underlying dankness. I wander around a dim maze. None of the light switches work. Doors are nailed shut except to the kitchen and a half bathroom. Both rooms are Spartan and neat. Reminds me of his car.

Anger deserts me the way sweat evaporates and leaves me clammy and flustered. Why would a person nail doors shut inside his home? Why haven't I heard any commotion? Why don't I call to Rocky and Mike? To this last, I can only say that the last thing a person does when exploring a semi-abandoned building is draw attention to one's self. It's a survival trait culled from inhaling enough slasher flicks. No fucking in an empty room and no calling out, *anybody there?* as you sneak around in your Nancy Drew shoes.

Thump-thump-thump goes my rubber-tipped crutch on floorboards in a long hall. I instantly notice the lack of photos, paintings, or any form of decoration. Shit ain't right. At the end of the hall are stairs heading down into the basement. Of course, I hear Rocky's voice. He chuckles and so does someone else.

I get to the bottom of the steps and push through a heavy rubber sheet. Okay, creepy. The basement is a box and it's hot as a greenhouse. Afternoon light dribbles in at the edges of the curtains and there's a desk lamp glowing from a distant corner. TV monitor with the sound muted. Comedians are performing. A rich, earthy reek gets into my nose and gags me. Fertilizer, shit, dead leaves, wet copper, and green growing things. A squirmy smell. The J family used to summer in the Amazon. They brought some with, apparently.

Furniture is totally Steely J. An aquarium, or terrarium, not sure which, except it's economy sized. Two hundred gallons or more, pushed against the far wall. Racks of the sort you find in hospitals are positioned opposite one another and strung with IV tubes and baggies of what surely must be blood and other, clearer stuff. I've seen plasma; it's plasma. Wonderful.

Rocky squats in an inflatable pool near the terrarium. He doesn't acknowledge my appearance. He's in a zone. His jacket is unbuttoned. He's not wearing a shirt or pants. I linger on this image: Shirtless. Pantless. Unbuttoned jacket. Squatting in a kiddie pool of water. An object sticks to his breastbone. Fat as a big old rubbery turd from a novelty catalog. Grayish-brownish-black, and shiny-slick. Attached at his left nipple, it trails to his belly. Vaguely familiar, possibly a specimen I've seen in Mr. Navarro's biology class. My poor brain will catch up real soon. The lighting is bad, but the passing seconds improve my vision and I'm sorry. More crescent moons are spray-painted in white on the curtains and the walls.

Steely J reclines upon a bench seat torn from a truck. He's naked as a Greek statue. His eyes roll back and forth, white to black. Leeches, that's what my brain was trying to say. Leeches of varying length hang from his neck and his man-tits. One, swollen to the heftiness of a kid's arm, gloms onto his groin, its bulk flopped across his thigh like a nightmarish wang. Makes sense— femoral artery runs through there. A prime tap. He slurps from a mostly deflated bag of blood, his expression dreamy and fucked up. In with the fresh, right? Those are Mike's boots poking from behind the bench seat-couch, for sure.

Another man, stark-staring naked too, rises from behind the couch and moves around the side. He kneels and gently detaches the leech from Steely's groin. Cheeks gleaming sweat, the stranger glances at me and smirks the dopey, amiable peasant smirk that has enthralled nightclub audiences since 1970-fucking-four. He tenderly lays the leech on a towel and sticks it with a horse-needle syringe. Pulls the plunger and draws creamy black blood into the barrel.

Steely J rouses himself. His marble gaze rolls to me. "Hi, JV. What can I do for you?"

"Never mind." I turn and head for the stairs. No keys for the car. Mike's motorcycle is beyond my capabilities. Town is a major hike for a girl with a bum leg. Too afraid to look over my shoulder. Swear there's heavy movement behind me, though. The universe and its bullet-fast molecules slow to a crawl.

First things first. I have to make it out of the house and call for help (that should be an interesting conversation). What are the odds I'll make it? Everybody knows that when seconds count, the state troopers are minutes away.

The TV volume kicks in. A laugh track swells and booms and fills my ears.

There Is a Bear in the Woods

by Nadia Bulkin

Rick McFarland. Cass would have said she'd fallen in love with him at first sight, but people usually took that the wrong way. Hers was a devotional love – she would have said *divine* love if she didn't know that Rick took the Lord very seriously; the kind of love that expected nothing in return.

She had signed up with Rick's new Party, even though government propaganda called it a "radical fringe movement," because she strongly felt that the country had nothing left to lose. Her family, like most middle-class families in Des Moines, was content voting for the conservatives in every election and clucking their tongues in disappointment when the conservatives inevitably lost. But why, Cass asked her father, what kind of opposition keeps bending over for the Alliance and the broken gangster-welfare-state? What kind of opposition doesn't fight back? "They're the lesser of two evils, Cassie," her father said, but Cass was pretty sure that minor evil was still evil. Even the reformist history books had not been able to wipe away the fundamental truth about this nation: that it had been built by the audacious and courageous, those who had the guts to reshape the world... those who could see evil for what it was. *"There is a bear in the woods,"* as Reagan said, *"For some people, the bear is easy to see. Others don't see it at all."*

Cass saw the bear, and as such she knew she was responsible for leading the blind from ruin. The weight had been placed upon her like a Miss America's sash; she was just not very good at wearing it. "You're too aggressive," her mother said when she lost the race for student body president. "Oh, child, run along," the neighbors said when she went door-to-door with petitions. She never gave up, which was why she was stuffing fundraising envelopes in a small muggy office in a desolate strip mall on a Saturday afternoon when everyone else she knew was watching the game. On that particular Saturday, with the election still a year away, Congressional candidate Rick McFarland came striding in with his sleeves rolled up and his tie flung over his shoulder: a fiercely happy lion of a man. "Well, good afternoon, ladies and gentlemen!" Rick shouted, voice booming. "Are we ready to change the world today?"

It was like Rick took a hammer and broke the terracotta shell that Cass didn't even realize had hardened around her. He came over and shook her hand over the pile of envelopes – because he insisted on meeting all the new volunteers, but maybe also because he saw in her the spark of potential – and as he did so he leaned in and said, "Cassie Spano. You and me, we're going to save this country, aren't we?" And just like that, Cass knew that Rick could see the bear, too.

Weekend work continued throughout the winter, and then for one brutal Iowa summer, the Rick McFarland Campaign Team – Team Rick, for short – canvassed daily from sunrise to sunset. At first Cass kept tallies in her notebook for each little farm town they blazed through, but eventually the process drove her skin-crawling mad – for Anderstown, IA, for example, it went ten for Rick and his visionary new Party, twelve for the conservatives, an incomprehensible twenty for the Alliance, and another twenty lost souls who had no idea what they were going to do come the first Tuesday of November. Some of those "undecideds" were on meth or mentally ill, but many had simply been well and truly addled by years of routinized Alliance electioneering, such that they could not tell right from wrong or express a true opinion of their own. Rick said they were making headway, but as the leaves began to turn, it took a lot of squinting to see his point. Rick also said "never give up, never surrender,"

so they didn't, but every time a new set of poll results was released Cass felt like another spare second had been taken off the nation's doomsday clock.

For months, Team Rick was mocked and belittled for daring to suggest that President Michalek was a menace to decent society; in mid-October, Aaron Doyle was flat out smacked in the face by a farmhand for saying that hard work, not hand-outs, was going to get that farmhand's children into college. Cass, who was trying to organize an event at Iowa State, worried jealously that Rick – red-blooded leonine Rick, who sometimes talked about what he'd do to President Michalek if he ever got the guy in an old-fashioned barroom brawl – might give Aaron a personal commendation for being an idiot. Like all the greatest politicians in American history, Rick was not really made to be a politician. He was just a cattle rancher who had grown tired of watching the Alliance tax the heartland until it could bleed no more. To her relief, however, Rick told Aaron that he had to start picking his battles more wisely. He was firm yet calm; he was going to be a wonderful Congressman, if only his Team could get him there.

But Aaron was twenty-four and self-confident that those twenty-four years had made him a wise walker of the earth, and he left the campaign headquarters to prove himself to Rick, or so he might as well have said. Aaron really did say that he wore his father's 800-meter gold medal around his neck to remind himself that he came from a line of winners. He used that ditty on the sharp-faced Daughters of the American Revolution that had joined Team Rick as November closed in; Cass always found it funny how rarely it worked.

Cass watched him buckle up his SwissGear backpack and asked him what exactly he was planning to do, because frankly she could see the headlines now – *Smear Campaign By McFarland Aide Backfires*; *Attempted Break-In by McFarland Aide*. It was true, as Reagan said, that *"isn't it smart to be as strong as the bear? If there is a bear,"* but Aaron just didn't have the finesse to pull off a covert operation.

"I'm going to make sure Rick gets face time with real Americans," said Aaron, "Real Americans who are really going to vote, and are really going to make a difference." It felt like he was slamming the Iowa State appearance, so Cass coldly let him leave, hoping at least a little that he wouldn't come back.

At Iowa State's Stephens Auditorium, Rick was more than a congressman. He was presidential. He delivered his stump speech with a voice that quivered with a passionate honesty never-before-seen in a D.C. politician; yet he commanded those three-thousand strong like an orchestral conductor, such that he seemed to grab each and every one of them by either side of the head and give them the electric spark of recognition. With that spark, he passed to them the certainty that he wasn't talking to the powerbrokers at the top or the leeches at the bottom, but to *them*, the good men and women who'd spent their whole lives working hard and keeping their heads down and trying to ignore the atrocities being done to their country in the name of "justice."

The night left Cass euphoric. It was not happiness per se; more a burning in her heart that set her throat on fire. Backstage, she hugged Rick ferociously, trying to impart to him without saying it and embarrassing them both that he was the future of this nation and she would do — they would all do — whatever it took to make sure that he and Governor Todd Hunter and Senator Calvin Dodson got to Washington and took the wheel of this fishtailing car. Cass believed that he was blessed — and she didn't even believe in God.

In the midst of the congratulations and dollar-store confetti, Cass checked her phone and got that first bizarre message from Aaron, the one she would wonder for years afterward if she should have just deleted and dismissed as a drunken raving. It was something about a town called Spira an hour out from Council Bluffs, and "*the oldest haunted house this side of the Missouri?"* called The Circle, and how Cass had to make sure Rick came to this "attraction," because they were going to love him there. Her first reply was just *???????.* He wrote back: *Cassie, this is a game-changer. Just get him here.*

Cass had pictured a community Halloween party. A gaudy Victorian haunted house decked in cobwebs and bats and gravestones, maybe a hokey fog machine hooked up to a speaker transmitting crackly, ominous music. She pictured kids in superhero costumes and clumps of giggling teens and good-natured parents keeping their patience satiated with candy apples. She thought maybe this was a tradition the little town took great pride in, and maybe the mayor and the principal and some small business owners would be there (it was important, Rick said, to remain compassionate at all times given the Party's ambitious plans), and maybe they could get a photo of Rick giving out candy bars with cat whiskers painted on his face. Her main concern, as they sped down Interstate 80, was that Rick might be freaked out by the supposed paganistic or Satanic nature of the whole thing. Although he claimed to be fine, little darts in his gaze and gulps in his throat were giving away his nerves. She reached over and squeezed his hand, pressing his cold wedding band into her palm.

"You're sure this will go over well with the base, huh," he said, and she promised, "It's just Halloween."

But she was wrong. The place was wrong. The Circle was just a lonely farmhouse in the middle of nowhere, as pale yellow-white as a pioneer's wedding veil. There were no paper skeletons, no tablecloth ghosts, not even a pumpkin on the porch. There were no children. She would have been sure they'd gotten the address wrong – the street signs in Spira were so faded that in the dark they were barely legible, and their GPS had already failed to take a broken bridge and a roadblock into consideration – if Aaron hadn't been standing out in front of the house, waving methodically. He looked very pale and very plastic under the beam of headlights, as if he was wearing an Aaron-mask over his real face.

Cass ran out and fought with him for a minute. "What the fuck are you thinking, what the fuck is this place," etcetera, etcetera. While Aaron's answers certainly weren't making any sense, she became distracted by the fact that he seemed mildly, no, moderately cross-eyed, and the fact that his voice had sounded so different – livelier, more promise-filled – on the phone. Eventually Aaron started to refer her to Mr. Kamke, the house's owner, but the last thing Cass wanted was to talk to the black silhouette standing in the front doorway. Everything inside her body said *pull the plug!* but Cass was not a quitter. Cass never gave up; Cass never surrendered. And anyway, Rick came out of the SUV before Cass could have stopped him, because he wasn't a quitter either. He looked nervous as a house cat that had seen a rabid dog on the other side of a fence, but he still wouldn't slink away. He wouldn't have been Rick their rally-flag if he did. Aaron pointed up the hill at the house and Rick said, "Well, I'm always happy to chat with a member of the public," and went on in.

Mr. Kamke had to be pushing ninety. He had tense broad shoulders reduced to a wire hanger of a torso and that sad, confused, half-angry look that Cass recognized from her own Grandpa Morris at Peaceful Valley Home. Around him, the farmhouse was a whirligig – a frenzy of lights sparking on and off, cabinets swinging open, shadows without bodies crawling leisurely up the walls, and what sounded like scratchy folk music tumbling down from up a creaky set of stairs. Cass didn't know why the old man had the place running, considering it had to be expensive to run so many wires and magnets and pulleys. It was distinctly uncomfortable to be in a haunted house without an audience, like an empty roller coaster shooting up and down a midnight track. It made Cass feel like an external intelligence was playing with human machinery without a human's consent; she did not like it. Leaning against the dripping kitchen sink next to Aaron, she twitched.

Rick tried to engage Mr. Kamke along all the usual lines – how with Mr. Kamke's help, Rick was looking to rebuild this country from the ground up into a place that both their grandparents and their grandchildren could be proud of, how Rick was worried about the lack of principled leadership by President Michalek and the Alliance, and how Mr. Kamke could be sure that Rick would govern with his own moral compass firmly at center.

"Are you a church-going man, Mr. Kamke?"

The old man's eyes rolled up toward a bubbly lime green stain on the ceiling. "There is only one church."

Cass gnawed her bottom lip and thought that old man Kamke was probably a True Lighter; that was the sort of thing they said. She had joined the Church of True Light to convince an ex-boyfriend that they had a future together and she could raise his children, even if she didn't really buy into the "radical reinvention" doctrine. He had come back from Japan all clenched and bothered, mumbling that the world was burning down and you could either be a firefighter or be consumed by the flames, or something like that, and now all she could do was search for him in the newsletters the Church sent every other day.

"Well, on that subject, Mr. Kamke, we certainly agree. And that's why I'm hoping you'll join me today and say…" He stopped in naked shock, and Cass's heart almost stopped, too, until she realized what Rick had seen: the milk jug on the kitchen table had tilted over at a forty-five-degree angle and begun to spin counter-clockwise.

Cass asked Aaron how they were making it look so real,

and Aaron said, "Isn't it smart to be as strong as the bear? If there is a bear."

He was looking straight at her, meaningfully, as if waiting for her to reply. Then an isolated muscle in the back of his neck shuddered like a small waking animal and he straightened up and turned his gaze squarely back to Rick. Their candidate was gingerly reaching his hand toward the spinning milk jug as the media attachés angled for a photo that would tell a story – "Rick, Rick, take a picture. Stick your hand out. Mr. Kamke, could you step into the shot? Thank you" – but what story? For the first time since she joined the campaign, Cass had no idea what story was being crafted here. This fit no narrative she could imagine except maybe *McFarland Visits Lonely Senior* but even that, Cass felt, would be a lie.

Pictures were taken, though they predictably turned out blurry and overexposed, and everyone was packing up their notebooks and wires when Mr. Kamke said, "Are you ready to see the Circle now?"

Rick cocked his head. "I thought that's where we were, sir."

"This is the house my father built." He pointed a crooked finger at the screen door, which slammed open and let the night in, right on cue. Cass jumped; Aaron did not react. "The Circle is just beyond."

The Circle was a corn maze, though quite a poor one; quite an odd one. They should have talked about it, but they went in without discussion. It seemed natural to walk through an open door. First came Mr. Kamke, without even a flashlight, then Rick the lion-hearted, then Aaron, then Cass – because for some reason, she didn't quite trust Aaron to be alone with Rick. The path they followed was so narrow and modest that it looked like a deer run at first. Only after they had been walking for ten minutes in each other's footsteps did Cass understand the enormity of the Circle, and the realization of how many back-breaking hours the old man had to have put into this structure made her worry for Mr. Kamke's sanity and Rick's safety. Behind her, the rest of Team Rick was laughing at the absurdity of this moment, but the longer they walked in nearly single file in the dark, the quieter the rear guard became.

"Well, this maze seems like a pretty easy one, Mr. Kamke," said Rick, trying to keep spirits up. Like Cass, he had noticed that there were no junctions in this maze, just the one slowly twisting counter-clockwise path. Now and then Cass was tempted to look between the stalks for some hint of what they were walking toward, but a primitive, childish fear forbade her every time. "Can't exactly get lost in here, can you?"

"Depends what you mean by lost," came Mr. Kamke's ghoulish answer. "Every human on this earth walks this path and every one of them thinks they know which way they're going. Oh, they're sure. They've got their dreams. This little piggy's going to Washington and that little piggy's going to Hollywood and that little piggy's going to save the starving little piggies in that yonder pig sty. But they're always wrong. Everyone ends up turned into pork chops."

Cass looked away from the gleaming white cross on Aaron's black backpack, unsure that she had heard correctly. She saw Mr. Kamke glance back at Rick with a wide, carnivorous grin on his face, as if he expected Rick to laugh along. Rick didn't laugh – how could he? – but his legs still wheeled him forward as if by autonomous will. "I'm sorry?" said Rick. Cass had often heard Rick's voice buckle with emotion, with love of God-and-country or righteous anger at the passive gutlessness of the nation's so-called leaders or genuine remorse that he would have to disown a friend who had fallen afoul of a donor – but this was the first time she had heard it tremble in fear. "I don't think I follow you, sir."

"But you're already following me, boy."

They kept walking, though by now a real trucker's hitch of a knot had tied up all the floating viscera between Cass's ribs. Even when the path finally broke open into a clearing five minutes later, there was no relief. They had reached the mathematical center of the Circle. Cass was sure of this. She could feel the giant flattened heart of *something* under her kitten heels. In the center of the center of the Circle, a Longhorn skull was nailed to the center of a seven-foot pole.

Team Rick was silenced. People were looking around, crumpling their brows, but no one was speaking. No one was reaching over and grabbing Mr. Kamke or Aaron, God-help-him, by the collar and shaking them silly, saying *What is this, what is that.* Cass was about to move toward Rick and whisper, "we should go" but Mr. Kamke reached him first. The old man put his liver-spotted hand on Rick's shoulder and said, "Now, Rick McFarland. Are you ready to see?" Rick didn't say yes. Until the end of days, Cass would insist on this, not only on the issue of The Circle but on everything else, the rehabilitation centers and the social health laws and the thousands of disappeared – *Rick didn't say yes.* But it seemed he didn't have to. Cass only had to blink and a wash of calm – even placidity – suddenly washed over Rick's face, removing all tautness in his muscles and all the flushed fear in his cheeks. It reminded her of Aaron and his plastic Aaron-mask – but when she looked over to her left, to see what had become of the boy, Aaron was hyperventilating into his cupped hands.

"Oh my God, I see it," he was whimpering. At first she couldn't tell, from the expression in his eyes, whether he was ecstatically happy or sad. "I see it, oh my *God…*" Cass grabbed Aaron by one seersucker sleeve and tried to make him explain.

That rubber Aaron-mask that he'd been wearing seemed to be melting off with what Cass realized were his tears, but what was underneath? What was left? A wet, gross lump of flesh that barely passed for a man? "They promised that I would see."

"See *what?*"

But Aaron just screamed, "No, I can't!" and after throwing down his expensive backpack and even more expensive phone, he started to high-tail it back the way they'd come, back into the entrails of the maze. The explosion of action was so shocking, so sudden, that it took Cass a few seconds to catch up to it. And when she did, she was horrified to realize that her first instinct – something even more pathetic and primordial and literally spineless than the urge that just a few minutes earlier had her walking into this maze – was to run. To leave Rick in the company of mad Mr. Kamke and the incompetent aides who could never stop Rick from shooting himself in the foot. In that moment, the golden kernel of potential inside Rick didn't matter. Rick didn't matter. Congress didn't matter. America – and she hated how much of a coward she was for thinking this – even America didn't matter. All that mattered, for the first time in her life, was her survival. She looked over her shoulder once, at a captive Rick beneath the licked-clean Longhorn skull and a Mr. Kamke whose withered mouth was slowly forming words. Slow and steady as the spinning milk jug. She ran.

She hissed Aaron's name, but he was gone, and without warning the corn maze's gentle warping curves became break-neck hairpin turns. She could hear the stalks rustling and she wondered if Aaron had cut into the corn in his hurry to get back to the SUVs, but beneath this sound reasoning all her reptilian mind could think was *there is a bear in the corn there is a bear behind you there is a bear* – and then she saw it: a small, strange, shining object lying on the foot-stomped path.

It was Aaron's father's gold medal. The 800-meter. The mark of a champion, or at the very least an extra-special talent. It was covered in blood.

"Cassie?"

She was holding the wet medal in her hand when she turned around to see that Rick and Mr. Kamke and all the rest of Team Rick had soundlessly crept up behind her. Their eyes glazed over as if blinded. Was it a leader they were groping for, someone to follow? *No, they're not following you,* the molecules in her blood vessels insisted. *They are chasing you. There is a bear in the woods there is a bear —*

"Cassie, is everything all right?"

It took only a second. Just for a split second when Cass looked up, she saw some other thing where Rick should have been. It was a bear, but not a bear, because it did not have a face. It had a bear's dank forest of shaggy fur and a lolling tongue and a mouthful of teeth — including canines where its ears should have been — but no eyes. Maybe if an alien intelligence tried to sculpt a bear based on the fever-dreams of a starved and stranded woodsman, it would create this grotesque, teratoma-like monstrosity. Maybe.

But another blink and it was gone, and only her man Rick McFarland stood there with his hand outstretched to save her, his face frozen now in a worry that at least *looked* real. Slowly, her human brain got to ticking again, started putting the pieces back together: that vision was an optical illusion, brought about by too little sleep and too much caffeine; there is no bear; there is no Circle.

"I'm fine," Cass said, although her voice seemed to waft in from somewhere very far away. She dropped the medal, but couldn't quite take Rick's hand.

Maybe she would have believed herself if not for the odd splash of deep red that had preceded the appearance of the bear-not-bear. Maybe she would have stayed with Team Rick through November and onward; maybe she would have seen him chosen and triumphant. Maybe she would have moved to Washington and walked behind Rick in those gilded halls of power. But for the rest of her life, Cass would never shake the feeling that the swath of pulsing touchable red, like a gently-billowing theater curtain on opening night, had made the vision deliberate.

The next October, Cass found the "oldest haunted house this side of the Missouri" – the real one, the one with the web site and the lines of shivering, gum-cracking teenagers snaking around the block. In a fit of anxiety over the possibility that her neighbor with a weak heart had been turned in for sedition, Cass had gone for a stomach-settling drive up Highway 69 and then, nearly without realizing it, west on Interstate 80. She put the car on cruise control and imagined all the ways in which she could die: that semi-truck might drift leftward into her sedan, the construction beam on the back of that pick-up might dislodge and plow through her windshield, all the drivers in this mechanical herd might close their eyes and clap their hands. Her weak-hearted neighbor said, "You wear that guilt like a crown, munchkin," and maybe that was why she fantasized about mass casualty car crashes – or maybe she was just terrified that her neighbor might submit her name under interrogation, and thought this would be a better way to go.

This continued into the fading half-light, with Cass repeatedly failing to take an exit despite the promise of food and rest, until she saw the signs. *HELL ON EARTH,* the billboard promised, but what she got was a regular hell house called Inferno in a regular small town called Pikesville. Each of Inferno's rooms was dedicated to the blood-spattered fate that would befall the various state-approved classes of sinners: the abortion-seekers, the homosexuals, the blasphemers who just wouldn't accept the word of God. Children in braces were hysterically crying beside her and she couldn't move to comfort them; Cass had never been good with people, and martial law made it even more difficult to socialize.

By then she had deduced the inevitable truth: there was no Spira. There was, probably, no Circle and no Mr. Kamke. There was definitely no reason that she should still be seeing the eyeless bear-that-was-not-a-bear lurking and grinning with its too-many-teeth in city parks and intersections. Definitely no reason to dream of Aaron manically thrashing his head in the dark as a clump of hair and tissue tried to chew its way out of his neck. But those were only a few in a long list of things that Cass tried not to dwell on. She could not even dwell on Rick, nor on any of the legislation that he and President Hunter were working so hard to pass. "Your man's on television," her parents would say, and as soon as his image bubbled up in her mind's eye her mouth would fill with the taste of metal, her ears with the howl of a locomotive. "That's nice," she would say, so as not to arouse suspicion.

In the parking lot near the exit of Inferno, a woman and two small black-haired children were devotedly watching something moving on the concrete. It was a vortex of ants, Cass realized when she took a few steps toward them, racing in a claustrophobically tight spiral toward an impossible center. Maybe a thousand ants roiling in the most organized frenzy Cass had ever seen. From a distance this death spiral looked like a single heaving entity, a dark carnivorous galaxy. One child asked what the ants were trying to find. "Nothing," the woman said. "They're just following each other. Round and round and round and round and..." "But why?" "Because they're ants, my sweet. It's what they do. It's all they know."

That night, Cass found Spira. The words and the mileage had been spray-painted in white on a larger road sign, with a big bleeding arrow pointing north. She took the turn because she strongly felt that she had nothing left to lose, and not long after she made it she found Mr. Kamke's farmhouse, all bleak and lonesome on the windswept plain. Judging by the belligerent, misshapen shadows still agitating in the windows, the house was still running. For a moment Cass stalled the engine, half-listening to the radio – *"six terrorists responsible for the Gadney Park incident were apprehended today, thanks to the hard work of our men and women in law enforcement"* – and then she parked the car in the empty, weed-riddled driveway and went straight to the back of the house and into the overgrown maze.

In the center, at the beginning and the end, lay old man Kamke, face-down on the dirt with his arms crossed under his leathered body. There was a dried, cavernous hole in the back of his neck that Cass dared not look down into. There was also a note, written on a blank check and tucked under his forehead so it would not blow away: *"Though changed, I shall rise the same."*

A spotted calf lay beside Mr. Kamke, its tail swatting at flies with the slow and steady rhythm of a metronome. It seemed too young to be without its mother. The calf blinked at Cass and Cass blinked back, until eventually the little creature wobbled to its feet and began to cut a path through what was now entirely wild corn – dead wasted corn that had not been harvested, but still clung stubbornly to the stalk. The stars were unusually bright, unusually close. And after a few deep breaths, Cass followed.

The Smoke Lodge

by Michael Griffin

Creamy mist followed Robert Doret and his friends in from the beach, dampening their jackets and hair like rain, though no drops fell. As the five approached the blackened restaurant's shell, Robert told them about the night the Moby Schooner burned.

"We'd arrived that evening, just Milla and me," Robert said. "The commotion brought us outside through all this thick smoke, toward shouting and sirens and orange glow. The firefighters couldn't stop it. Wind whipped the inferno into such heat, it vaporized water sprayed at it. Sparks streamed into the black sky like outpourings from some occult ceremony."

Robert realized he'd conveyed how the fire had looked but omitted how he'd felt.

"What was this place?" Jack Irons asked. Only thirty, Jack was younger than the others by a decade or two, and accustomed to needing explanations for all he'd missed.

"An old fish and chips place, always packed. Best chowder in town." Robert stood looking over the charred foundation and beams. As far back as boyhood, he'd eaten here whenever his family visited Lincoln City. It was more than just the vanishing of the only restaurant in the Road's End area. The real sting was lost tradition, another familiar comfort gone too soon. Worse, a reminder everything and everyone was under that same threat and might vanish before its time.

"Been a year, why haven't they rebuilt?" Jon Paulsen asked, habitually stroking the bushy mustache portion of his beard.

"The neighborhood's zoned residential now," Robert said. "Moby Schooner was grandfathered in, now they can't rebuild, at least not here. They're moving up to Highway 101, but it won't be the same."

Robert knew his friends, all fiction writers and editors,

understood well enough notions like memory and loss. This group shared history, overlapping lists of places and events, yet crucial aspects of memory couldn't be shared. Robert remembered too much, some of which pained him. He wanted to get back to the house, to eat and drink and search out more pleasurable reminiscences.

"So here you have five writers," Paulsen said, "though in the case of the pup Jack Irons, such an appellation may be too generous. Some of us even award-winning." He slapped Robert's shoulder.

The day before, at the 96th World Horror Conference in Portland, Robert Doret's latest novel, *At Midnight the Demon Sings Morning,* had won the H.P. Lovecraft Award for Best Novel, beating, among others, Jon Paulsen's *The Harlot Oracle.* The award was Robert's sixth H.P.L., and would've been Paulsen's third. None of the other writers on this post-convention trip, Jack Irons, Michael Standish or his wife, Agni, had ever won.

Paulsen insisted each should declaim what story they'd tell of the burning of an oceanside restaurant, and himself suggested a ghost story in the aftermath of fire, the rebuilt place haunted by the spirit of a waitress who burned to death.

Though Robert declined to offer his own story, he was glad for Paulsen's carrying on, and the time it granted him to control his emotions. Memories of fire always got to him.

Jack Irons proposed a curse brought back to land by a trawler that delved into a cove where long ago fishermen killed natives.

"A fish curse?" Paulsen roared. "The halibut filet terror? Alright, pup. What about Standishes?"

Dr. Agni Standish spoke of folklore, campfire tales handed down over generations.

"Bzzzt, gong!" Paulsen said. "Sounds boring. What of your estimable husband, the lesser doctor?"

Michael Standish's idea involved an angry husband,

forced out by his wife who's divorcing him, and keeping the restaurant they co-own. If he can't have the restaurant, she can't either. He chains the doors and burns everyone alive inside.

The five walked beneath a sky already darkening. Surf roared, distant.

Robert smelled smoke, though the Moby Schooner was blocks behind. Maybe fireplaces in neighborhood vacation homes? More than just smell, a whole array of senses. The pop and sizzle of firehose spray hitting hot timbers. Steam rising, while something glided along behind and overhead. Ghosts of memory silent and invisible, yet personified.

From the crest of Keel Street, the Doret house came into view. Upstairs windows glowed where two women moved cooperatively in the kitchen: Milla, Robert's wife of two decades, and their partner Lisa, a recent addition to what had always been a monogamous pair.

"Back to the wives," Paulsen said. "Good wives, making supper."

"Hey, I'm here!" Agni Standish protested. "A wife, not making anybody supper."

"And we're glad you're not," Paulsen said. "I'm just trying to nudge the award-winning Robert Doret into explaining his new domestic triangle."

Robert unlocked the front door. "Maybe later."

In the entry hall, they banged sand from shoes, hung jackets, and shivered off the damp October chill. Upstairs, a fire burned. Robert went to his blond women, kissed short-haired Milla first, then younger, longer-haired Lisa. Always this ritual, both women, never just one, and always in this order. He felt eyes upon him, knew they watched and wondered, but he didn't mind. Observation of human behavior and relationships, especially the unconventional, was universal among writers. Study from life yielded crucial details which might someday lend characters or scenes more interesting shading.

Those who had been outside drifted toward the fireplace.

"I heard rumors of good single malt," Michael Standish said.

"Better be more than rumor." Paulsen patted his belly. "It's the sole reason I let myself be dragged to this hell of tangible mist."

"I picked up a Lagavulin 16-year," Robert said. "Thought it was time."

Michael Standish's head turned. His expression shifted, surprise to wistfulness.

Paulsen smiled sadly.

"What's this?" Jack Irons asked. "Another tradition unknown to the new guy?"

"Karlring," Robert said.

Agni Standish was apparently more able to compartmentalize this emotional subject than the others. "It was the favored dram of Edward Karlring. He brought a bottle to every convention, even when he couldn't afford it."

Robert went to the kitchen, returned with the bottle and seven glasses on a tray. While the rest sat by the window, or stood overlooking the sunset, he poured. As Milla and Lisa started in from the kitchen to join them, Robert asked them to bring another glass.

"An eighth?" Jack Irons asked.

"If it's time for Lagavulin 16," Paulsen said, "Karlring needs one."

"I sense him." Robert raised his glass. "Especially here. He loved the coast."

"For me, he haunts the HPL awards," Paulsen added.

"He won plenty, I know." Irons phrased it like a query.

"Ten, most ever," Paulsen said. "If he hadn't done for himself by fifty-one, it would've been more."

"Plenty more," Robert said. "If he'd stuck around, I'd never have won. He'd have my six, plus his ten, and...who knows?"

Michael Standish sipped. "The man was eternal. Even that word doesn't cut it."

"Not one of us is poet enough to name the loss of Karlring. To even try seems phony." Robert leaned down and touched the glass front of the fireplace. "Phony, like this damn fireplace. A fire isn't gas flames, it's wood burning. Smoke and unpredictability." He was still thinking about another fire.

Milla moved toward the kitchen, gesturing at platters on the counter. "Karlring wouldn't stand for wasting food. Remember your early years, all coming up together, poor and starving?"

Dinner was a buffet of local seafood: Yaquina Bay oyster shooters with lemon and sea salt; blackened razor clams from Agate Beach; Dungeness crab cocktail in martini glasses with sweet habanero cocktail sauce; smoked Pacific salmon with aged gouda and caper chutney. Each filled their plate and returned to eat near the fireplace.

By the final bite, the Lagavulin too had been depleted, dispersing a cloud that had loomed since the mention of Karlring's name.

Paulsen fell into teasing Jack Irons for being too young, fit, and trim for a writer.

"Is it true you're planning a triathlon? What, last time you ran a marathon you thought, that's not hard enough, maybe next I'll add a bike ride and swim?"

"It's just a Half-Ironman," Jack Irons said.

"And let's discuss that nonsense you spouted in that *Rue Morgue* interview. Dictating your book with a voice recorder on all-day mountain hikes?"

Jack Irons shook his head and laughed. "This weekend with you guys, it's like *The Big Chill* for alcoholic grey-beards with bellies swollen and backs ruined from too much sitting."

All laughed, not least the gray-bearded alcoholics.

"All right, pup!" Paulsen roared, striking a pose. "Which of us is Meg Tilly in a leotard, doing splits?"

"What next?" Michael asked. "More Scotch?"

Robert went to the cabinet, and came back uncapping a bottle of Glenlivet.

"I prefer Irish whiskey," Agni said.

"Fuck Irish whiskey," Robert said. "And I say that as half an Irishman. Tonight we'll be drinking this here single-malt."

"Scotch aficionados are such tiresome snobs." Agni briefly withheld her glass, then held it out.

"You're married to this woman, Michael?" Robert poured around.

"What should we toast to?" Michael Standish asked.

"Publishing," Paulsen said. "The only thing I hate more than ex-wives."

"To Karlring, and publishing, and Paulsen's ex-wives," Michael Standish said.

They drank.

Paulsen blinked, red-faced. "Please, no more Karlring talk tonight. As an alternative, I suggest we start a rumor as follows. The only reason our Doret won his latest HPL–"

"My sixth."

"–is because World Horror was in Portland this year. That's home field advantage. Not to put too fine a point on it, the fix was in."

"Scoreboard, chum." Robert clinked Paulsen's glass. "Six is more than two. Nearly twice as many."

"Cheers." Both Standishes toasted in tandem.

Paulsen slapped Robert's back. "Congrats, my brother."

"My sixth HPL." Robert sighed. "I should be on top of the world. I am, really."

"I feel a cloud hanging," Michael Standish said.

"Things feel heavy, like some persistent lament," Robert said. "Is it Karlring, the Lagavulin? Maybe I should't have. But we've been avoiding it so long."

"That's just life," Paulsen said. "The ultimate fade to black."

Agni took Michael's hand.

"Is that all it is, just recognition of mortality?" Robert asked. "Not just Karlring's. Ours."

"Our careers have progressed, especially yours, Robert." Michael Standish chewed his lip. "Yet I barely recall the enthusiasm that got me here."

"You hit the level of multi-book deals, then keep your head down. One house, one relationship." Paulsen hunched, stroking his beard.

Jack Irons made a rude noise. "One relationship. Do you even hear yourself?"

Paulsen's face remained serious. "You stop walking the edge, and that's good, the edge is dangerous. But really, you stop living life. When's the last time I got arrested? Woke up beside a stripper?"

"That's the experience you're missing?" Michael Standish laughed.

"Nah, you know. It's fuel for the work, certain experiences. Earlier we took risks, stared demons in the eye. Suddenly thirty years have gone, spent typing, vision wrecked from computer screens. The edge gone dull."

The Standishes and Jack Irons appeared occupied by thought.

Paulsen continued. "When's the last time you felt afraid?"

"That's it," Robert said.

"What?" Jack Irons asked.

"What we need, Paulsen's right." Robert hurried to the kitchen.

The others waited expectantly, wondering, looking to Milla. She shrugged.

Robert returned with a small branch of driftwood, a salt-bleached ornament from the window sill. He knelt at the fireplace, opened the glass and placed natural wood atop the artificial logs. It surged to life, flared. Blue flames turned orange.

"Tomorrow, we'll show you something." He looked meaningfully at Milla.

"You mean take them to Smoke Lodge," she said.

"Oooh!" Lisa jumped up. "I've never been to the lodge, only heard about it. Yeah! Big fire."

"Can't be an equal third in the Doret *menage*," Paulsen began, "sorry, I meant marriage, without that. Not that I know what this Smoke Lodge is."

"If they let me, I'm going to take the Doret name." Lisa glanced at Milla, suddenly embarrassed, and covered her face with one hand. "We haven't talked about it, but I just..."

"Three Dorets are better than two." Milla reached around Lisa's waist and squeezed possessively. "We're all libertines here, aren't we?"

"Maybe not all," Paulsen said.

"Think of Scott and Zelda, all their friends," Milla teased. "They really knew how to live."

"Worked out great for them," Michael Standish said.

"Listen, everybody wants this?" Robert asked. "I'm serious."

General laughter and lighthearted dismissal trailed off before Robert's continued sombre look. Finally, all assented.

"Tomorrow," Robert said. "Smoke Lodge."

After an oceanside lunch of chilled half-shell oysters and excellent bread and butter with spicy salted Bloody Marys all around, they continued down Pacific Coast Highway, then turned off at Siletz River.

Paulsen, riding shotgun, turned. "Milla, what's this secret lodge your Robert's taking us to? When Uncle Paulsen asks, you must tell."

Milla, seated in the second row between Lisa and Agni, ignored him.

Lisa laughed. "I'm just excited."

Paulsen hailed Jack Irons and Michael Standish in back. "Either of you know anything?"

"Be patient." Robert gripped the wheel one-handed. "Enjoy the scenery."

Dead piers spiked the inlet where bay transitioned to river. Mist drifted in the marshlands beneath hills of Birch gone yellow and orange. The gap between river and road widened enough to allow homesites and sodden grazing land.

Robert pointed across the river. "There's the *Sometimes a Great Notion* house."

"These little seats aren't fit for grown men," Jack Irons groused.

Paulsen laughed. "Luckily that doesn't apply to you, waif."

"Speaking of lucky," Michael said, "if Karlring were here, he'd displace three of us."

"I've seen pictures," Jack Irons said. "Karlring was a bear."

"A giant man," Michael agreed. "A lion's mane. A mighty beard."

"Heart the size of a yoga ball," Agni added.

"His girth exceeded most doorways," Paulsen said. "They had to be broken out to make way, and rebuilt after. And when he was in his drink, he grew six inches in height. Could raise two ordinary men overhead, one in each hand, as I might lift kittens."

Unlike last night, when mention of Karlring had left the mood heavy, this outpouring seemed to please everyone. The mood brightened, and talk of scenery and destination resumed.

Paulsen read a roadside sign. "Ichwhit Park. What's *Ichwhit?*"

"Allegedly it's *bear* in some Native American dialect," Robert said. "Siletz Indians...I don't know, does every tribe have their own language? Standish, don't you speak all languages?"

"All but three," Michael shouted, "and Agni speaks those."

"There are bears here?" Lisa asked. "There aren't. You're making jokes about old bear Karlring."

"No bears," Robert said. "Not around here."

"Good," Jack Irons said.

"Bears fucking scare me." Lisa shuddered.

"Plenty of *ichwhit*, though," Robert said.

In fields softened by encroaching water, a half-sunk Caterpillar tractor sat abandoned and rusting beside a fallen tree from which cut sections had been dragged to the house and split for firewood, the remainder sodden in the emerald marsh. This seemed to be the last house beside the river. Trees took over. Spruces leaned over the road from both sides, almost meeting above the center, and in the occasional lesser valleys which shot sidelong uphill, trees leaned more steeply and managed to intermingle dying leaves above the very streams which cut downslope.

"Almost to the turnoff," Robert announced.

"Beautiful land," Michael Standish said. "You're doing well, you Dorets. The Portland place, a beach house, plus this lodge."

"The beach place, my grandmother left us. The lodge, you'll see, it's pretty rustic. No electricity. We built on land owned by our friend Jarrett. He owns most of this forest."

Milla laughed. "Jarrett's crazy, shut away in his plantation-style mansion. All these weird collections."

"Permanent coast-dwellers," Robert added, "they're

pretty much all misfits and loony tunes."

"What kind of collections?" Paulsen asked.

Robert looked sideways. "All kinds, almost a museum. Wood sculptures, maritime paintings, old records. Mostly books, some that might impress you. Here's Lost Lake Road."

A yellow car ahead turned left into a gap between trees. Robert slowed the Expedition and took the same turn. Up the narrow gravel road a metal gate blocked the way.

"Where's that other car?" Paulsen asked. "It turned ahead of us."

Robert removed his seatbelt. "What car?" He jumped out, unlocked the gate, and swung it open.

Through wavering leaves, intermittent sunlight filtered gold. The road wound through trees falling barren, summer's overgrowth lost. In another mile, the incline diminished. To both sides, fields of wild grass were weighted by damp orange and brown leaves. To the right, beyond tumbled rocks and vines, an irregular lake reflected slate sky.

"Your own lake," Paulsen observed.

The road curved past a scrim of Alders to dead-end at a log structure.

"Smoke Lodge," Robert announced.

Out front, a bonfire burned in a stone firepit. In the field, overgrown corn stalks sagged in rows. Overripe pumpkins slumped on their vines.

"Who built the fire?" Lisa asked.

Robert set the brake. "Probably our friend thought we might come today, wanted to welcome us."

"Why not inside?" Paulsen asked. "There's a chimney."

"You need the outdoor experience first. Later, we'll go in."

Rain fell, visible but soundless. Perimeter trees swayed independently in surging wind.

"What's that rotten smell?" Agni asked.

"Pumpkins," Milla said.

Around the fire, upended crosscut log sections made eight stools. The seven sat.

Robert hoped nobody would say anything about the empty stool. "It's always damp here. The ocean uses the rain and mist to reach inland, and the ground's a sponge, but if you build big enough fires and leave them burning, eventually things dry out." He went to the lodge's outer wall where an ancient rake leaned, and with this, began gathering leaves into piles, some like yellow parchment, others red or brown and hole-shot with decay.

He took up one mound and tossed them in the fire. The leaves sputtered and hissed. "No matter how wet," Robert said, "they always burn."

A column of smoke rose to vanish against clouds. Darker, ground-level smoke wound tendrils among the visitors.

Jack Irons coughed. "Is this why it's Smoke Lodge?"

"Nope," Robert said.

From a paper bag, Milla produced a magnum of Shiraz, pulled the cork, and filled clear plastic cups.

"No wine for me," Paulsen said. "Anything else?"

"Inside." Robert stood. "I'll go. Enjoy the fire."

Michael Standish and the women sipped wine, while Jack Irons and Paulsen waited with empty cups.

Robert returned, carrying a brown glass jug full of obscure liquid.

"What's this?" Jack Irons asked.

"Mead." Robert poured. "Jarrett often drops off a gallon or two from a new batch."

"Fireside mead," Paulsen observed, "in the forest by Lost Lake."

Michael Standish angled his cell phone at arm's length. "Untethered from the world."

"Try this," Robert promised.

Paulsen tasted. "Extraordinary. Spice on the tongue,

sweet. Burnt grain."

Lisa quickly finished her wine and tried the mead. "It's like pumpernickel."

They sat a long time around the fire, fetching their own refills, mostly not speaking.

Finally Jack Irons stood. "Damn, I'm sweating."

"Feel free to wander," Robert said. "I'll start dinner soon."

"It's early, yet," Paulsen said. "Not that I couldn't eat."

Milla stood. "When people lived outside, they ate early and slept at sundown."

Agni looked around. "We aren't sleeping out here."

"We won't stay overnight," Robert said. "Explore the field or the lake. Just don't go far."

"Let's explore," Lisa said.

Milla led Agni, Lisa, and Jack through the pumpkins and cornstalks to the lake. Robert watched despite knowing Milla would keep track. He gathered more fallen limbs and leaves.

The fire enlarged, intensified.

"How do you transition from two married people to this?" Paulsen asked.

Robert shrugged. "It wasn't how you'd think. We just took her in, like roommates at first. She needed friends. A stable place."

Paulsen looked dubious. "But now you three…".

"Now, yeah," Robert said. "But that took a while. Actually, the women worked it out."

Pointedly ignoring the subject, Michael Standish indicated the lodge exterior, where hung constructs of branches, dried plants, and animal bones. "Pagan influenced, I think, also Native American."

"Maybe."

Robert reentered the lodge, shut the door, and emerged minutes later carrying a heavy cloth-covered basket and four yard-long metal skewers. He placed these on the table and ran each spear through chunks of seasoned game meat, whole potatoes, red onions and yellow squash, then poised these over the fire.

After a while, the meat sizzled and spit, and the vegetables steamed and blackened.

"Food enough for twenty," Michael observed.

"Where'd you get fresh meat?" Paulsen asked. "We didn't carry that in."

"Inside. Jarrett leaves provisions, if he guesses we're coming."

Robert refilled his mead, then Paulsen's.

"I'll try that." Standish shook out his cup, but drops of Shiraz remained in the bottom. "I'm sorry, could I get a clean cup?"

Robert poured and they all drank, contemplating the transformation of raw food over fire.

Paulsen sniffed. "Real caveman time."

Robert shouted toward the lake for the four to return.

Through the trees, shapes emerged into the field.

Agni ran ahead of the others. She kissed Michael's hand, and froze upon noticing his switch from wine. "What's this? Speaking of wild transformation."

"Wild food, drink, and fire." Jack Irons walked up. "Have you heard of the Paleo Diet?"

Robert crouched to remove the first giant kebab from the fire. He placed the cool end into one of several angled holes drilled into the table.

"Wondered what those were," Paulsen muttered.

"Can I help?" Lisa asked.

Robert shook his head. "No silverware. No plates."

"Bare-handed like animals." Milla selected a blackened oblong of elk. "Careful, it's hot."

"Our hands is tender!" Paulsen slid a blackened potato

off the spear. "Oww."

They ate carefully, fingers juice-slick, lips black with smoke char. Some complained at first of burned fingers or mouths, then gradually, as if remembering, each ate with solemn purpose.

After, following Robert and Mila's lead, all cleaned their hands with damp leaves. There was no water to drink. Agni finished the Shiraz.

"Regrettable the mead's gone," Paulsen observed. "That brew opened my skull rather nicely."

"I have a surprise." Robert started inside.

"Are we going in now?" Jack Irons asked.

"Not until true dark. But I've stashed more mead."

Robert shut the door behind him, and reemerged carrying two more gallon jugs, along with something else under one arm. He handed Jack Irons the mead, and showed the others a book. Worn black leather, thick as an old Bible. No words on the cover, just a silver hexagon bounding an asymmetrical asterisk. In six corners within were arrayed indecipherable letterforms.

Paulsen's eyes widened. "I've seen that before, on Karlring's shelf. He wouldn't let me see."

"I know it bothered you, Karlring making me his literary executor." Robert handed Paulsen the book. "You'd known him longer."

"I wouldn't say..." Paulsen opened the cover. Pages crackled like dry leaves.

"He never let me read it either, until he was gone," Robert said. "I figure it's why he picked me. Not to caretake his own work. This."

"Who wrote it?" Paulsen turned pages.

"It contains many hands, and languages," Robert said. "Diagrams, poems. Tables of figures."

"There's no title."

"*Wyentenja Isvosk Nia Tenjmako.* My best translation is

Through Smoke Into Fire." Robert indicated the symbols on the cover. "Every line I've translated, I've found referenced within Karlring's later stories. This book is the foundation of all Karlring's most acclaimed works." He paused, gave them time to absorb. "And all my own, since the book became mine."

None of the others spoke. None moved.

Robert took back the book, flipped pages. "Here's a taste, untranslated."

He recited, glancing up periodically to make eye contact. The lines were metric, strangely incantatory, almost songlike.

Michael Standish leaned in, head angled as if still listening, even after Robert stopped. "Some words are Latinate, but I can't...It's none of the major Romance languages. I'd recognize Galician, Corsican, or Catalan."

Robert offered Standish the book. "The languages are mostly obscure, not taught in universities. Those lines hybridized Quechuan and Andean Spanish, rare even in Chile, where Karlring found this."

"Karlring spoke only English," Paulsen insisted.

"No," Robert said. "He'd been using it."

"I can't..." Michael shook his head.

"It ends as follows, in Karlring's hand." Robert flipped to a later page. "'Many before tied their lines, end to end. Fix yours at the last; others will join. The thread lengthens forever.'"

Paulsen whistled. "Did you know about this?" he asked Milla.

"She knows everything." Robert looked up at the darkening sky. "See that?"

Paulsen followed his gaze. "What?"

Michael pointed. "Is it the moon, breaking through?"

"No moon yet." Robert picked up the mead. "But something's coming."

He poured while Jack Irons distributed filled cups.

"And when there remains no water or wine," Paulsen

intoned, "all the world's people must content themselves with what brew the devil provides."

Everyone encircled the dwindling fire except Robert, who set the partial jug between the full and empty ones, then ventured into the mist to gather more wood. He returned, threw limbs onto the fire, and went back for more.

"That's enough, Robert," Lisa said. "Join us."

"He knows what needs doing out here." Milla smiled, gently disarming.

"Getting cold." Jack Irons squatted before the fire.

Robert fed another armload to the blaze, then more damp leaves, which hissed out eye-burning smoke. The fire broadened, seething with the yellow ferocity of a captive sun.

"Lean close," Robert said. "Breathe it in. If smoke burns your eyes, you're not drinking enough. Let it darken your skin. Preserve you like smoked meat."

Michael Standish refilled his cup and went to Robert's side. He breathed deep, blinked his eyes, and laughed strangely through coughing.

Agni approached, touched her husband's shoulder. "Michael, you should–"

Michael roared like an animal at the fire. His cry ended ragged and hoarse.

"You're making me afraid," Agni said. "This is–"

"You should drink." Bug-eyed, hair upstanding like Eraserhead, Michael offered his cup.

"Try some, it's good!" Lisa leaned against both Standishes, then unzipped her tall boots. She stepped out of them, looking about, wild-eyed.

Despite seeming afraid, Agni drank.

"Who wants to run?" Lisa sprinted off, soon vanished into mist. Only her laughter and the rustling of disturbed leaves hinted her trajectory.

Jack Irons pranced, kicked off shoes, and started after

Lisa. He fell, laughing.

Agni Standish finished the drink. Michael forcefully clutched her to himself and kissed her with uncharacteristic animal passion.

"Is this for real?" Paulsen regarded his cup. "Is it? What's in this stuff?"

Milla leaned in close, as if confiding a secret. "It's not ordinary mead."

"Not ordinary." Paulsen laughed and roared, like Michael before, then pounded his chest like Tarzan and cackled as if surprised at himself.

"Good?" Robert asked.

Paulsen's red face beamed. "I'll take more, if you're pouring."

"Do you have enough smoke?"

"No, more please. More smoke."

"Is this what you wanted?"

"I did say...We talked about Karlring and–"

"Why did we come?" Robert insisted. "Remember what you wanted?"

Michael and Agni approached, huddled in.

"To remember," Paulsen said.

"Look up." Robert pulled back.

The sky above cleared to transparency, while ground-level remained shrouded. The moon loomed red, impossibly large, filling a quarter of the sky. The massive disc, no real moon but a looming world, occluded or outshone all stars.

"Now it's time." Robert held a branch into the fire, raised it burning. "We go in."

The interior log walls were honey-gold. A massive river rock fireplace, black mortar speckled with metallic glass, dominated the near end of the open rectangle. Within the hearth, already loaded with kindling and splits, Robert struck a fire.

The prospect of finally seeing inside seemed to calm the group. At least briefly, they reverted to themselves.

The fire surged, blasting heat and light. Robert held the book and watched his friends exploring. At the far end, a trio of double bunks, each with shelves of rough-sawn lumber, were separated by delicate scrims which first appeared to be Asian paper screens, but were actually stretched hide painted with the black symbols from the book's cover.

Milla helped Paulsen open the last jug of mead.

Cup extended, Lisa bounced on tiptoes. "Me, me."

"Gotta love ladies who tipple," Milla said.

"These ornaments," Michael Standish mused, facing the side wall.

Jack Irons shrugged. "Sculptures of sticks, colored leaves."

The arrangements combined natural browns and reds with other colors less organic, which lent these dead things, despite brittle desiccation, the vibrancy of persistent life. At their center hung a wide, unframed painting, frayed edges dangling canvas threads, depicting an orange seething globe whose surface spit tongues of fire. Visible outlines of continents indicated this was Earth, not Sun. Beside it, a bear straddled the white moon, arms outstretched with elongated needle-sharp fingers, striving toward home.

"Getting smoky, Robert. Your chimney's got the flue. Get it?" Jack Irons cackled.

"Ha," Milla said.

Agni approached stiff-legged, staring into mead dregs. "It feels like clockwork elves are controlling my body."

Michael alternately squinted and opened eyes wide. "I

have post-anesthesia fog."

Robert drained another cup. "The mead contains its own secrets."

"Where do you want us?" Paulsen's eyes bulged, his face red.

"On the floor, by the fire," Robert said.

"It's hard to look at it." Lisa rubbed her eyes. "Like staring into a foundry."

Milla sat beside her. "Nothing can cut this smoke."

Even as the fire burned hotter, the interior seemed to darken.

"Everyone here?" Robert faced them. "Anything missing?"

Paulsen coughed, waving a hand. "Some air would be nice."

Robert held up the book. "This didn't begin with Karlring. But he left it to me, and it continues."

Michael Standish reached. "Can I see it again?"

Robert ignored him. "Karlring studied languages, delved into arcana, trying to understand."

Milla rose and crossed the room to the shelves near the left corner bunk-beds. Robert's eyes followed her, and the others twisted to watch as Milla started dragging what looked like an unrolled sleeping bag, lightweight, as if stuffed with dry leaves.

"Starting where Karlring left off," Robert said, "I learned more."

Milla passed behind her husband toward the fire.

"What's in that?" Paulsen asked.

Milla easily lifted the bundle and tossed it onto the fire. The flames caught, made it part of their burning.

"It's Karlring." Robert held the book so they could see only the cover, and resumed speaking in the same bizarre tongue he'd intoned outside.

The others stopped questioning, merely watched.

Robert halted, turned and threw the book onto the fire, where the bundle still burned.

"Robert, stop!" Paulsen fell sideways and scrambled forward, as if he might snatch the book from the flames.

Michael Standish stood easily, straight up, eyes bulging in surprise. Blinking at the smoke, he stepped around Robert, who made no move to stop him.

Words emerged from the fire in a deep male voice. Not Robert speaking, but the same language as before. A pause, then new words in another language, stranger still. Robert stood away, Paulsen and Michael fell back to their places. Dark smoke swirled thick. Within the core of yellow-orange flame, a human shape clarified, sat up and slowly stood. No longer a formless bundle. A broad man-shape unfurled, details lost in the smoke. It was this shape speaking.

"What are these words?" Michael flinched, as if the sound caused pain.

"Ask him." Robert pointed. "Ask Karlring."

Giant's stature, wild mane, formidable beard, Karlring's voice.

It murmured, standing at the limit of the fire, yet not detached from it. Robert had seen this before, had never been sure whether the form was a solid thing, or merely some uncanny formation of fire. The bearlike physique, overlarge head crowned with bushy hair. Copious tears streamed from its eyes, glistening, flowing ever faster, pattering heavy on the fireplace verge. The ground remained dry. Not transparent tears but something darker, like dark tea or whiskey, which sizzled and steamed away.

"Heard you say." The voice creaked like a broken chair.

"I brought everyone," Robert said.

It resumed speaking, now English in short bursts, not Karlring's characteristically fluid complex sentences. Each fragment triggered sequential images, memories spun rapid and disordered.

A woman falls stricken, dying on cold concrete. Paulsen's second wife, Ellen.

Hooded figures hunch over scrawled vellums, edges curled. Corner insignia black, wax seal red.

Hotel bar, Karlring, his agent, and Len Totts of Euclid Press. Three hands toast whiskey.

Third wife, Anne, first encounter. Hotel suite champagne, she strips off green satin.

Anne remarries, Len Totts, Karlring five weeks buried.

Providence with Robert and Milla, New York with Agni and Michael, later all in Boston. Thai dinner meeting Jack Irons.

Tar smeared on stone by many hands. Firelight outlines robed shapes against cavern wall.

Faster, others flash, indecipherable.

The voice stopped. Robert heard his own breathing, saw other faces twisted in fear and distress. The images, if all had seen the same, as he assumed, what would the others make of them? When Milla first accompanied him here, their experiences had matched.

It had to be Karlring. Events they'd shared, also things after his death. What explanation?

The voice resumed. "A dream remembered is not the dream itself."

"You can't be Karlring." Paulsen's voice broke.

The shape faded, edges softening into fire, then resolved again. "Many different kinds of dying," the voice croaked.

"If it's you, Edward, what do you want to tell?" Agni asked. "What can you give us?"

"Nothing," he said, then repeated the word, the last almost a whisper, like candle flame sputtering in the wind.

The shape finally vanished. Nothing remained in the fireplace but flames and smoke. Already the fire shrunk as if starved. The embers diminished, yellow to orange to red, dying until finally the black remains gave no light at all.

Robert couldn't pinpoint why he believed. So much felt subjective, experiences that couldn't be shared even by those in the same room. But looking at his friends, their expressions made him believe all had undergone something similar. This relieved him, comforted him. Always he felt such desperation, urgency in the face of fleeting time, the need to forestall death's encroachment. Eventually, tempted to face this again, to delve into the book, trying to learn more. What would it grant him? Would it season him, toughen his resolve, allow him to squeeze more life out of what time remained? He didn't know by what increment he should measure. New mornings, breaths drawn, seized recognitions?

He couldn't stop time spinning, accelerating, could only grasp what lay within reach. Life wasn't done, not yet, not today. More books ahead, more travel, new discoveries and friends. And what he possessed already. Things with Milla, stronger than ever. Lisa, good and true. They needed each other.

Was that enough? Still the Earth raced its flaming circuit, each year dwindling under the widening shadow of the past.

Nobody spoke. Just breathing, all around.

Robert went to the fireplace, delved barehanded into ashes. He retrieved the intact book, unburned and steaming.

Dr. Agni Standish rubbed her eyes. "Did we all just…"

"We did." Lisa looked from Robert to Milla, visibly stunned by the secrets revealed, seeming to guess what other concealments might remain.

"He only remains long enough that we're sure it's him," Robert said. "No more. And every time, sometimes days later, sometimes within minutes, we find ourselves questioning whether he was ever really here."

"Did we bring him," Paulsen asked. "With all our remembering, our nostalgia?"

"Nostalgia, it's nothing but pain," Robert said. "It's memory poisoned by the anguish of loss."

He went to the doorway, opened it. The smoke drew out, sucked by cold wind, and dispersed. Robert inhaled fresh outdoor air.

"It's all new." Paulsen came outside, shaking his head. "Everything."

The mist had cleared and the moon stood overhead in brittle clarity, no larger than usual, no sign of the strange earlier redness and exaggerated size.

Michael led Agni out, heads swiveling as if observing an unknown world.

Leaves crunched underfoot, dry and brittle.

"Like I promised," Robert said. "Let the fire burn long enough, it dries everything."

"I never thought Karlring would terrify me," Paulsen said.

"Fear is something we used to love," Robert said. "Now we write stories meant to be scary, without ever feeling afraid."

Milla came to his right side, Lisa his left. Two decades had passed since Robert and Milla had decided against having kids. Lisa, though newly arrived, felt the same. They had no regrets, never felt any lack, but now Robert wondered who would summon him from smoke after he was gone. None of these friends had offspring.

"I know what I'll write next," Robert said.

Both fires had died, inside and out. Already, Robert was thinking about the next time these fires would come. Out of the chill night, a coil of wind swirled brittle leaves, and spun them so they screamed, one against another.

Cul-De-Sac Virus

by Evan Dicken

Darryl was finishing up Molly's fire pit when a U-Haul pulled into the driveway across the street. Like most houses around the development, the modest asphalt-shingled Cape Cod had been empty since Darryl moved into the neighborhood about a year ago, so it was something of a relief to see it sold. The street just didn't look right with so many darkened homes, like a smile with missing teeth.

He stacked the last of the bricks around the pit then pressed his hands into his armpits hoping the warmth would tease some of the ache from his swollen joints. The pain had never come this early before. Usually, he stiffened with the ground, winter's chill riming his bones like ice on a windowpane, but this year had been different—in so many ways.

Darryl stood with a sigh, half-expecting his breath to fog the air. It didn't. The afternoon was crisp, but not cold—barely jacket weather. Molly would've loved it. He regarded the ragged circle of bricks, swallowing against the sudden tightness in his throat.

Another one down.

Wind hissed through the leaves overhead, and for a moment it was like being underwater—the late afternoon light shining coral red through a canopy of oak and maple leaves. Above, shoals of starlings circled beneath a flat, cloudless sky. A truck door slammed, followed by an explosion of furious barking.

Lemanski's dog was loose again.

Darryl stomped across the yard, every step kicking up little puffs of newly fallen leaves. Rufus, a hulking German shepherd with a torn ear, stood next to the curb, paws pounding the pavement with each angry bellow. A youngish woman stood by the truck, her expression calm, almost curious. A moment later she was joined by a man, who mirrored her flat gaze, then took a step toward Rufus, hand outstretched. The effect on the dog was instantaneous. Rufus' barks changed to whines, and he backed away–head low and ears flat.

Darryl grabbed Rufus' collar, wincing as the leather bit into his palm. "Sorry, not my dog."

The man and the woman only stood, watching. They were deeply tanned, with dark eyes and black hair–his parted on one side, hers in a loose ponytail. Both were overweight, not fat, just vaguely soft in the way that had become the norm in America.

Rufus twisted, lips drawn back from teeth the color of old newspaper. Darryl considered giving the dog a good smack, then thought better of it. It wasn't Rufus' fault he had a shitty owner.

That was Molly talking. She'd always had a city girl's sensibility when it came to animals, even ones that needed to be put down.

The pain in his hands whetted Darryl's temper, and he dragged Rufus back across the street and up the cracked pavers that led to Lemanski's porch. Like Darryl's, the house had been built only a few years ago, but Lemanski's refusal to perform even the most basic upkeep had left it looking decades older.

"Get off my property, Jackson." Lemanski sat in a rusted-out rocker, almost invisible against the cracked siding in his ratty flannel jacket and John Deer cap. His face was weather-beaten cardboard, lined and hairless but for a wispy beard stained yellow by smoke. Eyes like potholes stared from under heavy brows, almost lost in the shadow of his nose–a big, bulbous thing spotted with burst veins.

"Your goddamn dog was out again," Darryl said. "Letting your house go to shit is one thing, but Rufus could've really hurt someone."

"He's a good boy," Lemanski said.

"What? Did you just see–?"

"Rufus, *heel.*"

All the coiled tension went out of the dog. Cautiously,

Darryl let go, then crossed his arms to hide the fact his fingers were still crooked into arthritic claws.

"A little barking is good." Lemanski turned to regard the Cape Cod, spat, then looked back at Darryl, an ugly smile deepening the wrinkles around his mouth.

"Just what do you mean by that?"

"I mean what I mean." Lemanski edged past Darryl to open the door. At his nod, Rufus followed.

"Listen, you have to restrain–"

"Sorry to hear about your wife." Lemanski shut the door.

"Next time your dog gets out, I'm calling the goddam cops," Darryl said to the locked door, breathing through his nose as he made his way down the stairs, pointedly not kicking over Lemanski's ash can like he really, really wanted to.

Jo's tan SUV was parked in front of the garage when Darryl got home. She'd been making a point to drop by every couple days. The little thrill Darryl got at the sight of his daughter's car faded when he recognized Greg's silhouette in the family room's wide picture window. It wasn't that he didn't like Jo's husband, it was just–well, there wasn't much to him.

"We let ourselves in." Jo gave Darryl a hug that didn't last nearly long enough.

"Hello, Mister Jackson." Greg said.

"I thought I told you to call me Darryl." He shared a quick look with Jo, who shrugged.

"I wanted to stop by before we headed up to Cleveland." She frowned. "The dishes are piling up again."

"I was going to do them after I finished the fire pit," Darryl said with a glance at the refrigerator, Molly's list pinned to it with a magnet in the shape of a cartoon octopus. Jo gave a little twitch of her head, then a soft sigh–the same gesture Molly used when she was working up to say something hard.

"Dad, can we talk?"

Darryl found himself tensing out of habit.

"Go on. I'll do the dishes." Greg began rolling up his sleeves.

Darryl shook his head. "You don't need to–"

"It's fine, Mister Jackson. I don't mind."

Jo took Darryl's arm and guided him into the family room, waiting until Greg turned on the water before settling onto the big blue couch. She patted the cushion beside her, and Darryl sat.

He ran a hand over the threadbare armrest. "Remember the *U.S.S. Princess Explorer*?"

"How could I forget?" She gave an absent smile. "We must've sailed this couch around the world a dozen times. The stories mom used to tell…"

Darryl closed his eyes.

"I worry about you." Jo laid her hand on his. "All alone in this house."

"I'm fine," Darryl said. "There's plenty to keep me busy."

"That's just it. This–" She waved in the direction of the fridge. "–it's not healthy. If you were closer I could drop by more often."

"I don't need babying."

"Long Pines is right down the street from my house. You'd be around people your own age. They have a pool, and aides to help when the arthritis gets bad." Jo slipped a glossy brochure from her purse. The cover showed a group of grinning mummies flanked by men and women in hospital scrubs.

"I said *no*."

"I want you close."

"Why? It's not like you need help with any kids."

All the feeling went out of Jo's face.

"I'm sorry. I didn't mean–"

"Take a look at the brochure. We'll be back in a couple days." She stood stiffly.

"Joanna, stop," Darryl said with a hopeful smile. "You're walking on lava."

She looked down at the carpet, picked up her purse, then went into the kitchen. After few moments of hushed conversation Greg went outside to start the car.

"I'm not worried about the list, Dad." Jo paused in the doorway. "I'm worried about what happens when you finish."

The SUV's headlights stabbed through the front window, bright enough to bring tears to Darryl's eyes. He sat until the engine rumble faded into the background hiss of I-70, then pushed himself to his feet and went into the kitchen. The pain in his hands was bad enough he couldn't wrap his fingers around the pen, so he settled for holding it between his palms and smearing the tip across one of the lines of looping cursive. Only a few were unmarked, enough to fill an afternoon, maybe two.

"And then what?" He asked the empty house.

Truth be told, it worried him, too.

Jo would've had Darryl carted away if she'd seen him wobble up the old stepladder to scoop fistfuls of cold, wet leaves from the gutters. It had to be done, though. Home ownership was a study in entropy.

He'd saved this chore for last, not because it was murder on his hands, but because it was something his wife wouldn't do. Although Molly never had a problem with hard work, there were a few jobs–scrubbing the toilet, fishing hair out of the sink trap, cleaning the gutters–that made her gag. Those had always been Darryl's favorites, mostly because of the look on Molly's face when he finished, like he'd spared her from something *terrible*.

From the roof he could see Lemanski out in the drive, elbow deep in the guts of his Ford pickup. Across the street, the U-Haul had been replaced by a beige Prius, but Darryl could see another moving truck down near the brick-fronted ranch at the corner. He'd heard the housing market was bouncing back, but it was nice to see real proof. Soon, the development would be a proper neighborhood.

A light went on in the big bay window across the street, and Darryl realized he ought to head over and introduce himself. He could finish the gutters tomorrow, or the day after.

He went inside to wash up and grab a dusty bottle of wine from the rack, then crossed the cul-de-sac to ring his new neighbors' doorbell.

The woman who answered looked almost identical to the one from yesterday, but with blond hair, and skin several shades lighter.

"Hi, I'm Darryl Jackson. I live across the street."

"You had the dog."

"Yes. I mean–no–it's not mine. Lemanski, he lives over there, he's kind of a–" Darryl cocked his head. "Was that you yesterday?"

"We were moving in."

Darryl smiled, thinking she was joking, but she only stared.

"Okay." He shrugged, at last. "Thought I could welcome you to the neighborhood."

"We're still unpacking. Maybe some other time."

"All right, sure." He held out the wine. "Housewarming gift."

She looked at his hands. "You don't need to–"

"Please, it's just chardonnay. My wife loved the stuff, but

it gives me heartburn." Darryl pressed the bottle into her hands.

"Thank you. Goodbye." She shut the door.

It wasn't until a breeze prickled the skin on Darryl's face that he noticed he was sweating. He shook his head, then started for home, getting halfway up his driveway before realizing he hadn't gotten the woman's name.

"You're wasting your time." Lemanski leaned against his truck, an unlit cigarette dangling from his lips.

Darryl kept walking.

"Wondering what happened to that nice *Mex-i-can* couple?"

That slowed Darryl a moment. His eyes weren't what they used to be, but he was sure the woman had looked different yesterday. She could've dyed her hair, but her skin–no, he must be remembering wrong. Lemanski was just screwing with him.

"It takes 'em a little while to get settled," Lemanski called as Darryl hurried to his house. "Drop by again tonight, see if blondie's still around. By tomorrow it'll be too late to–"

Darryl slammed the front door, cutting off the flow of bullshit.

It was just a walk–out to Baffin Road, cut through the woods, down along the single strip of sidewalk, then a quick loop around the cul-de-sac. Darryl used to stop by the office, too, but all the people he remembered were either retired or dead, and the new faces seemed to change too quickly for him to keep track of.

He walked every evening, weather permitting–there was nothing strange about it. This time, though, he felt like he was twelve again, taking the old gravel road on his way home from school in the hopes Milo Redding's older sister would forget to shut her curtains when she changed.

Lemanski's needling had stuck with him all day, festering until Darryl found himself peeking through the blinds at the house across the street. Unfortunately, while he had a good view of the Cape Cod's driveway, the crabapple tree in their front yard still had enough leaves to block most of the bay window.

Usually the walk took around a half-hour. This time, Darryl was back in twenty minutes. Most of the houses were dark and empty, and those few that were lit looked like ships on a midnight sea.

He turned off the sidewalk and consciously slowed his nervous hustle. Light from the Cape Cod's widows cast checkerboard shadows on the front yard. Inside, the new couple was eating dinner, watching the TV at the far side of the room. Their faces were the same, but their hair was black again, and their skin as dark as Darryl's.

As they turned to regard him Darryl realized he was staring. The woman raised her hand and waved. A moment later, the man joined her. Neither smiled.

Darryl eyed the row of empty bourbon bottles on the windowsill, wrinkling his nose as smells of ash and stale liquor overpowered the scent of wet leaves. His forearm made a muffled thump against Lemanski's door, not nearly as loud as a knock, but all Darryl could manage with hands that felt like someone had filled them with crushed glass.

It had taken him awhile to digest what he'd seen on the walk. He'd spent most of the night alternately sneaking looks at the house across the street, and trying to come up with a rational explanation for the couple's change. Sleep must have crept up on him, because he awoke to the construction site beep of a truck backing into the driveway of the house opposite Lemanski's. This, more than anything, had driven Darryl to brave the morning chill.

When another thud with his forearm produced no response, Darryl settled for giving the door a very satisfying kick. Curses joined the torrent of barking as a bleary-eyed Lemanski cracked the door. The old man's beard was matted to one side of his face, and he'd traded his jacket for a stained bathrobe and dirty grey socks pulled almost to his knees.

"What the hell do you want?"

"The new neighbors." Darryl glanced across the street, relaxing a bit when he saw the Prius was gone. "They're black, now."

Lemanski snorted. "C'mon in. Lock the door behind you, and don't touch anything."

Darryl stepped inside, grimacing at the musty, spoiled-milk smell of the place. Shutting the door was easy enough, but the deadbolt was one of the old key-in-latch models and defeated his clumsy attempts. After a few embarrassing moments, Lemanski reached over and twisted it shut.

"Sorry. It's bad today." Darryl held up a claw.

Lemanski grimaced, then turned to thread his way through the stacks of old magazines that filled the foyer. His kitchen was a riot of peeling linoleum bathed in the light of a single fly-specked bulb. The Formica table at which Lemanski sat was stained a patchwork brown, the circles left by the bottoms of dozens of coffee mugs like the rings of an old oak.

"What the hell's going on?" Darryl selected the sturdiest-looking chair and carefully sat across from the old man.

"Don't really know." Lemanski selected two filmy jam jars from the counter and slopped a liberal measure of bourbon into each. He slid one across the table, then glanced at Darryl's hands. "You want a straw?"

"What are they? Some kind of monster?"

"Better if they were. Then someone might be able to do something about it." Lemanski tossed his drink back, then poured another. "Bastards ran me out of two neighborhoods, but I ain't going easy this time. Don't even care if they come for me. We're ready, Rufus and I."

"What? Come for you?"

"You ever driven down a highway, Jackson? All those other cars, houses far as the eye can see. You ever wonder who lives in them? I mean, they can't all be full of people, right? Folks with lives all their own–dreams, families, things they hate–like you and me, you know, *real* people." Lemanski pointed a long-nailed finger at Darryl. "Well, they ain't, not like you and me, anyway. It's them what's out there–in the cars, in the houses, everywhere, chewing their way through the world."

"Bullshit."

"If you say so." Lemanski sipped at his bourbon. "That's the thing about it. They act just like us–driving around, paying taxes, buying houses–but they're not. It's not just the shifting– even after they settle in there's all sorts of little tells. Like cutouts of people, you know, just going through the motions of being alive."

"I can't believe–"

"Don't take my word for it. Ever been inside one of their houses? Like *termites*. Unnatural is what it is." Lemanski was obviously drunk, and maybe crazy as well, but after what Darryl had seen last night he couldn't just discount the old man.

He chewed his lip. "What do I do?"

"Ain't nothing you can do except leave or wait for them to get around to you. They've been moving in since last month. I can understand how you missed it with Molly dying and all. Frankly, I thought you knew, what with Jo marrying one."

"That's bullshit. Greg is boring, but he's not..." Darryl pushed up from the table. Lemanski had to be lying. Greg had never said or done anything suspicious—come to think of it, he'd never really said or done much of anything. "I knew this was a mistake. I need to go."

Lemanski waved his glass at the front door.

Darryl fumbled with the door latch, face burning as Lemanski shuffled over, checked the window, then opened the door.

"Think about what I said, Jackson."

Darryl all but ran out of the house, not stopping until he passed the fence that separated his and Lemanski's lots. There he paused, one hand on the rough wood, his breath coming in short, tight gasps.

This was crazy. Molly's death must've shaken something loose in his head. He'd heard about things like that—one spouse coming unhinged after the other passed. Yes, that had to be it, he was just going senile or insane.

The sun was high overhead, the sky empty but for a few wispy contrails. Faint scents of dry leaves and wood smoke threaded the air, the brisk morning chill mellowing into a perfect autumn afternoon. A few deep breaths were enough to stop Darryl's hands from shaking, although not enough to ease the anxious tightness in his chest.

The steady swish of the I-71 traffic was like waves on a distant beach. And yet, as Darryl watched the cars blur by, he couldn't help but wonder what was in them.

Flashing lights dragged Darryl from the warmth of uninterrupted dream. Blue and red, they skipped across the family photos and bookshelves, carnival-bright in the darkness. Darryl slipped from his too-big bed and over to the window. An ambulance sat in Lemanski's driveway, and a police car on the street out front.

By the time Darryl winced his way into shoes and a jacket, two uniformed men had emerged from the house with a blanket-covered stretcher, the fabric tented in a way familiar to anyone who had ever seen a cop drama.

"Sir, I'm going to have to ask you to stand back." A policeman stepped from the shadows as Darryl shuffled up.

"Is he—?"

"Heart attack," the officer said with practiced sympathy.

"Shit." Darryl ran a trembling hand across his stubble.

"We couldn't find any next-of-kin or contact info. Did you know Mr. Lemanski long?"

"We both moved in when the development opened, maybe a year ago. For a while we were alone, well, not alone. I was married. My wife, she had a stroke and—" Darryl grimaced, embarrassed that nerves had set him babbling. He peered past the man into Lemanski's house. None of the precarious columns of newspaper remained standing, and the floor was littered with trampled refuse. "Was there a struggle?"

"We think he was trying to get to the phone when it happened." The officer glanced over his shoulder. "Most of it was the paramedics trying to get the stretcher in."

"He had a dog. Did you see Rufus?"

"No, no dog. Did Mr. Lemanski have any family, anyone we can call?"

"Not that I know of."

"Would any of his other neighbors know?"

Darryl looked around the cul-de-sac. Soft porch lights illuminated brick, wood, and vinyl facades, but the windows remained dark and empty as the moonless night overhead. "No, I don't think so."

The policeman watched the ambulance back onto the street, then handed a card to Darryl. "Here's contact information for the High Street morgue in case someone remembers something."

"Wait."

The officer paused in the act of ducking back into his car.

"Who called you?" Darryl asked.

"What?"

"You said Lemanski was *trying* to get to the phone. If he didn't call you, who did?"

"Dispatch didn't give us a name." The officer shrugged. "Probably a neighbor. It almost always is."

The cruiser's lights flicked off as it pulled away, leaving Darryl alone in the driveway. He darted a wary look around the cul-de-sac, half-expecting to see silhouettes in the darkened windows. Nothing moved in the dim moonlight. But for the porch lights, the houses might have been unoccupied.

At home, Darryl made sure everything was locked up tight, propping chairs against the front and back doors for good measure. When that was done, he tried Jo's cell, but got no answer. Late as it was, she might already be asleep, or maybe she was still angry with him. Either way, he had to get her here, had to know she was safe.

"Jo, I'm sorry," Darryl said into the silence after the beep. "I'll go anywhere you want. Just please, please come home right away. I love you."

On the desk by the phone, there was a framed photo of the three of them at Buckeye Lake–Molly in her floppy sun hat, and Jo, ten or eleven, grimacing in the bright-orange life vest they'd forced her into. He didn't remember the day, but it must have been early in the season because the water wasn't crowded with boats and swimmers.

Outside, Lemanski's house had gone dark but for the porch light. Shadows moved just beyond the glow, arms full of empty bottles and crumpled newspaper. A procession of shapes passed in and out of the house, hollowing it out.

Jo would never believe him. Hell, *he* hardly believed him. Lemanski had mentioned looking inside their houses, but not what Darryl would find. Still, he needed something to show his daughter.

He took the picture from its frame, folded it, and slipped it into his pocket. Then he went into the family room and settled down on the big blue couch to wait.

It didn't take long to finish the gutters, but Darryl stayed up there anyway, picking bits of leaves and maple seeds from the downspouts. The ladder gave him a good view of the neighborhood, and it seemed a shame to leave things unfinished before heading out.

He'd stayed awake all night, watching the world bleed from black to gray to the muted colors of dawn. The husband left early, coffee mug in hand as he steered the Prius out onto Baffin Road. It would be a little while before the woman left, more than enough time for Darryl finish Molly's last chore. He wasn't sure what to expect when he'd finished—there was no sense of release, and any lingering grief was overshadowed by worry for Jo and anxiety over what he planned to do. So he dithered, hoping something would change inside him.

But nothing did.

At last, the Cape Cod's garage door grumbled open and the woman drove away. If she knew Darryl was watching, she gave no sign, not even glancing up as she thumbed the right blinker and eased onto Baffin.

The aluminum rungs of the ladder were cold even through Darryl's gloves, and he hissed as he climbed down. A breeze kicked up as he crossed the cul-de-sac, the insect skitter of leaves on asphalt strangely loud in his ears. He'd expected to have to search for a window they'd forgotten to latch, but the door wasn't even locked.

The front room looked normal enough—a table and chairs near the bay window, a couch across from the TV. Darryl padded across the carpet, looking for something, anything to show he wasn't just breaking into someone's house.

The kitchen was the same, appliances updated and cabinets freshly varnished, a white plastic phone in its cradle by the door. The door to the study was closed, as was the basement door across from it. It was almost a relief to find nothing out of the ordinary. Darryl was just about to slip back across the street and chalk the whole thing up to creeping senility when a muffled thud sounded from inside the study.

Darryl froze, he hadn't seen anyone come or go from the house other than the couple, but that didn't mean anything, the place could be crawling with—whatever they were. Still, he didn't have a lot of time. If she'd gotten his message, Jo would be on her way. Darryl needed something to show her.

Carefully, he pushed open the study door.

There was nothing beyond—no ceiling, no floors, no walls—just an opaque blackness that seemed to press outward with almost tangible force. Darryl stretched out a hand, half-expecting the darkness to ripple like water, but his fingers encountered only air, cold and slightly humid. Although the morning sun was shining full through the kitchen windows, Darryl couldn't see the other side of the room. The darkness didn't absorb the light so much as ignore it, giving the impression of a vast, cavernous space deep underground.

He backed away from the study, more confused than frightened, then jolted as the basement doorknob dug into the small of his back. Numbly, he opened that door as well, and found himself facing the same terrible darkness. The sight broke something within him, and he hurried through the house, throwing open closets, bathrooms, cabinets, every closed door he could find. Behind each was more nothing.

Soon, he found himself surrounded by holes, as if the house itself was nothing more than a blanket draped over the night. Everywhere that couldn't be seen from the outside had been hollowed out.

Darryl ran a hand through his hair, ignoring the stab of pain from his fingers. What had Lemanski called them?

Termites.

A growl sounded behind him. Low and threatening, it raised the hair on the back of Darryl's arms. He'd half turned when something wrenched the arm of his jacket, dragging him down. Points of painful light flared in his vision as his head glanced off the kitchen counter. He felt teeth through the quilted fabric of his jacket, but managed to slip his arm from the sleeve before they closed on flesh. Although the effort of forcing his crooked fingers to close on the edge of the counter wrenched a scream from him, Darryl managed to pull himself to his feet. Blinking back tears, he turned to see what had attacked him.

"Rufus?"

The German shepherd whipped his head back and forth, Darryl's jacket flopping like a broken neck.

"Heel!" Darryl shouted.

Rufus dropped the jacket.

"What the hell are you doing here?"

The dog's ears perked up. He looked past Darryl and gave a short, sharp bark.

The darkness made a sound. Arrhythmic, but insistent—book pages rustled by the wind, the skirling hiss of the wings of low flying birds—it came from all around, accompanied by a smell like wet leaves gone to mold.

A hand slipped from the cabinet in front of him, its fingers long and boneless. They brushed across the countertop, closed upon the edge of the cabinet, and pulled.

Darryl backed away, only to see another arm emerge from the basement door, and the study, and the row of cupboards lining the wall above the stove. They moved in perfect synchronicity, shadows cast by the same maker.

As one, the thing slipped from the darkness, singular in its multiplicity, alone, but somehow everywhere. The creature was vaguely humanoid, with skin the inky kaleidoscope of spilled oil. Its outline seemed to pulse, and as it passed through a shaft of sunlight Darryl caught a glimpse of slick, boneless bodies squirming in the darkness.

They—it stood before him, surrounded him.

Darryl moaned as the thing reached out, close to, but not quite touching, his face. He heard a soft click. The hand withdrew, holding something square and white. Dully, Darryl realized it had picked up the phone.

"Yes, police." The voice that came from the creature's misshapen lump of a head was that of the woman Darryl had spoken with yesterday. "I'm at 4129 Oak Court. There's someone in my house, please hurry."

Something warm and wet trickled down Darryl's forehead, and he knuckled it away only to see his hand come away red.

"What the hell are you?" Darryl's vision swam.

"Just calm down." Like a swimmer rising through murky water, the creature took on form and substance. "You hit your head, Mister Jackson."

"How do you know my name?" Darryl wobbled, tried to steady himself, but his hand slipped on the counter.

The arms that caught him were human.

"You told me yesterday, when we talked." She lowered him to the ground.

Darryl turned his head to see Rufus watching from the door of the study, now a carpeted room with a desk and a wall of half-filled bookshelves.

"Traitor," Darryl whispered.

Rufus cocked his head, tail thumping on the kitchen tile.

There was a flash of pain when the woman pressed a dish towel to the wound on Darryl's forehead, then a cold numbness. The world seemed to pull away as he slipped back into unconsciousness.

He realized that for the first time in a very long time, his hands didn't hurt.

The room was dark. At first, Darryl thought the woman had dragged him into one of the holes, but as his eyes adjusted to the gloom, he recognized the familiar contours of his bedroom. He thumbed the switch on the lamp, then turned it down when he saw Jo curled up in one of the chairs. Someone had set the Buckeye Lake picture on the nightstand.

"You're awake." Greg stepped from the darkness of the hallway with a blanket. He spread it over Jo, then put a finger to his lips. "She's had a long day."

"Just what the hell–?" Darryl quieted as Greg sat on the bed. Although there was no threat in the younger man's posture, Darryl couldn't help but realize how little he could do if matters turned violent.

"Paramedics bandaged the cut on your head." Greg leaned close as if to share a secret. "The Cullens aren't pressing charges, and–"

"Is *that* what they're calling themselves?""

"Of course. It's their name."

"So what happens now? Are you going to kill me like Lemanski?" Darryl might not be able to do anything about Greg, but he wasn't just going to sit here and pretend like none of it had happened.

"We didn't kill anyone, Darryl."

"Call me Mister Jackson."

"We're not what you think we are."

"I've *seen* what you are–termites, gnawing away at the world, leaving nothing."

"That's where you're wrong. There has always been nothing." Greg nodded at the window. The blinds had been drawn back to show the shadowed bulk of trees and the night sky beyond. "Most of *everything* is nothing."

"Why are you here?" Darryl asked.

"Why are *you* here?"

Darryl responded with sullen silence.

"Let me explain." Greg picked up the picture from the nightstand and handed it to Darryl. "Do you remember this day?"

Darryl nodded, his lips pressed into a tight line.

"What about the day after it? Or the day after that? Or the day after that?"

"Of course not."

"If you don't remember them, how do you know you were there?"

"I know."

"We live day-by-day, but when we look back most of our lives are filled with…" Greg gave a little twitch of his head, then a soft sigh. "Nothing."

"I don't believe you." Darryl said at last.

Greg stood, offering Darryl his hand. "I want to show you something."

Darryl tried to keep up a glare, but his gaze kept sliding over Greg's shoulder to where Jo lay. "Just don't hurt my daughter."

"I would never hurt Jo." Greg followed Darryl's gaze. "I *love* her."

Darryl slid his legs over the edge of the bed and let Greg

help him up. Although Greg's hands felt human enough, Darryl still grimaced at his touch. The two of them padded from the room, but not before Darryl stole one last look over his shoulder.

Light from the street beyond filtered through the hallway windows, turning family photos into dark blots on the wall. Greg led him through the family room and into the kitchen, shutting the door before turning on the overhead light. Someone had placed Molly's list on the counter, along with a black pen.

"It's important you finish," Greg said.

"Why do you want me to–?"

"It's not important to *me*."

The paper felt strange in Darryl's hands, brittle as fallen leaves. He took up the pen, and found, to his surprise, he could grip it without pain. Slowly, he marked a line through the last chore, then looked to Greg.

"What now?"

"Nothing." Greg turned to open the door.

The family room was gone.

"What did you do?" Darryl asked.

"It was always like this. *You* were always like this." Greg stepped into the liquid dark, tendrils of glistening shadow writhing up and around his body. "Some fight it, some accept it, most ignore it, but that doesn't mean it isn't there–before the first, after the last–always and forever."

Greg's features shifted even as they remained the same. Faces overlaid his–the woman across the street, Lemanski, Jo, Molly.

Darryl gave a soft moan. He took a step toward the door, hand raised, then paused as he saw his flesh had turned the same rainbow black as the creature he'd seen across the street. In his other hand, the list cracked and crumbled, sifting through his fingers like fine ash.

At last, Darryl understood. "We're *everything*."

"Some of the time, at least." Greg shrugged, now human

again. Behind him the darkness faded, replaced by the familiar shadows of the family room. A light went on.

"Dad? What are you doing up?" Jo stood in the hall, the blanket wrapped around her like a shawl.

"He had to go to the bathroom," Greg said. "I was helping him."

"I was worried. I thought maybe you were wandering again, and after your call, and what happened with the Cullens—" She bit her lip.

"It's okay, it's okay." Darryl gathered her into a hug. This time, she didn't pull away.

"Dad, I know you don't want to go to Long Pines, but—"

"I'll go. It doesn't matter. None of it matters." He stroked her hair, trying to recall their days together. So few, but all he had left.

He looked up to see Greg watching them, his expression blank. The big picture window behind him opened onto the cul-de-sac, the autumn shadows dark but for the scattered pinpricks of porch lamps.

Above, the sky was the same.

DST (Fall Back)

by Robert Levy

I drove down to Milford on a Saturday in late October to see Martin for myself. I'd heard how much he had changed, but when I first laid eyes on my one-time romantic rival I almost failed to recognize him. His face had gone bearded and haggard, though he still had his paunch, a decade passed since he and Jasper left the city for the quaint domestic appeal of small-town Pennsylvania. Jasper, however, was prone to callousness (as I myself had learned the hard way) and I'd wondered how much longer the two of them would last. I suspected Jasper had, in due course, broken Martin's heart just as he'd once broken mine, and that I'd been summoned in the spirit of newfound solidarity. I had nothing better to do, myself.

"I used to work here," Martin said, and cast a baleful look across the wide porch of the Fauchere, the boutique hotel busy at late lunchtime before the guests headed back out to catch the last of the countryside's technicolor array of fall foliage. "Got a bit long in the tooth for the management's taste, though I could never prove that was why they let me go. They just kept shortening my hours until I was forced to leave. I like to come back every once in a while, just to remind the staff of the decrepit future that awaits them. A kind of living momento mori, if you will. 'You are now what I once was. I am what you will one day be.' That sort of thing."

Martin reached across the table for the ceramic creamer, his shirt cuff divulging a stippling of encrusted sores along the length of his meaty forearm. I was beginning to regret accepting his invitation.

"So, what's this about?" I finally asked. "Is everything alright with you and Jasper?"

"Well, no, actually." He looked down at his coffee, the mug's milky depths as clouded as his eyes. "Jasper's gone missing."

"Missing? What do you mean?"

"It's been over a month now. Nobody knows where he is. The police are aware of the situation, but since Jasper and I are no longer together..." Martin winced as if pained.

"Sorry," I said, and my ears felt hot all of a sudden. "I didn't know."

"We broke up for good in March. But the trouble started before then, a year ago now. I woke up one night and his side of the bed was empty. The next morning, I found him on the front lawn, naked and passed out and nearly frozen; thank God I got him inside before the neighbors called the cops. When I asked him what happened, he told me he'd gone for a walk in the woods. I pointed out that his clothes were missing, but he didn't say anything else, just stared off queerly into the trees behind the house.

"He was never the same after that. Started staying out at night, coming home at dawn, if at all. Well, you know what a horndog Jasper always was, I figured he'd found someone else to hold his attention. But then the cutting started."

Martin exhaled and leaned in close, crossing his mottled arms as if chilled. "Little nicks at first. He'd come home with mud on his boots, so I assumed they were scratches from branches, from trudging through the woods. But then they got bigger, and I started to notice how symmetrical they were. Round marks, in the flesh of his arms and legs. Across his chest, even. He stopped getting undressed in front of me, but every once in a while I would catch a glimpse of some fresh wound. A BDSM thing maybe? Who knows? Either he was letting someone do it to him or he must have been doing it to himself."

"Jesus." It didn't sound like any Jasper I'd ever known. The vain and smooth-skinned dancer, who wouldn't leave the house with so much as a blemish, let alone an open wound. My stomach knotted and I swallowed. I was surprised by how much I missed him.

"Suffice it to say, we didn't last much past the winter. He got his own place, a little hovel above a thrift store over on Broad Street. Said he needed to devote more time to a new project. He came around less and less, until he stopped coming around altogether." Martin shook his head. "I suppose in his own way he was shortening my hours as well."

"I'm terribly sorry to hear all this. But I'm not sure what you want me to do about it. I haven't seen Jasper in years."

"I wanted you to come because he spoke of you, not long before he went missing."

"Me? Really?"

Martin nodded. "It was the last time I saw him, over the summer. He was far gone by then. He'd been fired from his studio, arrested around town for trespassing, vagrancy, vandalism, one thing after the next. I suspected it was drugs, but that wasn't it. He was losing his mind. I spotted him wandering beside the road along the highway and pulled over to try to reason with him. But there was no use. He wouldn't even stop walking, just kept staggering along the shoulder as if he were late for something but didn't know where he was going exactly. Like he was in some sort of trance.

"He kept ranting about the date, the weather, how he wasn't going to make it. To wherever he was trying to go, I suppose. Burnt red as a lobster, his clothes filthy, sneakers worn through, toenails yellowed and cracked. I pleaded with him to get in the car so I could take him to the hospital, to see a doctor, *someone*, but he just shrugged me off.

"Jasper claimed I couldn't know what he was going through, that no one could. That's when he mentioned you. He said you were the only one who could see, when it was time. And then something about playing disco in 2000. A disco race? Something."

"*Disco Death Race 2000?*"

"Yes, that's it. What's that mean?"

"It's the name of an old techno album."

I was a late-night DJ at our college station, and when I spun a track from the album on my weekly show I received a rare call from a listener, praising my taste. Jasper and I got to talking, and he popped over from the dance center across the quad. As the end of my shift neared, I was packing up my record crates when the station manager called: it was the end of daylight savings time, and once 3AM fell back to 2AM I'd have to add another hour onto my show. I ended up throwing *Disco Death Race* back on the deck, and Jasper and I let the album play to the end as we fucked in the cramped space beneath the sound board. I'd never felt so happy.

Martin surveyed the porch's outdoor dining area once more. "Look at this place," he muttered, and shook his head. "They have a twenty-five-year-old maître d in the main restaurant now. Twenty-five! Some twink from Germany. I asked him where he was from and he said Nuremberg. Then, get this: he asks me if I've ever heard of it. 'Nuremberg? Uh, no, sorry, doesn't ring a bell.' Little twerp. Kind on the eyes though..."

I glanced out the window at the trees between the hotel and the town's main drag, their leaves red, yellow, orange, golden, brown. "Martin," I said, "where do you think Jasper might have gone, exactly?"

"Honestly, I have no idea," He drained his coffee mug and wiped his mouth with the back of a cracked white hand. "But there's something I want you to see."

I followed Martin's pickup through town until we reached a turnoff leading us past a large gatehouse. We drove up a scenic winding drive, and soon a grand and imposing mansion arose before us in a stunning assemblage of turreted towers and bluestone. We pulled around the castle-like building and into a largely empty parking lot in the rear, where we both got out of our respective cars and rejoined beside a slate patio overlooking the impressive property, the rolling lawns a stalwart green despite autumn's onward march toward winter.

"What is this place?"

"Grey Towers. The estate of Gifford Pinchot, who was the governor of Pennsylvania about a hundred years ago. Before that he was the first head of the U.S. Forest Service. His wife was a big suffragette. Fascinating family, the mansion is to die for. But we're not going inside."

"Martin, I'd really like to head back to the city while it's light. And it's starting to get late..."

"Come." He pointed away from the estate, past the parking lot and toward a wide stand of trees where a path snaked its way into the woods. "We're going there."

We hadn't walked for long before the scattered hemlocks and white pines began to thin and we reached a clearing, on the other side of which was an unusual wooden structure. Raised up on iron piping and suspended about twenty feet above the forest floor, it was quite large and resembled a grain silo, or perhaps a water tower you might see atop an apartment building in the city. It was tilted, however, at what appeared to be a forty-five-degree angle.

"What is that thing?" I asked, shielding my eyes from the setting sun as it stole low beneath the weblike tree canopy.

"It's what I wanted to show you. This way."

The air crisped in a swelling breeze, the crunch of dry leaves underfoot its own steady pulse as we made our way across the clearing to the mammoth structure. Peering up at it, I could now see it wasn't barrel-shaped so much as conical. Or perhaps it could be best described as corkscrewed, the wood at its base narrowed like the mouth of a conch but still wide enough for someone to access through a narrow rusted ladder bolted to its frame that led up and inside the occluded interior.

"It's called a cosmoscope," Martin said, and placed a pale hand against the dark wood. "It's a kind of observatory. Conceived long ago by a scientist from New Zealand, a summer visitor at Grey Towers. The cosmoscope was built to his specifications by Yale School of Forestry students, between the world wars. Unfortunately, the damned thing has been in disuse for decades. Sad, really. They haven't had the budget to restore it."

"This is all very interesting, but..."

"But what does it have to do with Jasper? They found him out here. Just last month. In fact, that seems to have been the very last time anyone saw Jasper at all. He'd been living inside the cosmoscope. Not only that, but according to the guide who brought me out here, someone appears to have modified it." He pointed to a length of rubber tubing, one of many fastened to the exterior. They had an oddly intestinal look. "See these things? The guide thinks they're meant to transmit sound. So if you're inside the cosmoscope, they let you hear the noises of the forest without any background noise. Birds, bugs, the wind through the trees, but magnified."

I waited for him to head up the ladder, and eventually he cocked his head and laughed. "Are you kidding? I can't fit up there. I'm not a little guy like Jasper. Or you."

I pushed against the small hatch, which creaked open and hit against the inside with a hard slap, and a musty funk washed over me. Holding my breath as I peered up inside the cosmoscope's wide barrel, I began to ascend, an astronaut climbing into a soon-departing rocket ship. This sense of transition was coupled with an additional nervousness I was hesitant to place at its source: that Martin had brought me out here for some nefarious purpose I had yet to ascertain.

He was right about one thing, though: not only was the

entrance too small for him, but the interior of the cosmoscope appeared to be constructed with an almost labyrinthine relay of wooden compartments. What I could see from the small amount of light from the open hatch (though there must have also been an opening in the cosmoscope's roof high above) was a series of inner walls, hard stops that, due to the severity of the structure's tilt, resembled nothing so much as a canted rat maze. How Jasper could have managed to live inside this strange contraption was anyone's guess.

I reached into the wooden cavity above me. Below a section of rubber tubing my hand stuck to the curved siding, which was coated in a viscous texture not unlike tree sap; I had the fleeting thought that the cosmoscope itself was somehow alive. It was only once I closed the hatch and started back down the ladder that I could see a small triad of words carved into the structure's base. *George Vernon Hudson.* The name was etched in erratic lines, barely legible in the dying light of day but there nevertheless.

I dizzied, and when I reached the ground again I stared down at my hands and the rust-colored substance that had coagulated upon them, a black and red amalgam of some unknown provenance collected from inside the cosmoscope. *Everybody thinks I'm high*, I thought, and froze. They were the first words of *Disco Death Race 2000*, the song "Sixteen Bit Suicide." Jasper and I would whisper those words to each other once upon a time, apropos of nothing. *Everybody thinks I'm high.* I couldn't help but smile.

I wiped away the angry stains on my trousers, and as I did so the smell of raw meat tinged the air. An olfactory hallucination, perhaps. Martin was watching me closely.

"What was Jasper doing out here?" I asked him. "What did he want with this thing?"

"Observing, I suppose. Though I had hoped that you might know the answer. He said he'd tell you at the right hour."

Martin stared down at the forest floor. For a moment he shook his head as if clearing away an unpleasant thought or memory, then started toward the path back to Grey Towers and the parking lot. I stole one last glance at the cosmoscope before I followed.

Dusk fell in a contusion of purple light and shadow over the distant hills as Martin and I parted ways at the center of town, hands raised in salutation behind windshields as I headed back the way we had come. I was bone tired and wary of the drive home to the city, so I returned instead to the hotel and checked myself into a top-floor suite for the night. I picked at a pink steak in the hotel's chic restaurant, accompanied by a lovely glass of port, but I couldn't bring myself to finish either. Since Martin took me to view the cosmoscope, I had the disagreeable impression that time had begun to slow, that I was walking through the world as if attempting to traverse some kind of jellylike sea, my progress no longer assured. I couldn't remember the last time I felt so drained. Or so very alone.

I returned upstairs to my room, hung the Do Not Disturb sign on the other side of the door, and engaged the safety latch, and as I did so I recalled the name scratched into the base of the cosmoscope. *George Vernon Hudson.* A quick Google search on my phone revealed him as a London-born New Zealander who first drew popular attention to daylight savings time. An ancient concept, yes, but his advocacy was critical to the larger movement and its adoption over the course of the last century.

A peek out the windows – at the tall pines that separated the hotel from the tranquil street beyond – before I drew the heavy curtains against the vast sweep of night that had settled over the town like a black shroud. I fumbled my way out of my loafers, their striated rubber soles encrusted with dried mud, and collapsed upon the bed without so much as undressing. Instead I buried myself beneath the sheets, curled a pillow over my head like a crescent, and descended into sleep's sweet release.

Sometime later I awoke in darkness to a decided chill in the room, as well as a deep feeling of unease. I reached for the bedside lamp on the nightstand, just beyond the digital clock and its LED display that read 2:59AM in bold green bars.

"Don't," a voice said from the corner. I jackknifed to attention and suppressed a startled cry. Of fear, yes, but also one of anticipation, since I recognized the voice at once. It was as if I had only just been dreaming of it.

"Jasper?" I said, rubbing at my eyes. And there he was, his familiar lithe frame visible in the half-light from the now-parted curtains. From what I could tell, he was completely naked. "How did you get in here?"

He raised a finger and pointed it upwards, toward the ceiling; I took it to mean he must have climbed down from the roof. Indeed, the window nearest him was cracked wide, the drapery's lining fluttering and pellucid in night's steady exhalation. Once my eyes adjusted I could see more of him: his pale face colored or flushed or bruised, round black marks along his limbs and concave chest, ribcage protruding as if trying to escape.

"You scared me half to death," I said. "They're looking for you. Martin's looking for you. They have no idea where you are."

"We're all looking for something." The space between us was obscured by a vapor of condensation from between his lips; the room was colder than I'd thought. "But to find it, you have to look in the right place. At the right time."

He pointed his bone-white finger at the ground. "They weren't very nice to him," he said. "They ridiculed him. But he was a visionary. And eventually, he prevailed."

Jasper peered out the window, his face bleached in the moonlight bleeding through the trees. "He was an entomologist, as well as an astronomer. I find that interesting. Because you see, you cannot glimpse the multitude of the heavens without listening to the multitude of the earth. As above, so below."

George Vernon Hudson, I thought, and Jasper smiled. "Yes," he said, and nodded. "Starlight and stridulations. Together, they open windows. But only inside the gifted hour. Otherwise..." He sighed. "Otherwise, they won't let you see. And he was the one who saw, first."

"Jasper," I started, but he shushed me with that white finger pressed to his bloodless lips. In an instant he was beside me, in less than a blink of the eye. I heard the sounds of his movement as a distant afterthought, the crunch of bare feet on dry leaves, as if the floor of the room was carpeted in dead foliage. Always the dancer.

"We fitted together," he said. "You and I. Wore the same clothes, to boot. I remember one time at the theater we were mistaken for each other, do you?"

His breath on my face was beyond stale, beyond rank, the smell of the grave. I took a step away from him, toward the still-locked door. Yet as he reached out and caressed my cheek with the back of a dirty hand, I nevertheless felt the old stirrings within me, my dormant cock roused to new life. It had been so long since I'd been with someone, since I'd been held; it had been since I'd last seen Jasper.

We kissed, and I stung where his tongue touched mine, pins and needles pricking at my mouth, my lips. I tried to ignore the pain. His hand upon the back of my head kept me pressed to him, however, his fingers cupping my skull as if drinking from it, his hardness against mine.

"Manipulation of time," he whispered in my ear, and gooseflesh pebbled my skin. "Their gift is also our key. Only then can we be open wide. Only then can we let it in, during the twice-born hour. Sixteen-bit suicide. All the way down."

I tried turning away but his steadfast fingers held me in place, his expression unreadable. Jasper's lips dropped open, a dark void absent of teeth, and his throat emitted the cry of an injured animal dragging itself across a frosted tundra. Black ooze spilled from his lips and ears, from the small mouths carved up and down his limbs. I couldn't scream, though I tried. I couldn't scream and so I twisted from his grasp, falling back upon the bed. The dark fluid took hold of me there, hardening into a dozen gelatinous protuberances that pinned me to the sheets. My mouth formed a final cry of anguish as the thrashing tide forced itself down my engorged throat, my teeth cracking one after the next in the black fluid's relentless irruption.

Just before I lost consciousness, my bulging eyes caught sight of the clock on the nightstand. Its alien green digits still read 2:59AM, and they trembled and strained and failed to change over, to a new and other and unknown time.

The main gates at Grey Towers were locked. Once I rolled up my shirtsleeves and trouser cuffs, however, it wasn't difficult to hop the adjoining stone wall, and I kept low to the ground as I circumnavigated the rolling lawn on my way up to the woods behind the Gilded Age mansion. I waited until I reached the path to turn on the penlight retrieved from my glove compartment, no sound but the soughing of the wind in the trees, a distant or perhaps imagined scent of cedar smoke on the air as I hurried into the dark heart of the night forest. I checked my watch: 2:37AM. It was still within the gifted hour, the end of saving daylight that Jasper had spoken of, in the dream that was not a dream. I still had time to see for myself.

I reached the base of the cosmoscope. Clasping the penlight between my teeth, I climbed the rickety ladder and hauled myself into the first compartment within the immense wooden cavity. I could just fit inside. Jasper had known that, of course. We were the same size, on balance, and really had been mistaken for each other, not just that one time at the theater but so very often.

We always fitted together, it was true. Jasper had wanted me here, in the end and after all these years. I'd been needed after all.

I forged my way deeper inside, crawling and stretching and compressing my form, and it soon became clear I was traveling in spoked circles. It was as if I were traversing the interior of a gargantuan wagon wheel, a narrow course designed for another age of man, now past. My palms were slicked in sweat and the strange viscous substance I'd encountered earlier, only now I could sense that the whole of the cosmoscope was coated in it, rust-red ooze atop ocher lumber, sudden flashes of ragged scratch marks against the damp siding in the penlight's erratic beam.

After some time, I reached the center. It was a coffin-sized recess, puckered out from the rest of the cosmoscope to comprise its highest elevation. I pulled myself up and inside, and laid myself out against what should have been hard wood but was in fact pulp, with the moldable consistency of sponge. I turned off the penlight and waited for my eyes to adjust, all alone in the dark. And then, I saw.

High above the me – above the tilted round face of the cosmoscope and the vaulted tree canopy, branches bending away from the clearing in a wide and deferential circle as if woven by a godlike hand – was the wide and starlit sky. It was as clear as I'd ever seen it. As clear, I knew, as it could ever be seen. The stars were closer to Earth than would seem possible, smoldering crystalline globules of fire that appeared to hang no higher than the thermosphere. The celestial heavens rattled and hissed as if threatened, trembling and straining, the firmament awakened to new life. And now Jasper was on his way.

A rustling noise, the uneven lurch of something crawling over dry leaves, and I became aware of the perimeter of dark holes lining the small chamber around me, making themselves known by a rising susurration of whispered breath through their mouths. It was the sound of the forest, called forth and issued from the rubber tubing threaded through the cosmoscope. A droning buzz and the frenzied communications of insects flared, hungry and watchful, a piercing hosanna that refused to end, even as the wind from the holes began to take a shape all its own.

My skin. It hummed with a thirst for communion, for the total unity of matter that only oblivion could provide. Jasper, he wanted me to see what he had seen, to feel what he felt. He wanted us to be the same. Not just us, but all things, if only we could find our way together. And now I could really see.

The nebular sky ripped open, the pinpricked curtain thrust wide at last, and in a heaving of rent wood and bone the cosmoscope undulated and spun, expanded and contracted, suspended in air, in darkness, in light, tremulous, wild. The thing that Jasper had become a part of took hold of me, slender black coils lashing and sucking with a thousand hungry mouths, an anarchic rattle of spurned life crying out in pain, in rage, in exaltation, transmutation, ecstasy.

I bled into it, into dark light, into sound. I became part of the greater whole. Because we were the same, Jasper and I, just the same, and we would never be apart again. In this hour, we could see what we were made of, and we were insects, we were dust, we were light, everything in the brightest of high color and made of stars.

I saw his face. His wry smile, Jasper here beside me once more, joined as one in yet another cramped space among many, as we were meant to be. Together, we gave ourselves away, and what remained of the structure's provisional contents splashed against the internal walls as wet gristle in a mighty centrifuge. We were elsewhere now.

Silence. The cosmoscope was still. A withdrawal, that of a hypodermic syringe, its plunger pulled back from its barrel. A slowing, a swallowing, a satiety, the clearing hushed, the forest hushed, time beginning anew, and what was left of that bodily cage dripped down to the roughhewn wood flooring. The crunch of dry leaves, a skittering through the quieted underbrush, as night continued its slow and glutted retreat until morning.

The Black Azalea

by Wendy N. Wagner

Graham had planted the azalea in the shade of an elm tree, and when Dutch elm disease had taken the old tree, the sun had burned the green from the bush's leaves. It had given up one last sad burst of purple blossoms this past spring, and now it stood withered and skeletal, the bark of its limbs dry and gray. Graham would have mourned the azalea's passing if he had lived to see it.

Candace put down her coffee cup and reached for the clippers. This week might well be the last good weather of the year, today the last sunshine until spring. When she stood at the kitchen window watching the endless gray sift down over the garden, she would be glad she had gotten rid of this dead thing.

She made her slow way across the back yard, feeling the long night on the couch in her hip. She would have to go back to her bed someday, but even the company of her old tomcat couldn't blot out how large and cold the bed was without her husband. The whole house stretched quietly around her when she tried to sleep, the wood and cement as lost without Graham as she was. He had practically rebuilt the little cottage over the years since they'd bought the place. Her counselor said she ought to be glad she lived inside Graham's legacy, but Candace could not find any gladness within her. Graham was gone, that was all. Others had tried to make death something meaningful, but the absurd nothing of it could not be denied.

She chopped at the gray limbs. Closer to the trunk of the shrub, she found live wood, but it would only be a matter of time before it, too, withered. The whole plant felt dry to the touch. Crisp, brittle.

But when she switched to the handsaw to begin breaking down the main trunk, the blade stuck, gummed up. She yanked it free with some difficulty. She had to pull away—God, what a stink. Nose crinkled, she examined the cut, which reeked of old drains and a hint of fish. Some kind of blight, probably. It was a good thing she'd decided to get rid of it; she couldn't risk the rhododendrons catching this.

The azalea toppled slowly over, the sere leaves and branches crunching as they settled. Candace frowned at the stump. Its heartwood was black, damp, and strangely juicy. She would have to dig it up—all of it—even the roots had to come out of the ground. Whatever was wrong with it, she didn't want it in the rest of the garden.

She rubbed the small of her back for a moment, steeling herself to go get the shovel from the shed. It was pleasant out here in the sunshine, the air a little crisp and mellow with morning wood smoke. With a soft sequence of crunching, a yellow leaf tumbled through the greenery around her and settled onto the grass. Autumn had taken hold of the world around her and would soon make inroads into her back yard. A small black spider darted up on the leaf and hesitated on it for a moment before racing onward. It was the first spider she'd seen all day. Perhaps it was just autumn weather, urging the insects into their winter hiding spots, but Candace found their absence strangely lonely.

She got to her feet and made her way to the shed.

That evening, after some small excuse of a meal, Candace stood at the kitchen sink; the glow of the house and porch lights illuminated enough of the garden beyond to make the after-dinner washing just this side of monotonous. The crisp boxwood borders of her vegetable patch stood straight and sober, lending a sense of prosperity to the late season tomatoes and pumpkins. At the edge of the lit area, the hole where she'd dug out the azalea could just be seen, a dark, broken-toothed mouth in the soil.

Tomorrow she'd fill it in. It would be all too easy to step into a hole like that and break her leg. After all, she lived alone now. Who would come looking for her if she lay out there, the bones snapped through the skin and the blood seeping into the cold clay earth? Enoch the cat couldn't dial 911.

She had to look out for herself these days. She had to be careful. Even the cutting board felt dangerous in her grip, slippery and heavy and just the size to crush a fragile toe. Everything in the whole house could be a threat to an aging widow like herself: the tile floor, so slick when wet; the step down into the living room that was always in the shadows. The world was a vicious, ugly place for a woman alone. She had forgotten that after all these years of marriage.

Candace put the cutting board in the dish drainer and then wiped down the counter. She couldn't help looking outside. The hole looked bigger, darker. She'd fill it in tomorrow. First thing.

She and Enoch went outside as soon as they'd finished their breakfasts: brown kibble for both of them. Graham had eschewed cereal for hot breakfasts covering every food group, and now Candace found it a relief to simply wash her one bowl and spoon and leave the kitchen behind. It somehow seemed more virtuous to eat plain oat flakes and seeds. Given her family history and late-midlife status, she should try to eat light. Even Enoch was on reduced calorie chow nowadays. She stroked the big orange tom's back.

"Healthy food and exercise, that's what we want, right, cat?"

The cat rubbed his cheek against her shin and then trotted off to sniff the nearest boxwood. Candace watched him a second, then slipped on her gloves and marched toward the hole. She had a bag of potting soil in the shed that might be big enough to fill the pit, but she wasn't quite sure.

The cat gave a low growl. Candace turned to look at him. His gaze was fixed on the land beyond the vegetables, his posture very stiff.

"Do you hear something, buddy? Got a rat?"

She heard nothing, but cats were so much more sensitive to tiny sounds and smells. She'd always admired them for that. To her, the garden was all peace today, the shrubs still and graceful in the cool, dry morning. A few more golden leaves had fallen off the neighbor's maple tree, adding spots of gilt throughout the yard.

Candace frowned. The shasta daisies to the left of the azalea's hole sagged, the green toothy leaves hanging limp. She knelt beside them and covered her nose. The fish and mildew stink had spread. And the bases of the daisies' leaves had turned black where they came up from the ground.

She got to her feet. This was more serious than one azalea plant. This was something nasty, something that affected a wide variety of plants, a disease that could spread beyond her own property line. She needed to call the extension office right away.

The thought of such a seriously contagious plant disease made her sick. Candace had poured a great deal of effort into the garden. Graham had purchased a few specimens, but by and large they'd agreed that the house was his child, the garden hers. After long days at work, they'd each needed some kind of outlet. The garden was hers, her ever-expanding project, her art.

Enoch squeezed past her as she pushed through the French doors. She looked up the number for the university extension office and called it immediately. After some run-around with the automated system, she found a soft-voiced man who listened to her description of the rotten plants with quiet interest.

"It's not like anything I've heard of," he admitted. "Do you have any idea how much of the area is being affected right now?"

Candace reached for the yard stick tucked beside the broom in the pantry. "I can measure right now. I'm on my cell phone."

The smell was stronger now—she didn't know how she'd missed it before. Its stomach-churning waves rolled out across the yard. No breeze lightened the heavy blanket of stench.

"Good god, that stinks."

"What's that?"

She'd almost forgotten that the extension agent was listening patiently on the other end of the line. She wasn't in the office any more, with a hold button and a secretary to field calls. She was retired. She covered her nose with her free hand.

"The smell has definitely gotten worse." She knelt beside the hole, studying the ground. "Some of the grass around the initial site shows the same mottling as the daisies."

"Grass, daisies, azaleas—it's odd to find a disease that affects such a wide range of species."

"That's what I thought, too." Candace nudged a clump of blackening dandelions with her fingertip. Their leaves felt *damp* somehow, as if their internal juices seeped out of their pores, the black blight pushing their innards out to make room for itself. "Dandelions, too. The plants almost feel like they're bleeding."

She scrubbed her hand on her pants. What if this was some kind of plant Ebola? Could something like that spread to animals?

As if he read her mind, the agent—Michael, that's how he had introduced himself—warned: "If you touched anything, you should probably wash with an antibacterial soap."

"Could it make me sick?"

There was a second's hesitation before he answered. "I'm

almost positive you'll be fine, but you wouldn't want to spread this to any of your other plants." She could hear his keyboard clattering in the background. "Look, I can't get out of the office today. But first thing tomorrow morning, I want to stop by and take samples. Can I get your address?"

Candace passed along the information. She drew it out, giving a few relevant landmarks and a good description of the house. But when she finished, she couldn't think of anything else to ask or say. She held the phone tight to her ear, listening hard. The keyboard had gone quiet.

"Candace, I don't want you to be nervous, but...could you stay out of your garden for the rest of the day? It's best to be cautious if we don't know what we're dealing with."

She backed into the house, closing the French doors in front of her. Already the garden looked darker, the hole in the ground deeper and wider. "Absolutely." She couldn't imagine going back out there.

Michael signed off. Candace hung up, but stayed at the French doors, her gaze fixed on the diseased patch in the garden. She didn't want to turn her back on it, even if she was safely inside.

Enoch thudded his head against her shin. She had left the yard stick outside, she realized—she could see it laying like a bridge across the hole she'd dug when she pulled up the azalea. She'd been in an awful hurry to get away from the nastiness out there. Enoch stood on his hind legs, pressing his head into her palm. She rubbed his plush fur.

Candace snapped the deadbolt shut with a satisfying thunk. "I'm going to leave the damned thing outside," she told the cat. "I can just buy a new one."

When Candace awoke with a stiff neck and a dry mouth, the sound was off on the TV as a man in a suit ran out onto a black-and-white highway. She couldn't quite remember what he was shouting at the cars, no matter how famous the line. She'd never had a memory for movie quotes; that had been Graham's forte. The thought had an unexpected sting.

These little bursts of pain always took her by surprise. She had expected Graham's death to be difficult but manageable. She had gone into his illness knowing it was irrevocable. It had taken Graham six months to die, and his disease had progressed utterly without surprises, every advance along the way forecasted and scheduled like a stop on a train's timetable. Ride the Pancreatic Cancer Express: next stop, metastasis! Final destination: death.

The end screen rolled on *Invasion of the Body Snatchers*, and she turned off the TV, blinking away tears. Her hip complained as she trudged out of the den. From her left, the cat chirped a little greeting but did not get up from his bed in the laundry basket.

She had no idea when the extension agent would arrive. She kept checking her phone as she went through her morning routine, but she jumped when it jangled with a text from the man. "Almost there." She nearly ran to the bathroom to brush her teeth.

The doorbell rang before she was done. She hurriedly cupped water into her mouth and spat a plume of red-stained foam. Candace wiped her mouth on the back of her hand, frowning at the sink. She'd brushed too roughly, she supposed. She'd been in a hurry.

The doorbell rang again. This time she did run, and was out of breath when she flung open the door. The extension agent stood on the stoop with his phone out, his eyebrows knit above his glasses. In his other hand he held a white plastic case that reminded her strongly of her father's fishing tackle box. The agent wasn't quite young enough to be her son, or at least she'd like to think he wasn't. His light-weight denim jacket was much smarter than she'd expected a horticulturist to wear.

He slipped his phone into his jacket pocket and put out a hand. "Dr. Michael Gutiérrez, OSU extension office."

"Candace Moore. Come in, Dr. Gutiérrez. Please." She led him through the kitchen. "Would you like a cup of coffee? Tea? Anything?"

"Nope." He raised the almost-tackle box. "I'm pretty eager to get these samples taken."

"The stuff is right out these doors." Candace reached for the deadbolt's latch and paused. "The yardstick's gone."

"Yardstick?"

"I used it yesterday to measure the extent of the diseased area, and I left it out there. Couldn't make myself go back out to get it." She twisted open the latch, although she realized she had no desire to go out into the stench of her yard. Her breakfast cereal turned over in her stomach. The plants looked worse today; even from the doorway, the hole the yardstick had bridged looked dark and moist, the grass around it subdued into strings of black slime.

Michael put his hand on the door knob. "We'll get to the bottom of this."

She let him lead the way. Yesterday on the phone, she had thought that the agent's arrival would be comforting. His years of field experience and collection of scientific gear would be more than a match for the problems of her small garden, and she would rest easily, knowing she'd turned over the problem to the authorities. Perhaps waking up to apocalyptic sci-fi had put her in a dispirited mood, or perhaps it was the agent's young face and stylish jacket. She couldn't explain the listless, hopeless feeling she had, following this young man of science toward the black hole she'd dug in her yard.

"Hey, the yardstick's right here," he called, squatting

beside the pit. "At the bottom of the hole."

She stooped beside him. "But it didn't fit inside the hole yesterday. The hole wasn't even two feet across."

He gave her a kind look. "Well, it's here. You'll be glad not to have to buy another."

He didn't believe her. She folded her arms across her chest. How could he not believe her? "Mr. Gutiérrez, I'm not a senile old lady yet. I made very careful measurements yesterday. That hole has gotten bigger."

He used a pair of tweezers to harvest a few blades of grass. "You're sure about that?"

"Yes." An idea struck her. "Wait. If I didn't get all of the azalea's roots out of the ground, and this black stuff dissolved them, could that have caused subsidence in the ground? I mean, if the grass is turning into goo, maybe it can do the same to underground plant materials."

He popped the cap on a plastic tube and looked up at her, his face thoughtful. "I suppose so, but—"

"But what?"

"But I don't like the thought very much, do you? The roots of plants hold an awful lot of soil in place, especially up here in the West Hills. Could you image the kind of effect that would have on the neighborhoods around here?"

Candace folded her arms around herself. Even through her cardigan, the morning breeze had teeth. She couldn't bring herself to answer the man. The yard settled into a tense silence around them, the squirrels and birds as hushed as she was.

"I haven't seen any insects out here this morning," Michael mused. "Have you used any pesticides out here recently?"

"You asked me that yesterday." Candace looked around her. No birds perched on the fence. No big orb weaver spiders spun in the rose bushes, even though autumn was their season. Even the pair of squirrels who nested in the maple tree were not to be seen. "I'm strictly organic."

Michael stood up. He snapped a few photos with his cell phone. "I'm going to go back to the office and run some tests on the plant and soil material I just gathered. It may be a few days until I have anything solid to report."

Candace shook his hand. Some of her old faith had returned while they'd been out here. He'd wound up taking her seriously, after all. "The sooner, the better. I don't like to think of this spreading."

They walked toward the French doors. "Nor do I," Michael agreed.

Candace opened the door for him. Enoch shot past the agent's feet, an orange blur. In an instant, he was up and over the back fence. "Enoch!"

But of course he didn't come back. He always did what he wished. She refocused her attention on the extension agent, who had already made it halfway to the front door. He moved like a man pushing toward an exciting achievement, waving a brusque goodbye on the porch step and then rushing to his car. She could imagine him bursting into the shabby extension office, eager to show his colleagues something so new there was no Latin name for it.

She'd been like that once, the hot dog of the office, but she'd put such things behind when she had left her career to tend to her terminally ill husband. It had seemed right at the time, the only respectful way to end thirty-eight years of marriage. Now she wondered if perhaps she should have tried harder to keep her job. Standing alone in this house, watching the leaves float down to cover the crushed place where Michael had parked, she thought of her career and her work friends and the fresh coffee scent of her office. It tugged something inside her like a strained muscle. Graham's cancer had cut off her life, too. She could reclaim it with effort, but she wasn't sure she had the energy to rebuild like that: even just worrying about this crisis in the garden had drained her. She wanted nothing more than a cup of tea and then a long nap with the cat.

Candace went to the back door and called for the creature. He rarely strayed from the yard, but there was no sign of him. The big tomcat didn't even meow in response. The heavy silence she and Michael had noticed continued on.

No, it wasn't completely silent. Somewhere in the very distance she could hear a metallic clicking, very high pitched—almost a ping. It reminded her of the sound the train tracks made after a heavy freight train had passed by, metal winding down after some enormous stress. She rarely heard the train from the house. It must be a massive freight.

She closed the door and went back inside, too tired to keep calling for Enoch. Let the dumb thing miss lunch. He would appreciate dinner the better for missing it.

Candace slept much too long. If her cell hadn't rang, she might have kept sleeping, too, but the steady chirping brought her up out of dreamless dark. She laid there waiting for the call to go to voicemail, uncertain at first where she was. It had been two months since she had tried to sleep in the bedroom, coming in only to drop off and pick up laundry, and in the deep shadows of the sunset, the room was unfamiliar. The voicemail notification beeped once, twice, lighting the nightstand an electronic blue. She made herself sit up.

"Candace," the message began, in Michael Gutiérrez's voice, taut with excitement, and much too loud for just- waking ears, "I've run some preliminary tests, and the samples I took show none of the markers for any known bacterial or viral plant disease. This is something entirely new!"

Candace rubbed the back of her head and yawned. She was still so tired. Michael wasn't tired, though. After all, he had made the scientific discovery of a lifetime. He wasn't just *excited*, he was hungry. This blackening disease could write his ticket out of the boring university extension office and into some first-rate research facility.

"I have to take some more samples, more pictures," he continued. "I'm bringing the whole team out there tomorrow. Don't worry—you'll hardly even know we're there!" On that happy note, he clicked off.

Candace hung up the phone, plunging the room into darkness. For a moment, she thought about going back to sleep, but she turned on the bedside lamp and got to her feet. Even sleeping in a real bed hadn't helped the stiffness in her hip. She felt older than ever. She had to put her hand on the wall to steady herself as she bent to pick up the laundry basket. A rank smell rose up from it, the ripe stink of mildew and spoiled fish. She should have washed those jeans last night. She had no idea how Enoch had slept on that stench all morning.

Enoch. She dropped the basket and bolted out the door. The poor cat must be starving. She'd slept till, Jesus, 7:30, and she wasn't sure he'd even had any breakfast. She threw open the French doors.

"Enoch! Kitty!"

A thin, sad meow answered her. It came from across the yard, from the dark shadows beyond the range of the porch light, where the azalea bush had grown. She stepped outside unwillingly, conscious of the crunch of leaves beneath her socked feet.

"Enoch?"

The meow again. He only meowed like that when she put him in the cat carrier, a sound like a trapped kitten that a big cat ought not be able to make. She pulled her arms tight around her and walked faster toward the cry. The mildew-and-fish smell of the blight made her nose and throat hurt. The ticking sound of the train tracks was louder than before.

She almost fell in the pit. It had grown during the day; it was no longer large enough to fit a yardstick inside, but now large enough to fit a grown woman. Big enough to swallow her whole, she thought, big enough to serve as her grave. Thank goodness she'd cremated Graham.

"Are you in there, Enoch?"

She wished she'd brought a flashlight. The sun was fading fast and the depths of the pit were utmost black. She could make out Enoch's eyes: two dimes flashing that iridescent red that only cats' eyes made. She leaned over the edge of the pit and stretched her hand out to him.

"Here, kitty, kitty."

Cold and wet seeped into the knees of her pants, and the smell made her head ache. Her fingertips almost reached the cat. He mewed piteously. She couldn't see what held him from jumping up out of the hole, couldn't make out the bottom of the pit at all. Down here the metallic ticking was louder, as if it were coming closer and picking up speed.

She stretched out both hands despite the precariousness of the position. "Come here, sweetie."

He mewed again, and she could just feel the muscles of his shoulders against her fingertips. His eyes burned up her, red-bright, but a thread of black flitted across first one eye, and then the other. With a rush of fear, Candace threw herself forward and grabbed Enoch under the armpits. He cried out. She couldn't lift him; something held him fast.

She tugged him left, then right. He screamed horribly. The clicking and pinging grew louder—the sounds came up out of the pit itself, cold and metallic and loud enough to make her ears sting. It wasn't the sound of a train at all, but something else, something as horrible and alien as the stench that went with it. Enoch clawed at her arms and shrieked again.

"Enoch," she growled and yanked hard. He shrieked and came free and she almost slid into the pit with him. She managed to roll sideways and clutched him to her chest. Cold water dripped off him and soaked her shirt, but she didn't care.

She got to her feet and ran toward the back door, but when she reached the edge of the light, she stopped hard and thrust her hands out in front of her. Black goo ran down her arms and her shirtfront and she held a black-soaked rag of a thing with no legs and no tail and raw red flesh from the shoulders down. Her legs went out from under her and she gagged. The thing in her hands mewed again and then went stiff. A trickle of black ran out of the dead cat's muzzle.

It had gotten him. The—whatever it was killing the plants—it had gotten Enoch, and she understood why Michael couldn't recognize it as bacterial or viral: It was something else entirely. Something from beyond the bottom of that hole she'd dug, something from a darkness beyond anyplace she knew, but had perhaps dreamed of. Something that was coming to swallow them all.

She crawled into the house and all the way to the bathroom and ran the shower over herself a long time before she could wriggle out of her filthy clothes. But even after the hot water ran out, she couldn't get the smell of mildew and rotten fish off of her. She wrapped up in a towel and stood shivering at the counter. Where Enoch's claws had scored her arm, the flesh was black and puckered. In her reflection, her eyes were sunken, dark-ringed. Her mouth tasted of mildew.

Much later, she found her way down to the kitchen and stood at the kitchen sink, spitting out dribbles of blood that turned darker as she waited for dawn to show her the black hole in her garden. The edge of the sky showed gray, but shadows still hid most of the back yard. Nothing moved out there. It didn't matter. Even with the door shut, she could hear the pinging and ticking of the thing's imminent arrival. There was something hypnotic about it that made her want to throw open the French doors and crawl inside the dark, dank pit she had dug.

Yes, she'd just go out there and pull the darkness over her safe and snug and wait for Michael Gutiérrez and his team of horticulturists. Then she would show them what lay beyond the bottom of the hole, what the black azalea had reeled in with its roots and what was chugging along toward them all: right on schedule.

After the Fall

by Jeffrey Thomas

The fossils in the sky appeared after an unusual windstorm.

No weather forecaster had predicted this storm, and its wind gusted across the entire surface of the globe. The storm occurred in the day for those in the United States, but on the opposite side of the world, it shrieked in the night like a migration of banshees. Depending on the local climate and conventional weather conditions, in some places the wind carried rain, or snow, or sand, but nowhere on the Earth – from pole to pole, upon ocean or desert, city or cornfield – was there stillness. The continuous wind was strong, yet not of hurricane strength; it did not bring destruction or damage throughout the hours that it blew. And when finally the high, ululating howling died down and calm returned to the air, and the sky became clear across the whole of the heavens – whether they were bright with day or starry with night – the fossils had been unveiled.

"Are you kidding me?" Wayne's wife said, eyes wide with emphasis. "You're still going to this party with *that* happening outside?"

"Whatever happened seems to have finished happening," Wayne said in a mild tone, his back to her as he reached to the coat rack by the door.

"Oh, and you can tell that? Well, call Washington, Wayne, and tell them they've found their only expert on the situation."

"Tania, this isn't just some party for the hell of it…it's a family gathering for my *nephew*, for Chrissakes."

"The reception after the service wasn't enough? With all this craziness going on, your family still needs to have a cookout?

Drink some beers in honor of the guy whose drinking problem got him killed?"

Wayne paused from sliding his arms into a hooded sweatshirt to turn and stare at her. He didn't say "fuck you," though he wanted to. He didn't say he was thinking of divorcing her, though he wanted to.

No doubt sensing his mood, however, Tania veered from the manner in which Wayne's nephew Keith had lost his life. Instead, she reasoned, "What if in the middle of the cookout the storm comes up again? It came out of nowhere the first time."

It had.

The storm had taken place two days earlier, and Wayne had been at work at the time in his cubicle. It had been an exceedingly pleasant drive to work, marred only by the knowledge that he was on his way to work. A mellow morning in the first week of October, and as Wayne lived in a rural area, the roads were closely flanked by trees that were like atomic mushroom clouds of red/orange, yellow/green, the leaves almost fluorescent where the morning's rays shone directly upon them. The surface of the pond he passed every day was entirely covered in fog, luminous and golden, with thousands of wispy tendrils being teased upward, as if the pond were a deep crater into which clouds had descended from the sky.

But by noon, eating a sandwich from the cafeteria at his desk while he reviewed the quarterly inventory reconciliation, he overheard workers who had ventured outside for lunch remark on how quickly the clear sky had become overcast. In no time, his coworkers' voices grew more animated as they discussed the wind they said was rising. Within minutes, Wayne could hear it himself, whistling beyond the walls, and he finally left his desk for the lobby to have a look. He found others grouped just outside the building, gawping at the sky, which was not black as he had thought it would be. It was as solidly white as a canvas awaiting a brush.

"Oh my God," one of the women had said, squinting against airborne grit as her hair started dancing. "Do you think there's going to be a tornado?"

"Not in October," Wayne had told her.

The wind had finally driven them inside, as it chased clouds of dust across their cars, which looked timidly huddled in the parking lot. Leaves spiraled in the sky like the tails of invisible dragons.

Yet despite the eerily wailing wind, no tornado had come, not even rain, and Wayne had returned to his desk and his work.

He hadn't gone to check outside again after that. Not until a few hours later, when the gale had finally died down...and several of his coworkers, who did peek outside, started screaming.

Tania said, "Well, do what you want, and give my condolences again to everybody, but no way in hell am I going outside until they know more about that stuff up there."

"I wasn't asking you to go," Wayne said.

"And you aren't taking our kids, either."

"Are you joking?" their twelve-year-old, Emmy, said as she poured herself some soda at the kitchen counter. "Nobody could drag me outside if they wanted to. You just wait till those things start moving or something. Come crawling down here out of the sky."

"They're apparently dead," Wayne said, regretting he had shared this opinion before he had even finished uttering it.

"Emmy," Tania said, "get the United Nations on the line. Tell them your Dad's got everything under control." She wagged her head. "Jesus, Wayne! It's only been two days! Anything could happen!"

"I know you're scared," Wayne told them. "I think it's scary, too. But until they know what those things are, the world can't just stop, can it? People have to go to their jobs, keep things running. Things have to...you know...go on."

"It's Saturday, Dad," said Emmy. "*You* don't need to do anything. You should be here to protect us if something does happen."

"Your father always put his family before our family, Emmy," Tania said.

There was a time when Wayne would have exploded at that. Asked his wife to explain exactly how he put his family first...what it was that made her say such a thing, beyond the need to prod him, anger him, diminish their child's estimation of him. But he had grown too tired to fight anymore. He didn't ask Emmy, either, just what it was he was supposed to do to protect them if the seemingly fossilized entities poised above the Earth did come alive again.

Anyway, his family was expecting him at the gathering at the home of his sister Sherri – Keith's mother. He was already running late.

Without another word, he finished slipping on his hoodie and went to the door, thinking that if the world kept on maintaining itself in the wake of this manifestation, he would indeed go through with it and divorce his wife.

Maybe this event didn't herald the end of humanity, but a new beginning. He then thought: huh, such a typically human response...looking for meaning where none might exist. Looking for signs in the sky, animals in the clouds.

Just as he started his car, his other daughter – fifteen-year-old Crystal – came running from the house pulling on her own hoodie and grinning wildly. A bit surprised, Wayne watched as Crystal flung open the passenger's door and bounced in beside him.

"I want to go, too, Dad," she explained. "I loved my cousin."

"Does your Mom know you're coming with me?"

"Not yet, so you'd better hurry!" She laughed and locked her door.

In the past, Wayne would have been too afraid to incur further anger from Tania by driving off with Crystal just then. But he hesitated only a moment or two, smiled at her, then backed his car into the street.

Just because this event might not be designed as a new beginning didn't mean it couldn't be one.

Along the drive to Sherri's home in a neighboring town, Crystal repeatedly craned her neck to gaze up at the sky through her window with a mix of apprehension and curiosity. Meanwhile, in her lap she thumbed her phone's colorful screen, alternating between searching out stories about the phenomenon on the internet and exchanging dramatic text messages with her friends. "*It's doomsday, bitches!*" Crystal read out loud.

"Besides that observation," Wayne said, "are there any more ideas about this on the news?"

"Well," Crystal replied, "looks like regular airplane flights are still cancelled, but I guess helicopters and military planes have been going up for a better look. Sounds like the things look the same even if you go up there. Not any closer or clearer or anything."

"So the images aren't inside our atmosphere, but outside it?"

"Um, probably. They're like showing through our atmosphere. Yeah, so I guess...in space? I wonder if satellites can see them. Anyway, I'll bet the government knows more than they're telling. They always do."

They arrived at Sherri's home, parked their car behind others filling the driveway, and went around to her sizable back yard – its swimming pool covered till next summer, if next summer should in fact come – to find that the yard was decorated as if for an early Halloween party. Cleverly carved jack-o'-lanterns on the picnic table and elsewhere, candles in little paper bags stenciled with witches and black cats, black and orange crepe paper bunting, bowls of popcorn, dishes of candy corn, jugs of cider. From a CD player, Orson Welles reported on the invasion of Earth by Martians. All of this was Sherri's work; Wayne had often teased her about being a Martha Stewart wannabe. Mixed with these accoutrements, however, were other accoutrements left over from summer: coolers of beer, and aromatic smoke rising from the grill tended by Sherri's husband Dave. He had already filled several plates with burgers and hotdogs. The air had a bit of crispness to it today, but it was still comfortable. The sun shone. The sky was blue...and full of monsters. Sherri couldn't take credit for those.

Wayne realized he was grinning as he crossed the grass toward his sister, who had spotted him and came to meet him halfway. He explained to Crystal, walking beside him, "Keith always loved Halloween so much."

"Dad, we all do in our family."

His sister hugged him too tightly. "Very cool, sis," he told her. "Very cool."

"He would have loved it," she said. Her voice was cracked around the edges.

"I was just saying that to Crystal."

The funeral had been on Wednesday, the day before the event. He hadn't seen his sister since then, but he'd called her to make sure she was safe and doing okay.

Crystal drifted off to talk with some cousins, while Sherri walked Wayne over to where her husband was cooking. The two men shook hands, then Dave insisted Wayne grab himself some chicken. He'd been busy. Wayne was sure the busyness helped keep his focus off his son.

Wayne glanced toward a cooler, necks of pumpkin-flavored ale poking up from the crushed ice. He remembered what Tania had said, alluding to Keith's death. Keith had been a contractor, reshingling a roof that day, and had indulged in too many beers at lunch. Though he should have been accustomed to drinking too many beers, and the fall wasn't really that far – Wayne had heard of skydivers who had survived falls when their parachutes didn't open – Keith had landed just right. Or rather, just wrong. How fragile, humans. Like bugs crushed in an instant under the steps of vast, unthinking forces...neither of which could really see nor fathom each other.

"Fuck it," Wayne muttered to himself, and went to the cooler and pulled free a beer.

His father and mother sat in plastic lawn chairs nearby. His mother's face looked crumpled in on itself, her eyes reddened, as if she hadn't stopped crying since he had last seen her on Wednesday. She had lost her first grandchild. Wayne went to them, leaned down to hug his mother. His father raised his own beer, an Irish red. He'd obviously already had a couple already. "*Slàinte!*" he said.

Wayne clinked bottles with his elderly father, then sucked at his beer. It went down good. It was a good moment. If Crystal had come up to him just then and asked for her own beer, he would have given her one. Not to spite his wife, not even because the world had changed and might soon end, for all they knew, but just because it was a good moment.

He wondered then: why did it often take death to bring people together like this?

Wayne had rushed toward his company's lobby, again, to see what all the screaming and shouting was about.

Most of the spectators who had already gathered there were afraid to venture outside, despite the fact that the storm had abated, pressing themselves close to the full-length windows that lined the front wall. But some braver souls had gone out into the parking lot. Because he didn't want to nudge his way through the bodies massed at the windows, Wayne also stepped directly outside.

Like the others, he immediately tilted his head back to gawk open-mouthed at the sky.

The blank white cloud cover had been entirely blown away, leaving what would have been a pristine blue sky like glazed ceramic, were it not for the translucent white shapes that entirely covered the dome of the heavens like chalk drawings rendered by a brilliant madman on a surface of opaque blue glass.

"Those are clouds, right?" one woman asked shakily, holding onto a coworker's arm. "They're just freaky cloud formations…*right?*"

"I don't think so," murmured the man whose arm she squeezed.

"Is it a…mirage?" someone else asked feebly.

Perhaps fearing they were all experiencing a hallucination brought on by mass hysteria, one of the workers glanced at two men directly beside him and said, "Tell me what you're seeing."

"Teeth. Ribs. Snakes?" one man said.

"Legs…claws," said the other man. "Centipedes?"

"Bones," was all Wayne could say.

The cloud-like images in the cloudless sky were a mad jumble, a tangle, an interwoven tapestry of unthinkably immense bodies. It was difficult, often impossible, to tell where one body ended and another began, even though no two creatures were identical. Their detail was somewhat misty, but still clear enough to appear almost tangible…almost solid, like skeletons lying in a shallow blue pool. Eyeless maybe-faces, spread open like flowers, with multiple jaws or spiral whorls of fangs, reminding one of hagfish or lampreys. Ribbons of comb-toothed ribs, like the curtains of an aurora borealis. Exposed, seemingly calcified organs, torn or exploded, from which protruded bundles of ropy tendrils…reminding Wayne of a dog's heart preserved in a bottle he had seen in a veterinarian's office as a boy, cut open to show the heartworms nested inside. Over there: were those the struts of wings? And there: stag beetle mandibles, or a set of barbed antlers? And those: spider legs, or vast skeletal hands? Had the flesh all decomposed, centuries or millennia or millions of years ago, or had these beings never been covered in flesh?

Fish? Insects? Dinosaurs? Terrestrial comparisons ultimately failed, but it was all the workers had by which to process what they were seeing. Only one thing was certain: none of it moved. These were plainly the remains of expired lifeforms. That the creatures were dead was the only thing that insured the spectators' sanity.

"Come on," one employee said, "someone's got to be projecting these things. Like the ghosts in the Haunted Mansion, you know?"

Wayne heard someone else, trying to rationalize the revelation in similarly human terms, suggest, "That windstorm…someone must have released drugs in the air. Mind control drugs, to give us delusions. Our government. Or…an enemy government."

"Maybe it's some kind of advertisement," another said. "For a movie or something."

But Wayne overheard yet another of his coworkers, who originated from Haiti, mutter to himself, "It's Hell."

A breeze stirred to life, causing many of the leaves dislodged in the storm to scrabble across the parking lot like a horde of crabs. The woman clutching her coworker's arm (Wayne had long suspected them of an affair) pressed her face into his chest and sobbed. But the benign little breeze faded away quickly, and the leaves went inanimate again.

A young man emerged from the building then and blurted, "It's on the news! They're seeing the same thing all over the world!"

When the sun went down – no longer glowing through the dense web of ghostly bones, leaving only a pink/orange swath above the silhouetted treetops – Dave lit a metal outdoors fireplace against the growing chill. Those relatives and family friends who hadn't already headed home sat or stood around the fire drinking beer or coffee. Some of Keith's young friends lingered, including his former girlfriend, weeping and inebriated.

Sherri lit the candles in the little paper bags, and the jack-o'-lanterns, of course, which grinned and flickered to guide the dead, or repel the dead, or something – Wayne forgot the original meaning.

The fossils did not vanish in the darkness, but in fact became more distinct, sharper in outline, brightly luminous as if they reflected the sun as did a full moon – though they were lit by no sun of this solar system. Maybe, no sun of this dimension. But in the black spaces between the latticed bodies, familiar stars peeked and twinkled as if to offer some measure of reassurance.

Thick woods bordered the rear of Sherri's property, and a light wind came up, causing the trees there to rustle ominously as if something huge were making its way toward them. Wayne shuddered, and stared into the restless dark foliage, but the disturbance subsided. He figured a lot of people would be gun-shy about the wind for some time to come. Gun-shy about a lot of things they had once taken for granted…like the sky.

Wayne's father stood nearby unsteadily, and wagged his cane at the heavens as if to challenge the dome of phosphorescent bones. "I'll be glad when a regular goddamn storm comes along, so the clouds will cover up these bastards and we won't have to look at them for a while!"

"I'd be afraid of that," Wayne's mother fretted. "What if they're radioactive? I'm afraid the rain might be poisoned."

"I wonder," said one of Keith's friends, "if we could like shoot nuclear warheads up at them. Blow the motherfuckers right out of the sky."

"They're not really in the sky," another of Keith's friends said. "They just look like they are. They're, like, in some other sky."

"Say *what?*"

Crystal came close to her father's side. "Mom called again."

"Is she still furious?"

"I think she's gone from furious to merely pissed. She just wants to know when we're coming home. I think she's lonely, with no one to fight with."

"Hey, you said that, not me."

"Dad…do you think everything will change?"

"You mean with your Mom?"

"No. I mean, with the world."

"Maybe. Everybody's looking and talking and thinking about the same thing." Wayne sipped his beer. "Until the next celebrity goes into rehab, anyway."

"Yeah," his brother-in-law Dave said, listening in. "If we get through this...I mean, if this doesn't hurt us, you know...in no time we'll all take it for granted like we do everything else. We'll kind of stop seeing it."

"Were they always there, and we just couldn't see them before," Crystal asked her father and uncle, "or did they come here from someplace else just now?"

"I think they were always there," Wayne said. "Maybe always will be, even after we're long gone."

"I wish Keith could have seen them," Dave said, gazing upward wistfully. "He wouldn't have been scared. He'd have been excited. It's really a kind of miracle."

"Like everything else in the universe," Wayne agreed.

"But everything dies," Dave said. "You see that?" He pointed with his own beer. "Even them."

As Wayne continued staring at the display suspended thousands of feet or miles or light-years above his company – shuffling in circles to study different areas, like a tourist marveling at the ceiling of the Sistine Chapel – it became apparent to him that these impossibly colossal animals, or sentient beings, or gods had been the cause of their own extinction.

One creature that Wayne likened to an isopod, with a head like the skull of a prehistoric whale without eye sockets, had its jaws clamped around the body of another beast that resembled some kind of eel larvae, with a bunched head like a clenched fist and a crest down its back like a row of praying mantis forelimbs. Another titan that was all spiny vertebrae, with a featureless globe of bone at either end of its serpentine body, had died locked in combat with a thing that looked like an uprooted tree or section of coral, its branches having once tapered into strangling tentacles, its trunk constricted by its opponent's barbed coils. Wayne's eyes were able to untangle more and more of these scenarios from the chaotic scene above him, though the effort was giving him a stabbing headache.

It had been an orgy of killing. But had these heterogeneous entities all been enemies, or had they entered into some kind of suicide pact, having agreed that their reign must come to an end? Determining how they had died was something, Wayne supposed, but in the end it gave no larger answers.

Even then, on the first day, he knew that answers might never be forthcoming for the miniscule inhabitants of this tiny world...which might not even have existed when that epic battle or mutual extermination had raged.

"Imagine seeing them *move*," a coworker said to Wayne in awe. "Imagine the sounds they all made."

"I can't look at them anymore!" another employee cried out suddenly, turning and fleeing back inside their building.

More babbling voices.

"What if they come back to life?"

"They're *dead*, Moira."

"Well, what if living ones come?"

"I need to get home to my kids."

"Shit, why aren't I taking pictures?" This person held his cell phone aloft.

Others' phones rang as frantic loved ones called. Dogs were barking everywhere, as if they sensed something was amiss.

"So what is this, the end of the world or something?"

"The end of theirs, anyway," Wayne said, gesturing at the fossils.

Car headlights pulled into Sherri's driveway, then were extinguished. Moments later, two dark figures walked toward the group clustered around the fireplace. Tania and Emmy stepped into its glow. Tania hugged Sherri for a long time, then hugged Dave. Then, she turned and slung an arm around Crystal's shoulders, pulling her oldest daughter against her.

"Ack! Don't choke me!" Crystal cried.

"Brat," Tania said. She met Wayne's eyes in the dancing red light.

He nodded at her and smiled. She gave him a nervous little smile in return.

"Hey, there's still some chicken," Dave said.

They opened more beers. Wayne raised his bottle above his head. "We should drink a toast to our new gods."

"Oh Wayne, don't say that," his mother said.

"Hey, they're the only gods we have evidence of. Maybe that's how they died…fighting over who was going to be our god."

"Like they'd even care about us," Crystal said.

"I'll drink to them," Dave said, lifting his own bottle. "I bet we won't be the only people worshipping them."

"Got to stay on their good side," Wayne said.

"Aw fuck it," Wayne's father slurred gruffly, cracking a fresh beer. "I'll drink to the bastards." He thrust his Irish red in the air.

All the others lifted their drinks high, then, like a group of irreverent cultists.

Another little gust of breeze rose up, and the black trees massed at the border of the property shifted and hissed, as if the phantom gods were whispering something alien and unknowable to acknowledge those who followed them.

Anchor

by John Langan

I

Fire and ruin march on heaven, Surtur
Brandishes his sword, Loki and his awful
Brood come for revenge. Who stands with me now
Stands in my doom.

James Ogin "Odin Foresees Ragnarok"

For the rest of what will be a long, long life, every
October Will Ogin will dream of this night. It will be one of
those dreams so vivid as to be indistinguishable from waking; for
all intents and purposes, he'll tell Manda, his wife, when he
reveals it to her, he might as well be back at the far end of the
driveway to his parents' house, standing beside his father.
Although the calendar welcomed autumn a couple of weeks
earlier, the trees are still holding onto a few of their leaves; the air
is unusually warm. It is nighttime. His father has switched on the
green lamppost beside the mailbox, the one they refer to as Mr.
Tumnus's Lamp. Its yellow light concentrates around its top in a
sphere, as if the surrounding darkness is a physical medium
against which it must push. To Will's twelve-year-old eyes, the
night seems heavier, somehow, thicker, and not only because he
is awake far later than he's ever been up with his dad, sleep-over
late. If he cranes his head back, he can see stars overhead without
having to squint too much against the lamppost's glow. Tonight,
his father told him, is the second night of the new moon, which
no doubt contributes to the stars' brightness, but he can't shake
the impression that the sky looks different, the figures whose
outlines the stars are supposed to mark gone, replaced by other,
unfamiliar arrangements. He pointed this out to Dad, who raised
his eyes to the heavens, then lowered them without comment.

The two of them haven't been at the end of the driveway for that long, but already, Will's arms are tired from holding the Chinese spear, the *qiang*, out in a forward guard. This isn't the waxwood version of the weapon with which he's trained at his father's studio in Wiltwyck; it's the real thing, nine feet of polished hardwood capped with a sharpened blade. He noticed it leaning against the house, beside the front steps, as Dad led them outside. His father carried it as they walked down and up the driveway, but once they reached the road, he held it out to Will, who said, "Really?" even as he took it. (He *never* got to handle the actual weapons, not like this.)

"Really," Dad said, unsheathing the long, curved sword, the *do*, he'd slid into the belt of his robe before they exited the house. Like the *qiang*, the *do* was serious business, its edge razor-keen, brought out only for cutting competitions at the big tournaments. His father shucked off his bathrobe. He was wearing his usual nighttime attire of old karate pants and worn t-shirt. He took the sword in both hands, squared his stance, and let the end of the blade dip into a middle guard, so that it was pointing towards the woods across the road. Will followed his lead, and leveled the spear in the same direction.

He had no idea, could not begin to guess what the two of them were doing there. As a rule, his dad was not prone to much in the way of erratic or unpredictable behavior, his limit being the occasional, spontaneous trip to Boice's in Wiltwyck for a hot fudge sundae or milkshake. He had never roused Will from his bed in the middle of the night. It had been Will, sick or pursued by nightmares, who had hauled him out of his slumber. Sitting up in bed a short time ago, blinking sleep from his eyes, Will asked what was wrong, his voice croaking. In reply, his father told him to find his sneakers, they needed to go outside. More asleep than awake, he did as instructed, clomping downstairs to find Dad at the front door, the *do* in its ornate sheath in his right hand. The sight of the sword—of that sword, in particular—jolted Will fully

182 | AUTUMN CTHULHU

awake. His dad pushed the *do* through his belt, opened the door, and stepped out into the dark. Especially once he saw the spear, Will assumed there was some kind of threat in the yard, an animal, he guessed, though one of the perverts from the boarding house at the other end of their street was also a possibility. He wasn't overly concerned which it was, too excited at being included in the defense of the house.

The longer they've stood with weapons ready, however, the more mysterious their purpose has become. By now, surely an animal would have revealed itself, or fled, likewise, a person. Will feels his father's concentration weighting the space around him, lending the air the same density that fills it in the run up to a thunderstorm. It's not an entirely unfamiliar sensation, but he associates it in general with the studio, when his dad is training in a new form, and in particular during the weeks immediately before his most recent black belt test, the one for third degree. Yet even the longest of those forms didn't last much beyond two minutes, and anyway, there was movement involved. Nor did his father mind if Will interrupted him as he was practicing his *hyung* ("I do Tang Soo Do for you and your mother," his mantra, "the art is for you, not the other way around"). He's less certain how his dad would respond to a break in his focus now.

When he hears the sounds coming from across the street, somewhere deep within the trees that run down the hillside there to the country road, Will is momentarily thrilled, to the point of happiness. Beside him, Dad lets out the briefest sigh, and Will realizes that his father is relieved, that he, too, has had his fill of waiting. A sense of connection, of love so fierce it causes his hands to tremble, the end of the *qiang* to quiver, sweeps him. He readjusts his grip on the spear, readies it for the source of the noise advancing up the hill toward them. Branches rustle and snap. A tree cracks like a rifle shot and rushes to thud on the ground. Another tree groans, as if a great weight is sliding against it. Something grunts, the deep note of a steam engine venting pressure. Bushes hiss as they drag on whatever is pushing through them. The dead leaves and pine needles that carpet the earth make a sound like sizzling as heavy feet shuffle closer. Before it appears between the trunks of a pair of birches, as if framed in a doorway, there is a moment when Will sees the darkness beyond the trees become darker still, occluded by a shape whose outline does not make sense. He glances at his father, whose jaw has tightened. He's on the verge of demanding, "What is this?" when the cause of the clamor passes the birch trees and into view.

It's a bear. Not one of the black bears native to upstate New York, no, this beast is the deep orange of fire overtaking wood. And larger, by several orders of magnitude, than any local species. Its blunt head is the size of the barrel they use for catching rain; the paws it lifts as big as the tires on his mother's Camry. The creature must weigh an actual ton. *A grizzly*, Will thinks. It's the only description that fits; though this bear seems beyond the dimensions of even the largest of that breed. Not to mention, an actual grizzly emerging from the woods across the street raises so many questions, he doesn't know which one to ask first.

When the bear's paws touch the road, it pauses. Its head cocks to the left, as if it has noticed Will and his dad for the first time, which it may have: Will isn't sure how much attention bears pay to their surroundings. Its lips peel back from yellow teeth the length of his palm, and the bear bellows, a long, low wave of sound that Will feels all the way down to his bones. It may be the single most frightening thing he has ever heard. He wants to run, would like nothing better than to cast the spear aside and head for home as fast as his legs will carry him, which he suspects would be far faster than they've run before. He can't, though, can't control any part of his body, from his legs and arms, which won't move, to his lip, which won't stop trembling, to his eyes, which are dangerously close to pouring tears down his cheeks. It isn't only the bear's roar; it's the animal's very presence, which streams at them like heat from a burning building. More than at any point in his life previous to this, Will has the sense of being in a circumstance beyond his ability to handle.

"Will." His father's voice reaches him from a long way away. He has the impression his dad has said his name a number of times. He tries to say, "Yes," but his mouth refuses anything more complex than, "Uh-huh."

"I want you to drop the end of the spear—not the tip, the end—to the ground. Can you do that for me?"

"Uh huh." To his surprise, he finds he can. He lowers the butt of the spear to the driveway's packed dirt surface.

"Good," his father says. His voice is slightly higher, but otherwise calm. "Now, if our friend over there decides to charge us—which I don't think he's going to do, but just in case—I want you to use the ground as a brace for the spear. This way, when he runs up against it, we'll have the earth helping us. Sound like a plan?"

"Uh huh." Words spill from him in a question: "Where should I aim the point?"

"Anywhere in his middle should do," Dad says. "His neck would be super, but his shoulders or chest would be fine, too. After you do that—after he sticks himself—I want you to get out of the way. It's too far to run back to the house, but you should be able to reach the Smiths' front door."

"What are you going to do?"

"I'm going to see if I can't convince this fellow to head in another direction."

"*No, Dad.*" Panic of a different kind seizes Will, loosens his hold on the spear.

"Steady," his father says. Will re-grips the *qiang*, redirects it at the bear, who is watching their exchange as if it understands them. "Good," his dad says. "Like I said, though, I don't believe our friend is going to do anything, *because what he's looking for isn't here.*"

For an instant, Will has the absurd impression that his father is speaking to the bear. The impression vanishes when the creature advances onto the road. Will digs the butt of the spear into the driveway's dirt; his dad shifts his hands on the sword's hilt ever-so-slightly. "Easy," Dad says, and now Will is certain he's talking to the enormous animal, which has paused in the middle of the street, less than ten feet from them. "Easy," he says. The bear's eyes focus on him. Will aligns the tip of the spear with a point to the right of and slightly below the bear's head, where he feels pretty sure there's a major blood vessels, like the carotid or the jugular in humans. This close, the bear's breath thunders in and out its lungs. Its smell floods his nostrils, a pungent mix of torn vegetation, rotted meat, and urine. If it charges, Will understands, his dad is going to draw its attack, allow him a chance to spear it. "Don't," he wants to say. "Don't worry about me. Move in quick and strike. Do what you're always telling me to do. Don't worry about me." Standing watching his father and bear stare at one another, the lamp at the end of the driveway casting deep shadows over the road, Will is struck by the absolute certainty that he is seeing his father in the last moments of his life. A combination of dread and acute sorrow washes through him, but he keeps the *qiang* trained on the spot on the bear's neck.

The bear snorts. There's something almost contemptuous in the gesture. It swings its outsized head to the right, the rest of its mountainous bulk shifting in the same direction. Slowly, it ambles up the street, towards the dead-end. Dad turns gradually, tracking the bear's progress with the point of his *do*. Will does the same with the spear. After the bear has been swallowed by darkness, they maintain their positions, listening to the tumult of its passage into the woods bordering the end of the road. Will is exhausted, hollowed out by the confrontation. His surroundings swim in and out of focus. The light from Mr. Tumnus's Lamp burns brighter, as if the darkness has receded. Where the beast stood, the space looks different, the air blacker, as if scorched by the creature's presence.

At some point after the night has grown quiet, the only sound the rush of a car speeding along the county road below, Will's father lowers his sword and turns to him. Dad's eyes are sunken, his cheeks drawn, the short hairs of his beard flecked with white. He looks ten years older than he did at the beginning of the last hour. "Come on," his father says, "I think we can go home now."

Will carries the spear back down and up the driveway. Until they're within sight of the cars parked beside the house, Dad walks with the sword unsheathed, although he leaves the point down. This is the time, Will knows, to ask his dad what just happened, but he cannot summon the energy for any action more complex than setting one foot in front of the other and keeping the spear from striking the ground. His father pauses by their SUV to slot the *do* into its scabbard. Without looking at Will, he says, "I don't think we need to tell your mother about this."

It's a ridiculous statement; as his parents like to say, their household runs on honesty. But Will nods anyway. He stares at the parking space to the left of the Saturn, where, until recently, his dad's friend, Carson, parked his truck while he was staying with them. A connection lights his brain; before he knows what he's saying, he says, "This was about Carson, wasn't it?"

Dad's eyebrows raise. It's confirmation enough, but he nods and says, "Yes, it was."

"Are we safe?"

His father is about to say, "Yes," because that's what dads do, they reassure you, tell you everything's going to be okay, regardless of the evidence. Something he notices in Will's face, some difference, stops the word on his lips. Instead, his dad says, "I'm not sure."

II
The highway is not a symbol, describes
No mythic transition, is blacktop and miles.

Carson Lochyer "Driving East on I-90"

When Will Ogin is eighteen and in his first semester at SUNY Huguenot, his Freshman Composition I teacher will assign the class an autobiographical essay, its topic, "A Time of Change." Its purpose, he'll understand, is to ease the class into writing by allowing them to discuss the transition from high school to college, which, while not the only possible response to the assignment, will be the one the teacher discusses with the class with the clear intent of steering them in that direction. After a brief conversation with his mother, herself a professor in the college's English department, Will will decide to write on a different event. He'll seat himself at his computer with a bottle of Dr. Pepper and spend the next three hours in a state somewhere between memory and reflection, his room, the sounds of the house, faint. By the time he's finished with the essay, he's breathing heavily, covered in sweat, as if he's just completed a lengthy workout. Although his mom has advised him always to sleep on his work, he e-mails the essay to his teacher then and there.

The following morning, Will reads what he wrote the night before over breakfast:

My time of change began when I was eight and a half years old, and continued until I was almost twelve. For those three and a half years, my father's friend, the poet Carson Lochyer, stayed with my parents and me,

renting a room that had been the office in which my dad wrote his poems. At the time, I didn't realize that Carson living with us was having such an important effect on me, but do you ever recognize the truly significant times in your life while they're happening?

Carson drove cross-country from Idaho to our house in early April. My father, especially, was concerned about him traveling at this time of year, due to the possibility of snow storms in the mountains and on the plains. Carson told him he had to come now if he was going to come at all. The trip took him three days, and my father had him call to check in every day. After he hung up the phone each night, Dad would announce, "Well, that's him through Montana," and I would look up his day's route in my mother's old Rand McNally road atlas.

Although my parents had gone to great lengths to make sure it was all right for my father's friend to come stay with us, I didn't really understand why he was leaving his home in the first place. In all the time he shared our house, I never spoke to Carson about it, either. It wasn't until a couple of years after he left that I finally thought to ask my parents what brought Carson to us. His marriage had failed, they told me, taking the rest of his life with it. He'd lost his job managing a Home Depot. He'd been asked to leave the school where he taught martial arts. He was seriously past due to turn in the manuscript for his next collection of poetry. He needed a change of scenery, a place to regroup. My parents discussed it, and my mother told my father to tell Carson he could live with us until he was back on his feet.

For three and a half years, Carson was part of

our household. He found a job at the Huguenot True Value, which took him out most days. Once he returned home, and on the days he wasn't at the hardware store, he went into his room and wrote. He wrote, and he wrote, and he wrote. Usually, his door was closed, but sometimes he left it open, and I would sneak a look at him on my way to the bathroom or to use the family computer. When I did, I saw him seated in front of his computer, the screen taken up by a page of whatever poem he was working on. He might be reclining in his chair, his chin resting on his right hand. Or he might be bent forward over the keyboard, leaning toward the screen as if he were riding a motorcycle. He liked to listen to music while he wrote, but he wore headphones. During his first six months with us, he was wrapping up *The Broken Circle*. My father loved it, said it was one of the great long poems of the last decade. Carson wasn't too crazy about it. I guess that was because he'd started it when he was still married to his ex, so there was all kinds of baggage attached to it. Dad went ahead and reviewed it for the *Los Angeles Review of Books*, and it went on to a better reception than Carson had been expecting. He spent the rest of his time with us writing the poems that went into his next book, *Ardor*. This was the one that won him the National Book Award, though not until after he'd moved out.

I didn't spend a lot of time with Carson. That was my father, who passed almost every night in conversation with him. Dad tried to get him to come to his karate studio, which Carson did a couple of times, but he said that what Dad was doing wasn't for him. My father's *dojang* was a typical American school, family-friendly, the majority of its students kids, classes split between warm up, traditional curriculum, and an assortment of fun activities. If you were a serious student, you could train with the senior students, the red and black belts, whose sessions focused more on traditional material. The goal was student retention, which, Dad said, meant that he had to be willing to come and go with people. Carson had studied with an instructor in Boise who worked with only adults, and whose goal was to teach his students how to survive life-or-death confrontations. It was what the martial arts were originally about, Carson said. If students weren't happy with what his instructor was teaching them, they knew where the door was. I trained at my father's studio, and if Carson heard me complaining about the night's workout, he was ready with a story about the kind of training he'd had to do, most of it a lot of push-ups and sit-ups. There was a kind of purity to Carson's view of the martial arts, an intensity that came from his focus. He told me that he'd spent six months perfecting his middle punch, day after day working on the same technique. I was impressed by his discipline, but I preferred Dad's approach, which catered to my youthful short attention span. I guess you could say that Carson focused on the martial part of the martial arts, and Dad favored the art part of it.

They were like that in their poetry, too. Carson was a fan of James Dickey and Charles Simic. My father loved Robert Browning and Jorie Graham. Carson's poems were direct, concentrated. Dad's were evasive, diffuse. In Carson's work, what you might call rough men and women came up against a Nature that was even rougher, and sometimes beautiful, as well. In my father's poems, there are an awful lot of academics, who confront creatures borrowed from ancient myths, and who spend a lot of time thinking about what's happening to them. The funny thing is, they loved one another's writing. They always said that was why they had become friends. An editor who'd published both of them in her journal sent Dad an e-mail telling him he should check out Carson's poems. Dad did, liked what he read, and contacted Carson. "And thus," my mother likes to say, "was born the bromance of the century." They corresponded; they talked on the phone; they roomed together at conferences and festivals. Eventually, they lived under the same roof.

None of this, I realize, answers the question of what role, exactly, Carson played in my time of change. He didn't cause the change; although it began not long after he arrived at our house. My mother was away for a couple of weeks, visiting her mother in Scotland. I had become obsessed with a TV show called *River Monsters*, which was about an English naturalist and angler who traveled the world looking for rivers where people said they'd been attacked by monster fish. The star of the show, Jeremy Wade, would talk to the locals, do research, then go fishing for the monster. Of course, what he caught were never monsters, strictly speaking, but local fish that could have been responsible for the attacks: giant catfish, arapaima, bull sharks, sawfish, tiger fish, and more.

Inspired by the show, I asked my father if I could go fishing, and to my surprise, he said I could. (Maybe he was running out of ways to occupy me with Mom away; I can't remember.) We went to Wal-Mart, where he bought me my first fishing rod, a Zebco spincast that came with a little plastic tackle box. Dad, who was not a fisherman, had watched a couple of YouTube videos on basic lure tying. We set up the rod and drove to a small pond he'd read online was full of fish and good for beginners. Later, he told me he was waiting to see how I would react if and when I hooked anything.

He found out with my second cast. A good sized largemouth bass took my lure, and suddenly, I was in a situation right out of *River Monsters*, fighting to bring in a fish that was fighting hard against me, splashing the water, jumping out of the pond as it tried to throw the hook. My rod bent. The line vibrated. I held on and drew the fish in. Dad was somewhere beside me, murmuring encouragement. As soon as I had the fish close enough to shore, I handed the rod to Dad, kneeled down, and took the fish by the lower lip. He thrashed so hard I almost lost my grip on him. But I didn't, and I guess you might say that the fish never lost his grip on me, either. I knew, as surely as I've known anything, that I had found my life's passion, the same as my father had when he first read *The Ring and the Book.* On the drive home, I was already planning my next fishing trip—was already planning a lifetime of fishing trips.

I have to admit, right from the start, my parents supported my fishing. They took me to all the local lakes and ponds, rivers and creeks, and to some that weren't all that local, too. If they had friends who fished, they invited them to join us so that their friends could give me pointers on my technique. They found instructional videos for me to watch on YouTube. They subscribed to *Bass Pro* for me. But despite all of this, fishing wasn't something either of my parents truly shared with me. No matter how many spots they drove me to, they weren't interested in picking up a rod and joining me in trying to catch something. Instead, whichever one of them had taken me brought a book, which they would sit reading while I fished. Now that I'm older, I can appreciate how much they did for me just taking me out as much as they did. At the time, though, I wanted more of a connection with them over fishing.

This was where Carson came in. He had grown up fishing in Idaho. In fact, his father had been a professional guide in the Salmon River part of the state, leading parties of businessmen along the river for week-long fishing trips. Carson had accompanied his dad on numerous trips, and he had plenty of stories about his adventures trying to hook fish in all kinds of terrain, in all kinds of conditions. He was full of stories about his father's fishing experiences, too, though a lot of these had to do with the characters his dad had contracted to guide, including at least one group of *Mafioso* who flew in from Seattle. It was Carson who first gave me the idea that I could be a guide, too, and that I could have a good life doing so (which my parents were concerned about; although they denied it). If I returned home having made a big catch, Carson was there to give me his approval, fisherman to fisherman. A "Good job!" from him made me swell with pride, made my head feel as if it was brushing the ceiling. The funny thing was, in all the time he stayed with us, I can't remember him coming to fish with me once. It didn't matter. His praise, his support, did.

Carson left my house with much less warning than I'd had before he arrived. My father was the one who told me Carson was going. It was a Sunday night. I suppose I'd known that Carson would be moving out at some point. After all, from the start, my parents had said he was going to stay with us until he got back on his feet, which implied a time when he would walk off on his own. I did my best not to show how surprised I was (because I was almost twelve, and concerned with acting mature). Instead, I asked Dad when Carson was planning to go. "Tuesday, I think," he said. This seemed pretty soon to me. "Where's he going?" I asked. "To our friend, Gaetan's, in Gloucester," he said. This seemed pretty far away, too. "Why does he have to go now?" I asked. "It's time for Carson to move on," Dad said.

That was what he did, setting out for Massachusetts while I was at school on Tuesday. I tried talking to him on Monday night, as I was helping him retrieve the last of the stuff he'd stored in our garage and load it into his truck. He was distracted, as though his mind was already on the road east. I kept making conversation, mentioning fishing spots my father had yet to take me to, the species of fish that were supposed to inhabit them, the lures I planned to use. Carson answered in short, vague sentences. There was so much more I wanted to say to him, a lot of it things I didn't know how to put into words. I'm glad you've been here with us. Thank you for supporting my fishing. Please don't go. I left all of it unsaid, and then he was gone.

My dad and Carson stayed in touch, via e-mail and the occasional phone call. They saw one another at the occasional conference. After almost a year in Gloucester, Carson left for Toronto, where he stayed until this past spring, when Dad said he was on the move again, this time for Iceland. Over the years, I've talked to him a couple of times, when he's called for my father and I've answered the phone. There isn't much to our conversations. He asks me how the fishing's going, and I tell him. He might offer a suggestion as to lures. Before I pass the phone to my dad, Carson says, "Sounds like you're doing great. Keep at it. You'll be running your own guide business in no time." Absurd as it might sound, those words never fail to make me feel better, to hope—to believe that someday, I'll be leading men and women into the wilderness to fish. If and when I do, it will be because Carson Lochyer supported me, never stopped encouraging me.

Sometimes, I think it would be nice to have Carson with me when I set out on my first tour. Then I realize, he will be.

III
The blade burns in the grip of the noble
Heart. Take it, and your heart be made known.

James Ogin "Dyrnwyn"

Of course, Will won't mention the incident with the enormous bear in his essay, in part because his father will not have explained how the creature's appearance connects to Carson, exactly. In all fairness to his dad, Will will have avoided asking for such an explanation, on the let-sleeping-dogs-(or bears)-lie principle. On top of that, the event will seem too strange to write down and hope to be believed. Nor will Will mention something that happened a couple of days prior to

Carson's decision to leave, but that, with the passage of time, seems to have heralded it. It occurred in the evening, after homework and dinner. He was at the family computer, playing *Hungry Games*. Due to the unusually warm weather, the windows in the computer room were up, admitting a slight breeze, which nudged the curtains. So involved was Will in surviving to the death match portion of the game and then, once there, in defeating the other finalists, that it took a while for him to register the voices outside the windows: his father and Carson, promenading back and forth along the stone path that ran from the front steps to the driveway. As interested in the conversations of adults as any boy his age, Will rose from the computer chair and moved to the couch, which sat below the windows. Lowering his head to give the impression he'd switched places in order to read, he glanced outside.

His dad was wearing a pair of old karate pants and the black t-shirt printed with the *Famous Monsters of Filmland* cover showing Godzilla and Gamera squaring off. Carson was dressed in long, olive shorts and a faded red t-shirt with the Flash's yellow lightning bolt on it. Dad's hands were clasped behind his back, which, Will had learned, he did to aid the impression he was taking what you were saying to him seriously. Carson's hands were a flurry of motion, in front of him, at his sides, back in front of him, weaving through the air as they did when he was speaking about something that mattered to him. Will looked down at his imaginary book. He couldn't hear much of what his father, who tended to talk softly, was saying. It was easier to distinguish Carson's words, though not what they were referring to. "Absolutely," he said.

Dad murmured.

"The weather, for one thing. It was like this the last time."

Dad said something that ended in, "—incidence?"

"Not with the dreams," Carson said. "Not together like

this."

Dad asked another question.

"A sign."

"Where?" Dad said.

"Somewhere close," Carson said. "I don't think there'd be anything on your property, not yet. But somewhere close."

Will couldn't hear his father's next remark, but the nod he gave toward the driveway suggested he was inviting Carson to walk it. "Yeah, sure, that's a good idea," Carson said, and the two of them set off in that direction.

There was fishing gear in the back of the SUV that Will had been meaning to bring in since yesterday. He tugged on his sneakers and hurried outside. While he opened the hatch and unloaded his tackle box, net, and rods, he kept an eye on his dad and Carson. They were ambling up the driveway, pausing every few yards to peer into the woods on either side of it. Whatever they were searching for amidst the maple, oak, and cedar remained elusive, since they continued toward the road. By the time Will had run his equipment into the house and returned to close the hatch, his father and Carson had covered half the driveway's length. Will leapt, caught the hatch, and heaved it shut. Then he took off after Dad and Carson.

The two of them glanced back at the slap of his sneakers on the dirt. His father half-turned to face him. "Hey, wee man. What's up?"

"Oh, not much," Will said. "Whatcha doing?"

"We are looking for something," Dad said.

"What?"

"We're not exactly sure," Dad said.

"Something...with fire," Carson said.

"Is someone setting fires on our property?" Will said.

"No," Dad said. "We're just checking something out. You can help, if you want. Always good to have another pair of eyes."

"Sure," Will said. He liked being included in his father's and Carson's activities.

"Good," Dad said.

Together, they climbed the driveway as it rose to the street. Will stared into the ranks of trees, their branches stripped by autumn, but saw no tell-tale flashes of orange. This past week, the days had been hot and dry, dangerous conditions should a spark fall on the leaves matting the ground. His father wasn't acting all that concerned, but tension poured off Carson like a fever. Will was aware that his dad and Carson had continued the conversation whose fragments he'd overheard, only stopping when he joined them, and whatever its substance had been hung in the air between them.

They reached the end of the driveway a couple of minutes after the sun had lowered behind the ridge on the far side of their little valley. Like cobblestones, clouds formed a path that led down after the hidden sun, whose glow dyed the clouds a deep, purplish pink. Will, his dad, and Carson scanned the trees around them, on the other side of the street. From the placid expression on his father's face, Will could tell that he considered whatever he and Carson were discussing settled, and in his favor. Dad loved to be right. Once, when Will was younger, he'd run across the expression, "He'd rather be right than President," in an old comic strip he was reading. After his mom explained what it meant to him, he said, "Like Dad." Which made her laugh and tell him not to say that to his father. It was true, though, and one of the qualities he least liked in his father.

"There." Carson pointed across the road—at first, Will thought, to the trees over there, which didn't make any sense, because they'd looked at them already and not seen anything. His vision adjusted, and he realized that Carson had seen something through the trees, near the top of the ridge opposite them. It was a line of fire, as if someone had poured gasoline along a hundred foot stretch of the hill and touched a match to it. In the evening light, the flames rose and rippled orange. As the three of them watched, the line shifted. Its ends curved, the left lower, the right higher, the left swinging underneath the line, the right arcing over it, until the ends met in the line's center, turning it into a figure-eight. Almost as quickly as they met, the ends whipped out in their original directions. It was as if, Will thought, they were watching a performance, a group of dancers, each one carrying a torch, executing a series of carefully-choreographed steps. Except there appeared to be no breaks in the line, which you would have expected there to be, if it was composed of separate people. Instead, they seemed to be looking at a solid line of flame, behaving in ways Will had never heard of fire acting.

A handful of trees on the ridge had ignited. Will could pick out additional spots where the ground was burning. The flaming line writhed like a snake. Will was waiting for his father, for Carson, to say something, but neither man did, caught up in the distant spectacle. Finally, he said, "Shouldn't we call 911?"

Dad and Carson started, jostled from whatever thoughts the spectacle had kindled in them. The whine of a local siren, followed close behind by those of neighboring stations, announced that someone had notified the fire department first. The three of them witnessed the line of flame curl into a spiral, which tightened into a circle, which fell apart into a dozen smaller conflagrations that splashed themselves onto trees, lighting them. Dad and Carson took this as their cue to turn around and start back toward the house. Will accompanied them.

Later that night, the odor of charred wood drifted into Will's room, through the windows he'd left open because of the heat.

IV

The eyes are difficult.

Carson Lochyer "Taxidermy"

The July after he turns twenty-seven, Will and Manda (then still his girlfriend) will drive to a spacious house outside of Brattleboro, Vermont, for a week's stay. It will be a working vacation. Manda brings books with her so she can study for the New York State bar exam. Will brings his fishing rods, tackle, and notebook so he can explore possible destinations for the fishing guide business he's finally started. The house at which they stay is a blended living room and kitchen surrounded by eight plain bedrooms and two and a half bathrooms; in the winter, it rents to ski parties. Will has the idea that, in the summer, it might accommodate fishing groups, which he's shared with the house's owner, gaining a modest discount on the charge for the week.

There's a half-stocked bookcase on one side of the living room, its shelves full of thrift-store rescues. Will flips through them, a habit picked up from his parents, who are unable to enter a room with a bookcase without inspecting its contents. The majority of the books are split between mysteries and spy thrillers, Agatha Christie and Sue Grafton rubbing elbows with Robert Ludlum and Len Deighton. In amongst them, Will finds a thick paperback, its red cover faded to burnt orange. On the spine, he reads *Shardik*, and under it, Richard Adams. He recognizes the name from his mother's bookshelves: it's one of the novels she's taught in her young adult literature class, *Watership Down*. She encouraged him to read the book; he started it, but can't remember finishing it. He slides *Shardik* out for a look. From the center of the cover, a bear's head stares at him. The artist has drawn it mounted on a wooden disk like a hunting trophy, but has left the eyes empty, giving the head the appearance of a mask. Though hardly the most realistic illustration he's encountered, something about it makes him pause, consider it before slotting it back between its companions.

Later that same day, though, after an exploratory trip to a local creek and a dinner of Chinese take-out, Will returns for *Shardik*. Manda is on the living room couch, surrounded by law books. He carries the novel to the easy chair across from her, settles into it, and opens the book. Between the drive here and the afternoon's fishing, he's pretty tired, and anticipates nodding off after the first couple of pages, especially in such a comfortable chair.

To his surprise, he doesn't fall asleep. He stays awake until two in the morning, long past Manda's retreat to bed, unable to stop reading Adams's story of Kelderek, hunter in an invented land, and Shardik, the great bear Kelderek takes as a god. The narrative begins with the bear crashing through the trees of a forest on fire, and that image, of a creature prehistorically-large, wreathed in flame, lights his mind's eye for the remainder of the night, and for the next four days, which is how long it takes him to finish the book.

It's been a while since a work of fiction has affected him this profoundly. During his visits to nearby creeks, part of him remains inside the narrative. Or it remains inside him: he isn't sure which statement is correct, only that, were Shardik himself to burst out of the sugar maples, his fur smoldering, and plunge steaming into the stream Will is wading, he would not be surprised. Planning this trip, he was worried that he might be bored after he finished his day's fishing and Manda was still deep in her textbooks, as she had cautioned him she would be. Adams's novel solves the problem before it arises.

Will does not dream of his and his father's confrontation with their own enormous bear, almost fifteen years gone by. If asked about this, he might admit it strange, or might shrug it off. A couple of times as he's reading, that distant night bobs at the surface of his thoughts, but it's swept away by the novel's progress.

When he and Manda leave the house, Will takes the book with him, something he has never done before. For the next ten years, the copy of *Shardik* accompanies him whenever he sets off on a fishing trip of any length. He rereads it on airplanes, on trains, and on ferries. He rereads it by the light of campfires, of ancient light bulbs, of assorted flashlights. Over time, the glue binding the book fails, and he resorts to a heavy rubber band to maintain the novel's integrity. At last, when he's guiding a group of advertising executives up French Creek in Idaho (not that far from where Carson grew up), the rubber band breaks, sending the pages of the novel swirling off on the breeze that's been blowing. Will succeeds in retrieving a few of the pages, but the majority of the book is gone, floating on the surface of the creek, above the trout with their empty gold eyes.

V

Here, in the combustion of dry wood, may
The pistoning of creation's engine be
Glimpsed.

James Ogin "Pyromancy"

February of his thirty-fifth year, Will will be struck by the worst case of the flu he ever has had or will have. It's a direct result of his skipping the year's vaccine, which he did for no good reason that he can recall. He was busy: with the guide business that's gone much better than he'd hoped; with Dana, his and Manda's older daughter, whose kindergarten class encourages active parental participation in its curriculum; with Flora, their younger daughter, who's been putting her big sister's record of the terrible twos to shame. Manda, returned to her law firm in Wiltwyck after a long maternity leave following the complications of Flora's birth, had been preoccupied with a defense for which she was supposed to be junior counsel, but which she was pretty much running, and Will has tried to step in to allow her the extra time she needed for the case. He meant to have himself vaccinated—he always does—but the early report pronounced this year's flu neither particularly contagious nor virulent, especially compared to those of the last couple of years, so if he couldn't find the time for his annual inoculation, he figured he'd probably be fine.

The extent of his error becomes clear the moment the disease overtakes him. He's sitting on the couch in his study, reading a memoir of fly-fishing the Catskills one of his mother's colleagues published a couple of years ago, and that he's been meaning to open ever since a copy arrived in the mail, autographed and with a personal message to him. The room is uncomfortably warm around him. He wonders if Manda, always complaining that he sets the thermostat too low, has adjusted it upward. His head is light, the way it is when he's gone too long between meals and his blood sugar crashes. Bookmarking his page with his index finger, he goes to stand, and the shivering starts. It begins as a trembling that keeps him seated, and swiftly escalates to a shaking that convulses his arms and legs as if he's having a seizure. His teeth rattle together with such force, they blur his vision. He loses his grip on the book, which flops to the floor. The sound catches the notice of Manda, on her way into her study. She alters course and enters his room. "Hon?" she says. "Are you okay?"

"Flu," Will wants to say, because that's what it is, he knows, but all he can pronounce is a stuttered "f."

It's enough for Manda, who says, "Oh God, you're sick, aren't you?" While he's trying to nod, she places her hand on his forehead. "You're burning up," she says. "Hang on. We'll get you taken care of."

For the next week, Will spends his days and nights on the pull-out bed in his study. Much of the time, he's asleep, which is fine, because when he isn't, he feels terrible. Every muscle in his body aches, as if he's received the mother of all beatings. If he has to stand to go to the bathroom, his arms and legs seem to be wrapped in lead. When he coughs, his chest is full of razor blades, his temples pound. Worst of all is the fever, which quickly soars to the dangerous heights above 104 and dips only a little with the administering of aspirin. After a day and a half of the highest readings she's seen on a thermometer, Manda phones the family doctor. The nurse to whom she speaks gives her a list of instructions, most of which she's following already, and tells her that if Will's temperature persists at this level through the night, she's going to have to take him to the emergency room. At the nurse's recommendation, Manda fills the bathtub with cool water and empties all the ice trays in the freezer into it. Through a combination of jollying and bullying, she raises Will off the pull-out bed, leads him into the bathroom, and undresses him. Standing this near his bare skin, she feels the fever burning in it. She guides Will into the water, cold and clattering with ice cubes, as their two girls watch from the doorway in wide-eyed fascination.

For Will, the ice-bath happens at a distance, as if he's watching it on the TV on the other side of the living room. He sees himself leaning forward so Manda can scoop water from the bath with one of the girls' bath toys and pour it over his head and neck. The spill and splash of the water sounds faint, as if the volume on the TV has been lowered almost to zero. Ice cubes bob against his legs and back; the contact registers as a faint disturbance. He understands that the water in which he's sitting, which his wife continues to tip over his shoulders, his back, is cool, blessedly so, but his understanding makes scant difference to the conflagration raging beneath his skin. Absurdly, he remembers a phrase from a poem his father read to him, years ago, about a man on fire, consumed by a gift he had not asked for, but had earned. Who wrote that, Dad or Carson? Or someone else?

While the bathroom, Manda, have remained at a remove from Will, another vista has opened for him, as if someone has switched on a second TV, this one closer to him. On its screen, he sees the end of a driveway, the portion of road to which it connects. It's nighttime, the only illumination offered by a green lamppost set back ten feet from the street. Will recognizes Mr. Tumnus's Lamp, the driveway to his parents' house. The trees bare of all but a handful of leaves tell him that it's autumn. At the limit of the lamppost's glow, a pair of figures stand facing the road and the woods across it. One is holding a *do*, a curved Korean sword, in a middle guard. The other has leveled a *qiang*, a Chinese spear, toward the opposite side of the street. Will knows the scene from twenty-three years before, but a number of the details are wrong. His father and he look not as they did then, but as they do now. Dad is thinner, slightly stooped, his beard and hair fully white. Will is wearing the white Joe's Flies t-shirt and grey sweatpants that are his sleeping attire. The woods across from them have changed, the maples and oaks replaced by a thicket like simplified drawings of trees, tall trunks leading up to round crowns of green leaves. From somewhere within the new trees, orange light flickers.

As this scene appears closer to him, its images more distinct, so are its other details more vivid, as if he's drifting into this space. The spear's polished wood is smooth in his palms. His shoulders and upper arms ache from holding the weapon in one position for so long. The night air is warm, threaded with an odor like oranges on the turn. A breeze rustles the weird trees, whose leaves clash together with a metallic sound. His father's breaths are deep, steady. In a low voice, he's reciting a poem he and

Will's mom have quoted back and forth to one another for as long as he can remember:

> So rested he by the Tumtum tree
> And stood awhile in thought.

> And, as in uffish thought he stood,
> The Jabberwock, with eyes of flame,
> Came whiffling through the tulgey wood,
> And burbled as it came!

The orange light brightens, tinting the trunks and crowns of the trees. A wave of heat rolls over the road, enveloping Will and his dad. He blinks at the sudden dryness in his eyes. A chorus of creaks and moans issues from the trees. Their leaves crackle and crisp, shriveling brown. Sweat slides down Will's face, soaks his t-shirt, his sweatpants. The wood of the *qiang* is warm in his hands. Orange light floods the woods across the street, joined now by a rushing sound, as if a great wind is sweeping up the hillside. Will's mouth is tacky, his clothes drenched. He removes his right hand from the spear long enough to drag the back of it across his forehead and eyebrows, to wipe the sweat from his eyes. Inside the orange glow, there's something moving, a patch of darker orange mixed with yellow and red. It brushes against a tree, and the trunk detonates with a *BANG!* that Will feels in his chest. The crowns of the strange trees, full moments ago, are naked, each stripped to an intricate weave of branches, their leaves reduced to a fall of dust. The moving form draws closer, gaining definition with each step. The bark of the weird trees blackens, seems to bubble as if metallic and melting. Each breath burns Will's throat, his lungs. Another tree bursts, almost at the road. Will ducks, jerking the spear up in defense. Pieces of sizzling wood fly past him.

"Steady," his father says. "He's almost here." He's panting with the heat himself.

As if to fulfill his dad's prediction, the shape at the heart of the light steps between a pair of trees onto the road. It's a bear, its massive bulk wrapped in flame. Fire runs up its front and rear legs in long, orange tongues. Fire rages along its sides, its back, in flickering sheets. Fire envelops its blunt head, vents from its eyes, its mouth, its nostrils. Despite the inferno surrounding it, the bear is not consumed, nor does it move with the panic and agony of a creature dying. It raises its snout and considers Will and his dad through fiery eyes.

Somehow, Will manages enough spit to speak. "Dad?"

"Uh huh?"

"What the fuck is this?"

"Language," his father says.

"Seriously?"

"Seriously."

"Fine," he says, amazed to find that even in a situation of such extremity as this, his dad can exasperate him. "What is this?"

"This is our pledge," Dad says, "to a friend."

"Carson."

"Yes."

"I don't understand."

"I'm not certain I do, either."

"Dad?"

"Uh huh?"

"I'm scared."

"Me, too," his father says. "Every time, I think it'll be easier. Somehow, it never is."

"What do you mean?"

"Never mind. Don't worry if you're afraid. My sphincter's got all it can do to control itself. Just stand and be true."

"Huh."

"What?"

"That's nice," Will says. "'Stand and be true.' Did you write it?"

"Thank Stephen King."

"If this thing comes any closer, I won't be thanking anyone for anything."

"He won't," dad says. "*What he's searching for isn't here.* It hasn't been for a long, long time."

The bear narrows its eyes. The flames swirling around it flare, too bright to endure. Will shuts his eyes against the blaze, the insides of his eyelids lit red. This would be a perfect moment for the creature to charge, while the two of them are blinded. Although the *qiang* burns in his hands, he keeps its point aimed at the bear, hoping that, should it rush them, it'll strike the end of the spear before the rest of the weapon bursts into flame.

"Steady," his father says. "*What he wants isn't here.*"

The interiors of Will's eyelids glow white. Heat scorches his face, his arms. His clothes smolder.

"Stand," Dad says. "*Stand*, William."

"WILLIAM!"

Manda's shout is accompanied by a pail full of water dashed in Will's face. A single ice cube smacks his right cheek, directly below the eye. Will splashes backward in the tub, hands raised against the second pail of water his wife is preparing. The bathroom telescopes right up to him. "Okay," he says, "okay, okay."

"Are you all right?" Manda says. "Because for a second there, it looked like you were having a seizure."

A seizure? he thinks. *Is that what all that was?* "I'm okay," he says, lowering his hands. "I'm still sick, but I think the fever's gone down."

"Really?"

"Yeah." He says this mostly to reassure Manda, but the words sound as if they might be true.

They are. The worst of his fever has passed, and while he will continue to feel the flu's effects for days to come, he will not experience the same sense of dislocation—of relocation, of what he supposes must have been a febrile hallucination. (He doesn't believe it was a seizure.) For a couple of weeks after he's better, Will considers phoning his parents, sharing his overheated brain's invention with his dad. *Maybe*, he thinks, *the old man can get a poem out of it.* A couple of times, he has the cell in hand, his parents' number onscreen.

He doesn't, though, for a reason he can't specify. Next year, however, he's first in line for his flu shot.

VI

Do not run, the Park Service pamphlet warns—instead, turn,

Raise your arms, make yourself menacing,
Or the big cat will pounce.

Carson Lochyer "The Puma"

September of the year he turns forty, Will and Manda will take the girls out of school for two weeks for a family trip to Provence. They'll go to meet Will's mother and father, there for a two-day conference devoted to his father's and Carson's poetry, which is being held at the *Université d'Avignon*. There's a chance Carson will join them. After moving from Toronto to Iceland, his dad's friend has continued eastward across the Atlantic, first to the northwest of Scotland for almost five years, then on to Holland, Germany, and now Finland, to a small town in Lapland whose name Will has saved on his phone because he finds it impossible to remember.

Through his father, Will has learned of Carson's rumblings of another departure, this one for a destination still more remote, Nepal or Mongolia. For the foreseeable future,

Provence is likely his best chance to introduce Carson to his wife and children, none of whom has met him, since Carson rarely ventures back in the direction from which he came. Even his Pulitzer a couple of years ago could not dislodge him from his log cabin above the Arctic Circle; instead, Will's dad collected it for him. Will himself has not seen Carson in person since his departure from his parents' house almost three decades gone by. The desire to do so now grips him. From brief phone conversations and e-mail exchanges he's had with Carson over the years, as well as from what his father has told him, Will knows that Carson is aware of his career as a fishing guide, has read the write-ups on him in *Bass Pro* and *Sports Illustrated*, and has watched the clips of his appearances on a couple of the better fishing shows. But Will wants to see him in person, to shake his hand and thank him for his long-ago support. He wants to show him his wife and children, the best parts of his life. These last few years, there have been a couple of times he's been in close enough proximity to Carson's current address to consider dropping in for a visit, only to be dissuaded by his father. "You know Carson," Dad's said to Will's calls to check his address, "he's funny about his privacy." Will has heeded his dad's words and respected Carson's privacy; now, though, if Carso is joining them, then there's nothing to be concerned about. He even nourishes a secret hope of convincing Carson to accompany him for a little fishing on a couple of the local streams, and has packed an extra rod in case that hope becomes reality.

It does not. In fact, Carson does not fly down to meet them after all. In response to the news, Will's parents offer one another a philosophical shrug. Dana and Flora barely register the news, while Manda expresses her regret for Will's sake. His parents know the region, to which they've been traveling since before Will's birth, sufficiently well to take the family on a number of day trips: to Nîmes, Les Baux, Arles, Les Saintes Maries de la Mer, and Aigues-Mortes. Both girls demonstrate a facility with French that surprises and pleases Will and Manda; by the end of their first week there, Dana and Flora are carrying on short, basic conversations in the language with their grandparents. Informed by their previous trips to the area, plus the advice of some of the professor and students from the university, the six of them search out fine restaurant after fine restaurant for lunch and dinner. Even Manda, whose parents ran a restaurant in Wiltwyck and is usually difficult to please in such matters, has no complaints. Will fishes here and there, but not as much as he—or any of the other members of his family—was anticipating. Strange as it sounds, he can't move past his annoyance with Carson for not showing up. *How many more chances*, he thinks, *are we going to have to see one another?*

He talks to his father about it over lunch on a day when his mom, Manda, and the girls are away at the open markets outside Aigues-Mortes. Dad doesn't say anything while his speaking, eating his *croque-monsieur et frites* with his head cocked slightly to one side in what Will thinks of as his listening pose. The depth of emotion in his voice, the venom with which he treats Carson's peculiarities, surprises Will. Once he's finished, he sits watching his father, half-eager for him to argue with his complaint.

Instead, his dad says, "You're right. Carson can be a real asshole."

"What?"

"How hard would it have been for him to fly here? He could have spent a night and left the next morning. The university would have paid for everything; although, it's not as if he couldn't have afforded it. Trust me: the Pulitzer does wonders for your bank account."

The bitterness in his father's words shocks Will. "Dad," he says, unsure what to say next.

"Never mind," his dad says with a grimace. "You brought another rod with you, right? Let's go fishing."

Will recognizes his father's tactic, attempting to use fishing to distract him from what's bothering him. It's a familiar technique, one his dad has employed to meet any number of disappointments in Will's life, from the end of high school romances to failing his driver's test the first time he sat it. He hasn't used it for years, since a particularly difficult spell he and Manda went through after Flora was born. While his father has written about fishing in some of his poems, he's never been enamored of actual angling. For him to suggest it to Will is an index of his concern and love. "All right," Will says. "Why not? Let's go catch some trout."

No clear destination in mind, the two of them take his parents' rented Renault south, toward the Camargue with its marshes and canals. The afternoon is warm and bright. A French pop song neither of them can understand pulses from the radio. A series of right-hand turns down increasingly-smaller roads takes them, eventually, to a dirt parking lot off the left hand side of the road, next to a canal running between tall, thick reeds. It's as likely a spot as any. Will ties a couple of multi-purpose lures to the ends of their lines, and they set out along the water, following a path through the reeds made, Will supposes, by other fishermen. Within five minutes, the car is out of sight behind them. Were it not for a contrail tracking a jet's progress across the blue bowl of the sky, he and his father might have stepped back one hundred, two hundred, five hundred years into the past. On their left, the reeds fall back from a patch of grass sloping to the water. "This should do me fine," Dad says. Will fishes the spot with him for a few minutes, then sets off deeper into the reeds. He isn't worried about his father catching anything; already, Dad's eyes are focusing on that middle distance in which he appears to sight most of his poems. Reeds clatter against one another as Will pushes them aside. Ahead, on his right, there's something beside the path.

It's a piece of stone, rectangular, rising out of the earth

like a headstone. Gray-white, its upper left corner worn away, its surface spider-webbed with cracks, the marker gives the impression of considerable age. This feeling is reinforced by the image barely-visible on it. Executed in the plain style of a medieval woodcut, a strange animal rears on its hind legs between a pair of simple trees. It's been carved in profile, and at first, Will thinks it's supposed to be a lion. The tail is wrong, though, segmented, insectile, capped with what appears to be a miniature sun. Nor is the head any more accurate: rather than following the line of the back, it rises into what might be a man's head (the wear is especially bad here). Unfamiliar symbols have been cut into the picture's border, a circle broken at about the five o'clock mark, a double arch, a downward-facing crescent, others faded beyond identification. Will glances side to side, on the lookout for other markers. He isn't sure what the purpose of the stone was. Neither its position nor its decoration indicate it stationed a pilgrimage route; nor is Will aware of major local battles it might commemorate. Probably a legend or tradition of the region. His father will know; he'll ask him on the way back.

The two hours Will passes fishing the canal slide by in a dazzle of late-afternoon sunlight and sweltering heat. A couple of times, a fish investigates his lure, only to swim off without taking it. The sun turns the water platinum. Something rattles the reeds across the canal from him, but does not show itself. Random mosquitoes brave the heat and light for a chance at his blood; he crushes them against his arms and neck in red asterisks. Brightness fills his eyes, makes everything around him seem faded, less substantial. ("Easy," his father says, somewhere in the recesses of his memory.) Finally, he decides he's sat beside this stretch of water long enough. He hooks the lure to his rod and heads back toward the spot he left his dad.

On the way, he intends to have another look at the stone marker with its strange creature. He should have taken a picture of it with his phone. He'll remedy that oversight when he reaches it. At the place where the stone rectangle stood, however, there's nothing. Did he misjudge the marker's location? He walks ahead fifteen, twenty feet, doubles back, peering into the reeds. Nothing. Could he have taken another path? It seems unlikely: there's the canal a few feet behind him. He must have passed the rectangle longer ago than he realized. He shakes his head, still fuzzy with the heat.

As he continues on the path to the spot he left his father, Will notices that the landscape around him has fallen silent. There's the clack of the reeds striking one another when he brushes them, the pad of his shoes on the earth, and that is all. No birds chirp or cluck or take flight with a whir. No insects whine or buzz or hum. No cars are faintly audible in the distance. He looks up, and sees no airplanes crossing the sky, the contrail he observed earlier long since blown away. It's as if there's only him, the canal, and the reeds.

And something else, he realizes. A kind of quiet within the quiet, out in the reeds maybe twenty feet to his left. He's spent enough time out of doors—sometimes very far out of doors—to know that there's animal in the reeds, keeping pace with him. He isn't certain what it could be. A deer? A dog, patrolling the border of whoever's property he's encroached upon? Hasn't he read about an uptick in the number of feral pigs in Europe? No, it's bigger than that. What if whatever it is came upon his father first? He knows he should maintain a measured pace, in order not to provoke a predator to the chase, but the best he can hold himself to is a kind of race-walk.

He finds his dad where he left him, slumped forward: asleep. Will shakes him awake a hustles him to the car before his father completely understands what's happening. He grumbles that Will interrupted a perfectly wonderful nap, but his voice is more amused than irritated. "Thought I'd checked out, did you?" his father says.

"Dad," Will says.

His dad assumes that the tightness of Will's jaw, the speed with which he drives back to the hotel in Avignon, are symptoms of his panic at thinking he'd found his father dead. Not until dinner, when they have met up with Manda and the girls and his mom, does Will reveal the true cause of his agitation, the animal pacing him. Manda, Dana, and Flora find his account of the experience giggle-inducing, and his concern at a possible feral pig pushes them to outright laughter, which his mother cannot restrain herself from joining in. Only his father does not laugh; although his lips grow thin from suppressing a smile. "Well," he says, "what do you think it was now?"

"I don't know," Will says. "Probably a rat," an answer which provokes a fresh burst of hilarity from the women at the table. "I'll tell you, though, it felt like whatever was out there was huge. Like, if I had seen a giant head rising out of the reeds, it wouldn't have shocked me."

Dana controls her laughter long enough to ask, "What kind of head?"

"A head," Will says. "I don't know, a person's head."

Over the girls' laughter, his dad says, "What makes you say that?" He is no longer fighting a smile.

"It was just how it felt," Will says. He's tempted to attribute the image to what was carved on the stone marker he found, but the continuing giggles of his wife, daughters, and mother has soured his desire to offer fresh material for their amusement.

"Huh," Dad says.

"You going to use that in a poem?" Will says.

"Could be."

Later that night, while they're preparing for bed, Will tells Manda about the marker. She isn't sure what its purpose was, either. Somewhere in the depths of the night, he dreams he's facing a wall of reeds behind which something enormous is lifting into view. He sees flames. If he sees any more, though, it remains locked in the dream.

VII
Within this round might two men find friendship,
The fraternity of shared interest
In the world's secret language.

James Ogin "Rosenkreuz Serves Tea"

Much of the year he turns forty-two, Will will spend away from home. In the late winter, he'll accompany a pair of investment bankers to the Salmon River in western New York state, where he'll instruct them in fishing for salmon. Throughout spring, summer, and a good part of the fall, he'll be booked solid taking groups of aspiring anglers into the Catskills to try for trout. Early the next winter, he'll fly to Peru with a group of lawyers to a lodge with whose owner he's become friendly, where he'll teach those members of the legal profession to bait a hook for the local fish. It will be the busiest he's been since he started the guide business, in part because he won't feel able to turn away any of the bookings and the money they'll add to the household budget. Dana will tag along on a couple of trips to the Catskills, and both girls will travel down to Peru with him, but otherwise, he won't see a great deal of them.

At the same time, Manda, who made partner in her firm the previous year, will be lead defense counsel for a case in which a local ophthalmologist is being sued for malpractice by a patient whose eye essentially collapsed during routine cataract surgery, which would be tricky enough, were the plaintiff not the mother of the state's attorney general. Her life will be an unending stream of phone calls, text messages, e-mails, and meetings, meetings with fellow counsel, with their client, with expert witnesses of various stripes. Between them, she and Will will joke, they contribute significantly to the local take-out places; though they'll strive for at least one sit-down family dinner every week (or two).

During this time, Will's mother will come for two extended visits, the first early in the summer, when she'll stay for four weeks, the second in the fall, when she'll stay for the five and a half weeks of Manda's trial. While she prepares dinner for whoever happens to be around, it's mostly to be with her granddaughters that she makes the trip from the house out in Bourne to which she and Will's dad have relocated since she retired from the college and he turned his *dojang* over to the black belt who'd been his right hand woman for years. At twelve and nine, respectively, Dana and Flora still require the presence of an adult (though Dana contests this). Will's mom talks books with Dana, who is an inveterate reader, and listens to the chapters of the novel her older granddaughter is writing. She drives Flora to the farm where her pony boards, and assists her in Clover's care. She takes the girls to the movies, on excursions to local parks, and to the art museum over at Penrose College. She makes them waffles for breakfast, grilled cheese sandwiches for lunch, and chicken korma for dinner. When she comes in the fall, she brings her dog, Dinah, with her. A gold and white boxer-bull mix, Dinah licks everyone and everything with her long tongue; the girls adore her, and argue passionately over whose turn it is to walk her.

At the end of his mother's second stay, Will takes her to dinner. Manda, whose case has concluded in victory for her client, has taken Dana and Flora for a girls' night out to their favorite restaurant, and though she invited her mother-in-law to accompany them, Will's mom demurred, saying that the girls needed time with their mother. Home from a late-season trip out near Roscoe, Will suggests a jaunt into Joppenburgh for a meal at

Widow Jane's, a new-ish restaurant whose smoked fish pie has drawn a number of favorable reviews, including one from the *New York Times*. She agrees, and in short order, the two of them are seated at a small table at the front of the busy restaurant. His mom has a Guinness; he has a Coke with lemon. Much of their pre- and dinner conversation concerns the girls: Dana's struggle with an obnoxious clique at school, Flora's newfound anxieties about death, and the girls' spats and squabbles with one another. As their plates are being cleared, dessert menus produced and considered, Will relates a couple of anecdotes about his most recent client, both of them of the can-you-believe-how-the-rich-behave variety. When his Irish coffee and Mom's apple-berry crumble have been served, Will says, "So: what do you have planned now? A month of rest and relaxation?"

His mother laughs. "No, I'm afraid I'm off again the day after I get back. Your father's accepting Carson's Bollingen for him, so we have to drive to Yale. Dad's doing a reading and signing while we're there. He might be visiting a couple of classes, too. At least it's close."

"Dad's accepted so many of Carson's awards, I'm surprised no one's tried to prove they're the same person."

"Once upon a time, someone might have. These days, though, there's enough documentation of Carson online for anyone who wants to verify his existence to do so. Not to mention, every few years, an enterprising young scholar tracks him down to whatever location he's retreated to and flatters an interview out of him."

"When was the last time Dad saw him?"

"They video-chat once a week. They haven't seen each other in person for a few years. The last time...I'm pretty sure it was while we were in Amsterdam for the Tang Soo Do internationals. Carson was renting an old farmhouse on a canal. Your father went out to have dinner with him. He said he might come in to watch Dad compete, but..."

"He didn't."

"He's always been funny about crowds."

"Unlike Dad," Will says.

"Yes," his mom says. "Protest all he likes to the contrary, Dad never met a group of people he didn't immediately try to win over. And succeed, most of the time. It helped him make the karate school such a success. It's the reason people will travel three hours to hear him read his poetry."

"Opposites attract, right?"

"You mean your father and Carson?"

"Well, yeah. It never occurred to me while he was living with us, but afterwards, I remember thinking how weird it was that these two guys should be such close friends. Here's Dad, who grows up in the country, but not that far from the nearest town. Grandma and Grandpa were in favor of education. From what I can tell, they pretty much left him alone to read and write as much as he wanted. He's Mr. Literature, almost all the way to the Ph.D. It seems as if he's read or at least heard of everything.

"Then you've got Carson, who's raised in the middle of nowhere. His parents don't want to educate him any more than the bare legal minimum. It sounds as if they were more interested in putting him to work at their guide business. He works a million odd jobs; it seems as if there's nothing he hasn't learned how to do, from clean a fish to rebuild an engine. I guess the two of them have martial arts in common, but even there, Dad always treated it as a mix of sport and performance, while Carson was more interested in being able to cripple and maim people."

"I suppose all that's true," Mom says. "It's funny. Your father and Carson have been friends for so long, all I see now are the similarities. I don't mean the karate, either. Their lives had more in common than you think. Yes, Dad's parents were in favor of education, but they saw it as a means to an end. You went to school in order to become a lawyer or a doctor, so you could be your own boss. That was what your grandfather used to say to Dad, that he wanted him to work for himself."

"Isn't that what writing poetry is?"

His mother frowns comically. "Not if it doesn't pay the bills. Your father's parents were deeply suspicious of education for its own sake, let alone of a career writing poetry. I'm sorry," she says, shaking her head, "I'm being unfair to them. They had been poor when they were very young—this was during the Second World War—and for them, being financially secure was very important. College was great because it allowed you to achieve that security in a way that going out and getting a job after you graduated high school didn't. To use that opportunity for something else was...self-indulgent, and if you had a family, irresponsible. I don't think I ever saw your grandmother as happy—as relieved—as I did at the opening of Dad's *dojang*. She was still nervous about him teaching karate, but as far as she was concerned, it was a big step in the right direction. Had your grandpa been alive, he would have felt the same way. Dad writing poetry made them deeply nervous. Grandpa used to say, 'But how can you know if it's any good? It's all just someone's opinion.' Grandma treated it as a phase Dad was going through, as if he were experimenting with drugs, or voting Democrat.

"On the surface, you're right, Carson's upbringing was completely different. But his parents wanted him to be financially successful in the same way as Dad's family. For them, formal education beyond junior high was a distraction, a delay in earning money. They had a plan to make themselves comfortable, moneywise, and they assumed their son would help them fulfill it. If he talked about anything else, showed an aptitude for reading and writing, that was fine, he could write the brochures and ads for their guide service when he was a little older. Carson wanting to put his talent to other uses made no sense to them. Why would he want to go off and compose poems when there was money to be made at hand? From what I understand, there was some resentment at their son's desire for a life so utterly removed from theirs, as if he was criticizing them with his dream, belittling theirs.

"Both of them had it, though, a...a fire for language, for what you could do with it. Sometimes, I imagined Dad's work as a great library, like the one at Penrose, all Gothic revival, its windows ablaze with light. And sometimes, I would picture Carson's work as a bonfire roaring in the center of a forest clearing, its light falling on redwoods a hundred feet high. They recognized that flame in one another. For as long as he's known him, your dad has said that Carson does what he does with absolute integrity, absolute commitment. Carson's written the same thing about him. So..."

"The bromance of the age," Will says. His mother hasn't spoken of either his father or Carson in such terms before; he's moved, unsure how to respond beyond gentle ridicule.

"Something like that," his mom says. "There's really nothing your father wouldn't do for him."

"I'm just grateful Carson didn't ask him to sacrifice his firstborn son for him."

"Don't be so sure," his mother says.

VIII
You start with a sharp knife.

Carson Lochyer "Cleaning a Trout"

Autumn of the year Will's father turns eighty-three and Will fifty, his dad will publish a memoir of his friendship with Carson Lochyer titled *Carrying the Lamp into Darkness*. A mix of essay and poetry, its occasion will be the fifth anniversary of

Carson's disappearance and increasingly-presumed death within the wilds of the Kamchatka peninsula in far-eastern Russia. Though he'll bring the slender volume with him on every fishing trip he takes, Will will put off reading the book for an entire year, until a series of ferocious storms will strand him in Seattle's Sea-Tac airport overnight. He'll remember some of the exchanges his father relates, some of the scenes from Carson's time with them his dad describes. The book skips around in time, moving from conversations recent to those of decades prior, and in subject, moving from poems to sports, from family to fellow poets. Dead-center in the book, Will reads:

There aren't many poems I haven't been able to write. This is not to say all of my work has been of equal success, only that I can count on one hand the number of subjects to which I could not fit an adequate verse-form. One of those was a story Carson told me in the weeks before he arrived to stay with me and my family following his divorce. The split from his wife had been sudden, swift, and merciless, and he came east in rough shape. For the first few months he was with us, he and I spent a couple of hours each night in front of the TV, watching reruns of *Family Guy* and *American Dad*, brightly-toned idiocy whose principle purpose was to kill time, to help move my friend thirty minutes further from his recent catastrophe. Some nights, he would retreat to his room afterwards; others, I would remove a bottle of single-malt from the liquor cabinet and pour each of us a couple of fingers' worth. I didn't know many of the particulars of Carson's divorce; strange as it may sound, I hadn't known much about his marriage in the first place. Our conversations and correspondence had focused almost exclusively on poetry: our own, that of our contemporaries, of those

who came before us. I expected, though, that at some point he would want—would need—to relate the story of his marriage's collapse, as a kind of therapeutic exercise.

One night in particular, I was certain Carson was about to unburden himself to me. This was in late September, after he had been living with us for five months. Until this moment, all Carson had said on the subject of his divorce was that it was entirely his fault. This declaration, combined with his lack of clarification of it, had led me to wonder if he hadn't been unfaithful to his wife, or guilty of something worse, violence mental or physical. Nothing in his behavior around me and my family gave my suppositions any support, but there are relationships that bring out a unique beast in us, and perhaps this had happened to my friend.

On the night of which I'm writing, Carson had two glasses of Balvenie I served him, a third, more substantial pour he served himself. Revelation trembled the air of the kitchen. He drank half his glass and said,

I ran away from home when I was eighteen. For the last time, I mean. I'd been trying to get away from my parents since my thirteenth birthday. A couple of times, I made it to Lewiston. There's a harbor, there, the furthest-inland seaport in the western U.S. I had an idea I'd play Jack London, sign on board a merchant ship and see the world. Couldn't find anyone to take me before my dad found me. When I was older, I tried jumping trains, but that was harder than I expected, too. The one time I actually succeeded in climbing inside an open boxcar, the train stopped an hour later, and the cops discovered me. Made Dad drive all the way there to get me. You can imagine how thrilled he was to have to do that. Eventually, I turned to hitchhiking, which a lifetime of my mom's warnings about perverts in cars had heretofore caused me to avoid. I encountered a few of them, too, though nothing I couldn't handle. None of my attempted escapes ever took me far enough away from my parents' reach. I might have a day or two in a town, but Dad always seemed to know right where to find me. He never failed to remind me that he knew his way around towns and cities; he'd lived in plenty of them before he and Mom pulled up stakes and headed for the country. I, on the other hand, was just an ignorant hillbilly, ill-equipped for any life but the one he and Mom had raised me to.

How I hated him during those long drives back to whatever hovel he and my mother had christened home that month. The thing was, he owned two large footlockers full of books, a lot of them old hardcovers he and Mom had picked up at library sales and flea markets. There were a lot of the classics, Homer and Dante and Shakespeare, the Romantics, as well as paperback copies of Twain and Hemingway and Steinbeck. I was allowed to read whatever I wanted, as long as it didn't interfere with my chores. I went through every last one of those books, at least twice and in some cases half a dozen times. I could not understand how my parents could own all of these books, could cart them from place to place—and read them, yes, they read a lot of them—I could not understand how they could have this portable library and yet want nothing of what it represented. You know what I'm talking about.

I did.

That was what kept prodding me to get away from them. Sure, there was plenty of physical deprivation, beatings when I misbehaved, unhealthy and inadequate food, outrageous work conditions, and forget a doctor if you got sick, let alone a dentist if you had a toothache. But I sometimes think that, if I had shared their vision, embraced their plan to become the pre-eminent fishing guide service in central Idaho, I might have been willing to put up with those hardships and more, beside. Since I didn't, since I wanted a life completely removed from theirs, the lashes with the belt and the plain spaghetti and the carrying a fifty-pound pack fifteen miles upriver—and the strep throat, the bronchitis, and the pneumonia—all of was just piling insult on top of injury.

When I decided to run away the last time, I hit on a different plan. Before, I had always set out for civilization, for town and cities. It dawned on me that if I went the opposite direction, headed deeper into the wilderness, my chances of evading my dad would improve. We were staying in a trailer outside of Stanley, beside the Salmon River. You stepped out the front door, and there in the distance was the Lost River Range, like the teeth of a great, broken saw. I'd been up in the mountains with Dad dozens of times. I knew the course the Salmon River took through them, and I knew the smaller rivers and streams that fed into it. The Salmon's also known as the River of No Return, and that struck me as a good omen.

On a Saturday night my parents were out at a

dinner party at a rich client's ranch, I left. I loaded my outdoor gear into an old beater truck I'd bought the past summer, and headed for the mountains. The only thing I took from my parents was a copy of Yeats's Selected Poems. There was no doubt in my mind I was going to fail. My parents would come back early, or just as I was pulling out of the driveway. One of the neighbors we rarely saw would pick this moment to drop in for a visit. My truck would die. I wanted to race up the road with my headlights off: there was a full moon, and visibility was pretty good. But there was a state trooper who liked to ride around Stanley from time to time, and I didn't want to provide him an excuse to pull me over.

There's one major road that runs through Stanley. Smaller roads branch off from it. A lot of them don't go much further than a couple of hundred feet, to a clearing or someone's old cabin. A few of them extend a considerable distance, trails the loggers and miners used. After maybe half an hour, I turned onto one of these. I took the truck as far as it would go into the forest, parked it as best I could on what shoulder there was, so it wouldn't hinder anyone else's passage, and set out into the mountains.

For me, Eliot has it right: "there, you feel free." I was up in them for twelve months. There were a couple of deserted cabins I'd run across during my previous trips to the area. I made for nearest one of those, and set it up as my base of operations while I waited to find out if Dad and Mom had worked out my ruse. Once I was satisfied they hadn't, I moved to the second cabin, which was in better shape, better-suited for the coming winter. There was a lean-to beside it under which someone had stacked enough firewood to take me a good portion of the way through the approaching season. Tell the truth, I was half-expecting whoever had cut and stacked that wood to show up and take possession of the place. In that event, I didn't know what my plan was going to be.

Nobody appeared to lay claim to the cabin, though, and I remained there for the rest of my time in the mountains. Much of what I did every day related to staying alive, chopping wood to add to the store under the lean-to, setting traps for small game, foraging for plants that were safe to eat, fishing, and making the cabin more weatherproof. I set aside time every day to read Yeats and to write. I'd brought a bundle of legal pads with me, and a handful of pencils, and I used them to write poetry. I'd read somewhere about Virgil writing ten lines in the morning, then spending the afternoon whittling them down to two. I took him as my model.

It was not an easy time. I rarely had enough food. No matter how sick or well I felt, the day's chores had to be seen to. Love Yeats though I did, I was soon desperate for something else to read. My poems were stale, derivative. I could have left, found my way down to Boise, but I was superstitiously certain that, within a day of setting foot in any sizable settlement, I would be found by my dad.

Winter arrived, and everything grew worse. The temperature plummeted outside and in. The warmth my fireplace gave ended about three feet from it. Snow fell for days, drifting to the cabin's roof. One night, a grizzly made a half-hearted attempt to get through the front door. I say "half-hearted" because I'm sure that, had it really wanted to, it easily could have broken in and had me for dinner.

Carson emptied what remained in his glass, tipped another couple of fingers of Scotch into it. He held out the bottle to me; I declined.

That bear. I don't know why it wasn't hibernating in a cave somewhere. I wish I could convey to you how afraid I was, to have this giant animal on one side of a flimsy barrier and me on the other. This was fear of an almost-entirely physical sort, in the pounding of your heart, the tightness in your balls, the shaking of your legs. The bear snuffled the edges of the door, snuffled them like a dog. It leaned on the door, and the hinges rattled. It pushed against the wood, and the door moaned. I had a rifle in my hands, a .22, but I had little faith in its ability to stop the grizzly before it reached me. I was as certain as I've been of anything that I was not going to survive the next five minutes.

But I did. I made it through the night, and I made it through the winter. That spring was most beautiful, the most astonishing time I'd ever known. Living with Dad and Mom, I had learned to hate and dread the end of winter, because that was when the guide business kicked into gear, and what respite I'd enjoyed while the snow was high was over. Months of frozen whiteness, however, gave me a fresh appreciation for the warmth that trickled into the air throughout the day, for the colors emerging around me. Green—I hadn't realized how many shades of green there were around me, from the emerald of the new grass to the chartreuse of the moss, from the mint of the weeds to the jade of the evergreens. And the wildflowers opening all at once, gold and violet and vermilion and lavender. The air was clamorous with bird song. The streams and rivers were fast and frothing with the spring melt, but I brought my tackle to them and pulled fish bright and fighting from them. I was leery of a return visit from the bear or one of his cohort, but the few grizzlies I saw were at a considerable distance, and uninterested in me.

In late June, around the solstice, I came upon an unfamiliar stream while fishing the Salmon. I was in a spot where the banks were growing steeper, and I was wondering if it was time to turn for home. On my left, a broad stream tumbled down into the river. I didn't remember a stream in this location, but I wasn't overly familiar with this stretch of the Salmon, so I chalked up the discrepancy to poor memory. The stream descended from a canyon a hundred yards back. I couldn't recall the split in the surrounding hills any more than I could the water emerging from it. I decided to investigate.

I had the crazy notion that the canyon hadn't been here, previously, or the stream, either. There'd been a pretty serious earthquake in these parts when I was thirteen. Damaged buildings for miles around, killed a couple of kids on their way to school. Left twenty miles of broken ground. I hadn't felt anything in the way of an earthquake during the winter, but a smaller one could have happened, cracked open this hillside.

From the look of the stream, though, that wasn't likely. The juniper and fir lining its banks were thirty feet high, tall enough to have been growing for a time.

As far as I could see, the stream bed was smooth, with no signs of any late upheaval. Where the banks drew up into canyon walls, there were no rockslides, no evidence the hill had been pried apart in the recent past. There was a narrow beach at the base of my side of the canyon. I walked up to and along it far enough to see that the walls opened out again after another twenty yards. Some kind of light was flickering in that area—I thought it was a fire, but the color was wrong, platinum instead of red and orange. Nor was there any sound of trees burning. I continued towards the other end of the canyon. My eyes wandered to the rockface across the stream from me. It was difficult to be positive in the canyon's dim light, but I couldn't pick out any of the striations you'd expect to find in a patch of exposed rock that size. A single unbroken wall of rose-colored stone faced me. There was a patch of shadow at its base, a little ways back from me, which resembled a door, but I figured the similarity was due more to my imagination than what it was acting on.

Where the canyon walls fell off to either side of me, the stream collected in a small lake that caught the rays of the afternoon sun and angled them directly into my eyes. For a moment, I saw nothing but dazzle. I could hear something over the rush of the water exiting via the canyon, a kind of low, irregular humming. Gradually, my surroundings swam into view. Low hills surrounded the scene. Directly in front of me was the lake, which collected water that flowed into it from a stream on the right. Beneath the sunlight wavering on its surface, the water in the pool and of its tributary appeared black. I took this as an after-effect of the sun overwhelming my eyes. Across the lake, the light I had seen from the canyon twisted and blazed. By walking the shore to the left of the lake, I soon came to a flat expanse of pale, chalk-colored rock which extended into the water. It was the dimensions of a modest church or auditorium. At the other end of the rock shelf, in the approximate center of the lake, a tower of white fire shone like liquid metal. It was a squat construction, slightly taller than I was, as wide as it was tall. Even at the distance I was from it, a flame of that volume and color should be uncomfortably hot. I felt nothing. I advanced closer to the burning tower, and saw that it hovered above a round depression in the rock, which was full of a liquid that did not reflect the fire writhing over it. A stone cup sat on the rock in front of the pool.

I don't know what I was thinking. Or, it was as if my mind was running on multiple tracks, simultaneously. I was wondering if the flame might be the result of some kind of gas vent, and if that might account for its color and its lack of heat. I was also wondering if what I took for fire was water, steam, full of a mineral that was catching and reflecting the sunlight. I was thinking that this was among the stranger sights I'd witnessed, and debating the wisdom of being so close to it. If I'm being honest, then I have to admit that I was telling myself, "Dad and Mom might be able to make some real money off this thing." And I was watching myself, too, approach the shining fire, which never grew hotter. Some part of me must have been shouting, "What the hell are you doing?" but I don't remember it. What I recall is the sense of absolute rightness that came over me as I walked toward the fire, as if I were doing exactly what I was supposed to.

Shielding my eyes from the glare with one hand, I knelt and picked up the stone cup with the other hand. The surface of the cup was rough, sharp in places, as if recently and quickly fashioned. I dipped it into the liquid beneath the tower and held it up for consideration.

The cup was full of water. Dad's years of warnings about the perils of unfamiliar water sounding in my ears, I raised it to my lips and drained it. The water was cool but not cold, tasting of nothing but itself. I weighed taking more, decided against it, and returned the cup to its place before the pool. I stood and retreated from the white tower. The humming I'd noted earlier had grown louder, become words I couldn't quite make out, delivered in a slow chant by many voices. All around the perimeter of the rock ledge, the air was alive with figures, men and women, robed in pale flames, the ghostly echo of the blazing tower. It was difficult to say for sure, but I thought I recognized a couple of them. There was a man whose fiery beard framed the features of Whitman, another whose crown of flames sat above Dante's aquiline nose and melancholy eyes. I couldn't decipher their chant, but I understood that it was old, far older than even the oldest poems we know. This was what the hunters had sung in celebration after they brought down a mammoth. This was what families keened over their dead after they were done piling stones on them. These words had welcomed the spring and begged mercy of winter. They had named the constellations, enumerated the deeds of the beings they represented. I could feel my lips beginning to move in time to the chant's rhythm, my tongue shaping itself to its sounds.

And then a great brass shout rang off the surrounding hills, a clanging note that drowned out the words of the fiery company and made me clap my hands to my ears. A wind rose from the ground and whirled around the stone ledge. The poets around me faded. Something was approaching. I felt it as a thickening in the atmosphere, as if something vast was pushing a wave of air in front of it. I couldn't judge the direction of its travel; I had the impression it was going to bound out of the very air.

Before it could arrive, I ran. Pack bouncing on my back, I fled that place and its fantastic sights as fast as my legs would go. At my back, the wind roared. I sprinted through the canyon, along the shore that had taken me here, kicking stones into the stream as I went. I shot out of the canyon down the slope to the Salmon, already veering right, in the direction of my cabin. I knew I could hike for the better part of a day, and cover substantial ground in the process. I hadn't known I could run like this. My legs were in agony, my lungs burning, but I did not slow my pace until I had the cabin in sight. The moment I was through the door, I dropped the pack and went for my rifle. I passed the rest of the day and all of the night, until the sun rose the next morning, positioned at the front door, which I had open a crack, scanning the long meadow in front of the cabin for whatever had been on its way from the wind. Nothing showed. Not then.

I didn't return to the place. That's the question, isn't it? Did you go back? Was it still there? Did you invent the experience, hallucinate it, or did you stumble through a gap in our world to...some other place? I knew what I'd seen, what I'd heard, what I'd tasted. At least, I thought I did. I weighed another trip to the spot on the Salmon, but couldn't make up my mind about it. I wasn't especially worried that I'd imagined the place on the other side of the canyon, the flaming tower, the fiery poets. There was nothing in the rest of my behavior to indicate that I'd suffered a psychotic break. To be honest, I was more, much more concerned that the stone ledge had been real, that by drinking from the pool in it I'd drawn the wrath of...I didn't know what. I didn't want to find out, either.

Anyway, I was busy writing. In the days after my excursion up that stream, I started a series of poems that sounded less like poor imitations of all my reading and more like distillations of it, filtered through a style and a voice that felt like mine. You know, there are times you begin work on something, and right away, you can tell, this is going somewhere. There may be some bumps on the road—let's be frank: there may be blown head-gaskets, and washed out bridges, and sudden thunderstorms—but you can just about see your destination at the outset. These were the sonnets about trout-fishing with Dad. I had full confidence in what I was doing in them, and I was pretty sure that they were going to announce me to the world. I worked on them daily, tirelessly, for eight, ten, twelve hours at a time. Beyond what was necessary for my immediate survival, I neglected everything in favor of the words pouring out of me. Wood lay ungathered, uncut, and unstacked. My traps had not been reset in weeks. The cabin had not received the maintenance it required, rotten boards replaced, gaps in the walls filled. By midsummer, it was obvious that I would not—could not—stay in this place another winter, not if I intended to continue writing. I decided that, come fall, before the weather turned too bad, I would pack my gear and head for Boise.

This was what I did; although I left about a week ahead of schedule. The fall had been and remained unusually warm, summer-like. I was reluctant to depart the location where I had broken through to my own voice, where I had written poems that seemed beacons lighting the way to what I might do, next. I may have been a little anxious about the effect a change of scenery would have on my poetry. The days were getting shorter, though, and I had no desire to be in the mountains when the weather changed.

I kept writing. Each night, I stood from the table where I worked, stretched, and went outside for a walk around the cabin. It was one of those things you do to give yourself momentary distance from whatever you're writing. I brought the rifle; I hadn't forgotten my encounter with the bear. I startled a fox, once, but that was it. A couple of weeks before I was planning to hike down to civilization, I strolled outside to see the top of the peak to my left in flames. Two-thirds of the way to its crown, a belt of red-orange encircled it, lighting the low-hanging clouds. While I knew forest fires were a possibility, the sight of the flames was shocking. I wondered if I'd have to clear out that night. I couldn't see for sure, but the fire appeared to be burning above the tree line. I hadn't heard thunder, seen lightning strike, nor had I noted hikers or climbers in the vicinity, earlier. As absorbed as I was in writing, though, it was conceivable I might have missed any of those.

As I watched, the band of fire rose up the

mountain, as if it were a line of climbers carrying torches, ascending the summit. It moved faster than a person could, and with more uniformity. I couldn't figure out what it was, what natural phenomenon I was witnessing. The fire gathered at the very top of the mountain, then leapt straight into the sky. It pierced the clouds and was gone.

How could I not have drawn a straight line between what I saw that night and the place beyond the canyon, with its tower of white fire? I tell myself that I must have made such a connection, but if I did, it failed to signify. I thought something to the effect of, *Strange things happen in the mountains*, but that was all. I did not recognize this incident as a consequence of my actions months before. That came three nights later.

It was after I'd put down my pen for the day and was lying in bed, reading Yeats. There was a sound in the woods at the far end of the meadow in front of the cabin, the crack and crash of a tree falling. I lowered the book and listened. Something big was pushing through the brush. At the same time, light stabbed through the gaps in the walls, beams of red-orange that filled the cabin with a dull glow. I rolled up from my bed, grabbed the rifle, and crossed to the front door. In spite of the light shining into the cabin, I was thinking it was the bear from last winter, come back for another visit. I opened the door the barest sliver, and at first, what I saw prowling the edge of the woods was a bear, the biggest kind I'd seen. It was enveloped in fire, an orange inferno that should have killed it immediately, whose heat I could feel a hundred yards away, but which the animal seemed not to notice. It voiced a roar that was the clashing of a huge bell, and I saw that it was no bear at all. It was nothing I'd seen before. The face was more like a man's, only bigger, and when it opened its mouth, it was full of rows and rows of teeth. I didn't want to look at the rest of it—I couldn't; the sight of it sent a sharp pain through the middle of my head. There was a tail of some kind, arched over its back.

I eased the door shut and stood with my back against it. The light within the cabin brightened as the creature moved out of the trees, into the meadow. I didn't think the .22 would make any impression on what I'd seen, but I didn't dare flee the cabin, lest I provoke it to chase me. There was nothing to do but stay where I was and await the thing's next move. It thrashed through the meadow, voicing its heavy, metallic roar. The air in the cabin warmed. Sweat weighted my clothes. I white-knuckled the rifle. This, I had no doubt, was what had been coming for me after I drank from the pool below the flaming tower—what I had summoned. It was near enough that the interior of the cabin shone with a red-orange light, as if dawn were throwing its rays over the mountains. The structure shook with the creature's roars, dust dropping from the ceiling, lifting from the walls. The door was hot where I was leaning against it. I straightened away from it. There might be a fire raging in the meadow.

Whatever I had come to this place to do, it was not burn to death in a cabin. I caught the door handle, turned it, and pulled the door open. At the same time, I stepped into the doorway, rifle up, sighting along it to the spot where I guessed the beast was. There was a purity to the act that was wonderful, that filled me with elation, even though I was certain I was passing to my death.

Except I wasn't. The meadow was empty. The traces of the creature's presence were in evidence: the tall grass and wildflowers had been burnt down to the baked earth, where scattered flames continued to flicker. The outside of the door, that side of the cabin, were scorched black. Keeping the rifle at my cheek, I retreated inside to pull on my boots. Feet protected, I went outside and made, first a tight circuit of the cabin, then a foray into the meadow to stomp out the remaining fires. Once the last flame had been extinguished, I retreated inside and started to pack.

Carson emptied what remained in his glass. He did not refill it.

The next morning, I hiked out of the Lost River Range. I brought with me fifty-four poems, which I began submitting to literary journals as soon as I was settled in a room in a boarding house in Boise. The first was accepted for publication late the following winter. Days, I worked a succession of odd jobs. I started to take classes in combatives. That was how I met Willa, at my martial arts school. She'd received one too many advances from pushy guys who thought they should be the ones to date Boise's hottest meteorologist. She and I got together. I was promoted to assistant manager at my job, then manager. And while all of this was happening, the pages on the calendar peeling away, I wrote, what had started in the cabin in the mountains continuing to the room in the boardinghouse, then a small apartment, then Willa's condo once we shacked up, and finally to the house we bought in Hayley after she accepted the job there. I published a chapbook with a micropress. Robert Haas said some complimentary things about it. The University of Virginia published my first full length collection of poems.

I know you know all of this. What you don't know is that the creature, the fiery monster, pursued me. It took years for it to track me to my apartment. At first, I didn't know it had found me. I looked out the living room window one night and saw flames on the roof of a building down the street, and assumed it was a normal fire. Only when the flames gathered into a sphere, which hung over the roof before bursting apart like a firework, did I understand that I had been located. The same night, I carried my meager belongings to my car and drove to a motel on the south side of the city. I stayed there for a couple of days while I considered my options. Willa had been asking me to move in with her, and she owned a nice condo in a suburb about a half-hour outside of Boise. I could chance taking her up on her offer, or I could get onto the interstate and let it take me where it would. The second option, I understood, was the prudent, the responsible one. But I loved Willa, loved the life I thought we could have together. I called her, told her I'd decided she was right, it was time for us to take the next step in our relationship.

Well. You see how right I was about that. Funny thing is, the beast didn't catch up with me again until the very end, after Willa had decided it was time for her to move onto bigger and better things, a move that did not require the encumbrance of me. Our marriage had been the axis holding the rest of my life in orbit. When it was over, everything went spiraling off in its own direction. Willa moved out, told me I could keep the house if I could afford it, which I couldn't. I didn't know what I was going to do; I literally could not think of it. I guess I was waiting to see what would happen, how much worse things could get. Then one night, one very late night when I was most of the way through a bottle of Scotch not half as good as this one, I gazed out the window and saw fire dancing on top of a hill about a mile away. This time, though, I decided I was going to confront the creature, was going to face it and let whatever happened, happen.

What was that?

Nothing. I left before it reached me. I saw it three days after the flames on the hill prowling the woods across the street from the house. For the last two days, I had been loading my truck, not in any particular order, more as it occurred to me I didn't want to leave this book or that blanket behind. I'd been keeping an eye on the other side of the street, which was where I had a sense the creature would appear. I had a rifle, a Remington, better quality and caliber than the gun I'd carried in the Lost River Range, but I was no more optimistic of its efficacy against the beast. In the early evening of the third day, I heard the creature's roar, that metallic clang. I was finishing the second-to-last knot in the tarp I had thrown over my truck's bed. The front door of the house was wide open, as was the garage; all the lights were on inside. The house sat on a rise, which permitted me to look down into the woods opposite to where the air was flooded with orange light. From deep in the trees—from somewhere *deeper* than that—the creature padded towards me, flames twisting around it. Its broad face was blank as a statue's. My keys were in the front pocket of my jeans. I slid behind the wheel of the truck and pulled out of the driveway. I'd like to say I didn't look back, but of course I did.

A couple of weeks at another motel, you and your wife's generous invitation, and here we are. I don't know how long it'll take the thing to find me on the other side of the country. I'd like to think I've given it the slip, but I suspect that isn't the case. When it shows here, I'll throw my gear into my truck and hit the road. I fantasize about striding out to meet it, playing Hercules with the Hydra, Theseus and the Minotaur, but what chance would I have? I'm pretty fond of this life; if I can avoid leaving it too soon, I'd prefer to do so.

Now I reached for the Scotch and poured a generous portion of it into my tumbler. The story I'd sat listening to was impossible, more for the pages of the latest Stephen King than anything resembling daily life. Yet I never doubted its veracity once. I swallowed the single malt without tasting it and said, "Are you positive the creature is hostile?"

"It burned my house to the ground. Willa wanted to pin it on me, but the arson investigator said the fire originated from a point across the road, possibly from a lightning strike. Said it was the weirdest thing he'd ever seen."

"All right. And there's no way to fight it?"

Carson shrugged. "Nothing certain. I've done a little research here and there, but I've yet to hit on anything in the way of a definite solution. Until I do, I'm reluctant to experiment."

"Could you placate it?"

"What do you mean?"

"Obviously, it came in response to your drinking from the pool. Is there any way you can apologize for that, atone for it?"

He shook his head. "Not that I've read. And to be frank, I wouldn't if I could."

"Come again?"

"You're the classics guy. What do you think that water was? It was the Pierian Spring, or something like it. Do you think it's a coincidence I found my voice after I drank from it?"

"As I recall, none of the myths mentions a monstrous guardian."

"That's because this was the thing itself, not some earthly analogue. Taste its waters, and you're trespassing on what's supposed to be the gods'."

"Then why hasn't the creature caught and punished you?"

"I don't know. I ran across something online that said there are very specific ways something like this can intersect our world, our reality. Maybe that's it. I'm not complaining."

"This website, the one that gave you this information, did it offer any suggestions for dealing with the beast?"

"No." Carson stared straight at me as he said this. I had the momentary impression that, within the depths of his pupils, I could pick out twin points of fire, burning white. For the first time that evening, I was almost certain my friend was lying to me.

There is nothing else in the book like this. The memoir, if that's what it is, contrasts sharply with the remainder of the volume's more prosaic contents. It's like finding a shark swimming amidst a school of trout, incongruous, absurd. The reviews of the book he pulls up on his phone express a similar sentiment, with greater and lesser degrees of pique. The *New York Times* accuses his father of having "turned Carson Lochyer into a character in an elaborate fantasy intended to elevate his late friend to mythological status (thereby, one suspects, accounting for his own failure ever to equal Mr. Lochyer's achievement)." The *Washington Post* compliments his dad for "an inspired bit of ventriloquy which makes Carson Lochyer into a kind of Ahab-in-reverse, relentlessly pursued by the same monster that gave his life its purpose."

Will intends to ask his dad about the piece himself. He wonders if it's a kind of stealth tribute to Stephen King, one of his father's favorite writers. (Carson, he remembers, preferred Cormac McCarthy's novels.) He dials his parents' number, but the call is shunted to voice mail. Ah well, it can wait until he's home.

When Manda greets him at the front door the following afternoon, however, it is with tears in her eyes, and the news that his father is suddenly dead.

IX
Gone the grim gods of my grandfather, who
Demanded a man meet mortality
At the stroke of a sharp sword, and arrive
Among them a fit companion, worthy

To sing his own deeds.

James Ogin "The Death of Wiglaf"

There will be a larger crowd at Will's father's wake, and funeral, and the reception after the funeral than he will anticipate. Family will come, of course, his father's surviving siblings, his younger brother and his wife, and his youngest sister and her husband, along with a mass of cousins and their children and, in a couple of cases, grandchildren. Manda's parents will fly in from their retirement villa in Arizona; her older brother and his wife and two children will drive over from Boston; and her younger sister and her husband and daughter will rent a car and drive up from Brooklyn. He and Manda will host her parents and Will's mother, who will alternate between stunned acceptance of her husband's death (from a stroke) and torrential weeping. The members of both families will be joined by friends ranging from close to acquaintance. There will be former colleagues of Will's mom's, from when she taught at SUNY Huguenot. A large contingent of his dad's karate students will appear, each of them bowing to Will and Manda as they shake their hands and offer their condolences. There will be white-haired, wrinkled poets whose younger selves stood laughing or talking with his father in photos forty years old. There will be poets Will's age and younger, who will hold his hand too long as they tell him how important his dad's work was to them when they were younger, the possibilities it suggested to them. There will be a few complete strangers, come to pay their respects to a man whose lines signified something to them and some crucial juncture in their lives.

Surprised and pleased by the number and variety of women and men who appear to mark his father's passing, Will has the odd sensation that his dad is slipping away from his private recollection of him to the collective remembrance of the public. Since his teenage years, he's been aware of his father's identity, his persona, as a poet, a literary figure. It's always seemed to him that there was the slightest bit of daylight between who he thought his dad was and who his father's readers thought he was. With his death, already Dad is becoming a Name, which Will supposes he must have wanted but which weights him with melancholy on top of his grief.

Because Carson Lochyer has not been declared legally dead, there has been no formal memorial service for him, nor is one planned for any time in the near future. Due to this, and to their long-time friendship, Will's father's wake, funeral, and post-funeral reception become an impromptu memorial for him, too. Dad, Will supposes, would approve.

The night of his father's funeral, after his mom has taken a sedative and retired to bed, and his in-laws have gone off to the other guest room, and Manda and Flora have kissed him good night, Will sits at the kitchen table with Dana, a bottle of eighteen-year Talisker open between them. They drink the Scotch slowly, allowing it time to loosen their tongues and unlock their memories. The stories they exchange of Dad, Grandpa, aren't all that different from those he imagines most people tell in such situations. Will talks about the time his father dropped everything to drive out to Wood's Hole so he would be in time to meet the afternoon ferry from Martha's Vineyard. On it was the twenty-year-old son of one Will's mom's friends from college in Scotland. The son, whose name was Lance, had taken a summer job at an expensive hotel on the island for which he had been disastrously unsuited and from which he had been fired in short order. For reasons Will can't remember, Mom's friend was unable to get to her son. Dad volunteered to pick him up from the ferry and bring him to their house, which he did. A couple of days later, he drove Lance to Newark for his flight back to Edinburgh.

Dana speaks of her years studying in Grandpa's *dojang*, of how amazing it was the first time she saw him break a pair of boards with a jumping front kick, this big man leaping into the air, the boards snapping with a sound like a book slapping shut. How old would she have been? Six, seven? Old enough to remember the event. And afterwards, he was still Grandpa, his hair a mess, his face sweaty, his hairy chest visible at the top of his *dobak*. At the same time, he wasn't Grandpa, or not the same Grandpa. It was as if there was all this energy radiating from him, this...fire. Does that make sense? his daughter asks and, Yes, Will answers, it does.

At some point after the kitchen has been reduced to a quasi-cubist backdrop that spins whichever direction Will turns his head, Dana pushes away from the table, mumbles that she has to get some sleep, kisses the top of her father's head, and sways away in the direction of her room. There's a scrim of alcohol coating the bottom of the bottle of Talisker. Will lifts the bottle, pronouncing, "*Slàinte Mhath*," his father's preferred toast, and downs the last of it. He should find his way to his and Manda's room, but the combination of whisky and exhaustion makes this appear an insurmountable challenge. Nearer by far, the living room couch seems a safer bet. Almost knocking over his chair, he stands and, hands out to either side to aid what balance remains him, he wobbles into the living room where the blue and white striped couch is waiting to receive him. Will sinks into its cushions. Briefly, he has the sensation of falling, as if unconsciousness is a pool he's plummeting towards, and then he's asleep.

The dream that envelops him is of the kind so vivid as to be indistinguishable from waking. It begins with him sitting up on the couch. The air around him vibrates the way it does in the immediate aftermath of a great sound. Dim light sketches the contours of the living room's complement of seats and cabinets. He must not have turned off the kitchen light. Rising on stiff legs, he crosses to the kitchen doorway, reaches through it, and flips the light switch. The kitchen darkens, but the living room remains full of a soft orange glow. It's coming from the windows, seeping into the room around the edges of the curtains. Dawn? It can't be: the sun rises on the other side of the house. Will walks to the picture window and parts the curtain veiling it. Through the glass, through the trunk and branches of the cedars in the front yard, he sees flames at the edge of his property. He rushes to the front door, unlocks and opens it, and runs outside onto the front porch of the house in which he grew up.

Startled, he looks from side to side. To his right is the wooden rocking chair his father liked to sit and read in when the weather was mild. To his left hangs the hummingbird feeder in the shape of an oversized strawberry. Before him, the ground runs level for the length of the short yard, dips into a gully, then rises in a steep hill to the road. Fire burns up there, too—or maybe it's the same fire. At the top of the stairs descending to the yard, he sees the *qiang*, the Chinese spear, leaning against one of the posts. He steps forward and grabs hold of it. The haft is smooth to the touch. Does this mean his father...? He hurries down the steps.

Holding the spear at his side, Will jogs along and up the driveway. Red-orange light makes a Halloween scene of the woods to either side. His thighs protest the driveway's grade. Ahead on the left, he spots Mr. Tumnus's Lamp, a black sketch on orange construction paper. There's someone a few feet to the right of the lamppost, a silhouette whose slight stoop causes his heart to pound. Eyes focused on that figure, Will forces himself to sprint the last few yards to the road.

Bathed in red-orange light, his father is waiting for him. He looks much as he did the last time Will saw him alive, his beard in need of a trim, his hair thin but not gone, his brow and the sides of his mouth grooved with deep lines. He's let the robe he was wearing drop to his feet, which are bare. He's dressed in a pair of worn karate pants and his favorite *Famous Monsters of Filmland* t-shirt, the one that shows Godzilla squaring off against

Gamera. In his right hand, he holds the *do*, the curved Korean sword, point to the ground. He's smiling, as if he's about to share some groan-inducing piece of humor.

Will stops, says, "Dad."

His father nods, reaches over and pulls Will into a hug. His dad feels real, far more so than the body in the casket against whose still, cold brow he pressed his lips before the coffin's lid was secured. Will steps back, his throat full. "Dad," he says again, because he wants to speak and can't think of anything to say.

"Will," his father says. "I wasn't sure you'd make it. I should have known."

"What do you mean?"

With his left hand, his dad gestures at the other side of the street. Will supposes he must have seen what his father directs his attention to as he crested the driveway, but ignored it, all his attention focused on his dad. Now he sees the half-dozen trees across the road burning, their crowns great torches casting fiery light about them. The trees behind them are aflame, as well, and so are the trees beyond them. Several details strike him at once. Instead of descending the slope on the opposite side of the street, the trees continue back on a level surface. That surface is a white sand rich in crystals, which catch the light and flare like miniature stars, describing strange constellations on the ground. Though the tops of the trees are balls of fire, the trunks below them are unblackened. In fact, Will feels no heat whatsoever from them.

"*Luceo non uro*," his father says.

"What?"

"A private joke." Dad raises his sword, takes it in both hands, and assumes a middle guard. Will grips the spear in his hands and holds it in front of him. "This," he says, "is not what I remember."

"No," his father says, "I don't imagine it is."

"What is it?"

"It's what we actually saw, that long-ago night. Or close enough."

"What are you saying?"

"I'm saying your mind constructed another memory to stand in for this one, because this was too much for it. A bear, wasn't it?"

"The biggest one I ever saw."

"For me, it was a man. He stepped onto the road in hand-tooled leather cowboy boots. He was wearing jeans, a white shirt, and a leather jacket. His hair was long and black, and he had no face."

Will shakes his head. "I can't... All right," he says, "if I didn't see a grizzly, and you didn't see a guy without a face, then what did we see?"

His dad tilts his head toward the burning trees. "It's coming."

Squinting against the glare, Will peers into the ranks of trees facing him. Amidst the trunks, something moves, winding its way between the trees toward them. Big as a Clydesdale, bigger, it pads forward, its shaggy head low. Will sees muscular flanks, huge paws, thinks, *Lion?* Its tail hoists behind it, a segmented arc that extends almost to its shoulders. A knob bristling with spikes caps the tail. *Not a lion.* He says, "What *is* it?"

"The guardian," Dad says.

"You mean like in that thing you wrote about Carson?"

His father's eyebrows lift with pleasure. "You read that."

"I did."

"Then, yes."

"It was true—the story?"

"As true as I could make it. Carson found his way to another place, where he drank from a spring and summoned the creature appointed to guard it."

"It doesn't sound any less crazy, hearing you say it."

His dad shrugs. "There are more heavens and earths—

250 | AUTUMN CTHULHU

and hells—than are dreamt of in your philosophy."

"Great."

"If it's any consolation, I didn't believe Carson's story, either, the first time I heard it. Not as literal truth."

"What changed your mind?"

"A couple of days before Carson left, he and I walked up here—"

"And saw the fire on the other side of the valley," Will says. "I was there, remember? It...moved, danced."

"Yes," his father says. "That's right, you were there. Anyway, watching those flames move on the side of the ridge did the trick."

Across the road, the creature reaches the edge of the tree line and pauses, its armored tail thrashing behind it. Although its body is that of a lion—a monstrously-large lion—the face framed by its heavy mane is a man's, grown to a giant's proportions. Its eyes shine, windows to a furnace. It opens its mouth, and Will sees row upon row of sharp teeth receding down its gullet. Its roar is the metal song of a full complement of cathedral bells. The fiery tree tops shiver at it.

Will winces, but does not release the *qiang*. He expects the thing to take advantage of its roar's effect to charge him and his father. It does not. Once enough of his hearing has returned for him to hear himself speak, he says, "Remind me what we're doing here, again."

"We're the anchor," his dad says.

"The anchor?"

"Like a distraction, but more lasting."

"How so?"

"The guardian doesn't have the same relation to space and time as we do. What little information Carson had been able to turn up on it told us this much. In order for it to spiral in on its prey, it was necessary for the creature to maintain its focus on them. If you could find a way to draw its notice away from its target, you might be able to split its concentration."

"To what end?"

"Ideally, the beast would become confused, lost, like a dog off the scent. If not that, then the red herring would act as a drag on the guardian, slowing it enough for Carson to maintain his lead on it."

"An anchor."

"Exactly."

"I take it this has something to do with why I dream about that night every October."

His father nods. "You aren't remembering it—it's still happening."

"What do you mean?"

"Having confronted it, you and I became entangled in its time. Not enough for us to be trapped in it, but sufficiently for a part of us to remain in this moment. Carson was not happy with the plan; he said there was too much risk in it."

"It sounds like Carson was right," Will says. "Didn't you think it was maybe a little dangerous to bring your twelve-year-old son with you to confront a Goddamn monster?"

"Language."

"Answer the question."

"Of course I recognized the danger," his dad says. "But we had to make a convincing display to the creature, and you knew how to handle the spear. You thought the world of Carson. I assumed if I'd told you what I was up to, you would have wanted to join in. Plus, I was reasonably sure the guardian wouldn't attack us."

"Reasonably isn't the certain I prefer," Will says. "Though you're right, had you asked me, I would have agreed to help."

"Well, I'm sorry I didn't."

"Don't let it happen again. So did your plan succeed?" Will says. "I assume the thing finally caught up to Carson in

Russia, but until that point, he seems as if he was doing okay."

"Look," Dad says, dipping the point of his sword at the waiting creature.

Enlarged, its features are exaggerated. Will sees the deep-set eyes, the high cheekbones, the rounded chin, and recognizes the face as Carson's. He steps back. The tip of the *qiang* drops. It's as if he's been punched in the solar plexus; he can't seem to draw enough air into his lungs. He leans forward. Of all the fantastic sights to greet him tonight, this is one too many, the piece of straw that cripples the camel. He finds enough breath to whisper, "What the fuck?"

His father's hand falls on his shoulder. "Steady," he says. "It's all right. It's okay. Come on. It's all right."

Gradually, his chest loosens, and Will straightens. His dad is watching him. His right hand remains on Will's shoulder; his left keeps the *do* trained on the creature, which observes the two of them with its burning eyes. Will lifts the spear and centers it on the thing's chest.

"Carson finally confronted the guardian and killed it," Dad says.

"What? When?"

"The first time was during his stay in Scotland. He'd rented a house in the Highlands. It sat at one end of a glen to which a narrow valley gave admission. He'd selected it precisely for its layout. He spent a summer digging a deep pit where the valet was at its most narrow. He filled the bottom of the hole with Punji sticks he fashioned from eight foot two by fours. He stitched together three of the biggest tarps he could buy, and secured them over the pit, scattering dirt on them to disguise the trap. The night the guardian appeared, he stood on one side of the tarps, a homemade spear in one hand, an axe in the other. The creature ran at him, and plunged into the pit. It heaved and sank, dealt a half-dozen mortal wounds. Carson waited until it was quiet, then lowered himself into the hole and beheaded it. He buried it right there, shoveled all the dirt and rock he'd excavated on top of it.

"He was pretty happy. He talked about returning to the States, coming to visit us. First, he had a book to finish, interviews to respond to, introductions to write. All of it took him longer to complete than he'd anticipated, but what difference did that make? He was free of his pursuer.

"Late the next summer, it returned. There were the familiar warning signs: he dreamed he was back at the pool in the rock; the weather was unusually warm; he heard the faint echo of the creature's voice, somewhere in the surrounding hills. He tried to dismiss them, discount the dreams and sounds as byproducts of stress surplus from years of being chased, the spike in the mercury as a fluke. When he looked out the window one evening to see fire lighting the top of the nearest hill, he knew his previous effort had failed, and the beast was on its way. He considered fleeing, but the success he'd had made him bold, and he decided to stay and fight. There was no time to construct another elaborate trap, so he settled on a simple one. He built a number of rudimentary bombs and positioned them just beyond his prior trap. As the creature stepped into their midst, he detonated them. The storm of shrapnel cut the guardian to pieces. This time, he dismembered it and disposed of the limbs at considerable distances from one another."

"I'm guessing this didn't work, either."

"You're right; it didn't. He spent one more year in Scotland, and left after his first dream of the creature. He killed it several more times, once in Germany, once in Finland, twice in Nepal, and once in Mongolia. There may be another I'm forgetting. He used everything he could lay his hands on against it, shotguns and rifles, wolf and bear traps, dynamite. He drowned it; he electrocuted it. The creature died and died and died, and returned and returned and returned, never any less relentless. Had it not been for you and me, restaging our confrontation with the guardian year after year, adding weight to our anchor with each repetition, the creature would have had Carson on a couple of occasions.

"Eventually, he grew tired of running. He had come to Tilichiki, a small town on the northeast coast of the Kamchatka peninsula. When next the guardian came for him, he told me, he was going out to meet it with an axe and a machete. There would be no more traps, no more experiments to discover if this means of death might be the one to slay the beast for good. He had called to say goodbye; he knew his chances of surviving such an encounter, even with our anchor, were slim.

"There was nothing I could say, not really, but I did offer a suggestion. If he overcame the creature again, this time, maybe he should try eating it?"

"Eating it?"

"It's an ancient means of absorbing your opponent's power. To be honest, what suggested it to me was an essay I'd been reading, in which the writer compared the job of the critic struggling to come to terms with a poem to that of a hero fighting a monster. The only solution, the writer decided, was for the critic to consume the poem. All of this was clever metaphor, needless to say, but it occurred to me as a tactic Carson had yet to employ."

"Obviously, he did."

"He phoned a couple of days after that last fight. Although the connection was terrible, I could hear the severity of his injuries in his voice. He'd lost an eye, an ear, had his scalp laid open. His torso was riddled with puncture wounds, from the creature's tail. He suspected its spines were envenomed, because the wounds had swollen and were leaking pus. His left hand and forearm had been crushed, and his left foot torn most of the way off. But he had done it, he said, had stabbed the beast in two of its three hearts, severed its tail at the base, and split its skull with his axe. As soon as he could move, he bound his wounds as best he could and started gathering wood for a fire to roast it. Its hearts were tough, he said, and he burned them but he'd had better luck with its liver, or what he thought was its liver. What was bizarre was he'd had no appetite at all, but the second he put that first piece of flesh into his mouth, he'd been ravenous.

"That was the last I heard from him. I assumed his injuries had been too severe for him to survive. Apparently, something else happened."

"Apparently," Will says. "What do we do now?"

His dad studies the creature facing them, Carson, or what Carson has become. He lowers the *do*, and holds it out for Will to take.

Will does. "What is this?"

"I think I have to go with him."

"You have to?"

"I'm supposed to—it's what makes sense."

"Makes sense? How?"

"Symbolically."

"Are you serious?"

"It's the kind of logic these types of places follow."

"And if you're wrong?"

"Avenge me, oh my son," Dad says, and grins.

"This is not funny," Will says.

"It is what it is." His dad turns to him. "You're a good man, and I'm proud of you. It's been my privilege to be your father, and I love you."

Their embrace doesn't last as long as Will wishes it would. How could it? He doesn't bother wiping the tears that fracture his vision. "Why?" he says. "What made you agree to help him?"

"He was my friend," his father says. "I had to. Not to mention, how could I pass up a chance to see an actual monster?"

And then he's away, striding across the pavement to where the creature that bears his old friend's face waits beside trees whose blooms are fire. As he walks, he calls out, "Hail, guardian of the sacred spring! Hail scourge! Hail psychopomp!"

The beast opens its mouth, full of fangs, and roars its awful welcome.

> Tell me a story.
> Make it a story of great distances, and starlight.
> The name of the story will be Time,
> But you must not pronounce its name.
> –Robert Penn Warren, *Audubon: A Vision*

For Fiona, and for Justin Steele

End of the Season
by Trent Kollodge

Jamie's Burned Down Bar looked naked without the gray and blue striped summer tent stretched overhead. The original building having been destroyed by fire years ago, its empty deck sat under the overcast sky at the corner of Marina and Bay. A handful of barstools stood against the counter, three of them occupied. A freestanding wood stove drove back the October chill with an older couple huddled near it in private conversation. And the rust-pocked, semi-trailer bar back threw out a welcoming light that beckoned me in from the street. For the first time since spring, I approached as only a customer. Not that that would matter much if Jamie caught me around, he was as likely to put a customer to work as an employee, more likely in some cases.

"I thought you were gone," Amber said as I slid onto the stool at the end of the bar.

"Missed the boat," I said. "Guess I'll be another night on the island."

Her wide blue eyes caught mine the way they had all summer. I don't think either of us knew what it meant. Maybe we could have had a good thing going if either of us had made the first move. Maybe the timing wasn't right for either of us. Or maybe it was just me.

"It's good to see you anyway," she said. "What'll it be?"

"Two shots of the Jim Beam and a Leine's." I knocked my knuckles on the bar and turned to take in the empty scene. I had occupied Jamie's through so many moods: from the spring cleaning and tent raising with the fresh paint for the old boards and new screws for the loose joints, through the summer storms rolling in off the lake and all hands on deck to lash down what the wind could take, to the hot July afternoons with the daiquiris grinding in the garage sale mixers and the tourists burning in their shorts, and the August nights thick with the final revelries of summer, the bands jumping loud on the makeshift stage, and the crowd pouring out into the streets. A season of drunken days and inebriated nights, and now the autumn came, stripping the tourists like so many leaves. And the last of the summer help flew south while the natives fattened their stores for the long Midwestern hibernation.

I unzipped my jacket for the space heater over the bar, rapped my shots against the counter to knock the devil out of them, and tossed them back in quick succession. My tolerance for alcohol both shocked and impressed me. I had arrived on the island thinking two or three drinks in an evening was a pretty good drunk. By mid-summer, I wouldn't even start feeling a buzz until the fifth: the wages of bar life and depression.

"Where's the crew?" I asked. The faces at the counter were those of lingering summer people, and with five o'clock coming on, there should have been at least one or two locals about.

Amber caught my eye again. "First full moon of fall," she said. "Private party. Islanders only."

"Do you know where they hold this shindig?"

She glanced down at the summer people two seats away. "You know where," she said.

"The little village."

Amber nodded and held my eyes. She looked concerned.

I had heard whispers of the little village since my first week on the island. In some ways it was as well-known as the island's famous tentacled petroglyph. Though likely a nineteenth century fake, the petroglyph carved in the cliff overlooking the bay was the island mascot. Its spirally image; the logo on the t-shirts, festival flags, and promotional pamphlets. The cliff's location pointed out by signs on every street corner, and proudly cordoned off with a fancy chain and historical plaque. The petroglyph was the island's claim to fame, its tourist attraction; the village was its mystery.

A dollhouse village, the whispers said, a perfect miniature

of the town, complete with streets and bushes and tiny piers, set back in the woods somewhere on the north end of the island. It was the local legend, the rumor among the tourists, the place everyone knew about but no one had actually seen. The knowledge of its location was what separated the locals from the tourists, but when questioned, few locals would admit its existence, much less let on that they knew where it lay. I'd asked Jamie about it the first night I'd found him drinking at one of the rival bars.

"Tell me about this little village of yours," I said with all the subtlety of an amateur drunk.

"This is me," he said, holding up a three-inch brass screw that had been twisted out of true. "Slightly bent and completely screwy." Then he laughed a crazy overbearing laugh that leapt out after any joke within earshot, particularly his own.

After a week in his employ I'd grown accustomed to these non sequiturs, and went on as if he hadn't spoken. "I've heard stories," I said.

"Yeah, stories," he muttered with an unconscious wink. "Nothin' in 'em but a bit of titillation to keep the tourists coming back."

But his wink told all. The gauntlet had been thrown. The place did exist, and I was going to find it. In the fleeting moments between working and drinking, I spent a few hours looking through the local library but nothing came up. Across the bay, I had better luck. The historical society there had several mentions of the little village rumor dating back to the 1830's. The articles took decidedly disparaging tones, as if the place were unwholesome, but revealed nothing helpful about its location.

Over the rest of the summer, I kept my ears open, gleaning veiled references from old timers and edging ever closer to the truth behind the mystery. By fall, I had narrowed its whereabouts down to a two-mile stretch of gravel road lined with PRIVATE PROPERTY signs, but its precise location had eluded me until now. If the islanders were out there having some kind of party, I was sure to find it. I chugged my beer and reached for my cash.

Amber shook her head and waved off the tab. Her eyes still held mine. There was something more on her mind. "Don't go," she said. "You don't want to get that deep into this place or these people."

Maybe she knew what she was talking about. Being from across the bay, she was local without being islander. She'd grown up with the rumors and spent half a dozen summers working the bar and watching the islanders. But what did I care? My ticket back to the west coast had tomorrow's date on it. One way or the other, I'd be out of state by the following evening.

"What are they going to do, kick me off the island?" I said.

Her expression never changed, but I could feel the concern behind her eyes vying with the very pointed distance we had kept between us all summer. "How are you going to get out there?" she asked.

"I'll take the bar truck," I said. "No one will miss it for a few hours, especially if Jamie's not around."

"Take mine," she said. "They'll hear that rust bucket a mile away."

"Wish me luck," I said, and headed out.

No one locked their cars on the island, or even bothered removing the keys from the ignition. What would be the point? Everyone knew everyone, and there was nowhere to go. I bought a bottle of bourbon and a fresh pack of cigarettes from the one and only corner store in town to keep me company on my way out to the north end.

The road turned gravel about a mile out of town and threaded through a forest that offered few vistas but the occasional peek at a rocky coast and the great lake beyond. As I drove, I wondered if the island had accomplished what I'd come there for. Six months before, a seven-year relationship—the longest I'd ever known—had broken, calling an end to love and kicking me out of my home. When a friend of a friend mentioned summer jobs waiting at a tourist bar on an island on the Great Lakes, nothing in the world sounded better than a drunken season three quarters of a continent away.

Well, the island had done its best by me. It had given me passion in the arms of a summer fling, distractions in the continual party roving from bar to beach to concert to rented room, and curiosities in the insular small town culture that lurked beneath the friendly tourist town façade. After a month and a half, I'd even begun to have nights mercifully free of the breakup nightmares that plagued my sleep.

Yet I had to admit, as the sky gloomed darker and the dust plume rose behind me, I was still a very broken man on the inside. Most mornings I woke thinking my ex was still there beside me, or maybe in the next room reading her web pages over coffee, steam curling in the sun like the curls of her freshly-washed hair. Then the realization would hit me right in the stomach, raw and wretched as a virus: she was gone from my life, she wouldn't be back. The reasons had always seemed vague and senseless. They could never add up to the cataclysmic conclusion.

I took another swig from the bottle between my knees, lit a fresh cigarette from the one I was smoking, and flicked the old butt out the window of Amber's Honda. There wouldn't be anyone on that road for miles. Plus, it was Tuesday: the one cop on the island would be down at the marina bars. He wasn't local enough to be out at the village, never would be, even if he spent the rest of his life out there.

The islanders were a strange breed. Though not in a physical sense. They traced their ancestry to the same immigrants most of the region was related to. Hell, even my family tree wound through the American Midwest. But psychologically, spiritually, they seemed different somehow: distant but intense, as if the outside world were interesting but not in any way important, and this attitude inspired a vague prejudice against them across the bay and throughout the surrounding region.

To me they all seemed to have a disturbing authenticity, a deep, innate sense of who they were that decried the self-consciousness and doubts I thought of as essentially human. Good or bad, big or small, their knowledge of themselves permeated everything they did, and everything they were. At first I had attributed it to the small town culture I had never experienced firsthand, to the way their lives were so intimately connected. With only a few hundred people living permanently on the island, there was a good chance that any two locals at a bar were related to each other within a couple of generations. The musical beds and loves and animosities had all happened between these people, and would happen, again and again, flaring up in the late night booze or the long hard winters or the summer decadence. They knew each other's secrets, shared each other's hardships and joys, grew up and lived and died together. With that kind of communal feedback, I thought, it would be difficult *not* to know yourself. But the same could likely be said of any of the towns in the area. There had to be more to it than that.

After two months of observation, I felt I could put my finger on it. Old or young, seventh generation or three-month resident, the true islanders had a vision of the world. They could laugh and cry and dance with the minutiae of the moment, but always behind their eyes glittered the sharp edge of a knowledge that all of humanity's passions were nothing more than a fleeting pareidolia in the wrinkles of the veil hiding a dark truth. What that truth was, I didn't yet know. Was it something I wanted, something I was looking for?

Navigating that gravel through the trees with a cigarette in one hand and a bottle in the other, what I wanted was to snatch that final peek at the island's most secret secret before being on my way and back to whatever it was that awaited me on the coast

I had come from.

About half a mile into the stretch I thought of as my target zone, I began to see familiar cars parked in the dead leaves along the side of the road. There was Jamie's beat up Buick, old Mr. Olsen's vintage orange muscle car, Rachel's pickup, and dozens of others. Another hundred yards along I saw Bill Patterson stumbling into the woods. Bill was what the locals called a 'man who likes a drink,' which by west coast standards amounted to a raging alcoholic with one foot in the grave. Personally, I didn't have a problem with Bill, and as his sometime bartender, he seemed to like me well enough in return. I gave a wave out the window and kept driving like I was just cruising the island loop until he was well out of sight. Then I parked Amber's car, downed another swig of whiskey, tucked the bottle in an inside coat pocket, and hiked back through the forest to the spot I'd seen him enter.

With the last of the sun sinking behind the trees, the evening was getting colder than I was comfortable with. The chill was laughable compared to the frozen months ahead, I'd heard, but being from the west coast, it may as well have been mid-winter. I lit another cigarette, zipped my collar up high, and balled my fists around the bottle near my belly. The woods, which I had seen teeming with growth and dripping with an outbreak of tent caterpillars over the summer, looked thin, dead. The heavy sky visible through the half-barren branches loomed low. Beneath my heels, the ground felt soft and fleshy from the accumulation of wet, newly-fallen leaves.

At the place I had seen Bill enter the woods, I found a trail leading north. The repeating and increasingly-threatening signs let me know I was on the right track: PRIVATE PROPERTY KEEP OUT, TURN BACK NOW, and YOU WILL BE PROSECUTED WITH PREJUDICE. I could feel the guilt of trespassing and the fear of backwoods reprisals clawing around in my gut with a giddy anticipation. Another swig tamped that down fine. My summer quest was about to come to its end. The little village would be secret no longer.

Distracted by my thoughts, I stumbled over a root. Worried that the noise would draw the attention of the islanders, I listened intently, but for all I could tell, I was alone. By the time I reached the final warning sign, which dropped its threatening tone and pleaded for respect of property and history, I began to wonder where the islanders could be. There had to be at least a hundred of them out there somewhere. I field stripped my cigarette, and moved cautiously.

The little village revealed itself slowly in the failing light. Buildings representing the outlying homes on the island were strewn back through the woods a good thirty yards from the main street, hidden in the lee side of trees or perched jauntily on small hillocks. Their intricate construction impressed me. Tiny stones, no more than an inch in length, had been ground flat and mortared into place, with concrete roof tiles to keep the rain out. From the lack of leaves and moss around them, I could tell that they had been recently maintained.

The village itself was incredible. The streets and buildings I was so intimately familiar with after a summer of wanderings were all perfectly reproduced and laid out in a clearing no bigger than a studio apartment. Here was the church, its simple lines going back to pre-revolutionary days. There was the octagonal library, a former Masons building from the late eighteenth century. Off to the left sat the shops, the bars, and the strip with the bank and the laundromat. Toward where the docks would be sat a tiny reproduction of the tentacled petroglyph. Even the empty deck of Jamie's bar was represented by a small slab of carved stone.

Interestingly, the miniatures the of older buildings in the real town looked significantly more weathered than those of the newer buildings, as if each miniature had been built contemporary with the building they represented. How long had the little village been there, I wondered. Had there been dollhouse versions of the fur trader forts that existed on the island before the country was a country? Or miniature wooden lodges of the native communities before?

Cautiously, I stepped onto the main street, smaller than a sidewalk, the tallest steeple of the church no higher than my knee. The wonder and magic of the place made me inhale a deep and purposeful breath even as the alcohol in my blood reached a pleasant warmth. Standing there, towering over the tiny buildings, I felt as if I were a part of the history of the town, a part of the island, a vital moment of its interminable existence. I felt the island talking to me, flowing through my veins.

The sound of singing broke my reverie. Approaching from where the marina would be if the miniature town continued through the forest, the islanders were singing in unison, like a congregation at Sunday prayer. I had almost forgotten them in my private moment.

I retreated back the way I had come. I had found their secret, seen their village, I thought, why get caught? But then curiosity got the better of me. What were they doing out there? Why was the event so private as to be islander only? With the darkness growing, the V of two trees provided excellent cover from which to watch the proceedings unobserved. I took another swig from my bottle and settled in.

They came in procession, four and five abreast, singing an eerie, droning, wordless hymn that fluctuated from minor to augmented harmonies and crept into my chest like fear. I saw Martha and Tommy, Bill Patterson, the Harvey girls, and Jamie, all the islanders I knew and more that I didn't due to their absence from the bar scene. Their fervent expressions bordered on zealous. As they reached the village, each one placed an item on the ground at the central crossroads: a scrap of cloth, an old rag doll, Bill's lucky bottle cap, Jamie's bent screw. Then they split into two lines, flowing out and around to form a ring, effectively blocking my view of the buildings and streets.

I tried to wedge my boot between the trees and hoist myself up to see over the crowd, but the bourbon was catching up to me. My foot slipped and my head knocked against the bark. With a wincing grimace to bite off a curse, I sat down hard on the cold soil, and rubbed furiously at my forehead.

Without warning, the song of the islanders ceased. I froze and strained my ears at the darkness of the woods. In the silence that echoed, I could hear the thumps and susurration of something large lurching and flopping across the forest floor. Something had followed behind the procession of islanders. Something that cracked trees and shook the ground with its passing. I couldn't see it from where I sat, but I could feel it in my chest, unnerving the warmth of the booze. Then the stench of fish guts and rot hit me and turned my stomach.

I retched violently, and stumbled to my feet, spitting and coughing without a care for who heard. The nauseous reek, the aqueous squelching, and the overpowering presence of something beyond reckoning held me in terror. And yet, it enthralled me as if the fervor of the congregation were contagious. In that moment, it didn't matter that I could not see or name the island deity that moved through the miniature village. I didn't question the incongruity of the glimpses of cnidarian flesh that occasionally peeked above the heads of the worshipers. I didn't need to be a believer; I was there. And even through the alcohol blur, I knew that this was the secret. This was what made the islanders islanders. I didn't understand it, but I would not run away.

When the creature retreated, shambling back toward the depths from which it came, the islanders broke ranks and began examining the little village with handheld lanterns and flashlights. At first, I didn't know what they were looking for, but then I saw Michelle burst into tears. Michelle had been the happiest local I had known on the island. She was young and in love with a lucky young man named Daniel. Her talismanic item had been the rag doll. I had seen her place it carefully next to Daniel's silver lighter. Now though, the rag doll was alone on her father's porch at the far end of the street, and Daniel's lighter was entwined with the hair band of Miss Erica Samwell, moved there by the motions of the creature from the depths. The implications of her anguish were obvious: prognostication or command, cosmic intent or happenstance, this was the way things were going to be.

From there I watched the stories unfold. Most were expected, people placed where they had been, or where they were obviously headed: Jamie at his bar, Martha in her shop, Bill in the graveyard where his doctor had predicted. Some couples shifted partners, not bothering to wait for the emotional causes to precipitate the actions, but simply abandoning their old lovers and leaving hand in hand with the new arrangements dictated by the items in the tiny town.

Realizing that it no longer mattered and too drunk to care, I left off any attempts at hiding and leaned hard against the tree. Most of the islanders walked by without noticing me in the gloom, and those who did just gave me a knowing nod. I rinsed the vomit from my mouth, lit another cigarette, and finished my bottle of whiskey, contemplating fate and future and the curse of knowing versus the curse of ignorance. I'd had no future since my breakup ten months before. All of my plans and visions of possibilities had been wrapped up with my ex, and I had been unable to formulate anything meaningful since. The ticket back to the coast was in my pocket, but the coast wasn't home, she had been home, and she didn't want me. She didn't want me.

I wiped the tears from my eyes as Jamie stepped up and put a hand on my shoulder. "This is you," he said, taking the empty bottle from my hand and holding it up before me, "empty on the inside and completely drunk." He turned to look down the path where the creature had retreated. "We all sing alone the first time," he said. Then left me, his voice finding a bawdy sea chantey as he wended his way back to the road.

Alone in the darkness I swayed and smoked three more cigarettes before the temperature forced me to move, to choose: the path to the car, the bar, the train to the coast, or the path to the lake and the knowledge from the depths? The clouds cleared away, and the big full moon poked its beams into the clearing, casting shadows from the miniature town. I took the path to the water.

The wind blew cold over the black lake. I set my bottle on the beach between the road back to the little village and the rocky pier with the miniature ferry boat built beside. Then I stood back and sang, tentative at first, unsure if my voice could follow the strange tune that still rang in my head. But as the gentle lapping rhythm of the lake worked its way into my bones, the song grew stronger, more confident in longing and sorrow, flowing out of me in a prayer of pleading and misery. Take me in or set me free, I sang to the island and its unearthly visitor. Tell me my place and I will obey.

As I sang, the last of the whiskey made its way to my brain. The world began to blur and spin, and I found myself lying on the ground, my eyes struggling to stay open, my voice trailing off to a murmur. Did I see something rise from the lake and snake up toward my bottle on the shore? Or was it only the moonlight on the waves twisting through the distortion of my inebriation? I'll never know for sure. What I do know, is that when the morning light woke me stiff and chilled, the only mark upon the sand was a deep clear line where my talismanic bottle had been dragged into the depths.

Two weeks have passed since that night. My train to the coast has long since come and gone from the shore across the bay. It's the last night of the year for Jamie's bar, everything stowed and locked down for the long winter ahead. Jamie himself poured the drinks from his private shelf. No one but islanders left now.

I suppose I could laugh at the omen, defy the fate decreed, or try to take up residence on the island and live a long contemplative life, but that's not the way fate works. Everyone here understands that this is goodbye. There are no jobs to be had through the winter months, no rooms to rent, no place for me. I've got a ticket for the ferry. It leaves in an hour. I don't expect to make the opposite shore. There is a freedom in knowing your fate, in walking your path without the pull of plans and dreams or the prodding of cause and effect. There are islanders and there are islanders, and for this brief time, I am one.

Water Main

by S.P. Miskowski

First the vine maples began to shiver, leaves of bright burgundy shot through with translucent veins forming a blood-red wall along the western edge of the park. Alders caught the rhythm and shook loose their amber, jagged leaves onto the yellow grass below. A final ray of sunlight struck the spot where the boy stood afraid to take another step. The sun seemed to roll down the far shoulder of the earth to be consumed by the cold waters of Puget Sound.

That final shimmer lasted only a second; when the boy looked up, night came tumbling down through the clouds. The air was bitterly cold. An underground rumble became a roar with a monstrous echo as it traveled. Bystanders in the park clapped hands to their ears and ran.

"This is what struck me about the grownups and never wore off," the boy said years later when he was a man, when he was a father. "They ran in all directions. Not one of them knew what to do! No one was going to help me. So I ran like hell.

"I heard the ground splitting, the asphalt and the sidewalks cracking open. A Volkswagen rolled over in the street. On both sides of me the slopes and hills were rippling. The giant was waking up, stretching his limbs, and shaking loose anything in his path.

"I was running so fast I couldn't breathe, my heartbeat throbbing in my ears and throat. That's when I heard the worst thing, the worst sound you can imagine. Crashing against the ground close behind me I felt his footsteps pounding the earth. The giant was following me. He was chasing me down."

At this point in the story Nancy's father would sometimes wink as if to assure the girl he was much more sensible as an adult. Nancy winked, too, anxious to ignore whatever was wrong with her dad, or whatever was still chasing him through his nightmares and into morning. She was forbidden to admit she heard him crying behind closed doors, her mother saying his name over and over until he fell quiet in her arms.

As for the ending to the story, he told a different variation depending upon his most recent dream. In one version he escaped by climbing to the top of a totem pole in the park. In another he ran to a nearby pier and leapt aboard a ship headed to Victoria. He never explained how he got down from the totem pole or returned from British Columbia.

These tacked-on happy endings didn't satisfy Nancy. When she was small and naive enough to believe in the giant, she wanted to know if it tried to shake her father loose from the totem pole. Did it follow him onto the pier, and drown in the bay?

After the age of nine or ten she understood the basic conditions that caused earthquakes. She became curious about the scale of it and the duration. She realized it could only have lasted for a couple of minutes at most, not the amount of time needed for a boy's epic adventure. As she grew up, the facts of the quake were the only parts of the story that interested Nancy. But for her father the childish fantasy of that day and its aftershocks lingered a lifetime—a lifetime being the four decades it took for him to drink himself to death.

A crisp day in autumn not long before Halloween always reminded Nancy of her father and his warnings. Throughout her childhood he had doled them out like candy. In fact, candy was at the top of the list of things she was supposed to avoid, especially holiday treats from strangers. But there were also dire warnings about public toilets, dogs (even on leashes), convenience stores (especially at night), unsupervised children and teens, electrical outlets (during storms), unlit rooms, steep staircases, carnival rides, banquet or buffet food, cocktails on a date, and all weather conditions.

Nancy trudged uphill from the bus stop. When she reached her apartment building she took a deep breath and resisted an urge to kick the jack-o-lanterns piled next to the front door. She wanted to. She wanted to slam her boots right into the crooked mouth of the biggest pumpkin and spread its orange, gooey guts all over the sidewalk.

Jim wasn't waiting for her to get home. He was playing one of his games, the lights from the TV screen sparkling in his otherwise vacant eyes.

"If you don't fix the plumbing by the end of the week," she told him. "I'm calling the manager."

"I'm on it," he said. "I'm all over it."

"What does that mean? I'll bet you haven't done a thing today, have you? Call the manager. Let him send a real plumber this time."

"They'll make us pay a fortune for it. They think this is our fault."

"I don't care, Jim. If you don't fix it by the weekend, I don't know what I'll do."

Vague as it was, this was Nancy's most emphatic threat so far. She had given him more than enough time. Her tender request in July had been followed by earnest pleading in August, sarcasm in September, and then came the October of shouting and angry tears. As they approached Halloween, the prospect of one more weekend tiptoeing around an icy puddle to reach the toilet, or changing clothes for work after getting spattered with meat-scented water from the kitchen, made Nancy want to strangle someone. She never drank tap water anymore, only bottled. She blamed Jim for the added expense.

He had made a useless promise every week since they leased the place, a spot he'd scoped out for its scenic beauty rather than practicality. Perched halfway up Queen Anne, the steepest hill in the city, the four-story Pacific Willow Arms afforded one quarter of its tenants—those, like Nancy and Jim, facing west and living above the second floor—a panoramic view. Tenants on the east side had to be content with a view of trash dumpsters lining a concrete alley.

"On a clear day we'll be able to watch whales from our living room!" Jim had said the day they moved in. He'd bought a pair of binoculars for each of them and spent hours spying on the bars, cafes, and rooftop gardens down the hill. Clear days, clear enough to see Puget Sound, were unusual. Even in summer they never spotted any ocean life, only massive clouds *shaped* like whales, gliding morosely parallel to the water.

From the second month of the lease, they'd had plumbing problems. The compact washer-dryer only operated when balanced at one corner by a wine bottle cork. The cold water handle in the bathroom sink was loose; jiggling it prompted a jolting noise from somewhere beneath the wood and porcelain vanity. One day the dishwasher erupted, sending an inch-deep lake of foam across the kitchen floor. Later their basement storage unit flooded, ruining a sofa bed and a trunk full of photo albums and mementos; renter's insurance only covered the sofa bed, and the lease agreement left management exempt from responsibility.

"It's probably that water main again," the manager had explained while munching wasabi and seaweed crackers. "That's a *force majeure*. Happens every few years. You could sue the city for negligence but good luck with that. Ever try fighting a parking ticket? Bureaucracy's gonna outlive all of us."

Recently the garbage disposal seemed to run in reverse, drawing up from the bowels of the Pacific Willow Arms a sulfurous sludge Jim had dubbed "the ick." In less than a week, the ick had spread beneath the floor, under the living room, to the hall bathroom and lingered until they had stopped using the garbage disposal altogether. Nancy was mortified to learn their downstairs neighbor had complained about the smell emanating from his ceiling fan.

"I told him we can't be accountable for natural occurrences or unsanitary personal behavior," the manager said.

Finally that morning, on the last Friday in October, the shower had come to a stuttering stop. Nancy had toweled dry and dressed for work. All day long she detected a vague underlying funk, a dried layer of sweat trapped between her skin and her clothes. She hated the feeling but she didn't dare cover it with perfume. Nearly everyone at the office was allergic, or claimed to be.

Through a team meeting, an executive tour for the Korean investors, and a couple of video conferences, she kept yearning for a bath—a long, hot, lazy bath with aromatic salts in a tub lit with rose-scented candles. Meanwhile she stank of sweat with a hint of something oily like herring. It seemed as if the day would never end. By the time she stepped off the #8 and began the slow, sweaty ascent to her building—now that she examined it closely, the whole structure of the Pacific Willow Arms appeared to rest uneasily on its carefully graded foundation—she was almost convinced her imaginary bath would be waiting for her because she deserved it.

Instead, as usual, she found Jim slumped in his favorite chair, wearing pajamas and munching a slice of pizza. Cheese stuck to his teeth and he reeked of garlic, anchovies, and onions. Behind him, arranged across the kitchen linoleum, lay a vast array of plumbing tools.

"Why can't you put those on a drop cloth?" Nancy asked while she peeled off her coat.

"What's a drop cloth again?" he said.

It was a constant source of irritation, this fantasy Jim had of himself as a handyman. His parents had been in construction, his dad a sub-contractor and his mom the company bookkeeper. Jim hated helping his dad with home repairs when he was growing up. Yet ever since his dad passed away he'd been nursing this delusion that he had absorbed the old man's knowledge. Not through practice or study but the way Jim claimed to learn everything—by magic, by osmosis, by picking up signs and clues in the atmosphere.

What he actually picked up were tools. Every time he tackled another section of pipes, he spent hours at Home Depot. When he finally came home he brought wrench sets, clamps, and tube cutters. Then he arranged everything on the floor and spent days in slow motion repairing the most recent trouble area. Within days or even hours of each fix another section would fail, and Jim would start the process all over again with another three-hour trip to Home Depot.

Nancy was sick of it. The leaks and damage now felt like reminders of their incompatibility, as if the place couldn't contain the multitude of differences erupting between them. Her habit of setting aside money from each paycheck was wasted on Jim, who considered earned cash to be instantly expendable. She had no idea how much he spent streaming his latest obsession—a series of poorly produced 1970s cartoons that left Nancy grinding her teeth. The art direction was terrible. All of the characters, both animal and human, were nothing but blobs. Every episode revolved around a different blob getting stuck or lost until his blob friends came to the rescue and all the blobs joined blobby appendages and sang the insipid theme song.

She wondered if she was being mean for not appreciating Jim's idea of fun. Then she blamed him for inciting her guilt and self-criticism. All she wanted was a hot bath or shower and a glass of clean tap water, things she once took for granted and was now beginning to think of as luxuries.

"I'm going for a walk," she said.

She pulled her coat and scarf from the closet and put them back on. She didn't expect him to object. She knew he wouldn't follow, or make sure she was bundled up against the cold, or give her a kiss. Over the past few months he'd grown negligent. They'd stopped taking day trips, stopped having an occasional lunch together. She couldn't remember the last time they'd had sex. He just wasn't interested. He never asked where she was going or how long she would be gone. Most evenings when he wasn't tinkering with the plumbing he sat completely mute, playing the latest version of his favorite games or staring at his blobby cartoons on TV. In every way, since they'd moved in, Jim had become the opposite of what she wanted. They never talked about getting married, these days. They never talked about anything except the apartment.

She knew all of this. She'd been thinking it through for a long time. Yet she was infuriated when he waved goodbye without a word, without getting up from his chair, and turned his attention back to his game. She yanked the door shut and felt it reverberate in the frame.

A gust of wind spiked with drizzle greeted her when she emerged from the stairwell and stepped outdoors. She tightened her scarf and shivered. Traffic was slower than usual. All of the stores down the hill on Mercer and 1st Avenue were decorated with cobwebs, spiders, witches, and black cats. It only reminded Nancy how much time had gone by, and how much of her life had been wasted on the peculiarities of men she loved.

Not that they would have gotten along. Her father would have warned her away from Jim. Her father would have vetoed the slim, soft-spoken young programmer with reddish brown hair hanging down in his eyes. But her father was dead, and before he died he was crazy. All of his paternal advice could be summed up in one word. *Don't.* Don't trust cab drivers. Don't talk to people on the bus. Don't go anywhere without cash in case a disaster shuts down the electricity and all the ATMs are broken into. Don't tell anyone you carry cash. On and on, all of it based on fear.

She considered walking down to the new bar for a martini. But then she would have to trudge back uphill to get home. The alternative to walking downhill and then up, or uphill and back down, was to turn east and follow Halloran Street alongside her building. There was never much traffic there, thanks to the topography. This was one of the odd areas the early white settlers had failed to conquer by re-grading. The best the city planners could do was to chart around natural inclinations. Landscaping gave way suddenly to rock formations, streets ended abruptly, and a death-defying set of concrete stairs had been laid against the bluff as a grudging accommodation to pedestrians. No one took the stairs unless they were drunk or stupid.

By following Halloran east Nancy would eventually reach another, smaller hill and more exclusive housing protected by low brick walls, but there were a good three blocks of neighborhood before that. She hoped the round trip would give her time to stomp out her anger and prepare for a decent night's sleep.

As soon as she started off she regretted leaving her gloves at home. She had peeled them off and slapped them down on the table in the foyer. The sight of Jim had sent a final electric charge through her veins. In her rage she had forgotten to collect her gloves.

Going back wasn't an option. If Jim turned to her one more time with his dopey, sleepy grin she wasn't sure she could be trusted not to murder him in his sleep. So she clenched her fists, shoved them deep inside her pockets, and pressed on into the soft, icy drizzle.

She took Halloran, crossed the first intersection, and passed the house Jim called Dead Poet's Corner. The 1950s mansion reminded Nancy of a trophy house for some ancient movie star like Doris Day. Its dove-gray walls spread from both sides of the portico like welcoming arms. In fact, it was a haven, bequeathed to an obscure department of the city as an artists' retreat. At all hours, in all seasons, the lawn was dotted with scruffy bearded men and women with long white hair, most of them wearing loose fitting garments, wandering in a daze or staring at nothing.

"Communing with their muses," Jim had said the first time he and Nancy spotted the house. "Or just waiting for the

Man."

"Who's the Man?" Nancy had asked. "You mean, the guy with their drugs?"

"Show some respect for the hippies," Jim had said. "They're a sacred race. This is where they come to die."

She remembered laughing and linking arms with him. They never had silly conversations anymore. She never caught him studying her with an expression of abject devotion. Somehow this year everything between them had dwindled and fallen away.

As she passed Dead Poet's Corner she peeked at the lawn. Tonight a couple walked hand-in-hand there, each step as delicately executed as a Himalayan climbing expedition. Both figures were soft, whisper-thin, with long shawls draping their shoulders and the crocheted hats perched high on their heads giving a tiny shimmy with each movement.

Night was spreading across the neighborhood. Nancy walked on. The sad grace of the couple on the lawn made her shudder but she couldn't say which emotion was stronger, disappointment or dread. She didn't like to think of the future any more.

In the shadows between streetlamps a pair of sparkling eyes followed her movements. When she reached the darkest point the creature let loose a yowl and pressed its body against her ankle. Nancy tripped and then righted herself, and the cat went galloping across the street.

"Stupid thing," she called after it. "Go home!"

The chill arc of the next streetlamp revealed a three-story house with a yard full of red, yellow, and orange maple leaves, and a cluster of jack o' lanterns on the porch. Fussy Victorian trim decorated every surface, and amber light glowed from an attic window.

In the past this would have prompted Jim to tell a story, some awful tale from one of the horror movies he loved.

Something about a scar-faced woman hunting children in the dark, or a maniac hiding in the basement.

Nancy winced at the pain these trivial memories conjured. There had been a time when she could tell Jim anything, and he would make a story out of it.

"But what if the giant under the earth was real?" Jim had said, the first time Nancy recounted her father's bedtime story.

"My dad dreamed up a monster to make himself feel less afraid of earthquakes."

"Did it work?" Jim asked. And she laughed bitterly.

"Terrible things happen," she said. "We can't change that. We have to go on living every day in the real world."

"I don't know," Jim said. "Maybe everyone should be a little bit afraid of the things we can't explain."

In hindsight, Nancy wondered if she should have taken this conversation as a sign of all the differences between herself and Jim. Maybe his strange view of life wasn't healthy. She recalled the most frightening thing her father had ever told her, not long before he died.

"If the giant ever finds you, Nan, don't ask questions. Don't try to reason it out. Don't stop. You run like hell, all the way home."

She wasn't afraid of real things. She was only afraid of her father's nightmares. He was such a fearful man, never at ease. His imagination had poisoned him over the years.

She passed a well-lit house where two children sat in a picture window, gazing out. The drizzle had let up but the air was still damp, the light diffuse. Through the haze Nancy could see the children—a girl dressed as a devil and a boy dressed as a ghost—staring out at her as she walked by.

The elms lining this part of Halloran Street were losing their leaves. She marveled at how the solid trunks in autumn and winter resembled arms; the branches at middling height fanned out like fingers.

Jim wasn't a terrible person. She bookmarked this phrase, to use later. She would begin by telling Jim he wasn't a terrible person; he simply wasn't the right person for her. He would be fine after they split up. He made a fair living programming phone apps, he had friends, and he was still young. She would resist the urge to call him childish.

Yet he was childish. Nancy was tired of playing the grownup. She had to manage every aspect of their lives, or risk disappointment. Anything left to his judgment was bound to go wrong. If she let him choose a restaurant they ended up eating pizza at a water-stained table where the kitchen door hit them every time it opened, because Jim was fine with it. If she asked him to locate a comfortable apartment while her team at work crunched a ludicrous number of hours on a big project, they ended up living in a swamp because Jim imagined whale watching from home. Indulging his plan to repair the swamp resulted in misery because Jim didn't see the problem. If she'd left birth control up to him, she would have been pregnant as well as fed up.

He didn't understand how important it was to make plans and follow through, to consider options, and build on what was accomplished. He brought to mind a story she'd read as an undergrad about an incompetent engineer who bid low to win a contract with the city back in the 1890s. There was an urgent need to stem the spread of cholera following a series of natural disasters that left the downtown flooded. The engineer won his contract and designed a tunnel between the lakes and the bay, to provide a better sewage system. But he disregarded certain geological foundations; his plan was entirely theoretical. He cut corners and hired inexperienced labor. While digging was underway, the workers hit an underground lake causing a rupture that flooded the tunnel and consumed them.

Fortunately, Jim's profession didn't require him to lead people into harm's way. But there were other ways to ruin a life.

WATER MAIN 281

The way Nancy's parents had ruined one another's lives. Slow leaks gradually eroding the ground until the moment when concern and compromise gave way to catastrophe.

A flash of light interrupted Nancy's reverie. She froze with one foot on the curb and the other in the street, and a Mini Cooper whipped past in the wrong lane. In the driver's seat a man wearing a leopard costume and mask glared at her. From the passenger's seat his companion, wearing rabbit ears and whiskers, shouted something Nancy couldn't make out.

She backed up onto the curb and waited, trying to catch her breath. Her impulse was to bolt, to dash home and jump into bed, to let it all out by sobbing herself to sleep. Her father was gone, and Jim was useless. She had to take charge of her life, somehow, without help.

As she turned to head home she noticed a building directly across Halloran. She was surprised to see apartments nestled between the well-tended single-family dwellings. She thought the zoning for such a structure ended at Queen Anne Avenue. But then she remembered Dead Poet's Corner and decided there must be exceptions for old buildings of architectural or historical value.

From where Nancy stood the building resembled bordellos she had seen in photos of the French Quarter in New Orleans, cake-tiered, lined with windows. As she approached, the impression altered. There were no balconies, and the windows were as round as portholes and ringed with brass. In the haze she might have been looking at a cruise ship docked at the end of a pier at night. The light on its surface wavered as if it were floating with greenish waves splashing across the white walls.

A man sat on a folding chair under a square awning at the front door, which was made of brass to match the portholes. The man wore a white shirt with blue trousers and no jacket despite the cold. He was studying his fingernails.

Nancy followed the walkway until she stood directly

before him. She glanced at either side of the building but the houses flanking it were in shadow.

"Perambulating on a fine evening," the man said, and looked up at Nancy.

His eyes were a color her mother would have called seafoam green, luminous and startling, framed by loose, white tendrils of hair that fell to his shoulders.

"Yes," Nancy said when she found her voice. "Walking. Just wandering around."

"Such a pity," he said.

"Walking helps me think." She didn't know why she offered an explanation. She told herself she was being extra polite since she was the one trespassing.

"For a moment you might have been the woman I'm waiting to see," he replied. "But the time has passed. Time to go indoors."

"Sorry," Nancy said.

It was a sad thought, the man sitting outside waiting for a woman who didn't show up. He was old but she couldn't say whether he might be sixty or eighty.

"And you have no interest, then?" he asked.

She didn't know what to say. He couldn't be serious.

"The deposit is very small," he said. "Very cozy here. Private kitchen and bath included of course."

Relief came with a quick exhalation, and then she felt like laughing.

"You have an apartment for rent?" she asked.

"Yes," he said. "Yes. Small, very comfortable for one person, very reasonable rates." He quoted an amount, far less than she was paying for her share of the place with Jim.

"You want to view?" He asked.

"Oh," she said. "Well, I don't know. What if the person you're waiting for shows up after all?"

"She isn't coming." He shook his head dismissively.

"She's lost her appointment here."

The brisk night air made Nancy shiver. She could hear the noise from Queen Anne but it traveled lightly, more music and voices than traffic.

She was curious about the interior of this peculiar building. What could it hurt? She wasn't ready to leave Jim this weekend but she could report on her expedition. Maybe it was exactly what he needed to shake him up. If she threatened to move out, he would shrug and go back to his video games. He wouldn't take her seriously. But if she came home with a price quote, it might do the trick. At the very least it might scare him into calling a real plumber.

"Yes," she told the man. "I'd like to take a tour."

The hour was well past twilight. All she could see was the walkway, not Halloran Street beyond. When she turned to face the man again, he was holding open the brass door. She stepped through the rounded archway, impressed once more by the eccentricities of the architect.

"My name is Nancy," she told the man.

"Good," he said. "I'm the manager and I live here. Felix."

"Who designed the building?" she asked.

"A man of great means," he said. "Not of this century."

"In the shipping business?"

"No," he said. "Why would you say so?"

"The nautical theme," she replied. But Felix ignored the comment.

Instead of entering a foyer Nancy stood before a narrow, circular stairway with a brass handrail. It crossed her mind that the novelty of such a place could lose its charm after a while. Although she was fit enough to handle the stairs, she didn't imagine the place was up to code in terms of disability access. Her train of thought was interrupted by the sound of Felix pulling the door shut, a whoosh of pistons and a sudden sense of being sealed in.

"Built to keep out cold," he said. He raised one palm toward the stairs. "Please."

"Maybe I should follow you, since I don't know the way," Nancy told him. She was determined not to be silly. Recalling her father's advice about strangers and fast cars and men with long hair, she decided she was perfectly safe taking a brief tour of an apartment three blocks from where she lived. Hers was absurd, useless training, the ignorant advice of an older worldview but also the product of a disturbed mind.

Up and up they climbed. She caught sight of a wide hallway painted bright white with blue baseboards. From her limited perspective it appeared that most of the doors on this level were wide open.

"Do you rent studio space?" she asked. For it occurred to her that the artists down the street might have living quarters at Dead Poet's Corner and workspace here.

"No studio," Felix said over his shoulder. He continued up the stairs and Nancy followed.

She saw someone gliding through one of the doors below on the level they were leaving. She couldn't tell if the figure were a man or a woman shuffling sideways and out of sight again. The halting, nervous quality of this motion made Nancy feel queasy, and then ashamed. A practical question occurred to her. If the person she'd seen was disabled, there must be another route through the building. She thought of turning back and descending the stairs but a glance downward brought an unexpected rush of vertigo.

"Excuse me," she said. "Do you mind if we stop at the next floor?"

Above her Felix replied, "Yes, yes, this is where we want to be. At the very next floor."

Nevertheless, when he reached the level above he continued climbing the stairs. This time when Nancy emerged she was sure another figure went scuttling from the hallway to an open door, disappearing before she could determine the reason for his or her shuddering gait.

"Aren't we there yet?" Nancy asked.

"Yes, yes," said Felix. "Very much so."

He stepped off the stairs at the next level and offered one hand to steady her. She touched it for a second but his softly tapered, damp fingers repulsed her. She let go and resisted the urge to wipe her palm on her coat.

"Here we go, then, yes," said Felix. "Come, follow me." He gave no indication he had noticed her disgust and she tried to act as if it hadn't happened.

On this floor the corridor was identical to the ones below but only a few of the doors were open. Wafting through was a distinct odor of boiling cabbage and fried salmon, and the shrill cries of infants. Felix approached a door with no number and unlocked it.

"Oh, yes," he said as though he'd just remembered something important. He knocked briskly on the door, holding it half open and calling out, "Showing these premises now!"

No one answered.

"Good, good," he said. "We're here at the right time. Come in."

He pushed the door open and proceeded inside. A few steps into the dimly lit quarters he beckoned to Nancy to join him.

She leaned in with one foot on the threshold and scanned the room. Filthy rags and soiled clothing lay in piles on the hardwood floor. A closet was sectioned off with a maroon curtain, half open, and the contents appeared to be random— boots, lampshades, inflated beach balls, stacks of vinyl records, and some sort of medical equipment with dials, tubes, and funnels.

Felix had reached the opposite side of the room and was still gesturing for Nancy to join him. She might have stepped forward just to be polite if she hadn't noticed the narrow mattress shoved against the wall to her left, covered in stained sheets. It looked as if it had been used by dozens of people and had never been cleaned. Some of the stains were brown and some were as black as oil.

"You want to see, yes?" Felix asked. "Come, come, Miss. Come in. Don't be shy."

Nancy backed up a step, and another. "You know what?" she said. "I'll have to ask my boyfriend if he wants to move."

"Come inside and see for yourself," said Felix. He took a step toward her.

The lie made her feel vulnerable and foolish but she didn't care. All she wanted was to get out of there as soon as possible.

"My boyfriend is right outside. He's waiting for me. I'll ask what he thinks." She turned away from Felix, who was still beckoning and moving closer. She heard his voice rising in the background.

"You will be foolish not to take this chance, Miss," he called out. "Don't be childish!"

For a moment she blanked and couldn't figure out where she was in relation to the stairs. She heard a shuffling noise and sensed movement on the floor around her.

She forced herself to look down at three babies crawling in sodden diapers, all of them wailing. Their faces glistened with tears and snot and as they crawled they left wet trails like slugs.

Beyond the open doors came the unmistakable sizzle of a frying pan, and Nancy pictured hotplates with glowing rings. The cabbage and salmon returned in waves, a nauseating, overpowering stench.

She headed for the stairs and started down, fighting dizziness. She descended several steps and stopped, gazing at eye level at another floor full of screaming babies. A large figure emerged from one of the doors. This time she didn't try to decide if it was male or female, gender hardly mattering to a creature without legs, a thick torso shuddering forward on its long, split tail.

The rattle of the stairs coiled beneath her reminded Nancy where she was, or she might have fallen to the floor. She had to reach the brass door before the creatures converged on her. She let instinct guide her body, one foot and then the other landing with a thud on each step, moving robotically and trying not to trip.

As she passed the first floor she saw them coming, more of the crying infants, at least a dozen of them, crawling toward her. She saw them for an instant but it was enough to confirm they were not wearing diapers. Their naked bodies shimmied on the wet trails they left, and their tapered, split ends slid from side to side in the tears and snot.

Nancy stumbled and landed hard, tailbone slamming against the final step. Pain seared her pelvis but she didn't slow down. On all the floors above her the larger creatures were slithering into view, their screams echoing and expanding.

She grabbed the handle of the brass front door with both hands and tugged with all her might. Above her on the last floor she could hear the slobbering of babies, the shrieking of the other creatures, and the voice of Felix calling her back.

"You belong in your room, Miss!"

From every shadow above, the shuddering figures emerged. One of them stretched out and began the descent toward Nancy, walking on its hands and then sliding on its belly down the spiral staircase.

Nancy pounded the brass door with her fists and screamed. She gave the handle another yank and cried out with relief when the pistons let loose with a rush of cold air. She jumped out onto the walkway and began to race through the darkness. She could hear the portholes breaking, the wailing of all the creatures mingling with the rumble of earth beneath her.

She wanted to run all the way home, and she would have, but something more familiar than anything she knew told her to stop in her tracks or she would never escape.

"Don't try to reason it out. Don't stop."

But she did. She stopped. She let reason flood her mind and body as surely as the creatures pursuing her were flooding the stairwell behind her. Shaking, freezing, with tears running down her face, and more afraid than she had ever been in her life, she turned around.

The Stiles of Palemarsh

by Richard Gavin

"Says here your reservation is for two, Mr. Morrow," remarked the concierge.

Ian Morrow neither needed nor wanted reminding of this fact, and he couldn't help but feel that the overfed man at the reception desk was taking perverse pleasure in grinding this verbal salt into Ian's wounded pride. The man even went so far as to spin the computer screen around to evidence his claim. The chunky, archaic monitor creaked on its nest. Ian didn't bother to look at it.

"It was originally for two," he muttered. "But I'm here alone."

"Can't give you no discount," the concierge returned, jerking the monitor back into place. "Set rate, you know."

"I'm not asking for one," Ian said curtly. The tone was so unlike him that a feeling of shame gave his insides a painful twist. He snapped his credit card onto the reception desk and tried to avoid any further eye-contact.

"It's a very fine room; plenty of space, nice soft bed. Air-conditioned of course, which is a blessing on days like this, yeah?"

"Sounds perfect, thanks."

The concierge nodded noncommittally.

June heat waves were hardly uncommon for Ontario, but Ian (naïvely, he now realized) had expected his Welsh destination to be ideally temperate. Perhaps this was because, to hear Cari describe it, Wales was awash in milk and honey. But then, anything, no matter how banal, could be made to sound fantastical if Cari's mood was in an upward cycle. Honeymooning "across the pond" in the hamlet of Palemarsh had been her idea, as had been the June wedding date, the traditional Welsh vows, and the marriage site of Saint Tudwal Church.

Her familial roots stretched well past the new world boundaries of Canada and ran deep in Wales. Ian had been happy to indulge Cari in this area, having always felt only a tepid kinship with the stew of British and European cultures that informed his own family bloodline.

Wales and her family's connection to it had been but one of Cari's many fixations. Ayurvedic medicine, the silversmith's craft, speed reading, and so many more had each been her raison d'être at one time or another. But their allure would bleed out whenever she experienced the inevitable emotional downturn.

Her depressive phases were unquestionably worse than her manic ones. Unnerving or frustrating as it was to be awoken by Cari compulsively waxing the kitchen floor at three in the morning, or to try to keep pace with her breathless chatter, Ian would have happily taken them over seeing his lover become the grey, maimed creature to which her downward cycles reduced her. In those tedious spans, Cari could scarcely do more than sink into their bed or, at best, their living room sofa. She would stare sightlessly, her chapped lips twitching reflexively and mutely every now and again as though she was a beached fish.

Throughout those interminable low days and nights, Ian could almost comprehend the impulse to consent to a loved one receiving electroshock therapy. Without the merest wisp of sadism, even, he was confident, in the roiling deeps of his subconscious, he would have signed any waiver, accepted any radical therapy. He simply wanted Cari to be free again, for that was precisely as he viewed her: as one prematurely interred in a vault of negative forces. But she was in there somewhere. He *knew* she was. If only the controlled electric surge could press into her temples, if only those eels of unthinkable wattage could pierce through that catatonic shell and bore out the woman he loved…

Ian unlocked the handsomely carved door with the key the concierge had given him.

The suite was much slighter than its online photos had suggested, and one step into the room made it clear that what the Welsh considered air-conditioned differed from what Ian was accustomed to. He flung his suitcase onto the bed, causing the box spring to squeak like startled mice. Ian experienced a mild, if ironic, relief that he would be using this conspicuous furnishing for sleep and nothing besides.

Upon the mirror-backed desk, a complimentary bottle of champagne stood between a pair of long-stemmed flutes. A tented card offered its congratulations. Ian couldn't help but feel mocked by the display. He wrung the foil from the bottle's neck and uncorked it. He took a swig, and then tossed the card away without reading its inscription.

Glaring out the window, he saw a sloping meadow whose grasses bowed and were righted by the wind. Cari's relatives were somewhere beyond those glens and orchards. The thought made Ian's insides chill. He then randomly flashed back to the curt exchange with the concierge and once more felt pangs of guilt.

He needed to clear his head. From his luggage he fished out his runners, a pair of shorts and a t-shirt. Humidity be damned, he needed a run.

Crossing the crowded lobby made Ian feel the burn of self-consciousness, imagining as he did that every pair of eyes was upon him, mocking his athletic attire and the pale flesh of his exposed legs.

Palemarsh's high street was, Ian wagered, about as close

to bustling as the village ever knew. Figures moved in and out of the charming, if antiquated, shops. But Ian found displeasure in their company. He couldn't help but feel that they, too, were studying him, judging him. As he passed the window of the furniture maker's and the butcher's, faces seemed to draw toward the glass as though he was a flame and they moths. A delivery van and a pickup truck rattled over the hills that were paved with ancient, uneven cobblestone. The motion distorted Ian's perception of the driver, for the face was an inhuman smudge.

He began to jog faster, and his legs, stiff from the transatlantic flight, throbbed painfully in protest. There was the temptation to pause to stretch them, but Ian adjudged that he deserved this punishment.

Rounding the corner, Ian welcomed the sight of a dirt road that led away from downtown Palemarsh, into a more bucolic setting. Briefly he noted the road sign, Wheat Sheaf Lane, before the town gave way to old-growth trees, and farmland. Ditches lined both edges of the lane, reducing the road to something only nominally wider than a footpath. Ian followed the gentle bend, wincing as the water that sat pooled in the ditches created a greater, more pungent humidity. Every time he moved beneath a taller tree Ian was grateful for the scrap of shade, even though such respites only made the long stretches of open sun-soaked road more uncomfortable.

Eventually all the shade was behind him and he found himself flanked by sprawling fields of what he assumed by the colour to be wheat. Yet they looked more bleached than golden, and the shoots were limp, as if wilted or trampled. Were they harvesting dead grass here? Motes flitted above the flat fields, and these desiccated visions alerted Ian to his own parched throat. He reached down to pluck his water bottle from its belt clip, then realized that in his emotional state he'd neglected to bring anything to re-hydrate himself.

All at once the distance he'd run dilated into something

hopeless, a journey of a mythic scale. His pace began to slacken and his head began to swim, so much so that Ian only became aware that he'd been sharing the road with a hatchback car when the driver laid down on her horn. It let out a thin peeping noise, keen as a shrieking child. The vehicle veered around Ian, who was also trying to leap clear of it. He stepped too near to the ditch and quickly found himself lying face-first in the mud. Pain flared in his left ankle.

As the woman sped off, she extended an arm out the driver's side window and gave Ian a gesture that he presumed was meant to both chastise and offend him.

With care, he righted himself then limped over to the wooden fence that distinguished the lane from the open field. The beams creaked when Ian leaned against them. Looking down at his clay-spattered body, coupled with the unfortunate knowledge that his ankle might be sprained, nearly brought Ian to tears.

'Why am I here?' he asked himself. 'What am I *doing*?'

Drawing in a calming breath, Ian willed himself to become re-centred.

'I'll walk back to the inn,' he thought. But the pain in his left leg instantly shot down this solution.

He needed assistance: water, a drive back to the inn, and possibly medical attention. Glancing over his shoulder, he noticed the barn at the far end of the field. There was likely a farmhouse somewhere on the property as well, but the less distance he had to walk the better.

A wooden step-stile was arched over the fence. Ian cautiously scaled and descended it on the other side.

Dried grasses crunched beneath his runners as Ian, slowly yet impatiently, crossed the field. The sun pressed beams of white light and heat against him. Seeing the condition of the barn quashed his thin hopes for assistance, for the structure was nearly dilapidated. Gaps stretched open between several of the wall boards, giving Ian the impression of extracted teeth. The roof sagged as though struggling to brace an unseen weight. The interior appeared empty.

"Hello?" Ian cried.

Silence.

But a figure then stepped out of the murk and into the sunlit mouth of the barn's doorway.

The man was tall but his rod-straight posture did not betray his age. Only after Ian had gotten close enough to see the man's long-receded hairline and the drooping flesh of his face did he realize that the farmer was old. An antique two-pronged hay fork was clutched in one hand. He was dressed in corduroy trousers and a pale chambray shirt, both of which looked uncharacteristically clean.

Ian couldn't be sure, but he thought that the sight of his own lame step brought a twinkle of delight to the old farmer's grey eyes.

"Sorry to bother you," called Ian. He shuffled forward to narrow the gap between himself and the farmer.

"Looks like you could use some help," the old man replied. His Welsh accent lent his voice a melodic lilt, not unlike birdsong.

"Yes, I could."

Ian noted, with curious relief, that the man's face was rather benign. He was looking closely at Ian.

"That accent, lad; are you an American?"

Ian shook his head, "Canadian." He slightly lifted his injured leg. "I twisted my ankle running on the road there. I was hoping you might be able to drive me back to my hotel."

The man raised a hand, flexed it in a strange and seemingly noncommittal gesture. "That's a problem."

"I'm staying at the inn just on the high street back there. And I'll gladly give you some money for gas."

"Begging your pardon, lad," the man returned, "but the

problem is that I haven't anything for you to put petrol in. These old legs o' mine are the only carriage I have!"

"Oh."

"I can offer you a rest though. And a spot of food if'n you're peckish."

As though on cue, Ian's stomach gurgled noisily, reminding him of the many hours he'd gone without nourishment.

"Uh...okay."

The farmer moved his skullish head in a nod and began toward the wooden house, which Ian only just then spotted. He was grateful that his host's pace was geriatric, for he was able to keep in step with his injured leg.

"Mind the railing, it's in need of a good sanding," the man advised once they reached the porch.

Within, the farmhouse's walls did little to fend off the heat. If anything, their purpose was reversed. Ian leaned against the doorframe long enough for his eyes to grow accustomed to the dim interior. The living room to his right was framed in wooden shelves that bowed under the burden of seeming junk. The room was made impassable by four bulky picnic tables, the tops of which were also smothered under bric-a-brac: costume jewellery, lanterns, books, and plastic dolls with grubby faces. Ian recalled a reality show Cari had loved to watch that dealt with compulsive hoarders. He also recalled, much to his dismay, the crime scene photos from the home of Ed Gein.

"This way," the farmer advised. Ian followed with boyish obedience. Once inside the kitchen, he accepted his host's offer of wobbly wooden chair.

It felt as though he had entered a brick oven. Everything Ian touched seemed ember-warmed. The kitchen was another over-packed nook of the house, with a chunky refrigerator that looked only faintly newer than the woodstove that squatted in one corner. The windows were all fully ajar, but their lack of screens gave the bluebottles freedom to crawl in and buzz about the room. It also allowed the hot winds to deliver blasts of fine field grit.

There came an unpleasant creak as the farmer pulled the doors of the Victorian pot dresser open. From this he extracted an iron saucepan. He tugged hard on the oversized chrome handle of the fridge, which clunked as it gave. From the sour-smelling icebox the old man produced a large mason jar filled with brackish liquid. Ian felt his stomach flip.

Wordlessly and with an ease that comes with habitual actions, the man fired up the woodstove and began to heat the green-brown liquid inside the iron skillet. Either he knew exactly how much wood was required to cook this dish or Ian was too overheated to notice any further increase in the room's temperature, either way the fire from the black iron hull was hardly noticeable.

Ian was about to lie to his host about lacking an appetite when the aroma of the warmed dish reached him. It made his stomach rumble eagerly.

"Barley soup," the man announced as he set a steaming wooden bowl before Ian, "made it myself."

Ian smiled crookedly and took up his spoon. His initial sip of the broth was done purely for etiquette's sake, but it was the finest thing Ian had ever tasted.

He ate greedily and when his dish was emptied he felt sated, almost dozy.

"How's that ankle?" his host asked.

"It feels a little better. I must not have actually sprained it. You know, I just realized that I didn't even introduce myself. My name is Ian."

The man slid his fingers around Ian's offered hand. "A pleasure."

Ian waited for the old man to reciprocate, but it was not to be.

"Tell me, Ian, what brings you to Palemarsh? Not many folks venture this far from Cardiff."

The room's tightness and sweltering temperature assailed Ian. He was so reluctant to answer his host's question that he very nearly rose and exited the house.

"Holiday," he uttered at last.

"Alone?"

Did the old man know something? Was he related to Cari? What if he and the woman in the hatchback had conspired to bring Ian here in order to mete out some familial punishment?

Ludicrous...

"I was originally supposed to be here with someone... It didn't work out..."

Who was *he* to pry into Ian's affairs? A bit of hospitality did not render him Ian's Father Confessor.

"Did she stand you up at the altar?"

He did know. Ian was certain.

"I'm not... Look, I don't want to go into this. And I'm sorry; I didn't catch your name..."

The old man rose with a grunt. "If you're able to walk, why don't I show you a shortcut back to the high street?"

"Um, sure, okay."

The sun practically blinded Ian as he trailed across the yard behind his aged host.

Precisely where the field merged with the forest stood a pair of lean stones. They were, by Ian's estimation, roughly six-feet in height and were set slightly askew, one planted just ahead of the other. This gave the impression not of a barrier, but rather a passage.

"You see that squeeze-stile there?" The man's pointing finger tapered toward an unpleasantly overgrown fingernail, scuffed and ragged and yellow.

"I see the stones. Is that you mean?"

"Aye, that's a squeeze-stile. They were used to mark the

boundaries between one man's land and another's. You slip between those stones and you'll find yourself on the path. It's a fine walk. Eventually you'll come to a wooden step-stile at the far end of the trail. Climb that and you'll set down at the head of Wheat Sheaf Lane, right at the high street."

"Sounds straightforward. Thanks for everything."

"Remember," he advised, raising higher his finger with its unsightly nail, "you always want to keep the sun on your left shoulder when you're passing through that glen, lad."

Ian nodded, despite not caring to understand the wives' tale advice of rural folk.

He crossed the last of the field. Perspiration was already beginning to dampen his underarms and back. The tree-shaded glen would be a welcome relief.

The stones of the squeeze-stile seemed to radiate coolness, as though they were righted ice floes instead of granite slabs. Vein-like ribbons of moss suggested the stones' age as well as lending their appearance a strange texture, like a relief map of some remote land.

'Squeeze' was an apt name, for, as Ian soon discovered, the gap between the off-set rocks was claustrophobic, and their uneven faces were made almost hazardous by jutting keen ridges. When he was pressed between the two standing stones, desperation flushed hotly through Ian, followed instantly by a tarry sense of despair. Childishly, he shut his eyes and held his breath before pushing through to the other side of the stile.

The grove expanded all around him. The velvet leaves of the oaks pulsated and the insects offered up a subtle fanfare. While he knew that his passage through the squeeze-stile had not been anywhere near as dramatic or traumatic as he'd imagined, Ian was nonetheless grateful for the verdant expanse at his elbows, the soft trail under his soles. This new environ seemed to lessen the dull ache in his ankle. He was already fantasizing about lying on that King-size bed, his bad leg propped, the air conditioner blasting at full-power and the television playing loudly.

In what seemed to be no time at all, Ian spotted the wooden step-stile that marked the trail's end.

Age and the elements had smoothed the wood steps to such a degree that they felt ice-slick beneath him. Ian scaled and descended the inverted-V carefully, experiencing an unwarranted sense of achievement when his feet struck Wheat Sheaf Lane.

But this spike of exuberance became lost in a sudden blast of terror; a terror that was as inexplicable as it was unbearable. About him, the midday sun shone warmly through the screens of healthy leaves. Swallows trilled and a temperate breeze pressed the entire scene as rhythmically as the evening tide. There was nothing that should have upset him. Ian scanned his surroundings more closely, hoping yet at the same time *not* hoping that he might glimpse whatever obscured threat had aroused in him this pulsing dread. But there was no danger to be seen, not even the potential for danger. All was thoroughly pastoral. Ian could even see the rooftops of the high street; a reminder that civilization was but a few steps away.

But it was all still somehow unbearable. The openness of the lane, the visibility of the cloudless sky was too immense, too open. Rather than providing airiness and relief, the space aroused a reverse claustrophobic response in Ian, who began to view himself as exposed; a speck of tender prey standing unprotected and wholly visible.

This, Ian realized, was true panic.

Instinct urged him backward, until he was up against the wood stile. Turning about, he clamoured up the rungs and down again, sighing with unalloyed joy at being concealed once more.

The forest, or rather some unseen aspect of the forest, enveloped Ian, wrapping itself around him, sealing him protectively, as a wolf-mother would her cub.

The woods had changed. Ian was aware of it the instant

he turned to walk back along the trail. Both light and temperature had noticeably diminished during his brief stint on the lane. He assumed that the density of the trees was capable of shielding the sun's rays and its heat to such a degree, but the further he walked the less likely this reasoning seemed, for there was an undeniable chill to the air, a crispness that was indigenous to October. Halting, Ian craned his head back, shielding his eyes with his meshed fingers.

A thunderstorm; yes, this was the obvious explanation for the sudden and drastic change to both temperature and light. It must have been rolling in swiftly, for the sky was now deeply leaden.

Reasoning that he should rush to shelter before the storm hit, Ian prepared to run when a detail of the woods froze him in place and forced him to look up again, and then, doubting his senses, a third time.

Why should there be so much more of the sky visible now than only a few moments ago?

Because the trees that lined the path were now leafless.

Ian stared dumbly at the naked branches that domed him like skeletal wings. He looked down the path, at the fire-vivid hue of the leaves that still clung to a few of the trees, at the brown carpet of fallen foliage. Mist swayed lazily above the slumbering soil, obscuring the further bends in the trail.

The words of the old farmer coursed through Ian's mind, about the need to keep the sun on his left shoulder. Had the farmer somehow entranced him? Possibly drugged his food?

The wooden stile exit was only a few feet behind him. Perhaps the panic he'd experienced on the open lane had also been part of the old man's spell. But now Ian knew better. He needed to get back to the high street. He turned about and ran toward Wheat Sheaf Lane.

After several minutes his predicament became clear to him, for the trail wended and curved in bewildering ways, stretching to an impossible length. The lane beyond the woods was nowhere to be seen.

He turned back around and retraced his steps, still running as hard as his aching legs and burning lungs would allow. The air was perfumed with smoke and damp earth. Perspiration cooled rapidly on his flesh, chilling him. To his right Ian spotted blotches of colour that brightened the otherwise uniform grey. An apple tree was in full bloom, its gnarled limbs flaunting red fruit.

As he rounded the next in a seemingly endless array of twists in the path, Ian caught sight of movement.

The carpet of leaves rustled as something rose up from the ground. Ian nearly tripped, so startled was he by the sight of the richly coloured moth that was hovering above the leaf-laden ground. The pattern on its wings was unsightly – a blotchy mess of purples and blacks and greenish-yellow. The moth had perched itself upon a chalky-looking stone. It was a hideously large bug.

But it was not a bug at all, and the pale slab that supported it was not old stone, but old flesh. Ian could now distinguish the head and the arms that were but skin-draped bones. The dark blotches were not moth wings, but the ugly patches where the figure's un-circulated fluids had pooled. Gripping branches for support, the shape pulled itself upright, turned, and made its way onto the path.

At fist Ian thought the figure hermaphroditic, for breasts sagged above the distended belly and the genitals were almost comically small. But then Ian could see the drooping testicles, the stubby penis. It was a young man, or had once been.

Its jaw was slack. The eyes were closed and sunken. Ian could distinctly see the manner in which the eyelids seemed to be drawing into the sockets, as though the jelly they guarded had deteriorated.

Within the gape of the mouth: leaves, a tangle of sharp

October hues. The thing's head was like an overstuffed yard-waste sack. Excess leaves were tugged free by the damp breeze and went flitting off like startled birds.

It raised one of its rope-thin arms.

Ian ran.

Slowly, as though time did not matter in the slightest, the pale thing began to follow him.

The pain in Ian's ankle flared up, wordlessly pleading for him to cease. But terror was his prime mover and it refused to let him yield.

Finally Ian found his way to the opposite end of the grove, near the farm with its standing stones. The squeeze-stile was visible, jutting up from the damp October mud like granite fangs. Well beyond it was the wall of the old host's barn. Ian shouted something, waved his arms, all on the thin hope that the aged farmer would step out from that crumbling structure.

Ian glanced backward. What he witnessed caused him to stumble, to fall and get partially subsumed by the cold, sucking clay of the path.

There were three of them now, a colourless trio shambling awkwardly along the path. One of them, the woman, was the latest to join. She stood up from her shallow resting place between two yews, then cut a wide and manic stride onto the path. Like the first boyish revenant, these others also stalked the trail with their eyes unblinkingly shut.

Ian unleashed a wordless cry then lunged toward the squeeze-stile. He could see the hay field basking under the summer sun whose heat he now yearned for. Here, the October chill seeped in deeper and deeper, causing him to shudder and curse his light attire.

From the still woods Ian now heard a low gassy noise. It was emotionless, meaningless; stray air passing through grave-withered throats. The sound encouraged him to press frantically between the squeeze-stile.

The righted stones were so deceptively keen that Ian didn't realize he was cut until he saw the fresh red stippling upon the sun-bleached granite. 'Are the stones weeping blood?' he wondered. Then he felt the stinging in his forearms and his wrists and upon the back of his neck.

"Jesus," he cried, staring in disbelief at his wounds. He was queerly offended by the very idea that he could be harmed in such a way. He pressed deeper into the gap in the stiles and was stricken with the cold and shrivelling realization that he was now stuck between the stones.

His attempt to call for help resulted in a stifled grunt as his lungs struggled for air. The further Ian tried to press, the tighter the stones' grip became. Every jerk of one of his bleeding limbs tightened the crag-vice. He shrieked and wriggled and, unexpectedly, began to sob.

He looked down to see his own tears and blood falling onto the tops of his runners.

Under his muddy soles lay an array of objects. There was an envelope whose inscription had been smudged to the point of being illegible. There was a thimble and a man's wallet and a St. Christopher's medallion.

There was also a ring.

As to the how and the why, Ian was at a loss, but as to what, he was certain. There was no mistaking it, not after he'd studied it so long in the jeweller's in the Mervish Village. Cari had adored it, worn it proudly. And finally, on that final ugly night, had twirled it around and around as she sobbed and kept repeating "Please, Ian. Please…"

But he'd run. Whether or not it had simply been a case of the proverbial cold feet, Ian couldn't say, but just nine days before their wedding, every one of Cari's needs, her afflictions, became inflated in his mind, until they were as smothering as this squeeze-stile.

So he ran. He'd shattered her world and then left her

there among the shards. Could he have endured such a blow, even with his supposedly healthy psychology?

He hearkened back to the flurry of 3a.m. voicemails, the mountain of emails (most of which were scarcely more than a sentence). She had begged him. This was, Ian now realized with an awful lacerating clarity, much more than obsessive attachment. Cari had been desperate. Her pleas were just that; not for Ian's hand in marriage, but rather his help. She'd been slipping. She'd known it. And on some level Ian knew it. His reneging of his proposal had blasted the scaffolding out from under Cari. Now she was clinging to the ledge, feeling the winds sucking her toward an endless freefall, all the way down into the abyss that was her own fractured soul.

He likely couldn't have cured her, but at the very least he could have been there for her. Perhaps something as minute as replying to an email or a phone call to Cari's sister, advising her of what had happened, perhaps these measures could have kept Cari from falling.

But he'd run. He'd raced out of his apartment at the time when he and Cari had supposed to be catching their honeymoon flight. Instead it was just him and a stubborn childish impulse. His landline had rung. He'd known it was Cari, *known* it. But he let the phone ring lonely and raced out the door.

His last sight of Cari had been of her curled foetal-like in her apartment hall, wheezing out a pathetic "Please" while she spun the ring on her finger. *This* ring.

Now he was racing still, running for his sanity if not his life.

Unable to press through, Ian resorted to pulling himself backward.

When the stile birthed him, he laughed with relief, an elation that was ruptured by the sight of the shut-eyed creatures shambling down the path. There had been three a moment ago (Or had he been ensnared for much longer? What else could explain the harvest moon gleaming blue and cool above the trees?); now they were too numerous to count. The figures moved in a great horde.

Ian then heard the low, thick awful growling of hounds. Their barking startled him, made him cry out.

His voice drew the attention of the sightless things.

Instinct caused Ian to reach back between the stile stones. He tried in vain to retrieve Cari's engagement band. His mind spun back to the image of the old farmer's house and he imagined Cari's ring soon being stored with the rest of the clutter.

He rose and he ran, this time back toward the step-stile at the head of Wheat Sheaf Lane. He argued with himself, first positing how futile his attempt to escape was, then reasoning that he had to try. There was no other option.

He ran off the lane, weaving and ducking between the old growth trees. A rumble of thunder shook the forest and when the storm clouds began to knit across the moon's face, Ian pined for its cold light.

Assuming he was hearing correctly, Ian swore that the throng of revenants were racing to one dead end of the path, then coming about and retracing their steps, again and again and again. Was this wild hunt for him, he wondered?

Exhausted, he wrapped his arm weakly around an old oak. He bent over and breathed deeply. His jaw was chattering from the frigid night air.

A figure bolted up opposite him. The leaves which had concealed it fell from the luminous body like wide black snowflakes.

The woman, whom Ian could only see from behind, stood.

Her body was familiar enough for Ian to shut his eyes and shut it out.

He ran madly, not daring to turn back. The hunt, he heard, had reached the far end of the path and was now circling back toward him. The woman from the forest, however, was much nearer. Ian knew he was within her reach, or would be soon.

He opened his eyes and saw the wooden step-stile once again. It was forty, perhaps fifty yards ahead.

The cabal of rasping creatures rounded the bend. He could see them, and though their thick eyelids remained closed, Ian was sure they were seeing him.

He slid down the decline and landed back on the footpath. He flung himself at the step-stile and scrabbled up its smooth beams. Reaching its topmost rung, Ian dove headlong into a blinding light.

The first clue he had regarding his safety was a blazing heat against his face. His eyes fluttered opened. The sight of the cloudless summer sky was too bright. Ian sat up.

He purposely avoided looking back into the woods. Even the peripheral image of the tapered hand slinking back between the slats of the wooden stile could not tempt him to peek. His eyes remained locked on the high street that was only paces away.

Crossing under the sign for Wheat Sheaf Lane, Ian examined his bloodied hands. His wounds required care but were nothing he couldn't treat himself.

The window for the druggist's shop hurled a shocking self-reflection. Ian took a moment to wipe the blood from his still-weeping cheeks and to pull the leaves and twigs from his hair. He tugged his torn T-shirt down and hobbled back to the inn.

The same concierge was on duty. At first he looked relieved to see Ian coming through the entrance, until he spotted his guest's condition.

"Mother Mary!" he called.

"I'm okay, I'm okay," Ian muttered, barely loud enough for him to hear himself.

The concierge moved out from behind the counter.

"I'm pleased you're back, sir," he said. A fan of pink paper slips was held in one fist. "There've been several messages for you, from back in Canada."

Ian glimpsed the names and numbers that had been scribbled on the Message slips; one was from Cari's father, three from her sister, and one from a mutual friend of his and Cari's.

"Not bad news, I hope," the concierge said, though his tone seemed to convey just the opposite.

"Yes," Ian said, his voice scarcely slipping past the fresh lump in his throat, "yes, I'm afraid it is."

Grave Goods

by Gemma Files

Put the pieces back together, fit them against each other chip by chip and line by line, and they start to sing. There's a sort of tone a skeleton gives off; Aretha Howson can feel it more than hear it, like it's tuned to some frequency she can't quite register. It resonates through her in layers: skin, muscle, cartilage, bone. It whispers in her ear at night, secret, liquid. Like blood through a shell.

The site they're working on is probably Early Archaic— 6,500 B.P. or so, going strictly by contents, thus beating out the recent Bug River find by almost 2,000 years. Up above the water-line, too, which makes it *incredibly* unlikely; most people lived in lakeshore camps back then, right when the water levels were at their lowest after the remnant ice mass from the last glacial advance lying across the eastern outlet of Lake Superior finally wasted away, causing artificially high lake levels to drop over a hundred metres. Then isostatic rebound led to a gradual return, which is why most sites dating between the end of the Paleo-Indian and 4,000 years ago are largely under water.

Not this one, though: it's tucked up under a ridge of granite, surrounded by conifer old growth so dense they had to park the vehicles a mile away and cut their way in on foot, trying to disturb as little as possible. Almost a month later—a hideously cold, rainy October, heading straight for Hallowe'en—the air still stinks of sap, stumps bleeding like wounds. Dr. Anne-Marie Begg's people hauled the trunks out one by one, cross-cut the longest ones, then loaded them up and took them back to the Reserve, where they'll be planed in the traditional manner and used for rebuilding. Always a lot of home improvement projects on the go, over that way; that's what Anne-Marie—Dr. Begg—says.

Though Canadian ethics laws largely forbid excavations, once Begg brought Dr. Elyse Lewin in to consult, even the local elders had to agree this particular discovery merited looking into. They've been part of the same team practically since Begg was Lewin's favourite TA, operating together out of Lakehead University, Thunder Bay; Lewin's adept at handling funding and expedition planning, while Begg handles both tribal liaison duties and general PR, plus almost anything else to do with the media. It was Begg who sowed excitement about "Pandora's Box," as the pit's come to be called, on account of the flat slab of granite—lightly incised with what look like ancestral petroglyphs similar to those found on Qajartalik Island, in the Arctic—stoppering it like a bottle. Incised on top *and* below, as Aretha herself discovered when they pried it apart, opening a triangular gap large enough to let her jump in. She'd shone the flashlight downwards first, just far enough to check her footing before she landed—down on one knee, a soggy crouch, too cramped to straighten fully—then automatically reversed it, revealing those square-cut, coldly eyeless faces set in silent judgement right above her head.

"How'd they get it here?" Morgan, the other intern, asks Lewin, who shrugs and glances at Begg before letting her answer.

"The slab itself, that's found, not made—shaped a little, probably. More than enough rockfall in this area for that, post-glacial shear. Then they'd have made an earthwork track like at Stonehenge, dug underneath—" Begg uses her hands to sketch the movements in midair "—then piled in front, put down logs overtop, used them like rollers. Get enough people pushing and pulling, you're golden."

Lewin nods. "Yes, exactly. Once the grave was dug, there'd be no particular problem fitting it overtop; just increase the slope 'til they had a hill and push it up over the edge, down-angled so one side touched the opposite lip, before dismantling the hill to lay it flat again."

"Mmm." Morgan turns slightly, indicating: "What're the carvings for, though? Like...what do they mean?"

"Votive totems," Begg replies, with confidence.

The forensics expert—Dr. Tatiana Huculak—just shakes her head. "No way to know," she counters. "Told us yourself they don't look like any of the ritual marks you grew up with, remember? So it's like a sign in Chinese, for all of us—just as likely to say 'fuck you' as 'God bless,' unless you know Pinyin."

Begg's already opening her mouth to argue when Lewin sees Aretha's hand go up; she shushes them both. "Oh dear, you don't have to do *that!*" she exclaims. "Just sing out if an idea's struck you."

Aretha hesitates, eyes flicking to Morgan, who nods. Courage in hand, she replies—

"Uh, maybe. I mean—Even when you don't know the language, there's still a lot you can get from context, right? Well…" She hauls herself up, far enough past the slab to tap its top, nails grating slightly over rough-edged stone. "'Keep out,' that'd be my guess," she concludes. "'Cause it's up here."

Lewin nods, as Huculak and Begg exchange glances. "Logical. And down there? On the underside?"

Here Aretha shrugs, uncomfortably in the spotlight for once, pinned beneath the full weight of all three professors' eyes.

"…'stay in?'" she suggests, finally.

Working this dig with Lewin's team was supposed to be the best job placement ever, a giddy dream of an archaeological internship—government work with her way paid up front, hands-on experience, and the chance to literally uncover something unseen since thousands of years BCE. By the end of the first week, however, Aretha was already beginning to dream about smothering almost everyone else in their sleep or hanging herself from the next convenient tree, and the only thing that's improved since then is that she's now far too exhausted to attempt either.

Doesn't help that the rain which greeted them on arrival still continues, cold and constant, everything covered in mud, and reeking of pine needles. Sometimes it dims to a fine mist, penetrating skin-deep through Aretha's heaviest raincoat; always it chills, lighting her bone-marrow up with sharp threads of ache, the air around her so cold it hurts to inhale through an open mouth. Kneeling here in the mud, she sees her breath boil up as cones fall down through the dripping, many-quilled branches, their sticky impacts signalled with rifle-shot cracks, and every day starts the same, ends the same: wood mould burning in her eyes and sinuses like smoke, impossible to ward off, especially since the Benadryl ran out.

"Jesus," Morgan suddenly exclaims, like she just hasn't noticed it before, "that's one hell of a cold you've got there, Ree. Does Lewin know?"

Aretha shrugs, droplets scattering; hard to do much else, when she's up to her elbows in grave-gunk. And: "Uh, well...yeah, sure," she replies, vaguely. "Can't see how she wouldn't."

"Close quarters and all? You're probably right. But who knows, huh? I mean..." Morgan trails off, eyes sliding back to the main tent—over which two very familiar voices are starting to rise, yet again—before returning to the task at hand. "...she's kinda—distracted, these days, with...everything. I guess."

"Guess so."

Inside the main tent, Begg and Huculak are going at each other like ideological hammer and tongs, as ever—same shit, different day, latest instalment in an infinite series. It's been a match made in hell pretty much since the beginning; Huculak's specialization makes her view all human remains as an exploitable resource, while Begg's tribal band liaison status puts her in charge of making sure everything that could conceivably once have been a person gets put right back where it was found after cataloguing,

312 | AUTUMN CTHULHU

with an absolute minimum of ancestral disrespect. Of course, Begg's participation is basically the only reason they're all here in the first place, as Lewin makes sure to keep reminding Huculak—but from Huculak's point of view, just because she knows it's true doesn't mean she has to pretend to like it.

"I'll point out yet again," Huculak's saying right now, teeth audibly gritted, "that the *single easiest way* we could get a verifiable date on this site continues to be if we could take some of the bones back and carbon-date them, in an honest-to-Christ lab…"

Aretha can almost see Begg curtly shaking her head, braids swinging—the way she does about fifty times a day, on average—as she replies. "Carbon-date the grave goods, then, Tat, to your heart's content—carbon-date the *shit* out of them, okay? Grind them down to paste if you want to; burn them and smoke the fucking ashes. But the bones, themselves? *Those* stay here."

"Oh, 'cause one of 'em might share maybe point-one out of a hundred-thousandth part of their genetic material with yours? Bitch, please."

Lewin's voice here, smooth and placatory as ever: "Ladies! Let's be civil, shall we? We all have to work together, after all, for a good month more…"

"Unfortunately," Huculak snaps back, probably making Begg puff up like a porcupine. Hurling back, in her turn—

"Hey, don't denigrate my spirituality just because you don't share it; is that so hard? Say we were in Africa, digging up Rwandan massacre dumps—things'd be different *then*, right?"

"You know, funny thing about that, Anne-Marie: not really. They'd be the same way anyplace for me, because I am a *scientist*, first and foremost. Full friggin' stop."

"And I'm not is what you mean."

"Well…if the moccasin fits."

At that, Aretha whips her head around sharply, only to meet Morgan's equally-disbelieving gaze halfway. The both of them staring at each other, like: *seriously?* Holy cultural slap-fight with potential impending fisticuffs, Batman. *Wow.*

"Knock-down drag-out by six, seven at the latest," Morgan mutters, sidelong. "I'm callin' it now—fifty on Tat to win, unless Anne-Marie puts her down with the first punch. You in or what?"

Aretha hisses out something that can't quite be called a laugh. "Pass, thanks."

Morgan shrugs, then turns back to her designated task, head shaking slightly. "Your loss."

Going by her initial pitch, Lewin genuinely seems to have thought hiring only female associates and students would guarantee this little trip going far more smoothly than most, as though removing all traces of testosterone from the equation would create some sort of paradisaical meeting of hearts and minds: cycles synched, hands kept busy, no muss, no fuss. The principle, however, was flawed from its inception: *just 'cause they ain't no peckers don't mean ain't no peckin' order,* as Aretha's aunties have often been heard to remark 'round the all-gal sewing circle they run after hours out of their equally all-girl cleaning service's head office. It frankly amazes Aretha how Lewin could ever have gotten the idea that women never bring such divisive qualities as ambition, wrath, or lust to the metaphorical table, when she's spent the bulk of her career teaching at all-girl facilities across the U.S., before finally ranging up over the border—

But whatever. Maybe Lewin's really one of those evo-psych nuts underneath the Second Wave feminist frosting, forever hell-bent on mistaking biology for destiny no matter the context. Just as well she's apparently never thought to wonder exactly what those pills Aretha keeps choking down each day are, if so.

On puberty blockers since relatively early diagnosis, thank Christ, so she never did reach the sort of giveaway heights her older brothers have, and her voice hasn't changed all that much, either; that, plus no Adam's apple, facial and body hair kept chemically downy as any natal female in her immediate family, even if the other team-members felt inclined to body-police. But the plain fact is, they've none of them seen each other in any sort of disarray since they left base-camp—it's too cold to strip for sleep, let alone to shower, assuming they even had one.

This is typical paranoia, though, and she knows it; the reason everyone here knows her as Aretha is because she *is.* That's the name under which she entered university, legally, and it'll be the name with which she graduates, just like from high school. She's a long damn way away from where she was born at this point, both literally and figuratively.

Aretha looks back up to find Morgan still looking at her and blushes, sniffing liquid, with nothing handy even halfway clean enough to wipe the result away on. "Sorry," she manages, after a second. "*So* gross, I know, I really do. I just—sorry, *God.*"

Morgan laughs. "Dude, it's fine. Who knew, right?"

"Yeah." A pause. "Think it would've been okay, probably, it just hadn't rained the whole fucking time."

"And yet."

"…and yet."

Morgan has a great smile, really; Aretha'd love to see it closer up sometime, under different circumstances. But right now, the little moment of connection under pressure already had, the only thing either of them can really think to do about it is just shrug a little and drift apart once more—Morgan back towards the generator array, which is starting to make those worrying pre-brownout noises yet again, while Aretha heaves herself up out of the pit and stamps slushily towards the tent itself, planning to sluice her gloved hands under the tarp's overflowing gutter. This brings her so close to the ongoing argument that she can finally see what the various players are actually doing through that space where the tent's ill-laid side gapes open: Begg and Huculak squaring off, with Lewin playing referee. It's not quite at the cat-fight stage yet, but if Morgan's placing bets, Aretha's at least setting her watch.

"Look, Anne-Marie…" Huculak says finally. "I know you want to think these are your people outside, in the grave—but I've been studying them hands-on for weeks now, and I just don't think they were at all. I don't think these were *anybody's* 'people.'"

"Jesus, Tat! What the hell kind of Othering, colonialist bullshit—"

"No, but seriously. *Seriously.*" Huculak points to a pelvic arrangement, a crushed-flat skull, and as much of the spinal column as they've been able to find. "Pelvis slung backwards, like a *bird*, not a mammal. Orbital sockets fully ten mL larger than usual and side-positioned, not to the front; these people were barely binocular—probably had to cock their heads just to look at something in front of them. Twice as many teeth, half of them canines, back ones serrated: this is a meat-eater, exclusively. And that's not even getting into the number of vertebrae, projection processes to the front and rear of each, locking them together like a snake's…"

"You've got three bodies to look at, barely, and you're already pushing taxonomic boundaries? Phylogenetic analysis by traits is a slanted system and makes it too easy by far to mistake clades or haplogroups for whole separate species—"

Ooh, bad move, Dr. Begg, Aretha thinks, even as that last sentence starts, and indeed, by its end Huculak's eyes have widened so far her smile-lines disappear completely. "Oh really, *is* it?" she all but spits. "Golly gee, I didn't *know* that, please tell me more! Hottentot Venus what?"

"You know what I'm saying."

"I know *exactly* what you're saying, yes; do you know what *I'm* saying? Or did you just start shoving your fingers in your ears and singing *lalalala I can't HEEEEAR yooou* the minute I started talking as usual?"

Begg snorts, explosively. "You've seen the dig, every damn day for a month—it's a *grave*, Tat, you just used the word yourself. Full of grave goods. Animals don't *do* that, if that's what you're implying."

"Of course I'm not saying what's in there is animals, for shit's sake; an offshoot of humanity, maybe—some evolutionary dead end. Like Australopithecus."

"You're telling me Australopithecus had snake-spines?"

"*No.* But just because we haven't found something yet doesn't mean it never existed."

"Good line, Agent Mulder."

"Oh *fuck you*, you condescending, indigenocentric *fuck*—"

Lewin raises her hands and goes to interpose between them, but they ignore her roundly—both wider as well as darker, more built for the long haul, able to shrug her off like a charley-horse. Huculak glares up as Begg stares down, hands on hips and braids still swinging, and demands: "Seriously, is that what we're down to, right now? The black girl and the Indian, calling each other out as racists?"

Huculak twitches like she's about to start throwing elbows, trying to divert the urge to punch first and answer questions later; the movement's actually violent enough to rock Begg back a micro-step, make her start to flinch involuntarily, right before she catches herself.

"You first," is all Huculak replies, finally, voice flat.

And: "*Ladies,*" Lewin puts in again, a tad more frantically. "We're scientists here, yes? Professionals. We can differ, even quarrel, but with *respect*—always respect. This is all simply theory for now."

Now it's Huculak's turn to snort. "For*ever*, she gets her way," she replies. "And she will."

"Bet your ass," Begg agrees. "'Cause this is Kitchenuhmaykoosib Inninuwug First Nation land, and that's *not* a theory, so those bones go right on back in the ground where we found them, just like your government promised. No debate."

Lewin looks at Huculak. Huculak looks away.

"Never actually thought there would be," she mutters, under her breath.

The grave goods Huculak finds so uninteresting are typical Early Archaic: a predominance of less extensively flaked stone tools with a distinct lack of pottery and smoking pipes, new-style lanceolate projectile points with corner notches and serration along the side of the blades suitable to a mixture of coniferous and deciduous forests, increased reliance on local chert sources. What's odd about it, however, is the sheer size of the overall deposit—far more end scrapers, side scrapers, crude celts (stone axes), and polished stone *atl-atl* weight-tubes than seem necessary for a mere family burial, which is what the three bodies Begg talked about would indicate: one male, one female, one sexually indistinct adolescent (its pelvis missing, possibly scavenged by animals before the capstone was laid).

Folded beneath a blanketing layer of grave goods so large it almost appears to act as a secondary grounding weight, the three bodies nevertheless take pride of place, traces of red ochre still visible on and around all three rather than just the male skeleton, as would be customary. Weirder yet, on closer examination, the same sort of ochre appears to have been painstakingly applied not only to the flensed bones themselves but also to all the grave goods as well, before they were piled on top.

In burials from pre-dynastic Egypt to prehistoric Britain, Aretha knows, red ochre was used to symbolize blood; skeletons were flensed and decorated with it as both a sign of respect and of propitiation, a potential warding off of vampiric ghosts: *take this instead, leave us ours.* With no real sense of an afterlife, the prehistoric dead in general were thought to be eternally jealous, resentful of and predatory towards the living...but particularly so if they'd died young, or unjustly, and thus been cheated of everything more they might have accomplished while alive. Like the Lady of Cao, Aretha thinks, or the so-called "Scythian Princess," both of whom died in their twenties, both personages of unusual power (the former the first high-status woman found in Moché culture, the latter actually a Siberian priestess buried in silk and fur and gold), and both of whose tombs also contained the most precious grave good of all, startlingly common across cultures from Mesoamerican to Hindu to Egyptian to Asian: more corpses, often showing signs of recent, violent, *sacrificial* death.

Retainer sacrifice, that's what they call it, Aretha thinks, her head spinning slightly, skull gone hot and numb under its cold, constantly wet cap of skin. *Like slaughtering horses so they can draw the princess's chariot into the underworld, except with people: concubines, soldiers, servants, slaves—maybe chosen by lots, maybe volunteers. Killing for company on that final long day's journey into whatever night comes next. In Egypt, eventually, they started substituting* shawabti *figures instead, magic clay dolls incised with spells swapped in for actual corpses; an image of a thing, just as good as the thing itself. Unless it's not.*

Text taking shape behind her eyes, wavering: she can almost see it on her laptop's screen or maybe even a page somewhere, whatever reference-method she first encountered this information through. How in Mound 72 at Cahokia, largest site of the Mississippian culture (800 to 1600 CE, located near modern St. Louis, Missouri), pits were found filled with mass burials—53 young women, strangled and neatly arranged in two layers; 39 men, women, and children, unceremonious dumped, with several showing signs of not having been fully dead when buried, of having tried to claw their way back out. Another group of four individuals was neatly arranged on litters made of cedar poles and cane matting, arms interlocked with heads and hands removed.

Most spectacular is the "Birdman," a tall man in his forties, thought to have been an important early Cahokian ruler. He was buried on an elevated platform, covered by a bed of more than 20,000 marine-shell disc beads arranged in the shape of a falcon with the bird's head appearing beneath the man's head, its wings and tail beneath his arms and legs. Below the Birdman another corpse was found, buried facing downward, while surrounding him were piles of elaborate grave goods...

Cahokia was a trade centre, of course, the apex of an empire; makes sense they'd do things big, lay on the bling. This, meanwhile...this is different: smaller, meaner. The faces of the three prime skeletons have been smashed, deliberately, as if in an attempt to make them unrecognizable, a spasm of disgust or desecration; God knows, Aretha's spent more than enough time piecing them back together to know how effective that first attack was, how odd that it should be followed up with what reads as an almost equally violent avalanche of reverence. But then there's the capstone, the lid, the flensing, and the ochre, plus the ochre-saturated grave goods pile itself—all added later, at what had to be great cost to the givers. Like a belated apology.

No retainers, though. Not here.

Not where anybody's thought to look, as yet.

This last thought jolts Aretha out of half-sleep at last, making her sit up so sharply she almost falls over, a blinding surge of pain stitching temple to temple; she holds herself still on her sleeping bag, breathing as slowly as possible to thwart nausea. She presses her fingers up against the edge of her eye sockets until white dots flicker behind her eyelids, forcing the pain back by pressure and sheer will, until—gradually—the agony recedes. The minute she's able, she slips her boots back on, grabs her excavation spade and trowel, and ducks out of her tent.

The mist, cool on her flushed face, brings a moment's

relief. Not sure if her giddiness is inspiration or fever, Aretha heads for the grave pit as fast as she can.

The light is dimming; she won't have long. She can't see anybody working, which suggests they're at dinner in the chow tent. But no, not all of them, it turns out. Because as she pauses by the main tent, she can hear Dr. Begg arguing with someone yet again—over the sat-phone this time. Who? Curiosity gets the better of her. She edges up to the tent's outer wall, holding her breath.

"...don't know *who* she knows, is my point, *Gammé*," Begg says. Aretha frowns, translating: *Gammé* for grandmother, the elder who helped swing the tribal council towards permitting this dig in the first place; Aretha's never heard Begg sound this uncomfortable with her. "But if it's somebody with enough clout, somebody who decides they don't want to honour the arrangement any more—" She stops, sighs. "Might be more money involved, sure. Maybe not. And maybe money's not what we should be thinking about right now."

A longer pause. "Well, you saw the pictures, right? Yeah, they're the ones Tat already sent. So if people start agreeing with her—" A beat. "Okay, what? No, I'm not going to do that. *No*. Because this is *science*, not story-time, that's why, and by those standards, what Tat says makes *sense*. Muddying the waters with mythology isn't going to—hey, you there? Hello? *Hello?*"

No reply, obviously; the receiver slams down, *bang*. Sometimes the phone cuts out for no reason, even with satellite help—vagaries of location, technology, all that. "Oh, fuck *me*," Begg mutters, and goes trudging away, still swearing at herself under her breath.

Mythology?

There was a moment, back in Week One...yes, she remembers it now. Sitting around the one smoking camp-fire they'd ever risked as the tarp above dipped and sloshed, Lewin asking Begg to fill in the tribal history of this particular area and

Begg replying, slightly snappish, that there wasn't one, as such: *Lots of stories, that's all; heroes and monsters, that kind of shit. "We don't go up there much, that place, 'cause of the—"*

—and a word here, something Aretha'd never heard before, clipped and odd: *buack, paguk, baguck.* Something like that.

(*bakaak*)

Bakaak *in* Ojibwe, pakàk *in* Algonquin, a version of Begg's voice corrected, from somewhere deep inside. *It's an Anishinaabe* aadizookaan, *a fairy tale. They split the difference, usually, and call it Baykok.*

Like the Windigo, Morgan suggested, but Begg shook her head. The point of the Windigo, she replied, was that a Windigo started out human, while the Baykok never was.

It's a bunch of puns stuck together. Bakaak *means "skeleton," "bones draped in skin"; thus* bakaakadozo, *to be thin, skinny, poor. Or* bakaakadwengwe, *to have a thin face—*bekaakadwaabewizid, *an extremely thin being. Not to mention how it yells shrilly in the night,* bagakwewewin, *literally clear or distinct cries, and beats warriors to death with a club,* baagaakwaa'ige. *Flings its victim's chest open,* baakaakwaakiganezh, *to eat their liver...*

Why the liver? Aretha asked, but Begg just shrugged.

Why any damn thing? It's a boogeyman, so it has to do something *gross. Like giants grinding bones to make their bread.*

You could do that, you know, as long as you added flour, Huculak put in, from the fire-pit's far side. *Just a flatbread, though. Bone-meal won't bond with yeast.*

Thank you, Martha Stewart.

Is that what Begg's grandmother just said, over the phone? That the skeletons look like Baykok—Baykoks? That Huculak's right, and also wrong? That Begg—

Oh, but Aretha's head is burning now, bright and hot, like the Windigo's legendary feet of fire. So hot the raindrops should sizzle on her skin, except they don't; they just keep on falling, soft-sharp, solid points of cold pocking down through the sodden, pine-scented air. And the pit gaping open for her at her feet, a toothless, mud-filled mouth.

She drops to her knees, scrambles over the lip, slides down messily inside.

By the time Morgan comes by it's...well, later. Aretha doesn't know by how much, but the light's just about completely gone, and she's long since been reduced to scraping blindly away at the grave's interior walls with her gloved fingers. She looks up to see Morgan blinking down at her through a flashlight beam, and smiles—or thinks she does; her face is far too rigid-numb at this point for it to be any sort of certainty.

"'Lo, Morgan," she calls up, not stopping. "How was dinner?"

"Uh, okay. What... What're you *doing* down there, Ree? Exactly?"

"I have to dig."

"Yeah, I can see that. Are you okay? You don't look okay."

"I *feel* okay, though. Mainly. I mean—" Aretha takes a second to shake her head, almost pausing; the pit-walls blur on either side of her, heave dangerously like they're breathing. Then: "It doesn't matter," she concludes, mainly to herself, and goes back to her appointed task.

"Um, all right." Morgan steps back, raising her voice incrementally with each new name: "Tat, Dr. Huculak, c'mon over here for a minute, will you...like, right now? Anne-*Marie?* Dr. Lewin!"

They cluster 'round the edge like flies on a wound, staring in as Aretha just keeps on keeping on, almost up to her wrists now in muck. "Aretha," Dr. Lewin begins at last, "you do know we mapped out that area already, yes? Since a week ago."

"I remember, Doctor."

"You took the measurements, as I recall."

"I remember."

"Okay, so *stop*, damnit," Huculak orders. "You hear me? Look at what you're *doing*, for Christ's sake! Anne-Marie—"

Begg, however, simply shakes her head, hunkering down. "Shut up, Tat," she says, without turning. To Aretha: "Howson, Ree…it's Aretha, right?" Aretha nods. "Aretha, did you maybe hear me, before? Up there, on the sat-phone?"

"Yes, Dr. Begg."

"Uh huh; shit. Look…the Baykok's just a story, Ree. It's folklore. You're not gonna find a, what—separate bunch of human bones in there, is that what you're thinking? Like a larder?"

Still scratching: "I'm not thinking that, no."

"Then what *are* you thinking?"

Aretha wipes mud off on her cheek, gets some in her mouth, spits brown. "Sacrifice," she answers, once her lips are clear again. "Like at Cahokia; slaves for the underworld, not food. But then again, who knows? Might've been both."

"Uh *huh*. How long you been down there, Ree?"

"I don't know. How long did they co-exist, Neanderthals and Homo habilis? 'Cause they did, right? I'm right about that. Lived long enough to share the same lands, even interbreed, enough so some people have Neanderthal DNA…"

"That's the current theory," Lewin agrees, sharing a quick, dark look with Begg. "The hell's she saying?" Huculak demands of Lewin, at almost the same time. "Elyse, don't you *vet* your damn volunteers? We need to get her out, back to the Rez at least, get her airlifted somewhere—"

"Just shut *up*, Tat," Begg repeats, still not turning.

"Morgan, you're her friend—on my count, okay? One…two…"

But that, precisely, is when the wall of the grave-pit finally gives way. Releases a sudden avalanche of half-liquid earth that sweeps Aretha back, pins her under, crowns and crushes her alike on a swift, dark flood of roots and stones and bones, bones,

bones.

Here they are, I was right, she barely has time to think, reeling, delirious, her arms full of trophies, struggling to raise them high. *See? See? I was right, they're here, we're*

(*here*)

But who's that, back a little further beyond her team's shocked rim-ring, peering down on her as well? That tall, thin figure with its cocked head, its burning, side-set eyes? Its featureless face carved from jet-black stone?

She hears its scream in her mind, thin but distinct, a far-flung cry. The wail of every shattered skull-piece laid back together and set ringing, tuned to some distant tone: shell-bell, blood-hiss. Words made flesh, at long last.

(*here, yes*)

(*as we always have been*)

(*as we always will*)

Aretha comes back to herself slowly, lying on a cot in the main tent, pain-paralyzed: hurt all over, inside and out. The out is mainly bruises, scrapes, a general wrenched ache, but the inside—that's something different. Like the world's worst yeast infection, a spike through her bladder, pithing her up the middle and watching her writhe; her whole system clenched at once against her own core, a furled agony-seed, forever threatening to bloom.

She'd whimper, even weep, but she can barely bear to breathe. Which at least makes it easy—easi*er*—to keep quiet while the other talk around her, above her, about her.

"Baykok, huh?" Dr. Huculak's saying, while Dr. Begg makes a weird snorting noise. "Looks more like a damn prehistoric serial killer's dump-site, to me. And how'd she know where to dig, anyhow?"

Morgan: "She said she had a dream. Whispered it, when I was taking her vitals."

Dr. Lewin sounds worried; Aretha wishes she thought it was for the right reasons. "Yes, as to that. How bad's her damage?"

"That's one way to put it," Huculak mutters, as Morgan draws a breath, then replies: "Well…she's fine, I guess, believe it or not. Physically, anyway."

"What about the—"

Morgan's voice gets harder. "Those scars are old, not fresh. Surgical. And none of our business."

Lewin sighs. "If they mean what I think they mean, I'm not happy with…'her' choice to misrepresent 'herself,' on the project application form."

"Can we not use bullshit scare-quotes, please?" Morgan asks. "I mean—check the University rules and regs, Doc. Pronouns are up to the individual these days."

"Is biology? Aretha is—is female, just because 'she' says 'she' is?"

"Uh, yeah, Dr. L, that's *exactly* what that means. Just like a multiracial person's black if they say they are, or anybody's a Christian if they say so, even if they don't go to church." The fierceness in Morgan's voice puts a lump in Aretha's throat. She cracks her eyes open, tries to find words to thank her with, but her lips won't work; all that comes out is a dry clicking, some insect clearing its throat from inside her mouth.

But Huculak's already moved into the pause anyhow, adding: "Like those things in the pit'd be human, if they could say so."

At this, Begg turns, confronting her. "Excuse me, *things*? We're back there again? What the fuck happened to parallel evolution?"

"Oh, I don't know—tell me again how your elders think

of them as ancestors, Anne-Marie. Tell me they *don't* call them monsters."

"Sure, okay: this is Baykok country, like I said that first week, which is why somebody non-tribal—some hiker from Toronto—literally had to stumble over the capstone for us to even know it was here, and why we had to cut our way in after. But all that proves is that superstition's a powerful thing. My *Gammé*'s in her eighties, and frankly, when it comes to archaeology, she doesn't know what she's talking about."

Huculak scoffs. "Yeah, and Schliemann never found eight different versions of Troy by looking where Homer said to, either."

"Oh, so what—folktales are fact disguised, is that the song we're singing? Schliemann using *The Iliad* as a guidebook was the exception, not the rule; he got lucky, and what he found was *not* what he'd been looking for, either. Which is exactly what's happened here, all over."

"A pile of bones that don't look human, with a much larger pile of bones attached that do," says Huculak, voice heavy with sarcasm. "Yeah, sure, no big mystery *there*."

"Well, in point of fact, no. You heard Aretha: retainer sacrifice, like in a hundred other places, and do you really think we need monsters for that?" For once, Begg sounds more exhausted than angry. "It's classic Painted Bird syndrome, Tat. Whatever makes a person different enough from the herd to be rendered...pariah, alien, monstrous: this little family with their wide-spaced eyes and their snake-spines, or my *Gammé* when she came back from Residential School, hair cut and wearing white kid clothes, barely able to speak her own language anymore. Or Aretha here, for that matter, once Elyse got a look at her chest..."

Lewin lifts her hands. "Don't bring me into this, please."

"But you're already *in* it. We all are." Now it's Huculak's turn to sound uncharacteristic, all her usual snark gone. With some difficulty, Aretha turns her head, sees the woman bent down over something long, greyish-brown and filthy: one of the freshly-dug bones, plucked from a teetery, cross-stacked pyramid of such, off the gurney she stands next to. "I mean, I'd need to do a full lab workup to verify, but some of these remains—they still have flesh on them, under the muck. Like, non-mummified flesh."

Dr. Lewin, blinking: "You mean they're—"

"Recent. Yeah."

"But they were buried. How—?"

"You tell me. Anne-Marie?"

Begg opens and closes her mouth. "Well," she starts, "that's obviously—um. Okay. I mean, that's…" She deflates, slumping. "I don't know what that is," she says at last, near-inaudibly.

You'd think Huculak would be proud to have thrown her chief rival off so thoroughly, but no; she looks equally taken aback, almost scared. Lewin just stands there, studying the tent's tarp floor, like she's misplaced something; above, rain drums the roof, incessant, a dull cold tide. Morgan's gaze flicks from one to the next as the silence stretches ever more thin, disbelieving, 'til it finally falls on Aretha, and her eyes widen. "Shit—Ree! You're awake!" She hurries over to the cot and kneels down, stroking Aretha's forehead. "How you feeling, babe?"

Babe. In Morgan's mouth, the word sounds good enough to make Aretha cry, or want to.

"Hurts," she husks instead through chapped lips. "All through my groin, lower abdomen…" She tries to move and hisses, agony spiking her joints. "Elbows and knees, ankles, too."

Morgan puts the inside of one wrist to Aretha's forehead then takes her pulse; Aretha's creeped out by how pale her own wrist looks when hefted slackly in the tent's lantern-light, its veins slightly distended and purpled. "Fever feels like it's gone down, at least," Morgan tells her, attempting an unconvincing smile. "But since that's as far as my Girl Guide first aid training goes, all I can tell you beyond that is you need a hospital, like *now*. Dr. Begg, is the sat-phone working again?"

"Um, no, not yet."

"Fine. You know what? It's half an hour back to the access road; give me that damn thing and I'll get it to where it can get a signal out, then call an airlift to get her down to Thunder Bay."

Lewin puts a hand to her mouth, Victorian as all hell. "Oh dear, not at night, in this rain! What if you get lost, slip and fall, or—?"

"Ma'am, I'll be fine, my boots are hiking-rated. Seriously."

"No, Morgan, trust me, bad *bad* idea," Huculak says, Begg nodding agreement. "Wait for daybreak, for the weather to clear, that'll free up the signal link—"

Both stop as Morgan, already bent to lace her boots tighter, slashes one hand across the air.

"I have a compass and a map," she tells them, not looking up, "a flashlight, a knife, and I'm not gonna melt. Plus, it's safer on foot than trying to drive when it's like this. Anybody wants to go instead of me, I'm amenable, but you better speak now or forever hold your peace: Ree's my friend, and I'm not putting her through one second more of this than we have to."

Straightening, she glares 'round, hands on hips, but no one objects. So she stuffs the blocky sat-phone away and ducks down with a shrug instead, planting a swift kiss on Aretha's forehead—too light to fully track, here and then gone, almost hallucinatory. Like a promise.

"See you soon," she murmurs, swinging her knapsack onto her back.

No, that same voice hisses, from inside Aretha's mind. *I*—

(*we*)

—*think not.*

Aretha doesn't remember falling asleep. When she wakes, the pain has diminished astonishingly; not gone, still twinging through her hips and knees when she swings herself into a tentative sitting position, but so much less it's near-euphoric. She feels light-headed, insubstantial; even the forest's damp pine-reek doesn't burn the way it used to. For a few moments, she simply enjoys breathing with something like her normal ease.

Then she sees the light, or lack thereof. The similar lack of company. No sat-phone on the table, just dirt and bones. No Morgan.

Shit.

Wrapping the sleeping bag around her like a puffy cloak, she stumbles out into open air, for once blessedly free of rain; no visible sky between the trees, but there's less sinus-drag, cueing a possible shift in air pressure. Lewin, Begg, and Huculak are huddled around a Coleman stove maybe ten feet away, clustered gnats and moths flying up like sparks; Lewin turns as Aretha nears, almost smiling as she recognizes her, which is…odd but welcome. Things *must* be bad.

"Aretha!" she calls out, voice only a little strained on the up-note. "You look—better. Than you did."

Aretha clears her throat, even as the other two shoot Lewin looks whose subtext both clearly read *are you fucking kidding me?* "…thanks," she manages finally. Then: "Morgan?"

Lewin sighs. "No, dear. Not yet."

"How long?"

"Two hours, maybe three," Huculak replies. "Anne-Marie went out looking, but—"

"I didn't find her," Begg says, a bit too quickly, too flat.

"Not her."

Aretha nods, swallows again. No spit.

"What *did* you find?" she asks.

Tracks, that's the answer; about five minutes' walk from the camp. They're narrow but deep, as if carved, each a slipper full of dark liquid, welling up from underground. The soil is saturated here, Aretha can only suppose, after a solid four and a half weeks of precipitation—but there's something about the marks, both familiar and un-. They look…wrong, somehow. Turned upside-down.

"They're backwards," she observes, at last. Bends closer, just a bit, and wavers, not trusting herself to be able to crouch; the water throws back light, Huculak's beam crossing Lewin's as Begg hovers next to them, holding back, waiting to see if Aretha can eventually identify that particular winey shade without prompting.

"Not water," Aretha says, throat clicking drier yet, and Begg shakes her head. "No," she confirms, and Aretha dips further, sniffing hard. Smells rust, and rot, and meat.

Blood.

Lewin recoils, almost tripping, but Huculak stands her ground, demanding: "And you didn't think to tell us? The *fuck*, Anne-Marie!"

Begg stays where she is, rooted fast, as though every ounce of protest in her has long since drained out through her heels. Doesn't even bother shrugging.

"Not much point," she says, simply. "You'd've found out eventually, too, once either of you thought to ask. But Aretha here's been a whole lot better at that than most of us throughout, hasn't she? Which is sort of interesting, in context."

"How so?"

"Things my *Gammé* told me over the years, that's all, about this area. Stuff I discounted automatically, pretty much, because—well, *you* know why, Tat: because science. Empirical data vs. subjective belief, all that. Because I've tried so fucking hard to never be *that* sort of Indian, if I can help it." She pauses here, takes a ragged breath. "But what do you know, huh? Sometimes a monster isn't a metaphor for prejudice at all, plus or minus power. Sometimes it's just a monster."

Huculak stares at her, like she's grown another head. "What?" she asks, yet again.

"What I just said, Tat. We should probably get going, if we're going to."

"Going to—?" Lewin apparently can't help prompting, carefully.

Begg sighs, windily, as though about to deflate. "Try, that's what I mean," she says, after a long moment's pause. "To leave, I mean. Before they get here."

"'They,'" Lewin repeats. "They...who?"

Now it's Begg's turn to stare, even as Huculak—possibly just a tad swifter on the uptake, or simply paranoid enough to connect the dots without being asked—draws a sudden in-breath, a choked half-gasp; hugs herself haphazardly, grasping for comfort, but finding none. Lewin just stands there, visibly baffled: it doesn't make sense to her, any of it, and *can't*, really. Not in any *scientific* way.

"They were here first, that's what *Gammé* always told me," Dr. Begg—Anne-Marie—remarks softly, as if to herself. "Hunted us like animals when we came into their territory, because that's what we must have seemed like to them, the same way *they* did, to us; things with some qualities of people, not people who just happen to look like things. So we fought back, because that's what we do, but there were more of them, and they were— stronger, fought harder. Started out taking us for food, then for slaves, then for breeding stock. Changed so they could hide everywhere. Hide inside of *us*."

"Neanderthals," Aretha says. "And Homo habilis."

Begg smiles, slightly. "The current theory," she replies,

echoing Lewin. Not looking 'round as she does, even to watch how Lewin—her cognitive refusal suddenly punctured, sharp and clean and quick—begins, at last, to buckle under her own words' weight.

Behind them, the grave-site still gapes uncovered, rain-filled, ochre seeping. From above, Aretha muses, the unearthed cache of grave goods must look like a huge, slightly layered blood-blotch, all that remains of some unspeakably old crime. An apology made on literally bended knees, pot sweetened with a pile of tools and corpses, yet left forever unaccepted.

Huculak—Tat—clears her throat, knuckles still knit and paling on either elbow. Complains, voice weak: "But...we didn't know."

"I did."

"You never *said*, though."

"No, 'course not, because I didn't want to think it was true. I mean, c'mon, Tat; seriously, now. Would *you?*"

"Well…"

(No.)

Deep twilight, now, under the trees, overlaid with even deeper silence. Deep enough Aretha can finally start to hear it once more, rising the same way her pain does, threading itself through her system: the song of the bones, set shiver-thrumming in every last wet, cold part of her; that note, that tone, so thin and distinct, a faraway cry drawing ever nearer. Like blood through some fossilized shell.

And oh, oh: *Anne-Marie was right, not to want to,* she thinks, faintly, as she feels her knees start to give way—as she droops, drops, ends up on hands and knees in the mud, the blood-smelling earth. *I'm not even Native, and I don't like that story much, either. Not at all.*

Not at all.

"Who's that?" Aretha can hear Lewin—Elyse—call out, faintly, squinting past her, into the darkness. Adding, hopefully, as she does: "Morgan? I—is that you, dear?"

To which Anne-Marie just shakes her head, while Tat begins to sob. And Aretha, looking up—seeing those familiar features hanging flat against the thickening curtain of night, mouth slack-hung and eyes empty, set ever-so-slightly askew—doesn't even have to wait to hear the bones' answer to know the trick of it already, to her sorrow: that skeletal shadow poised behind, head cocked, holding Morgan's skin up like an early Hallowe'en mask with the scent of fresh-eaten liver on its breath. That line of similar shadows fanned behind, making their stealthy, back-footed way towards them all, with claws outstretched.

Don't worry, the bones' song tells her from the inside out, as the Baykok sweep in. *This darkness is yours as much as ours, after all: a legacy, passed down hand to hand, from our common ancestors. Where we are, and were, and have been. Where you are, now, and always.*

The only place any of us have left to be.

Not so different, then, after all: cold comfort at best, and none at all at worst. Not that it really matters, either way.

Every grave is our own, that's the very last thing Aretha Howson has time to think before the earth opens up beneath her. Before she falls headlong, wondering who will find her bones, and when—what tales they'll tell, when dug free…what songs they'll sing, when handled…

How long it'll be, this time, before anyone stops to listen.

The Well and the Wheel

by Orrin Grey

After the divorce, my dad moved into the old house. Mom said that it had been in his family for years, though I'd never seen it, and he'd never talked about it. The first time I laid eyes on the place was a month after the divorce, sitting in mom's Suburban in the gravel drive with the engine running while she talked to him on the front porch, the collar of her coat turned up against the cold. A weathered, one-story building the color of unfinished wood left out in the elements, it looked more like a shed than a house, though it already had new windows and a little satellite dish bolted onto the roof.

The house was outside of town, on a twenty-acre plot of land that had once been part of a farm, and the corpses of old farm buildings still dotted the edges of the big yard. Not even ruins anymore, just jumbles of sunbleached wood. Out behind the house were what was left of some cattle pens, reduced now to splinters and rust. And on the top of the hill, an old stone well with a single dead tree beside it, denuded of branches, the trunk curling toward the well as if the tree was being sucked inside or trying to crawl in.

While my dad was alive, I never set foot in the house. I only ever saw mom go in once, but she told me to wait outside, and so that day I explored the yard, poking at the remains of fallen-down buildings with the toe of my boot. It was a few months after the divorce, the weather starting to warm back up, the sky gray and filled with moisture, giving the whole property the air of a Gothic novel. I saw the well then, but I didn't go near it, because at that moment my mom came outside and called my name. Did she look a little shaken on the drive back into town? That I don't remember.

Dad didn't get any custody rights from the divorce; didn't, I think, even ask for them, which hurt my feelings at the time, though I pretended that it didn't, even to myself.

Sometimes he would pick me up in his beat up old truck, the one that smelled of stale dust and seemed to let in as much air as it kept out, so that in the winter months the heater was waging a constant battle against the cold that froze your toes and fingers. He'd take me out to the mall where we'd eat in the food court and look in the shops, or he'd take me to a movie and buy me a giant Icee and a tub of popcorn.

When I was old enough to drive, I'd go visit him instead, but I still didn't go into the house. I was never told that I couldn't, but somehow by then it was just an unspoken rule, something that I accepted without question. I'd pull my Ford Fiesta into the drive and honk the horn, and my dad would come out onto the porch and wave at me, and then we'd go to dinner at Chili's or Olive Garden or shopping at Sam's Club, where he'd buy bottled water in enormous quantities. I assumed that the tap water in the house was no good to drink—probably hard as a rock, maybe pulled up from that old well out back—and I asked him why he didn't get a water filter, but he just shook his head, hefted one of the bottles, and said, "I like this."

Neither he nor my mom ever remarried. She had a regular boyfriend for years, and moved in with him after I went to college. Dad lived alone in that house until the day he died.

The day he died was the week after my twenty-eighth birthday, though he sat in the green metal rocking chair that he kept on the front porch for three days before anyone found his body. A neighbor noticed that she'd seen him sitting out there on her way to and from work every day, and on the third day she stopped, the wheels of her car crunching on the gravel, and got out to see if he was okay. She later told me that it "just looked like he was asleep."

The doctor said that it was a heart attack, "but not the bad kind." I had no idea what that meant. Was there a kind of heart attack worse than the one that kills you?

My dad had a piece of paper crumpled in his left fist

when he died, something torn out of a notebook and written in purple ink that had smudged from the elements. It was addressed to me, and all it said was, "Sorry, Emmy." Dad was the only one who ever called me Emmy. To everyone else it was Emma, and Emmanuel no place but on my driver's license. I didn't know then what he was sorry for, or why he was holding that note so tight when he died. Had he known, somehow, that it was coming? Does the not-so-bad kind of heart attack give you a nice warning in advance?

Because my mom and dad had been divorced for more than half my life, and he had no one else left, I inherited everything he had to his name: the house and everything in it, and the land on which it stood. While he was still alive, my dad had hired a lawyer in town, a short, round man named Mr. Beaumont whose office was in a square brick building that looked like a post office.

Mr. Beaumont handled all the paperwork associated with my dad's estate, and handed me the ring of keys that my dad had worn on his belt for as long as I could remember. He hadn't wanted a funeral, and besides, there really wasn't anybody to come besides me and my mom and her new boyfriend. His body was cremated, and they gave me his ashes in a plastic bag inside a cardboard box. I figured that I would dump them somewhere on the property, thinking that he must have liked it there. My eyes stayed dry until I pulled my car into the drive and sat looking down at the ring of keys in my hand, realizing that I didn't have any idea which one unlocked the front door.

I planned to sell the house. Mr. Beaumont had offered to take care of the "disposition of the estate" for me, but I wanted to at least see it all for myself first. Go through my father's things, see if there was anything I recognized, anything I might want to keep. When I pulled into the drive I already had a duffel bag full of clothes and toiletries in the back seat.

My roommate and I had fought about something stupid

maybe a week before I got the news, and it had been cold silences and little passive aggressive gestures whenever we had to be in the apartment together. Of course, Amanda forgave and forgot the moment I heard about my dad's death, but I still hadn't yet, and I wasn't ready to be around people, not even ones who meant well. Maybe especially not those.

So I took the opportunity to move into my dad's old house. I told Amanda that it would just be for a few weeks, while I sorted out his things, and at the time that's probably what I had in mind. Work had already told me to take as much time as I needed, and I'd already told my boss that I wouldn't be back for at least two weeks, after which I'd check in. Was cutting myself off from everybody I knew and moving to a new place forty minutes from town a great idea when I'd just lost my dad? Probably not, but it was the only thing that felt right to me then.

It was raining when I stood on the porch and tried keys until I found the one that unlocked the front door. Someone had removed the green metal rocking chair, and I was grateful for that, but nobody had so much as set foot inside my dad's house since he'd passed. That's the pleasant euphemism they always use, right? Passed? Instead of stopped, broke down, died.

If you've never walked into a house where someone once lived but no longer does, then you're lucky. I recommend avoiding it for as long as you can manage. It's a different feeling than walking into a house that happens to be empty, say because everyone is at work or out to a movie, or even a house that's sitting empty because it's for sale. There's a vacancy that houses only get when their occupants have vanished in the middle of things, as if you can feel the vacuum left behind by death. That's what I felt as I stepped through the front door of my dad's house for the first time.

It was dark inside. The walls felt close, the ceiling light in the front hall produced only a dull, amber-colored glow, and the sideboard was stacked with mail and papers. Walking slowly through the house, room by room, I could get some sense of the rhythm of my dad's life. There was a big room near one end of the house—we would have called it a living room in any normal place, though in my dad's house it seemed to be something else. There was a couch and a recliner there, both old and ratty with stuffing showing through, the former covered in a faded blanket. There was a fireplace that was cold now and dark, though wood was stacked beside it. I recognized the wood immediately as old lumber from the tumble-down buildings that dotted the yard.

I could tell just by looking that this was the room where my dad had spent most of his time. An electric blanket was plugged into the same outlet as the floor lamp and piled at the foot of the recliner, and I knew, without any more substantial evidence, that he had slept there more often than in the bed, which I hadn't yet seen. On the floor next to the chair was a stack of books, and there was also a roll-top desk in one corner of the room, and a TV in the other. The desk was locked, and I didn't bother right then to try any of the keys on dad's key ring.

A trail of clutter led from the living room to the kitchen in an elliptical pattern, as food made its way from the latter to the former, and then dishes, occasionally, made the return trip, though some of them had ended up stacked here and there on the living room floor, or around the brick fireplace. Next to the refrigerator was a stack of bottled water as high as I am tall, the top case opened and several bottles missing. The fridge had also been stocked with dozens of bottles, as well as cans of beer and food in various stages of going bad.

Walking through the rest of the house, signs of habitation dropped off sharply. None of the windows had blinds or curtains, and instead heavy blankets had been draped or nailed over them to block the light. There was a bathroom just off the kitchen, and at the farthest end of the house from the living room were two bedrooms across the hall from each other. One I recognized as my dad's—clothes that I had seen him wear hung in the closet—

while the other was locked from the outside with a deadbolt and held nothing but a bed with a heavy wooden frame.

The bed was made, and next to the pillow lay one of my old stuffed animals from when I was a kid, a bunny named Mr. Stuffles who had since turned gray with age and started to pill up. He was the first thing I noticed upon opening the door, and I crossed the room to pick him up before I saw what else was on the bed. Chains attached to the frame at head and foot, ending in thick leather cuffs that looked like they had been homemade from old belts.

Was that my first indication that something was terribly wrong? I can't really say anymore. I try to tell myself that something felt off from the first moment I walked through the front door; that a germ of concern, rather than simply too-late-in-coming pity, had started in my mind when I saw the state of my dad's living room. Maybe I had, after all, seen enough of the titles of the books that lay piled beside his recliner to make me worry. It's possible that I had even suspected something more sinister for months now, years, as long as he had been living his strange life in this strange house.

Whatever the truth of it is, I know that I didn't feel the surprise, the dread or shock or nausea that should have overwhelmed me when I saw those well-worn restraints dangling from the heavy wooden frame of that bed in a room that locked from the outside. Just as I know that I didn't suspect, not for one moment, that what I had stumbled on was nothing more than the secret of my dad's interest in some kind of kinky sexual fetish.

I don't remember making my way from the bedroom back to the cluttered living room, or sinking down onto the couch there. When I did, I was still holding Mr. Stuffles limply in my left hand, just as my dad had, perhaps unconsciously, clutched his apology. Was this what he was sorry for?

I can't say how long I sat there. Minutes? Hours? The blankets over the windows made time impossible to gauge, even if the wet October day outside had given any indication. All I know is that the room grew subtly darker still, until finally I had to stir to turn on the floor lamp. When I did, I noticed once more the pile of books that lay next to my dad's recliner.

When he had still lived at home, my dad seldom read anything at all, and on the occasion that he did it was mostly Tom Clancy and John Grisham novels. The closest he had ever come to the supernatural was an occasional dalliance with Dean Koontz.

The books in the pile next to his chair were, to a volume, put out by no-name presses, with uninspiring covers featuring blurry photographs or simple line drawings of pentagrams and something that looked sort of like the veins of a leaf. Their titles were filled with words like "occult" and "paranormal" and "Satanic" and "demonology." They were not the sorts of things that the dad I had thought I'd known would even have been aware of, let alone interested in reading about, and yet the broken spines and curling covers showed that his interest hadn't been an idle one. These books had been read again and again, paged through, consulted. Post-it notes flagged pages, corners had been turned down, and notes were written in ball-point pen in the margins. Whole sections were underlined, or angrily scribbled through.

I read enough to make me more confused, rather than less, and tossed books aside one by one, the pile beside my dad's recliner becoming a sort of avalanche of my frustration. Finally, I walked over to the roll-top desk. The drawers were unlocked, and contained the things you might expect to find in a desk drawer, along with a revolver that I had never seen before, but nothing that shed any light on what was going on. I started trying keys until I found the one that unlocked the top of the desk.

I don't know what I expected to find when I rolled it open, but it was tidier inside than I had imagined. There were scraps of paper here and there, covered in my dad's handwriting, but what drew my attention immediately—as, I think, it was meant to—was a binder, like a photo book or a wedding album, with a faux-leather cover. It was unmarked on the outside, but I could see that it was thick with whatever contents it held.

There may have been a moment, while my fingertips rested on the cover of the binder, when I considered walking away. Calling the police, perhaps, or at least Mr. Beaumont. Letting this all become someone else's problem. But I had to know, so I opened the cover.

Ever since I was a little kid, I've had a habit of opening books to the back pages first. I don't know why I developed it, but it has stuck with me most of my life, so when I opened the scrapbook, it was to the last page onto which anything had been pasted. The date was only a few weeks before, on my birthday. It started with the words, "Sorry, Emmy, but I'm beginning to wear thin."

I called the binder a scrapbook, and so it was. Newspaper clippings, photographs, and meticulous notes recorded in purple pen in my dad's handwriting. Not the grim trophies of a serial killer, but the careful records of a man who can't afford to make a mistake. One entry a year, going back twenty-eight years. Each one of them the same. A picture of a girl beside a set of vital statistics: approximate height and weight, eye color, hair color, age. Twenty-eight, then twenty-seven, twenty-six, twenty-five. The first entry in the book was a photograph of a newborn, the kind that they stick up in maternity wards. It was dated twenty-eight years ago, on my birthday.

Never having been in the house before, I nonetheless remembered seeing a back door that opened off the kitchen, and that was where I stumbled then, the shock and nausea that should have overwhelmed me before suddenly welling up inside, as I remembered birthdays that my dad had missed, arrived at late, left early. One girl a year, one girl my age, every year for my entire life.

I thought that I might be sick, that I might vomit up what little food I'd managed to eat in the last twenty-four hours out behind the house, but somehow, once the damp air hit my lungs, I seemed to calm down. Still, I wasn't ready to go back into that house, so I stood in the back yard and looked up the hill, past the old cattle pens, to the well and the bent tree.

It was a cold October day, getting on toward evening, and though it was no longer raining, fog hung thick over everything. The grass of the back yard looked jewel-green, and the fog closed everything in, so that the hill was the most distant thing I could see. It felt as if I had stumbled out of the house and into a different world, for more reasons than one. Without thinking, I started to climb.

By the time I had reached the lip of the old stone well, I knew, with a knowledge that went beyond fact, that this was where he had put them. I pictured them wrapped in canvas, tied with sturdy ropes. A slightly bigger bundle each year. Were they still alive as they went down, struggling and squirming? Did they scream as they fell?

I half expected to be hit with a fetid stench as I reached the mouth of the well, the odor of almost three decades of decay. But the only smell that came from the dark hole was damp stone. What I found instead was a series of metal rungs set into the side of the well, a ladder descending down into darkness. Was it some fatalism, some sense of assumed guilt that drove my actions as I gripped the first of those iron rungs and started down into the pit? What did I think to find down there, without even a light to guide me?

When I was still in high school, I had a boyfriend who abandoned me at the county fair. After he had gone and left me with no ride home, I wandered the midway in my bare feet— maybe my shoes were still in the car; I can't remember why I didn't have them, any more than I can remember why he left— until I came to a tent, far out on the edge of the fairgrounds. The sign above the entrance to the tent didn't have any words on it, just an enormous violet eye painted on a white banner, with lines coming off it that could have been lashes but that I saw then as beams or rays of some kind.

It was a fortune-teller's booth. The woman inside looked as old as sand, though there was enough light getting in from outside to let me know that at least some of it was pancake makeup applied to add years. I had been crying, I think, and my own makeup had run down my face, but she didn't make any mention of it, just accepted my crumpled five-dollar bill and proceeded to read my fortune.

The darkness of the tent flickered with light from outside, blinking on and off, first illuminated, then in shadow. The fortune teller laid down a card with a picture of a wheel, marked with symbols I didn't recognize, held up by a red devil and mounted by a blue sphinx. It said, "La Roue." Over it, at a ninety-degree angle, she laid another. A picture of a naked woman surrounded by some kind of wreath, flanked by stylized drawings of a lion, a cow, a bird, and a golden face: "Le Monde."

She must have told me something, to accompany that cryptic action. For it to have been a proper Tarot reading, she should have put down more cards. But I don't remember any of that. I don't remember her saying a single word. Maybe I wouldn't have remembered it, even if she did. What I wanted to know, in that moment, was about the boy who had just ditched me, about how I was going to do in school, about when I was going to get my own car, be able to get away. This fortune had nothing to do with my heartbreak, with my troubles, and so I'm sure that I blanked it out. All I remember are those two cards, the wheel and the world, in the blinking light of the midway. That's what I think about, as I descend the cold rungs of the ladder into the well.

How far down do I go, into that damp darkness? Far enough that what light remains in the gray sky above disappears, and I should be climbing in blackness, but I'm not. Far enough that I begin to think about theories of the hollow earth, of dinosaurs and ancient civilizations and inner suns. Far enough that my arms and legs begin to ache, and I should worry about how I'm going to climb back to the surface, but I don't.

When my foot finally touches the ground, I expect it to crunch among old bones, or to sink into icy water, but the floor of the well isn't even damp or muddy. It feels solid and dry. It should be dark, but I can see the stone wall in front of me, see the last few rungs of the ladder that I've been climbing down. I can feel the light against my back, and I can feel that which makes the light, waiting for me to turn and face it.

What is it that I see, when I turn around? Another world in the heart of this one, spinning clockwise? A nuclear flame, burning fetid green? A congeries of iridescent spheres? A formless mass, as big as the universe, fit inside a globe of finite space? Any of that, or none of it?

I'll tell you what I see. I see a fortune teller, in the blinking darkness of her tent, laying down first one card and then another. The wheel, and then the world. It's tempting to take the easy way out, to say that I hear the voice in my head, but that's a lie. I *feel* its longing inside my brain and my bones, just as I *know* what it wants, what it has always wanted, without the need for words. It wants me. It has wanted me for twenty-eight years.

The wheel knew me on the day that I came into this world, knew who and what I was, knew me better than I have ever known myself, just as my father knew his duty, and his father before him, and his father before him. Was it love of me that made my dad defy this calling? How could such a love kindle so quickly? Whatever drove his decision, he had found another way to do what he must. Year after year, another girl to take my place. Not what the wheel wanted, but enough to keep it spinning, year after year. Until he had grown too old. Until, as his note had said, he had worn thin.

And now, at last, I am here, where I was always meant to be. At the bottom of the darkness, with the wheel that turns the world.

Trick… or the Other Thing

by Joseph S. Pulver, Sr.

(for Marilyn)

Fuck all the asshole kids.
Jesus.

Go to the Lunden's, or to Steve Rader's, they had their lamps trimmed and burning, and their pumpkins, carved into grinning jack-o'-lanterns, displayed. The Carpenter's lawn, windows, garage doors, and front porch were fucking Halloweenland! Green and orange lights (most flashing or winking) illuminated the driveway, and there was a smoke machine in the manicured rose bushes on the right side of their steps. They had rubberish bats (some with blinking red eyes) and old sheets for ghosts and a 7-foot, plastic, glow-in-the-dark skeleton hanging from the maple tree in the center of their yard. Shit, they encouraged the kids to lie down in front of any of the six large Styrofoam R.I.P. tombstones and take goddamn pictures, and they had their all-weather patio-speakers in the bushes by the smoke machine, looping a self-burned CD of seasonal standards that included "Monster Mash" and "Thriller" and "Ghostbusters" interlaced with cartoonish screams and howling monsters. Kathy Carpenter (in a witch dress and hat) gave out extra candy for costumes that brought back memories of her childhood. Dave gave an ace-bandage wrapped mummy six extra KING SIZE Snickers bars; Dave loved The Mummy (adored Kathy—"Baby, you're *my* Princess Anckesen-Amon", for giving him the *The Legacy Collection* on his last birthday), Karloff was his go-to Halloween movie, and he had the 5-tray Sony DVD player loaded.

Go the fuck *across the goddamn street.*
Bell.

BELL.

bell

Trick or treat—Trick or treat—*Trick or treat.*

Trick or treat from a mouth of fire.

Tigger-treat.

Trick… *or treat.*

Trick

or treat. Bag out and open.

BELL.

Trick or treat—*Me too*, trick or treat.

Atticus could half-recall some poem he had to read in high school English about Halloween-in-the-burbs. *Yeah, Pests and harpies. All they do is laugh and beg and stare. I'd like to show them the tomb's black maw.*

Trick or TREAT.

Treat please.

Hi, Trick or treat.

Trick or treat.

Trick or treat. Unhappy eyes.

Treat please.

BellBell. Lightning laughter on the other side of the door.

Bell.

Trick or treat. Grimacing when nothing is offered.

Tricker-treat.

Nervous. *Trick…* or treat?

No "Thank you". No candy, no reason to.

BELL extended.

BELL

BELLBELL—

"Goddamn little fuckers."

Fuck the thigh-high princess and her goddamn soccer mom.

Fuck Pokemon.

Fuck the peacock with the giant slippers that was going to

tumble on someone's front steps and break their face and the Power Rangers and Super Mario and the stupid Cookie Monster, or whatever that was.

And fuck Pooh!

Fuck the Wal-Mart Wolverine… and that stupidass tie-dye ghost that reeked of weed—high school asshole should be at the mall with the other high school assholes.

His lights were off.

OFF!

Atticus Kenton had mowed and mulched, two hours to get it all done. Bagged what needed to be bagged, took the three bags to the dump. Hadn't decorated. Never decorated. Fuck Christmas and doublefuck Halloween. Little bastards wanted candy, let them get fuckin' jobs, or whine until their parents swatted their asses, or jammed some candies down their gobs.

Bell had been ringing since just before 4, group of three waist-highs (parents waiting at the bottom of the driveway) in cheap Wal-Mart and Target costumes. Group of six high school kids, sexy pirate, two matching Star Trek somethings, Captain America, Poison Ivy, and a girl Freddie Kruger—Atticus thought she had nice tits. Two. One with dad; she was some fuzzy pink & glitter critter and dear old dad was a clown, had her on a reflective leash. Four. 5 o'clock. 6. Three. One… and one more. Four groups of two less than a minute apart. 8:30—*Go the fuck home and go to bed.* 9 fuckin' pm. Didn't stop.

Nearly 11 o'clock. Insistent bell again.

"Fuck." Atticus opened the door. Glower, takedown power pushing the same energy that shotgun projectiles deliver at impact.

"Trick… *or the other thing?*"

Christ. Wasn't even a kid. Guy. Over seven feet by any measure. *Old* old guy, goddamn senior by the look of him. Black as Miles Davis poured liquid smooth from the coffinBLACK that lies between the stars. Asshole was wearing bright-red *pharaoh* robes—and *that eye*—

"I *don't* Halloween. No candy. If I did, it would be *for kids*."

Slammed the door. Turned the dead bolt.

Bell again.

Over his shoulder, "*Fuck*, **I just told you**—"

The door opened itself.

Thing had been locked.

"Good eve—"

"How the fuck?"

"The door? Just something I can do." It smiled.

Atticus Kenton, stomach and chest burdened by the madness of a fear held by defenseless men struck by unseen things—night stalkers hissing in the primal darkness, finished turning and stepped back at the same time. Faced with a wolf shaped by its desire, a beast with infernal coloring its eye, he wished he'd owned a gun. His bodyguard, Cuddy, had told him twenty times he needed one. "You been in "Rolling Stone" more times than I can count, and you've sold 15 million CDs. That draws freaks, stalkers, and a world of shit." Atticus hadn't been in a fistfight since he was in junior high school, he wondered if it came to shoving and fists what would happen. On the road he'd always had Cuddy for this shit.

Mounting alert without shrieks. His afraid out, quick, thick as non-stop desperation on a straight-for-elsewhere. Eyes the room for sudden weapons. Finds nothing, no way to hurry away. Nothing hard to swing or clip or cause bleed. All his agitation can hand him is his cell. "You know what 9-1-1 summons. Leave now, or you'll be in cuffs. Trooper station is less than a mile from here."

"I believe you'll find that device does not work."

He was right, no service.

"I have a gun."

"No, you don't. And you are out of future, that is, as

you'll soon discover, why I've stopped by this evening."

Out of future. He'd been hearing that horn blare for months now... longer. "Rolling Stone" said the same in a review two months ago.

ATTICUS KENTON IS OUT OF TOUCH (WITH EVERYTHING)

From *Take Me With You* to *Colorless Ground*, Kenton's blues-seared songs of pain and losin'-end prophesy have brilliantly explored the consciousness of the post-modern Steppenwolf, as he roams from Desolation Row to Nightmare Alley, broken heart to betrayed heart, until his last dead-on-arrival release, three years ago, *Personal Effects*.

My review (October 2010) called the release, *out of touch, and directionless, devoid of the passion and hungry poetry his fans had come to expect from this farmer of the city. There's not a whiff of Kenton's I'm-a-Chicago-bluesman guitar on this tonight-I'm-crooning-just-for-you/ cocktail-jazz piano-based experiment of limp and thoroughly diluted. Lyrically, it yawns with meme-based fragments, stitched together in hollow transmissions from a mainstream power-pop sensibility that has forgotten how to tap its foot.*

No treat for fans, my autopsy can only declare this train wreck killed the patient. We can only hope someone buries Kenton's remains at the Crossroads, and The Devil, passing by and in the mood to dole out treats from his trick bag, will pause and offer terms that inject mojo back into this shriveled soul.

Last week's largely-unattended concert at The Barris was further proof the patient is dead. Kenton, the former Pretty Poison frontman, stepped on stage fronting a four piece combo, and offered up songs from his soon to be released, *The Sorrow and the Search*. Four songs in, a third of the very small audience quietly made their escape. This reviewer stayed; it's what they pay me for. For an old fan it was ninety minutes of heartbreak and torture.

2 stars.

Dead.

It's going to kill me.

A frenzy of disease and devils erased the smile from its face. Behind the intruder, the lights directly across the street at the Carpenter's house were extinguished. The whole street went black, black not empty. There were *other phantoms* in the spaces on the other side of the doorway, things from a measureless, deeper table. Mindless things driven by must.

Atticus Kenton couldn't *see* see them in the dense eternal shades, but he could feel their measure. Drawing a breath, he could taste the activity and reflections of their consciousness.

"You sense my friends and companions." The smile was back. "Not to worry, Atticus, they're not coming in... *yet.*"

Hard frost after hard frost had beaten the auburn out of autumn. Tombstones and no silence. Lawns were stiff and wounded. "Antique" Sandy was on the radio, spinning a cold radiance of unfinished miserableness, K. D. Lang's "Busy Being Blue" followed Emika's cover of "Wicked Game" and Neko Case's "I Wish I Was the Moon". Three daggers were more than she could bear. Marilyn snapped off the radio and ran into the bathroom.

"'An apparition in the night'." *Have I reduced myself to that?*

She turned away from the mirror and the tears that keep you off balance, the tears that say you only have yourself to blame.

Tears didn't help. They didn't wash the pain off stage.

Didn't change the orchestration. She didn't want to face another attempted *C'est la vie* in the mirror, or another expression stimulated by obligation, or true (and mostly sisterly) concern. Tears didn't help, but they wouldn't stop. Night came, or there on her desk (waiting for her signature) would be a word in someone else's divorce decree, and she was back in it, the sharp that got in your blood, that sprouted horns in your mouth. The cold-hot fire you couldn't understand. The stiff, bitter-smelling looking back shriveled her.

"God-damn-it. God-damn-it." Marilyn felt like an exhausted, tragic ghost. "Get a backbone, or find a distraction."

An autumn exit. Screamed out of the living room and out the door. In the blow armed with chill. Crying that was too hot to medicate itself inside the house behind him. What he didn't say, a bluster of chipped moments (invalids now) and lies Atticus can't hide from, swirling, stabbing, louder and louder. October now the wrong color. And the volleys kept on coming. Feet on New York streets occupied by disquiet. Blocks that sing of cleaving and incapable. Wind pressing them, a few corroded-by-autumn leaves leaped an empty gin bottle and two beer cans. They manically swirled above the sewer grate, then were quick to dart.

"Too fucking cold to be *here.*" Wind answered with another blast of chill-you-to-the-bone. Stupid with rage Atticus kicks a cat-size pile of soggy leaves that has collected in the middle of the sidewalk. Curses his now-wet sneaker. "Nothin' pretty about New York in the fall when you're not in Central Park." Decided to head south and get a *warm* room. Saw less-pretty and what remained of *we did* when he turned the corner. A scarred, scab-covered rat and his hunger-frantic mischief in a sidewalk-garbagecan wonderland. Fear of the obsessed diseasecarriers; two steps back, hurry across the street. Maw of a cobalt alley saturated with a density to terrify. Atticus wondered what else was in its shadowed black belly. "Whole place is a highway to *fucked*."

Neighborhood with few autumn leaves and not a sign that Halloween, or any other holiday, would be celebrated here, but full of moist steady breeze. Few lights on. No cabs. Figured he wasn't going to see one soon, not here. Hurried to be out of the moist cold. "You Can't Always Get What You Want" was on a radio scratching its way out of some living room above. Jagger was lying about getting what you need.

Where was September and its possibility of remorseless, the August angel who opened the brief flight from misery with spoonfuls and skin? September, without this frost in it... now somewhere out of town, somewhere South with softer, warmer winds, somewhere too far to even to be seen behind closed eyes.

He'd stormed out, that's what he told himself, without his cell. Had his wallet, his credit cards, cash. Get a room. Get a bottle labeled *soothe*, or *I haven't got anything better to do*. Marilyn would calm down. Had before. Times before that too. Rock-'n'-roll wife knew deep, starfucker sweethearts released huge kisses and were gone, or flung rapidly. This one had been no different; he barely remembered her, blonde, big tits, had her own coke. She (a Manhattan Lorelei who was only too happy to take off her clothes—he didn't remember if she had a name, or if he'd forgotten it the second he heard it—) was a blur he fucked on a whim.

Across town. A hard frost in Central Park. The head of an overexposed bird is under a dead leaf. "Decapitated. Fuck." In summer the city lights surrounding the park would be pretty—an old friend, glimpsed now, in the pallor of autumn, they whisper, cry. Pierced by unease and the stare of the coroner moon eerie smolders around him.

Atticus shivered. "I need fucking coffee." *Followed by a good drunk.*

Skips coffee for beer. Grabs a quick burger and a bottle of single malt.

Bottle in a bag. Checks in. Nineteenth floor room of La Bibliotheque. TV on—some old bullshit creeper about exorcism, not that he's watching it. Forth double after the two beers he had with the greaseburger. *Deny* (vapored) sits with *give it time* (not far behind in the race to fool itself). There's a telephone within reach, but he's afraid of its teeth. Brings *the act of feeling* in his glass to his lips, gulps, goes down like bones. Looks over at the window. And suddenly, somehow, he's dragged himself to its reality, autumn's outside, but his drunk does not see the jewel tones of dying leaves or Central Park's pleasant lampposts. Home's that way. Marilyn's that way. "*Marilyn*—" He's trying to hold an image of her, 5'8", black tresses, smile that could turn on Bill Evans' turned-off stars, legs worthy of their own ZZ Top song, great curves, always fetching in that black dress from Warwick's—the connection to her softness is broken, she's sharp, merciless, full of war, her teeth bared, her eyes claw, he's choking on her rake and rant. Can't summon a soft dreamscape. Rolling with the anger, can't muffle the torment. Picks up the bottle of Glenlivet 12. Tomorrow would start with a bad morning.

While Atticus was holed-up with his bottles and room service nursing his stupidity, which he had sprayed (along with a hundred invectives) all over the hotel room, Marilyn dried her tears and talked to her best friend, Diana. Halloween was coming and they were going to do *something*. Diana said, "Put the *Lying Asshole* out of your mind", quoted Prince and laughed. Marilyn started the something by going up into the attic for her Halloween decorations. Atticus hated holidays, hated decoration—"An orange and black... *macramé* owl? That's stupid,

Marilyn."

"Screw the asshole." Marilyn hung a furry bat with lacy wings from the dining room chandelier. "Kicked, but not defeated." Two hours and many-decorations-brightening-her-mood later she sat and pulled out a Halloween recipe book. "Soul cakes." Allspice, nutmeg, cinnamon, ginger, had them. Flour, salt, butter, yes. Made a note to buy cranberries. Added, see if de Sedella's has any new Halloween decorations. Grinned.

Diana was right. "Look, Sweetie, you need a soul provider. Atticus was a trouble man, and not the good kind. We'll hit the Masquerade Party or Dances of Vice, or *both*. I'm going as the original swingin' chick, Mrs. Emma Peel, looking psychedelic and taking no prisoners." Diana laughed. "You?"

"If we're going to party like Prince, I think this girl needs a new dress. One that would make Smokey sing."

Back from de Sedella's with the cranberries and a few necessaries (and the cutest plastic owl ornament for the front door). Oven on, ingredients in the mixing bowl, the nutmeg and cinnamon were ground fresh. "Jumpin' Jack Flash" mojo? Hell no, Marilyn had The Doors—cranked—on the stereo. Yes, she loved Morrison madly—yes to L'America's Rimbaud, yes, to Texas Radio and The Big Beat. Two hours later she's done. Two trays of soul cakes stacked high. Her kitchen is filled with their aroma. The warm, sweet scent follows Marilyn to the porch when she goes to tack her new owl to the door.

Nyarlathotep catches the wafting smell as he passes her home. "All souls... *fade*." And as he turns into the aromatic aroma Marilyn Moorstadt catches his eye. "A sweet tongue now blackened by a foul soul's bullets." Nyarlathotep walked on.

From the corner he'd almost turned and looked back at her, but the whim never solidified. Stood stock-still on the beach, watched the cold Atlantic waves surge above the sea canyons. Heard murder, ambulance sirens, the modulations of black time.

Marilyn's on the boardwalk; he follows the scent of Chanel and cranberries.

In a bar called The Wharf. She sits alone admiring the owl art of her latte.

"*Trick...* or the other thing?" He asked.

She smiles at the elderly gentleman in the black wool Armani, at the exotic and grandfatherly warmth he radiates. "Treat, please. I really could use one." Fast, almost excited. Generally she's a listener, a good one, but if she warms-up to the person she'd dive into conversation. Marilyn's shocked how easy that slipped out.

Feels like she's been unlocked or unwittingly pried open. Out it comes, the chemistry—hopelessly, shamelessly blessed with desire; their immersion, the expansion of their wonder; watermelon-basil daiquiris and making a frog and a leaping stag and Jack and the Beanstalk out of clouds summering o'er their honeymoon cottage; the shape of his chaos; the internet video (scored with Marianne Faithfull's "Why'd Ya Do It") of that amphibian that blew him backstage; that Lunatic Slut who hated her in high school and screwed Atticus to spite her, that Lunatic Slut who *still* lived around the corner in Belle Harbor; the D. I. V. O. R. C. E., forced to digest the spilled entrails of once happily-conjoined. "I know it's been a year, and I'm better—*I really am*, but—" Marilyn Moorstadt wants payback. Wants to unleash the pain of her silent screams... in *his* head. Let him endure it. Let him shed tears until his tear ducts were filled with ashes. "Goodbye without rhyme."

"For you, my dear lady, done and done. The voyage that will recalibrate the velocity of his dispersal will begin soon."

She stared at Nyarlathotep. *Voyage. From here to nothing. Is that what it is?*

Marilyn, her hands trembling with a jumble of heated-anger and softer remembrances, was gazing at the barren vines of Atticus' fate and—*There was bottle of red... and current. Commences amplified New. Wish touched on fate, looming, You, about to follow, skin. Eyes textured by foreplay soared in Become. Atticus picked up his Strat and put together a boogie-and-blues medley of "Legs/A Fool for Your Stockings/Love Her Madly" for her. No one dimmed the lights as the immersion in belly-to-belly-math danced. After, he whispered, "One day I'll write one for you."* The day he did seemed a million miles away.

The ominously-cold expression seated across from her and the icy fingers of *lonely this last year* brought her back to the anger-part of the tangled equation. "*Merde.* Let the sky fall on him."

"Oh, I will."

His smile made her feel helpless in a way she could not describe.

Nyarlathotep left Marilyn in The Wharf Bar & Grill and looked to the north, toward Kenton, but time and the other 11 dimensions do not influence Nyarlathotep and the other celestial ancients in the ways they confront creatures leashed to the tapestry of the tomb, and he was turned. Beyond the concrete facades of 5th Avenue and the B-V color index of Celeano, vaster, incomprehensible to men, galleries and libraries contoured by *other odors* call the ancients to symphonies unheard by the swarms of gravebound human flesh. Stroked by whim, Nyarlathotep—outstretched, stepped over a bridge, hopping the vortical phenomena of the Outer Voidways, to probe a contentious affair. "There will be time for lessons and the scattering later."

No recovery in a 5-star Riviera paradise or the Caribbean this time, there's a cold quick divorce—Marilyn's uncle at Norwood Hathaway diced him up good, and the purchase of a pleasant colonial tucked away on the outskirts of the burbs, Upstate in the Adirondack foothills… and little else. Dust. Salt in the melody of his last dance.

The quiet world of forest and field does not quiet Atticus.

After balancing the scales of a slight disaster involving *Mindless Jaws* and the *Things in the Water*, Nyarlathotep turned to face a deranging corruption gnawing on the hearts of mortal rivers. As the mortal things departed their worldly-shells, he remembered his conversation with Marilyn about Atticus. Black stars and throbbing drums in his pockets, Nyarlathotep shifted and Atticus moved from dim margins to centerstage. The Black Man's smile looked like dungeon doors opening.

The Carpenter's had Halloweenland fully trimmed and burning. A cabinet-maker that Dave was training had been over for a beer last Saturday and given Dave a CD of heavier Halloween tunes to play. Kathy, while busy making pumpkin cupcakes for her daughter's 3rd grade Halloween party, told her husband Oingo Boingo's "Dead Man's Party" was delightful, but "Frankenstein" by the Edgar Winter Group, "Highway To Hell" by AC/DC, Van Halen's "Running With The Devil", and Donovan's "Season Of The Witch", were too upsetting for the kids. "They want fun stuff, Hon. They don't want to be too-scared to come up to the door." 10 p.m. they shut it down and went to bed.

Nyarlathotep looked over the Carpenter's inactive decorations. Grinned. *"Human fatedness…*Their strange need to connect and express. They're so charmingly clueless."

Moon lost to conquering clouds. Breeze that muscled-up, an enforcer cleaning the loitering leaves from Stony Creek Drive. Nearly 11 o'clock. The bursts and romance of their activities swallowed, most of the lights on the street have gone out.

Prominent face mangled, the discomfort of a pilfered jack-o'-lantern lies at the curb with several candy wrappers that just couldn't wait for the obsessive inspections of parents. Nyarlathotep eyes Atticus Kenton's door.

"I only have fifty or sixty bucks in the house. *You can have it.*"

"I have no need of money."

Psychos. Fuck. Kenton's eyes were on the man's hands. *No knife.* He was slowly inching backward, looking for a weapon.

"You once considered yourself something of a storyteller. "Man Driving West", "Out On Bail".   In interviews you said, your paintbrush channeled haunted hearts, delusions, and albatross." Nyarlathotep stepped past Kenton and walked into his dining room-cum-rehearsal studio.   He picked up Atticus' treasured Strat, strummed it once. "Needs to be tuned."

"Please don't touch that, it's—"

Nyarlathotep grinned. ""The Woman With the Standard Smile", "A Happy Hour Wedding"." Strummed it again. "Yes, it needs to be tuned. "The Bukowski-Beckett Swap Meet", "Hallucinations on a Blind Train", "Comforted by the Kindness of Marilyn's Poetry", what did you call them, 'self-help for the rock bottom'?"

Nyarlathotep set the black '55 Strat back in its stand. "If you go for Strats, she's a beauty."

Some kind of weirdass fan. Give him some autographed CDs and talk him outta here.

"I am not a fan, but I am very fond of stories. I heard an interesting one not so long ago. In a hive such as this, cluttered with preparing and haphazard, none of it new mind you, there are times things come to my attention."

Fucker's shitass-nuts.

"Lawns and emergency rooms. Segments considered, clumsiness, betrayals... everything is allowed and nothing matters. You speak of justice, and yet you fear cutting the rope that fastens your—what's that word you like, *shitass*—your shitass little boat to Moby-Dick. Do you not find any of this curious?"

It's good when they want to talk. I think?

Atticus looked at the hardcase his Les Paul was in. *I could pretend to play him a new song and bash his head in with the thing when he's not looking. All I'd have to do wait and—*

"I'm surprised you kept the Les Paul. You never liked the fingering."

"You can read—"

"Your mind. Yes. I can do *anything* that comes into my mind. *Anything.*"

Wiry, almost spiderish. Too tall. Hand the Black Trickster a scythe and he could have portrayed Death or an inmate in a facility for the criminally insane. Didn't need make-up. Nyarlathotep walked around the room, touching this and that, then wiped his fingers, as if he'd touched hot-August-rot compost. Long black fingers picked up a small stack of the musician's CDs, flipped them over, scanning titles, reviewing—

"All the atoms in the mirror that spelled poverty, how they screamed. What they screamed. Nothing soft, no semi-believable lie you could hide behind.'

"There was the face... stressed. Somewhere in it was the bull of rage. Somewhere in it were laws patterned by ash and rain, and what the eyes had seen when they undressed the horizon. The light. The shape of the statues at the gate, how they spoke of the prayers of the past. The long list of memories that were in her eyes, how they were over."

—tossing each CD back on the table after it failed to

impress.

Nyarlathotep had spent moments with other musicians; there had been one prominent piano player (who would only play nocturnes) and a bevy of guitarists—they were the worse, but it was mostly horn players that drew him. He heard them play, watched them strive and hustle, and never full enough, or able to take care of necessary and right-in-front-of-them, finally lose. He walked around the table and took the Martin D12-20 Atticus had composed Marilyn's song on from its guitar stand. He strummed it a few times. "Now, this one is in tune…Do you ever consider how fragile some things really are?"

"*Yes.* That's a *1970 Martin.* It can't be replaced."

"It has always been about sound to you, hasn't it? In PsyOps they love the effects of *sound.* But we're not going to fool with Barney's "I Love You", or "Enter Sandman"—two favorites in the PsyOps game, if you didn't know."

"PsyOps?"

"Do you have a preferred volume? Let's try concert level, 110dB. That's not too much to handle for an old rocker, is it? '

"Ready? I am. Hey, Mister DJ, we're ready to get this party started."

In a flood of deep darkness.

And momentary silence.

He's bound, wrists and elbows knees and ankles, to what feels like a hardback chair. "What the fuck? Hey?"

"Hush. We don't want to miss anything."

Sounding distant a tattered grey choir rises up, its grainy squalling solidifies. Kenton's ears tell him he's in a good-size acoustic space. His nose and gag response have been in a head-on collision with a scummy stench, rivaling a Bowery bar toilet that needed to be cleaned with an explosion. Irregular bursts of brittle light reveal the environment to be the expansive interior of a living thing infested with cell-like organisms, that, like maggots, feast on the lunatic deformity next to them, or an overgrown ecosystem dreamed up in a fungoid hell. Then comes the REALNOISE. Trick or treat and the buzzing of his doorbell were pinned to him—no start and stop, on-and-on, waves without ebb. Leaping above the upper registers of the looped and distorted bombardment of "TRICK OR TREAT" and the sound of his ceaseless doorbell there's an invading pestilence of spectral chittering and what coherence would describe as bizarre, freakish laughter. If a fox bark was kaleidoscopically reprocessed in a studio choked with delay units and ring-modulators it might resemble this pained clamor.

Off the map, beyond normal time. Wide open—this is a fever sharpened on blackness, this is pain that has no bottom—shrieking. Unsettled by what connected to his ear.

An extended period of pitchBLACK. A muscular moaning. Frequency and pitch and rhythms change and change and change again. Cyclical patterns sour. He's having trouble with simple and meaning. All the details that once rumbled and darted within him are being executed.

He screams, "STOP!", but cannot hear his own voice.

Every minute or so, Atticus can see Nyarlathotep, hear him, walking in circles around the hardback chair he's shackled to. Few times he gets a glimpse of the Black Man's head Atticus encounters faceless. In one flicker, Atticus thought the tall black figure was a winged fog in the form of a woman. His sense of time is worm-eaten and drained by the barrage of Trick or Treat and the door bell, and the intermittent light.

He's cold, scorched. Something in the sound is withering and leeching him, his throat is dry. His skin starts to flake, peel, as if he'd been critically sunburned.

Roaring silence. No sound. No. Sound. He's incarcerated in it for an eternity.

Light on—ON, crawling, screaming. 'neath *alone*, a predatory sucking flitters.

Spittle. Nyarlathotep's rank, wet breath on Atticus' face.

"end of care
obsolete bed.
Lou
and Jesus' son
dead.
no smell of you next to me."
Unfathomable BLACKNESS.
Soundlessness.

Belly, chest, throat, tight, hands balled into pale little fists. Atticus is waiting.

On and on NOTHING. He's counting, clinging to each number ...Counted. Lost track. "How... long?" In the darkest darkness. Swallowed. In the belly of some *thing*.

Lightning WHITENESS—BLACK ...ghostly light, slow, quitting... again in penal BLACKNESS—flicker of struggling illumination, misshapen cells of black grow in it, conquer it— BLACK—

Atticus is suddenly overcome by the scent of Marilyn's perfume. What was a road of delicate and sweetly that lead to radiance is stuffed into him like a disease that would only be blunted by ghostly. If there had been anything in his stomach he would have expelled it.

Nyarlathotep barks gleefully and returns to the song.

"no moon, stars,
above.
out on bail'

"One from your *thankfully-brief* Lou Reed period, as I recall. It's not very good, is it?"

The napalm of lights and bell and Trick or Treats roars again. He may have been here a week ...

His voice, groping, is raw. His words few, cracked snatches, weak and directionless as smoke.

Smoke torn to shreds.

His life torn to shreds.

All he could have, joy, Marilyn, should have, listened to her, learned from her, is being chiseled by extinguished. All she wanted to do that day was fly a kite. A simple thing. Fun on the beach, feet splashing in the foam. Stretch; soar with the oboeing gulls in the sunlight.

Marilyn. All the times they could have talked, engaged in a real conversation ...If he'd shut up and let her. If he had just shut up and drank the Darjeeling ...

Unable to move.

Mouth open... no scream.

Her eyes. The questions.

The times his tongue took over. Turned her way under his.

Pain—this is why cancer patients have tears in their eyes, and their screaming begs for the grave.

All the times—

In those days—

Dried up.

His first gig with Dom, Mike, and Ray at the VFW hall for their 4th of July barbeque—

Blown away.

Marilyn front-row-center at his first show in The Garden—Marilyn in his arms at the beach—giggling at his worn-out vulture joke—on top—Devouring her heavenly Key Lime Pie—"I wish you and your whores were dead."—*Marilyn—*

All the times—

Times it came up he always told Marilyn there was nothing after this life, nothing the searchlight of consciousness couldn't expose. She believed something was out there, but didn't know what.

Atticus could feel what was framed in the starry winds of The Beyond. He could tell her now. There were things, adders burning with poison urges, ancient things—older than the festivals of Samhain and Walpurgis, older than parietal visions of

Pech-Merle, ravenous things—shapes beyond understanding, right here. Nyarlathotep was one of them; he had a hand in controlling this game. The rules didn't work here. *Apart* worked on him. Vibrant misused, brittle. Rational was nearly gone, blown away. Off every map—farther down the line overrun. His resist in crisis, he couldn't flee. He shrieked. Cried. The End frolicked in his convulsions.

Silence.

"Still with me?" Nyarlathotep sings part of another one of Atticus' songs, "The Bukowski-Beckett Swap Meet".

"Rehearsals
And bit parts
This and that
Way gone away.

To there and not today
Watercolor maps washed out
Hopeless terms in a wooden box.'

"Seems that the reviewer was accurate, wasn't he? The patient really did die."

Atticus' corpse is in no condition to respond.

Nyarlathotep grins.

Halloween. September's flame has burned out. Marilyn's jack-o'-lantern is fully trimmed and burning; her soul cakes are fresh out of the oven. She's hung her furry bat with lacy wings from the dining room chandelier. Her pre-Atticus tradition of night-before-Halloween double feature revived, last night was spent on the sofa in her white flannel jammies and rag socks, with a bottle of Californian chardonnay, a bowl of hot-buttered popcorn (lightly sprinkled with sea salt), the Criterion *Carnival of Souls,* and *The Ninth Gate.* In a-little-over three hours she was off to Dances of Vice with Diana; this year Marilyn's was going as Dr. Frank-N-Furter. Diana, of course, said she was just going to have to be, Columbia the groupie.

She hasn't heard from Atticus in almost a year, she's not sure if he's still living Upstate.

Bell. Without waiting, bell-bell.

Rushing from the kitchen. Smiling. "What savage little predators."

Bell.

Filled candy bowl (of peanut butter cups) in hand, Marilyn opened the door. Steeped back deeply unsettled.

"Trick…" Pushes the bell again, grins. *"or the other thing?"*

"How do you know where—"

"It's something I can do." Nyarlathotep stepped around her. "Your soul cakes smell delicious. Do you have any coffee?"

"What do you think you're doing?"

"I'm here to report on Atticus."

That stopped her.

"About that coffee?"

Knows she should be firm, billow "No. Please leave." Seizure, throat can't. Odd, she's never been timid before.

Grasped. Compelled. Feels like she's on a leash she can't see.

Coffee in the kitchen, his black, burning hot. He gulps it.

Marilyn's scared, jumbled, staring at the figure seated on the bar stool in her kitchen.

"You will have to forgive me, my dear, but I get sidetracked… everyone has faults, I guess. But the good news is I did not forget you. I've just left your former beau. You'll recall me mentioning, recalibrating?"

She did. Nodded, yes.

"He hardly uttered a word as he passed. I was not paying

close attention, but it seemed there really wasn't much struggling."

The feeling he was dangerous was there the last time Marilyn sat with him, but she pushed it back. (*That's foolish. He's just a charming old man... but he might be off his rocker.*) It was stronger this time. He wasn't talking about ruining Atticus' life and career, Nyarlathotep was putting it right out there, annihilated—*gone*, fixed in a way her anger had not seriously embraced.

Closure or ghost (all that carrying one entails), which is the language of future? Marilyn's engulfed by a chill and certain she's never felt colder. Atticus had ruined part of her, stripped her as autumn strips the trees of their summer nature, and her misery had reached out, wanted to break him, to commit him to hell—the old-fashion kind (flesh forever burning in the Paradise of Torture), but hearing it, that she, her words, had been his death penalty... she shuttered.

She could have wept.

Nyarlathotep is up, walking around her kitchen, touching things—he's thumbing through her *Alice in Wonderland* cookbook—Portmanteau Bread, Ambidextrous Mushrooms, Treacle-Well Tarts. "Eat Me Cakes. I've served man to some of my associates." Looking in cabinets. Grins at the glass apothecary jars labeled arsenic, belladonna and hemlock, Marilyn uses for sugar and tea and coffee beans. His back to her, he laughs after asking, "What, no tormentilla?"

She's seen apex predators in animal documentaries on PBS, they moved with the same assured power and grace he does. Dread she cannot express gnaws in her blood. Marilyn can't stop shuttering. As she flashes on the Dr. Frank-N-Furter outfit laid out upstairs on her bed, her sixth-sense tells her it only gets *this cold* on Judgment Day.

She was going with Diana.

They were going to sip champagne.

They were going to dance.

They were going to laugh, to party and sing along with the Halloween hits of yesteryear.

Nyarlathotep started to quietly hum a passage from "Comforted by the Kindness of Marilyn's Poetry". The phrasing of the melody was off, ominous. Halfway through the verse his pitch descended into Georg Trakl's *Trauer*. It sounded like hearing an ugly song on the radio.

Marilyn's trying to reconcile the first time she heard the line 'With kind / And a boat sculpted of love / She opened a library of bridges' and this distortion.

"So many, many times." Nyarlathotep looked out the window. "I've opened pathways, helped many across the bridge." He can see—*a woman, who will soon be sitting in the Seahorse Grill with grubby men and their glasses of beer and hungry eyes, is putting on cheap lipstick. to a man, they'll climb over each other to spread her flame ...a husband sits in a fog of sullen years. his 4th beer is no comfort ...an aging alto played is stained by a sharp message that smells like rain*—He turned back to her. "I have always been a prisoner of my whims." The trickster was looking in the palm of his hand. "'what he *chanced* to mould in play' ...Yes, perhaps?"

She had no idea what Nyarlathotep was talking about.

"Yes, of course, you're right, I'm so easily diverted. We all are on occasion. Wouldn't you agree?"

Nyarlathotep waited for her to respond.

She didn't.

He shrugged. "Well, my dear, you've had your treat... it's time for the other thing." His featureless face is a livid EXIT sign.

(Hal Willner Weird Nightmare: Meditations on Mingus, *John Lee Hooker "The Healing Game", Scott Walker "Farmer in the City", Adele "Skyfall", Stevie Ray Vaughan "Cold Shot", ZZ Top "Legs", "A Fool*

For Your Stockings", The Doors "Love Her Madly", Oingo Boingo "Dead Man's Party", Jackson Browne "These Days")

A Shadow Passing

by Daniel Mills

These things he remembers.

The light is green, then gold. The elms are waving, and he is a child again, feverish and chilled. He smells smoke, leaf-mold in the gutters. His mother's eau de cologne.

She lingers in the doorway, dressed in widow's black with kid gloves buttoned to her sleeves and her hair in a bun with no strand out of place.

I'm going out, she says.

She speaks these words to no one. The others are upstairs (his grandfather, his aunt), and she does not see him where he crouches behind the settee, listening as the doors fall shut: the inner, the outer.

He leaps to his feet, running, and watches from the window as she rounds the far corner. Her shadow dwindles down the pavement, vanishing with the light through the elm trees.

He waits.

Later, his aunt finds him curled up in the window-seat, shivering as his fever climbs. Minutes or hours have passed, and his mother has not returned.

Poor child, she says. You needn't worry about her.

And he does not reply because he knows better. Because his mother has come to him at night when the fires have gone out and told him of the shapes that dwell between the buildings, the winged shadows she calls *them*.

His aunt helps him up. She places her hand across his forehead, sighs, and leads him to the kitchen that is her sanctum. It is warmer here, the flames kindled high and licking round the copper kettle. She sits him down at the table and sees to his supper in silence, as is her way, unspeaking unless spoken to and he has nothing to say.

The kitchen is quiet but for the rasp of her breathing. His

aunt makes herself coffee and rolls out the dough for her tea-cakes, which she keeps in a tin with the President's face on it and the words *Remember the Maine* inscribed below. This tin is forbidden him, as are so many things, and his aunt keeps it on a shelf where he cannot reach.

Six o'clock: the night is drawing in.

His aunt claps her hands to rid them of flour and lights the kerosene lamp. The wick she turns down to a glowering, a gleam—orange like the windows that look west to the street. She will not use the gas. She is thrifty, as is her sister, who lives near Boston with her husband and saves her hair in jars to use as stuffing for her cushions.

His grandfather does not join them. There will be no stories tonight, no tales of djinns and princesses, which his grandfather is fond of telling.

So they eat alone in the paneled dining room with the vast expanse of table between them and the lamp placed near its center, the flame burning low as the hour stretches, and the windows are black past the lamplight when he hears the doors slam shut: the outer door, the inner.

His mother enters. Her hands are bare, the gloves discarded so her knuckles show, the long fingers. Her eyes are blank, hair windblown and wild.

His aunt, rising, takes his mother by the arm before she can speak and walks with her down the hallway to the stair. It is some time before his aunt returns, and the boy is alone with the darkness gathering into shapes like wings all round him, beating out of the shadows.

Afterward, when supper is finished, he sneaks a candle from the tallboy and brings it to his bedroom upstairs. His aunt would disapprove, as would his mother, but he strikes a match and lights the candle and quickly falls asleep.

He is shaken awake. His mother looms over him, white and ghostly in the half-dark.

She says: I saw them. They came out of the canal, rising in a smoke where the sun makes patterns from the floating leaves. I ran. I fled over the bridge, up the hill. I was making for the church—I thought I'd be safe there—but the alleys swarmed with them, hundreds of them, with bodies made of corners so you see them only where they block the light. I lost my hatpin, my gloves, but still I did not stop, not until I reached the church on the hill. I fell down, gasping, but they would come no nearer. They unfolded their bodies, forming rings around me. The church was at my back, its black spire, and I thought—

Her lips are wet, her breathing strained and rapid.

She says: It's raining.

The elms are dripping, a gentle music. An arabber drags his cart down the street, whistling down the damp.

Then his mother notices the pilfered candle, and her face changes, her voice. Her mouth curls in on itself so that he scarcely recognizes her, this creature with a voice like the frost and the spittle flying from her lips.

You wicked thief, she says. You stole this from downstairs, didn't you?

She slaps him once across the face. She calls him ugly and selfish and cursed with his father's temperament. She snuffs the light and carries it with her when she goes.

His aunt is waiting in the hall. The two sisters argue in whispers, hissing through teeth as not to wake his grandfather, who is sleeping in the room next door.

The rain continues.

The boy lies awake with the blankets pulled to his face, the nerves vibrating in his gut. An omnibus, passing, drags the puddles behind it, and he recalls the first time she saw *them*.

Like winged shadows, she said. *But with hooks for teeth and long arms to reach.*

Beyond that, she would not describe them, or perhaps could not, for she said she spied them only from the edges of her vision, in the angles where two roof-lines met, or where a tall man's shadow divided on a slab of uneven paving.

In his dreams tonight, they surface out of the Moshassuck, with wings spread and mouths open, gums and lips flapping. They breach the water and hover in plumes above the river, coiled in darkness and merging with it before scattering themselves over the city with the rain that strikes the window, calling him from sleep.

It is Sunday morning, the curtains slightly parted. He fumbles at the bedside, fingers closing round the pocket-watch that belonged to his late father, whom he never knew.

Nine o'clock. Church bells sound throughout the city.

He dresses himself and descends the stairs, passing the parlor, where he is surprised to hear his aunt's voice. She is not at church, then, but is talking with her father, his grandfather, and with his other aunt, visiting from Boston, the door closed and fastened.

There is no one in the kitchen. The boy lingers over the hearth where the coals smolder in the grate. He looks west toward the street, the rows of gray buildings washed clean by rain, sending back the bells in echoes.

His mother has gone out—early this time. He imagines her footsteps, heels striking pavement then soundless where they drop like rain amongst the muddied leaves.

And silent in the same way he tiptoes down the hall to the parlor, where his aunts are arguing now, their voices indistinguishable from one another.

It cannot continue. Not like this.

So young. And such a fragile thing—

Not as fragile as his mother.

But surely that is the point.

His grandfather's voice: queer and creaking, scarcely audible.

Too much, he says. Sent away.

With these words, the fear settles over the boy. Terror fixes the bones inside him, binding the muscles so he cannot move, though footsteps cross the parlor and the door swings open to reveal his married aunt, who keeps her hair in tins beneath the bed.

She scowls. Listening at keyholes now? she says.

He turns and runs and throws himself into the window-seat. He pulls the blanket over him and presses his face to the window. The old glass vibrates with every bell from outside, blurring the light with the drips from the eaves and the elms beyond like yellow flags waving—and still his mother does not return.

An hour passes. He watches the married aunt depart with her umbrella, making for her hotel. She proceeds quickly, cheeks flushed and head down and so she does not see him.

His aunt enters the hall and lingers over the window-seat, wreathed in the smells of coffee and pipe-smoke. He lowers the blanket. She extends her hand to him with the palm open, a tea-cake nestled in the thatch of wrinkle and bone.

Take it, she says, and he does, and chokes it down quickly for fear that she might take it away or that his mother might see him with the sugar smeared about his lips.

His aunt nods, satisfied, and continues to the kitchen.

The boy retreats to his bedroom. He wraps the blanket round him like a shawl as to ward off the chill, returning now with his fever as the afternoon passes. He loses himself in the books he has borrowed from his grandfather's study, rereading the stories of heroes and dryads and gods from the sea. He is working on a tale of his own, a story of a ship. He opens his notebook—a gift from his grandfather—but finds he cannot focus on the page for thoughts of his mother and of the things that follow her.

Hours later, with night approaching, he hears the doors open and shut and listens for her step outside his bedroom. It does not come. He closes the notebook and steals across the hall to the carved railing that overlooks the staircase. His mother sits on the landing, marooned in a mess of skirt and crinoline and with her head held in her hands.

She lifts her gaze. Her eyes are dry and empty and she sees through him where he stands with his fingers round the railing and the terror bursting over him once more.

Too much, his grandfather said. *Sent away.*

His mother says: They waited so long. I walked for hours and miles and still they didn't show themselves so it was dusk before they came for me. I watched them approach. I waited with hands held out, expectant. They paused. They gathered themselves into clouds, which whirled and spun beyond my grasp for all I begged them to touch me, to take me. They parted with a ripple of wings, and I saw the hill beyond them. The church was clearly visible, and I knew at once what was required of me.

His mother hears footsteps, is quiet. His aunt emerges from the kitchen with a ladle in hand and her lips pressed together, a thin line.

His aunt says: You were gone all day.

His mother shrugs.

You might at least have told us where you were going.

Nowhere, his mother says.

Our sister has come from Boston. She wanted to see you.

His mother laughs. Is that so? She's staying at a hotel, isn't she?

We talked to Father. You've left us no other choice.

Father, she says, dully.

About your—sickness.

I am perfectly well.

Please, you must think of the child—

He is my child, she says. Not yours.

Anyway, Father is in agreement. The doctor is coming tomorrow.

Doctor.

The word drops like a thunderclap between them and his mother is on her feet, yelling and flailing out. The boy bolts down the hall to his room and slams the door on the noise from downstairs. The leaves of his story rise up in a storm from the desk and then float down softly, landing face-down on the floor.

He burrows deep into the bedclothes and closes his eyes as the shadows loom over him, slanting with the streetlamps through the curtains. He sees winged creatures with legs like thin cables and arms arrayed in writhing masses. A church spire long and sharp where it wounds the sky, the clouds pouring down blood. His mother surfacing out of the river. She grins, horribly, showing steel hooks for teeth. He does not go down for supper.

Midnight comes, and his mother enters the bedroom, souring the air with her perfume. He pretends to sleep. She places the candle on the nightstand and sits down beside the bed. She says nothing, makes no attempt to wake him, and he does not stir, though an hour passes or more until at last she rises and goes out, her perfume fading.

Hours later, he wakes with the same fever, familiar now. His legs ache, and his head is like crown glass. There will be no school today.

His mother is downstairs in the parlor. She is sleeping on the daybed while the glow makes patterns on her face: light through leaves and the leaf-shadows overlying it. Her brow is relaxed, hands falling open, her fingers half-curled like the smile on her lips.

He finds his aunt in the kitchen, leant up against the countertop with a teacup clasped in both hands and her gaze fixed on nowhere, the curtains drawn across the windows. She nods at him as he enters and wordlessly boils him an egg. As usual she takes no breakfast herself but merely watches him eat while sipping her coffee to the dregs, and her voice is hoarse and brittle when, finally, she speaks.

She says: Your Grandfather is asking after you.

She breathes out sharply, fumbles in her apron for her pipe.

She says: There is something you should know about. My sister reckons you're too young, but Father and I—well, we think maybe you're old enough.

She lights her pipe, waves him away.

Go on, she says. He's in his study waiting.

The door to the study is ajar, though the boy pauses at the threshold. His grandfather is slumped at the desk with his back to the door and his head bowed forward. The breath whistles from him, doubling the sound of the wind in the casement.

Come and sit down, his grandfather says.

The boy shuffles inside with head bowed and eyes averted, saying nothing as the old man's gaze strikes across him: his ugliness, his shame. He sits on the rug beside his grandfather's chair and crosses his legs.

His grandfather looks out toward the street, and his gaze lingers there a spell, as though watching for a long-awaited guest. He opens his mouth but then hesitates, closing his eyes—and with eyes closed, he tells a story. This time he does not take down a book from the shelf behind him but speaks instead from memory or imagination with the words and phrases trailing one another, a halting procession.

Once in Baghdad, he says, there lived a princess, who was the Caliph's daughter. Her hair was darkly luminous, as is the new moon, while her smile was coy and lovely as the crescent. She had many suitors, princes of Syria and Jordan, but the Caliph loved her more than life itself and could not bear to be parted from her. He turned them all away, princes and poets alike, and the princess withdrew into her loneliness.

He continues: Around this time a young man arrived in the city. This boy was the son of a magician and carried with him a sealed bottle, which his father had left him, though he had warned the boy against opening it. For within this bottle there dwelt a djinn, who was cunning and cruel, as are all such spirits. One night, at dusk, this young man chanced to spy the princess on her balcony and a kind of madness overcame him. He unstoppered the bottle.

The djinn issued in a vapor from the bottle's narrow neck and unfolded himself to stand in a cloud high over the boy. The spirit was tall as the tallest man and black as an eclipsing sun and curved the night about himself in the same way. The djinn proposed to him a bargain. If the boy would but break the bottle, giving the djinn his freedom, the djinn would grant the child his heart's innermost desire.

Now this young man could have had anything, but he was afflicted with love and thought of nothing save the princess. He wished for one night alone with her beauty, which was to him, the boy said, as pale and bright as the stars in winter. Saying this, he smashed the bottle.

The djinn kept his bargain. He gathered the boy and the princess into his arms and whisked them away to a mountain far from the city, to a place where no living thing grew and the snows lay deep and white as the Milky Way overhead. The djinn departed. He laughed as he rode the night winds, leaving the two lovers alone in that place of winter, just as the boy had desired, with the cold stars shining over them. There was nothing to eat, no wood with which to make a fire, and the young man, despairing, leapt to his death.

But the princess was the Caliph's daughter: she was born with iron in her heart. The tears froze inside her eyes but she trusted in her father and waited through the night for the rescue she knew must come.

His grandfather halts. The old man's voice trails off to a strangled pitch, his breathing slow and labored. His eyes stray to the window overlooking the street, where a coach has pulled up beside the house. A man alights from inside, wearing a black cloak and top-hat.

His grandfather says: And in the end he, too, betrayed her.

These last words circle the boy, unheard for the heat of his illness and the blood that pulses in his ears. The old man lowers his head to the desk once more. His story is over, will never be finished, and the leaves outside are shearing from the elm trees, burying roads and walkways. The doorbell sounds.

His aunt responds from the kitchen. Coming, she says.

The boy, standing, backs up toward the hallway, terrified by the thought of the cloaked visitor and the fate which has come for him.

His mother appears. She sweeps toward him down the corridor, dressed in black with her hair pinned up beneath a wide hat. Her face betrays excitement, relief.

This way, she says, and takes his hand in hers. She drags him down the corridor to the back door and outside onto the lawn.

She says: They are waiting for us. We mustn't be late.

And so they run. He flies with her down an adjoining alleyway, his hand folded in hers and her skirts billowing out behind. The folds engulf him, wrapping round his face and eyes so he follows blindly, their steps carrying them downhill and at such a pace that the speed of it threatens to lift him from the ground and send him sailing up behind her, a tethered balloon.

They reach the canal, the bridge, and the sea-wind blows her skirts free of him as they cross over. A teamster curses and draws up his horses, their hooves flashing over him as his mother pulls him hard to the right and the road turns to climb toward the top of the hill.

The church is ahead of them, the black spire of which she has often spoke. The street is empty with the trees in rows to either side, branches stripped by the winds and their leaves upon the ground: crimson and yellow and brown about the edges with the mud from the weekend's rain. The paving is slick, yielding. The boy's feet slip, give way, and his hand slides from her grasp. He strikes the paving with his knees then his hands and heaves onto his side as the light shifts and changes, sun compassing sky so the shadows swing toward him from the trees and alleys and from the doors of the church, left open to receive her.

The bare trees rattle. The shadows writhe and stretch and bend upon themselves, turning to fragments when his mother reaches the church and hurtles through the doorway, visible to him in that instant as she spreads wide her arms and the wind encircles her with its roaring. Her mourning dress shreds, spins loose from her body. Her corset next so the pale limbs show, her nakedness, though this, too, dissolves with the whirling shards of fabric and flesh that twist and circle, ringing the center which is her illness: a churning chaos.

The wind recedes, releasing itself.

The doors fall shut and his mother is gone. The pieces of her move away down the street like flapping leaves: shadows of the coming winter, a mountain he cannot reach.

A hansom pulls up. His grandfather is seated within, slumped against the far door with a handkerchief to his mouth. Beside him rides the man in the cloak and top-hat with a doctor's bag placed between his feet.

It's all right, the doctor says and offers his hand.

The carriage brings them back to the house, where all is quiet and cold. His mother is nowhere to be found and his aunt paces in the kitchen, pipe-smoke drifting from beneath the closed door. By now his fever is worse, and his grandfather carries him upstairs to his bedroom, gasping with the strain.

Evening. There are shadows on the wall, wings and hooks retreating with the elms that toss and sway. His grandfather departs but returns with a kerosene lamp. He lights the wick, sets it burning by the bedside. Then waits with the boy for the fever to break and for the sickness to go out of him, a shadow passing.

Lavinia in Autumn
(Sentinel Hill)
by Ann K. Schwader

Ancestral echoes from these hilltop stones
Erected by no hands the living know
Call shadows out of autumn: those below,
Who sated darkness with their blood & bone.
Such rituals are dust ...yet one alone,
Soul sister to the whippoorwill & crow,
Still wanders here. Still feels the star-winds blow
From distant space where chaos keeps its throne.

These columns hold no mysteries for she
Who traced their patterns from her freshest days
To final twilight shredding like a veil
Between the Ones who were – *are still to be* –
& summerlings whose lives must fade away
Before the sovereignty of sharper gales.

Thank you for reading *Autumn Cthulhu* – I hope you enjoyed it. If you did, please consider leaving us a review on Amazon. **Lovecraft eZine Press** is a small independent publisher, and your review will benefit it more than just about anything else you can do. Thank you!

Biographies

Scott Thomas is a native New Englander and author of 10 books. His titles include *The Sea of Ash* and *Urn and Willow*.

Damien Angelica Walters is the author of *Paper Tigers* (Dark House Press, 2016) and *Sing Me Your Scars* (Apex Publications, 2015). Her short fiction has been nominated twice for a Bram Stoker Award, reprinted in *The Year's Best Dark Fantasy & Horror* and *The Year's Best Weird Fiction,* and published in various anthologies and magazines, including *Cassilda's Song, Black Static, Cemetery Dance Online,* and *Nightmare Magazine*. She lives in Maryland with her husband and two rescued pit bulls.

Pete Rawlik is a long time collector of Lovecraftian fiction and is the author of more than fifty short stories, a smattering of poetry, and the Cthulhu Mythos novels *Reanimators* and *The Weird Company*. He is a frequent contributor to *The Lovecraft eZine* and the *New York Review of Science Fiction*. In 2014 his short story "Revenge of the Reanimator" was nominated for a New Pulp Award. His new novel *Reanimatrix,* a weird noir romance set in H. P. Lovecraft's Arkham, will be released in 2016. He lives in southern Florida where he works on Everglades issues.

Laird Barron is the author of several books, including *The Croning, The Imago Sequence,* and *The Beautiful Thing That Awaits Us All*. His work has also appeared in many magazines and anthologies. An expatriate Alaskan, Barron currently resides in upstate New York.

Nadia Bulkin writes scary stories about the scary world we live in. She once crossed the Missouri River in search of a legendary haunted house in Iowa, but her quest was unsuccessful. She now lives and works in Washington, D.C., tending her garden of student debt sowed by two political science degrees and waiting, impatiently, for November. Her additional pieces of Midwestern Lovecraftiana can be found in the *Letters to Lovecraft* and *She Walks in Shadows* anthologies; for more, check out nadiabulkin.wordpress.com.

Michael Griffin's stories have appeared in magazines like *Apex*, *Black Static*, *Lovecraft eZine* and *Strange Aeons*, and such anthologies as the Shirley Jackson Award winner *The Grimscribe's Puppets*, the Laird Barron tribute *The Children of Old Leech*, and *Cthulhu Fhtagn!* His debut collection *The Lure of Devouring Light* was published by Word Horde in 2016, and he has work upcoming in is work is upcoming in *Leaves of a Necronomicon*, *Nightscript 2* and *Eternal Frankenstein*. Michael blogs about books and writing at griffinwords.com. On Twitter, he generally posts as @mgsoundvisions and writing-specific news appears as @griffinwords. He's also an electronic ambient musician and founder of Hypnos Recordings, an ambient music record label he operates with his wife in Portland, Oregon.

By day, **Evan Dicken** studies old Japanese Maps and crunches medical data at the Ohio State University. By night, he does neither of these thing. His fiction has most recently appeared in: *Shock Totem*, *Pseudopod*, and *Unlikely Story*, and he has stories forthcoming from publishers such as: *Chaosium*, *Flash Fiction Online*, and *Beneath Ceaseless Skies*. Feel free to look him up at: evandicken.com

Robert Levy is an author of stories, screenplays and plays whose work has been seen Off-Broadway. A Harvard graduate subsequently trained as a forensic psychologist, his first novel, *The Glittering World*, was published worldwide by Gallery/Simon & Schuster and is a finalist for the Lambda Literary Award. Shorter work has appeared in *Shadows & Tall Trees*, *Black Static*, and the *Brooklyn Quarterly*, among others. He is currently working on a television pilot as well as a new novel, and can be found at TheRobertLevy.com.

Wendy N. Wagner is the author of more than three dozen short stories, as well as the Pathfinder Adventure novels *Starspawn* (August 2016) and *Skinwalkers*. A native northwesterner, she lives with her very understanding family in Portland, Oregon. To keep up with her misadventures, visit her at winniewoohoo.com.

Jeffrey Thomas is the creator of the dark future milieu *Punktown*. His many books include the novel *Subject 11* and the Lovecraftian collection *Unholy Dimensions*. Thomas lives in the autumnal state of Massachusetts.

John Langan is the author of two novels, *The Fisherman* (Word Horde 2016) and *House of Windows* (Diversion 2016), and three collections of short fiction, *Sefira and Other Betrayals* (Hippocampus 2016), *The Wide, Carnivorous Sky and Other Monstrous Geographies* (Hippocampus 2013), and *Mr Gaunt and Other Uneasy Encounters* (Prime 2008). He lives in the Hudson Valley with his wife and younger son.

Trent Kollodge is the author of the novel *Two-bit Angel*. He also animates, illustrates, and occasionally makes noises he calls "music." He currently lives in Austin, Texas with his wife and two children.

S.P. Miskowski's first novel *Knock Knock* and first novella *Delphine Dodd* were finalists for the Shirley Jackson Award. She has stories in the anthologies *October Dreams 2*, *Cassilda's Song*, *The Hyde Hotel*, *Leaves of a Necronomicon*, and *Sisterhood*. Her award-nominated series the Skillute Cycle is published by Omnium Gatherum. Her novelette *Muscadines* is part of the Dunhams Manor Press limited edition hardcover series, illustrated by Dave Felton. Her chapbook "Stag in Flight," illustrated by Nick Gucker, is published by Dim Shores.

Richard Gavin is the author of five acclaimed collections of supernatural fiction, including *Sylvan Dread* (Three Hands Press, 2016). His stories have also been selected for several Year's Best anthologies. *The Benighted Path*, his non-fiction book that explores Night Consciousness, was released by Theion Publishing in 2016. Richard lives in Ontario, Canada. Web presence: www.richardgavin.net

Born in England and raised in Toronto, Canada, **Gemma Files** has been a film critic, teacher, and screenwriter. Probably best known for her weird Western Hexslinger series (*A Book of Tongues*, *A Rope of Thorns* and *A Tree of Bones*, all from ChiZine Publications), she has also published two short fiction collections, two speculative poetry chapbooks and a story-cycle (*We Will All Go Down Together: Stories of the*

Five-Family Coven). Five of her stories were adapted as episodes of Showtime's *The Hunger*, an erotic horror anthology series produced by Tony and Ridley Scott. Her latest novel is *Experimental Film*. You can find out more about Gemma Files at http://musicatmidnight-gfiles.blogspot.com.

Orrin Grey is a writer, editor, amateur film scholar, and monster expert who was born on the night before Halloween. His stories of ghosts, monsters, and sometimes the ghosts of monsters have appeared in dozens of anthologies, including *The Best Horror of the Year*, and been collected in *Never Bet the Devil & Other Warnings* and *Painted Monsters & Other Strange Beasts*. He can be found online at orringrey.com.

Joseph S. Pulver, Sr. has released 4 acclaimed mixed-genre collections, including *Blood Will Have Its Season*, a collection of King in Yellow tales (*King in Yellow Tales Vol. 1*), 2 weird fiction novels, and he's edited *A Season in Carcosa*, the *Shirley Jackson Award*-winning *The Grimscribe's Puppets*, and *Cassilda's Song*. His fiction and poetry has appeared in many notable anthologies, including *The Children of Old Leech*, Ellen Datlow's *The Year's Best Horror*, and *Best Weird Fiction of the Year*. Joe is a regular contributor to the *The Lovecraft eZine*.

Daniel Mills is the author of *Revenants: A Dream of New England* (Chomu Press, 2011), *The Lord Came at Twilight* (Dark Renaissance Books, 2014), and the forthcoming *Moriah* (ChiZine Publications, 2017). His short fiction has appeared in numerous magazines and anthologies including *The Year's Best Dark Fantasy and Horror* and *The Mammoth Book of Best New Horror*. He lives in Vermont.

Ann K. Schwader's most recent collections are *Dark Energies* (P'rea Press, 2015 – poetry) and *Dark Equinox* (Hippocampus Press, 2015 – fiction). She is a two-time Bram Stoker Award Finalist, and a 2010 Rhysling Award winner. Schwader was also Poet Laureate for NecronomiCon Providence in 2105. A Wyoming native, she now lives and writes in suburban Colorado.

Mike Davis is a writer and editor, as well as publisher of *The Lovecraft eZine*. He is at work on his first novel. Find him on Twitter: @misanthropemike

ALSO FROM
LOVECRAFT EZINE PRESS

The King in Yellow Tales volume I, by Joseph S. Pulver, Sr.

The Sea of Ash, by Scott Thomas

The Lurking Chronology, by Pete Rawlik

Acknowledgements

I owe a debt of gratitude to everyone who helped me with this project. Those people include, but are not limited to: Salomé Jones, Kenneth W. Cain, Steve Santiago, Dave Felton, and Joseph S. Pulver, Sr.

And to everyone who pledged to the *Autumn Cthulhu* Kickstarter: Thank You!

By Sara Bardi, for *The Night is a Sea* by Scott Thomas

By Sara Bardi, for *After the Fall* by Jeffrey Thomas

By Nick Gucker, for *The Well and the Wheel* by Orrin Grey

By Sara Bardi, for *Lavinia in Autumn* by Ann K. Schwader

100 Thanks

I appreciate everyone who donated to the *Autumn Cthulhu* Kickstarter. People like you keep the small independent press alive. Thank you.

Below is a list of the first 100 people who pledged $20 or more.

Joe Kontor
Chris Kalley
Kaleb Maskill
Sam Gafford
Chad Anctil
Samantha Henderson
Paul McNamee
Andrew Nicolle
Robert Kassebaum
Lou Columbus
Benjamin Holesapple
Sandor Silverman
Jeremy Hochhalter
David Ploskonka
Ben Reeves
Kevin F. Wilson
Christian Wiessner
Vincent LaRosa
Matthew Carpenter
Jonathan Sprague
Matthew Plank
Laird Barron
Aaron Besson
Matthias Weeks
Michael LeSueur
Duane Stockton
Lee Clark Zumpe

Tro Rex & Eyo Bella
Fred Lubnow
Scarlett Algee
Rebecca Allred
Grant Stewart
Jason Aiken
Anya Martin
Lou Perry
C.M. Muller
Stephanie Graham
Jason Andrew
Chris Duncan
Stacy Hart
Thomas Pluck
Raven Daegmorgan
Leah Bond
David Chamberlain
Jessica M.
William Lohman
Brett J. Talley
Clint Hale
Philip Gelatt
James Kiley
Keegan Fink
Matthew Martin
Sarah Walker
Liv Rainey-Smith

Wim Baelus
William R. Rieder
Matthew Minnear
Chris Hyde
Jason Carl
Brian & Gwen Callahan
Mandy Farley
Paul Cardullo
Scott Cowan
Bjorn Smars
Cliff Winnig
Candida Norwood
Dan Alban
Jon Padgett
Ronald L. Weston
Nathan Carson
Scott Valeri
Nicholas Nacario
Rick Tillman
Conor Farrell
Renee Mulhare
Luiz Eduardo Neves Peret
Tobin Anderson

Thomas Corrigan
Amy H. Sturgis
Christian Wood
Ann McCann
Brandi Jording
Jason Duelge
Seth Bradley
William Wood
Simon Holcroft
Jeremy Davis
Kennon James
Lorenz Thor
Scott Desmarais
Jim Parrott
Charles Allen
James B. Serfling
Heather Baker
Alexandra Dimou
Catherine Swidzinski
Adam Alexander
Benet Devereux
Penny Parks
Jesse Berrett

Made in the USA
Charleston, SC
06 May 2016